Henry Cresswell

A Wily Widow

A Novel

Henry Cresswell

A Wily Widow
A Novel

ISBN/EAN: 9783337044282

Printed in Europe, USA, Canada, Australia, Japan

Cover: Foto ©Andreas Hilbeck / pixelio.de

More available books at **www.hansebooks.com**

BY THE AUTHOR of 'INCOGNITA'

A WILY WIDOW

LONDON: SPENCER BLACKETT

A WILY WIDOW

A Novel

BY

HENRY CRESSWELL

AUTHOR OF

"A MODERN GREEK HEROINE," "THE SINS OF THE FATHERS
"INCOGNITA," "THE SURVIVORS," ETC.

" Beware of the wrath of the dove '

LONDON
SPENCER BLACKETT
(Successor to J. & R. Maxwell)
MILTON HOUSE, 35 ST. BRIDE STREET, E.C.

BLACKETT'S
SELECT SHILLING NOVELS.

99 Dark Street. By F. W. Robinson.
A Wicked Girl. By Mary Cecil Hay.
Gabriel Allen, M.P. By G. A. Henty.
The Argonauts of North Liberty. By Bret Harte.
The Abbey Murder. By Joseph Hatton.
A Mere Child. By L. B. Walford.
Love Until Death. By R. Whelan Boyle.
The Queen's Token. By Mrs. Cashel Hoey.
The Pretty Sister of Jose. By F. Hodgson Burnett.
The Haunted Fountain. By Catherine Macquoid.
                                                    [Shortly.
Favour and Fortune. By Minnie Young.   [Shortly.
A Rainy June. By Ouida.
John Needham's Double. By Joseph Hatton.
Don Gesualdo. By Ouida.
James Daunton's Fate. By Dora Russell.
Betty's Visions. By Rhoda Broughton.
Topside and Turvey. By Percy Fitzgerald.
Beforehand. By L. T. Meade.

*** This Series will be exclusively reserved to the works
of well-known Authors. Other volumes are in course
of preparation, and will be published at short intervals.

LONDON : SPENCER BLACKETT

(Successor to J. & R. Maxwell),

Milton House, 35 St. Bride Street, E.C.

And at all Booksellers and Bookstalls.

A WILY WIDOW

CHAPTER I.

"YES, Brown, you are right. It will make a deal of difference who gets the place. Well: good-night."

With his great-coat collar turned up high about his ears (for the October night was cold), Dr. Gregg descended the steps of the South-Western Bank, Lynham, and directed his steps towards his own house at the other end of the street.

Brown was quite right. It would make a deal of difference who got the place. For instance, if a large family came to live there, wealthy, but none of them in good health, that would make a difference to Dr. Gregg himself. Or a man of position with a little public spirit; that would be a godsend to every one. Whereas, on the contrary, if the place again fell into the hands of a miserly old hunks, there would be one more chance lost for Lynham. And at Lynham, "chances" were rare.

The little town of Lynham—it is not worth while to look for it on the map—lies hidden, in one of the most sequestered parts of the Dorsetshire coast, in a narrow and secluded valley, shut in on every side from the surrounding world by high, steep hills. No one has yet thought of making a "sea-front" at Lynham, nor of inventing curious diagrams to show

how much more the sun shines and how much less
rain falls there than anywhere else in England ; nor
even of discovering that the climate—like that of all
the known watering-places—is a certain cure for most
of the ills that hurry poor humanity to the tomb.   So
Lynham remains a primitive little place.   Down by
the beach there is an old church on one side of the
narrow valley, and on the other side a small, and
very tolerable, old-fashioned inn that calls itself the
" London Hotel."   Between the two a little esplanade extends, built by the munificence of a former
lord of the manor, and believed by the natives to be
one of the finest promenades in Europe.   Then there
is a High Street, and a Church Street, and three or
four other streets, with about a dozen houses in each of
them ; and after that only cottages and the rectory, and
a few picturesque little houses dotted here and there ;
one, untenanted, up the Mill Lane, a pretty little place
covered with jasmine, and another, even more secluded,
nearly a mile out of the town in a hollow on the cliff,
called Cliff Cottage : of which more anon.

In the same direction, but further inland, is Lynhurst, once the country seat of the Lynhursts of
Lynhurst, lords of the manor of Lynham, and county
people of a little importance.   The family is now
extinct.   The last of the Lynhursts (he who built
the esplanade) ruined himself with speculation, and
expensive faddles, and afterwards died childless.
Lynhurst was sold, and passed rapidly from owner to
owner, faring ever worse and worse, until the poverty
of some, and the neglect of others, and the indifference of all, had reduced the estate—sadly curtailed
of its original proportions—to a miserable condition
of ruin and dilapidation.

It had been a pretty spot.   Not, it is true, one of
those stately homes that are fairylands of rolling lawns,
and glassy lakes, and lordly forest trees ; but a fair
place, with woods climbing the hills, and a broad,

well-timbered valley opening before the house, and a glimpse in the distance of the Channel. The mansion itself, the last of the Lynhursts rebuilt. It was a largish house, of two storeys, forming three sides of a square, with a long verandah in front, not very picturesque, but, within, roomy and comfortable; though, like everything else at Lynhurst, fallen into a shockingly ruinous condition.

Still, of course, the place might be done up, the house restored, and the dilapidations of the estate put into repair, and then Lynhurst might be as pretty a spot as ever. Nature does not wear out. And if some one would come with a pocket full of money, and do all that, that would be a fine thing for Lynham.

For the last fifteen years Lynhurst had been in the possession of a particularly sour and unsociable old bachelor, who had been in evil odour with every one. Undeniably he had allowed the place to go to rack and ruin in a shameful way, and he was niggardly and mean to a degree. But perhaps the old fellow could have told some things his neighbours little suspected. How hard it was for him to find the money to pay the interest on the crushing mortgages, and what sort of weight that is which falls on an old man's heart when his circumstances demand of him the spirit and energies of youth. At any rate, the old gentleman's shortcomings do not concern this story. At the time when it begins he had been buried just a week, and all Lynham was on the tiptoe of curiosity; and every one, except the very poorest— the only persons in the place whose occupations were large enough to fill their lives—was talking about who would have Lynhurst, and what would ensue.

As Brown the banker said, it would make a deal of difference who got the place. And Dr. Gregg was not the only person who agreed with him.

A tall, thin man was the doctor, with light hair

and whiskers, and a rather cadaverous face that seemed to be entirely made of sharp points—sharp cheekbones, a sharp nose, a sharp chin, sharp pointed lips, sharp ends to his short whiskers, and a sharply prominent forehead.

But the doctor had not at all the air of being intellectually a sharp man. Rather the contrary. As is mostly the case with these pointed-faced people, he looked like a vague man.

The doctor soon reached his own home. It was a double-fronted house, with iron railings before it, and wire blinds in the lower windows. Two very large brass plates, one attached to the iron railings, and the other to the surgery door, announced that Dr. G. Gregg was M.D., surgeon, and M.R.C.S., and neither the doctor himself nor any of his patients had ever observed that that was saying the same thing twice over.

The doctor hung up his coat and hat in the hall, and proceeded towards the drawing-room. A sound of eager conversation, mingled with merry laughter, came through the door. Mrs. Gregg had a Cambridge man staying in the house for a few days, and had asked one or two friends to tea. When the doctor entered, he found them all sitting round a table on which a pack of cards had been thrown aside. There is no occasion to describe particularly either the doctor's wife or the rector's daughters, two plain, ladylike, countrified girls, without a trait to distinguish them from a thousand others of their class. But two other ladies sat at the round table who merited attention.

One of them was a young widow; a handsome brunette, in the opinion of some people a very handsome brunette, of five-and-twenty, who looked younger than she was, in fact, of so girlish an appearance that her title of "Mrs." seemed to be a mistake. Scarcely above the middle height, she had a pretty

figure, and a charming head and neck. Her face
was a striking face, finely chiselled, delicate, intellectual, with deeply cut features, and an expression
a little sad, a little arch, a little reticent, a little
romantic, and altogether very difficult to decipher.
Men who looked at her once invariably looked at her
again, to get some better understanding of her wide,
low forehead, of her deeply shaded, dark, enigmatical
eyes, of her round, wilful chin, and of her little
mouth, firm, with narrow, blood-red lips. And if
the low forehead appeared, on a second view, a
morsel cruel, if her lips seemed to close a little
coldly, who would have a brunette without steel in
her composition? At moments she looked like an
unhappy woman, and she was no flirt, as the Cambridge undergraduate, who had been smitten on the
spot, had discovered with regret.

The charms of the other were of a different kind.

This was simply a lively, pretty, frank, young
girl, fresh as a rose, with a broad dash of spirit in
her fine eyes and her easy bearing. One look at her
open brow, her clear blue eyes, sparkling like two
stars, her guileless lips, and her fearless, direct
regard, was enough to tell that she was of a generous
nature, innately noble, and untainted, hitherto, by
contact with the world. She was taller than the
widow by a good inch, and so distinctly above the
average height, with a slight, girlish figure, a small
waist, sloping shoulders, and a long, flexible neck.
Her face was rather small, a mignonne face, full of a
certain artlessness, but saucy too, with a touch of
childish *espièglerie* that lurked in her soft eyes, and
her rosy cheeks, and about her little dimpled chin.
Her eyebrows were exquisitely pencilled, arched, and
two or three shades darker than her hair, of a light,
soft brown—crisp and abundant. Her ripe little lips
had a look of such sweetness, with such an air, too,
of " Why don't you kiss us ?" that the temptation

to comply would have been altogether irresistible if there had not been about her, for all her childishness, and all her pretty mischievousness, clear evidence of other qualities in her character that would have made au impudence difficult to offer her. As she rose, with the rest, to greet the doctor, turning her head quickly, and smiling as she held out her small, uarrow hand, a charming dignity of girlish grace mixed with her rapid movemeuts. And, as she put her hand iuto the doctor's, aud, looking straight into his eyes, said, in her clear, musical voice, the commonplace " How do you do, Dr. Gregg ? " there was a sincerity in her regard, and in the tone of her greeting, which showed that, if she was artless and light-hearted, still she carried in her breast a soul intrinsically noble and sincere.

She was much better dressed than the widow, whose silk gown was a tiny bit shabby, and did not, iu the exactest acceptatiou of the word, fit. Indeed, she was by far the best-dressed person in the room. The fact may as well be mentioued at once : that, when Lily Hardwick became one-and-twenty, she would have a very pretty little fortune ; and so having nice clothes from Loudon was for her one of the simplest things in life.

They had all sat down again, and the doctor, alluding to the laughter he had overheard in the hall, begged that his arrival might not interrupt their amusements, and asked what was goiug on.

" Well—I was proposing a little problem—a sort of problem of the imagination," said the Cambridge man. "It was not origiual, but——" he paused.

" But I want to hear the end of it, please," demanded the young heiress, with that species of authority which pretty girls are very apt to assume.

The Cambridge man went on.

" Well—I was saying, Dr. Gregg, that suppose there was an old Tartar in Tartary—oh, you have

heard all about it, I am sure—and suppose that, if
that old Tartar died, you came into a very large fortune. And if you did something very simple ; say,
took this thimble "—he had a thimble under his
hand, and was rolling it about on the table—" and
put it down so "—suiting his action to his words, he
put down the thimble on the table-cloth, as if he
were extinguishing a candle with it—" and put that
old Tartar out, you see, without anybody but yourself knowing anything about it : well—would you
do it ? I don't mind confessing that I—well ; I am
afraid I should be much tempted to put out that
Tartar."

And he put down the thimble again, as if extinguishing a candle with it, and then, looking up
quickly at one of the rector's daughters, asked :

" Well, Miss Wood ; what do you say ? "

" But that would be murder ; just as if you killed
him in any other way," replied the girl.

" But I should not be found out, you know—and
the fortune ? "

" I should do it, I know," said the other Miss
Wood. " I know it would be awfully wicked. But
I'm sure I should not be able to resist the tempta-
tion."

" We ought to pray to resist temptation," remarked
her sister solemnly.

" I'd not do it ; not for millions," exclaimed the
heiress, in her clear, ringing voice, without waiting
to be asked.

" Not really, Miss Hardwick ? " asked the Cambridge man.

" Certainly not ! "

" You know he is awfully old. He can't last long,
anyway," said the undergraduate with a droll ear-
nestness that made every one laugh.

And, with his eyes fixed on Lily Hardwick, he
n bringing the thimble down again.

"No, you sha'n't!" exclaimed the girl, stretching out her arm and snatching the thimble out of his hand.

The doctor, standing by the table, laughed.

The Cambridge man turned to the young widow.

"And you, Mrs. Gainsborough?" he said.

Leaning forward with her elbows on the table the widow had been watching all that was going forward, with singular attention. Her thin crimson lips were tightly pressed together, and not a shade of change passed over the expression of her sculpturesque face, still as marble. But her strange, dark eyes went from one to another of the group before her as they spoke, and she seemed to watch for what each would say, and to con the expression of their faces with an inordinate interest. Every time, too, that the thimble slowly descended to extinguish the imaginary Tartar's existence, her eyes fixed themselves on it in a fascinated glance. Now that she was addressed she moved, almost as if unexpectedly awakened from a reverie.

"What do I say?" she repeated, and meditatively lifted her fingers to her lips. "But—you see"—she looked at the Cambridge man—"the thing is impossible."

"Unluckily," admitted the undergraduate so seriously that they all laughed again.

"Yet," he went on, "do you know, I once heard of something that comes very near it. If I may tell a little story?"

"Oh, do!" exclaimed the girls.

"Some years ago a scientific man, a friend of one of our tutors, was showing some chemical experiments to a number of schoolgirls. They were very intelligent girls, big girls, who had been attending chemical lectures at a first-class school. They asked him a number of questions, and got him to show them various elements and compounds that they had heard of but never seen ; and, among other things, they asked to be shown some of the poisons. Some days afterwards, going to look on his shelves, he found that one of the most dangerous of his poisons had been stolen. And he believed one of the girls had taken it. If so, there is somewhere in the world a lady—for she is of course grown up by this time—who could dispose of any of us as simply as I could of the Tartar—if Miss Hardwick would kindly give me back my thimble."

The girls regarded each other with wide eyes.

"What was the poison ?" asked Dr. Gregg.

" I believe it was aconite."

" Is that very poisonous stuff, Dr. Gregg ?" asked Lily Hardwick.

" Yes ; a very small dose is fatal."

" But can it not be easily detected, doctor ?" enquired the widow. " I have an idea that I have heard my father—he was a medical man, you know —say that it could."

" Well, Mrs. Gainsborough," replied the doctor, speaking gravely, and with much authority, " in some cases this poison can be very easily detected ; in fact——"

What more he might have said remained unfinished, for at this moment the rector was announced and entered the room. He had himself come to fetch his daughters home, because he had some news to bring the doctor. His wife had had a letter from a friend in town who had heard all about Lynhurst.

The late owner of the estate had bequeathed it to a Mr. Warrington. Mr. Warrington was a young man of some property, it seemed, and was shortly to be married. But Mr. Warrington had no wish to live in the country, and meant to sell the place.

So it still remained to be seen what would become of Lynhurst.

CHAPTER II.

BUT man proposes and—woman disposes.

Later this same evening the new proprietor of Lynhurst, who had recently been the object of so much curiosity in the Dorsetshire town, and his intended bride, sat talking together in the large drawing-room of a house in Welmore Street, Cavendish Square.

The *fiancée*—she was his cousin—was in a low seat a little distance from the fire, leaning back idly, and listening to what he was saying to her as he bent over her chair.

She was a good-looking girl—nothing more ; a blonde, with a blonde's fine complexion and a graceful figure, and a classical face, a trifle passionless and reserved.

But he was a distinctly handsome man. Tallish, dark, about six-and-twenty, with a well-knit figure, athletic, and justly proportioned, with a strong, deeply cut face that had aristocratic features and keen, penetrating eyes of the sort that attract those women who like to feel a little awe for what they admire. There was, however, nothing awe-inspiring in his appearance this evening, as he stood leaning over his betrothed with that easy, masculine grace which appears merely natural, but is never achieved except by perfectly well-bred gentlemen, chatting to her in a pleasant playful tone of his fine flexible voice, and compelling her to be amused, even in spite of herself, in a manner that revealed him—whatever resoluteness or inflexibility he might have in reserve —as a good-natured fellow, with a strong vein of chivalry in his character, and a natural penchant for honest, perhaps almost blunt, straightforwardness.

The girl listened apathetically, dropping now and

then a few words, and smiling softly when he said anything that amused her; for the rest employing herself merely with holding her fire-screen between her face and the flames, and remarking from time to time, " I wonder where Essie can be." To all appearance she was a little bored.

Presently the door opened softly, and a girl came into the room—the expected Essie. As her eyes fell on her sister and her lover by the fire, she stopped, and entertained herself for a minute or two with regarding them. There was a twinkle of amusement in her eyes.

She was prettier than her sister, though her features were less correct. She had all the appearance, too, of being a good deal brighter. Her light, tall figure seemed created for rapid motion, and in her playful face, with its high cheekbones, sharp nose, little roguish lips, and laughing eyes, stood a pretty plain confession of a waywardness, capable when the humour took her, of pranks that at one-and-twenty, which was her age, may be serious.

All she said to herself, while watching the couple at the other end of the room, was, " Ah, Mr. Frank Warrington, make the most of it, my dear cousin ! " Then, with the step of a cat, she crossed to them.

She had stood a full minute close to Frank Warrington's side before he or her sister saw her.

Then, laughing, he said :

" Ah, here you are at last. I've persuaded grandfather."

" And he will let us go ? " exclaimed the girl, with an eagerness in which appeared some seriousness.

" Yes ; both you and Violet. I have told Violet."

" And I have told Frank, Essie, that he had better breakfast with us to-morrow," said Violet.

" Yes, do, cousin ! " said Essie.

" Well, I will then."

"And we will all drive to the station together. And, Violet," she continued, turning to her sister, "as we shall have to breakfast to-morrow at nine instead of half-past ten we had better go to bed soon."

"Well, then, I'll be off," said Frank Warrington.

Violet rose and he put his arm round her and kissed her, and, having shaken hands with her sister, took his departure, saying:

"To-morrow at nine."

Essie listened for his steps descending the stairs, and for the front door to close after him. Then she turned quickly to her sister.

"Oh! I say, Violet!" she exclaimed. Struck with a sudden thought, she went on, "Violet, Frank has over-persuaded grandpapa for the instant, but nothing is more likely than that the horrid old thing will change his mind again. And you know how he went on at dinner. Let us go to bed before he comes upstairs."

"What for? What does it matter?" asked Violet, who had sat down again, leaning back idly in her chair.

"It seems to me it matters a good deal," replied Essie. "Suppose grandpapa should not let us go?"

But her sister would not move.

CHAPTER III.

However, when the next morning Warrington appeared for breakfast at a little after nine, the girls welcomed him with their things on, already dressed for their journey.

It was a bright October morning, calm and rather cold.

An hour later the northern express, standing by the long departure platform at St. Pancras, was rapidly taking up the last of its passengers and their luggage. The minute hand on the giant clock-face at the end of the imposing station had nearly reached the hour, and the clipping of tickets had commenced, and the closing of carriage-doors.

Warrington, standing on the edge of the platform, by the window of one of the first-class carriages, was talking to Violet, and from time to time looking over his shoulder at the bookstall.

" I don't see Essie," he said.

" Oh, Essie is sure to come in time, Frank," said Violet, reassuringly.

And, as she spoke, Essie slipped out of the booking-office, and, passing through the crowd on the platform, came over to where Warrington stood, coming up to him with her noiseless step just as the ticket-inspector reached the carriage, which he opened for her.

She sat down opposite her sister, by the window. At the other end of the carriage was the lady's-maid, a discreet-looking *Parisienne*, with an impenetrable and imperturbable French face.

Whilst the official clipped the tickets, Warrington for the moment stood back from the window. Then, resuming his place, he said, speaking to both the girls :

" I shall tell grandfather that I saw you safely off, and that you had a compartment to yourselves. The guard has promised me not to put any one in at Kentish Town, and the train does not stop afterwards until you reach Kettering, so you will have the carriage to yourselves all the way. Mrs. Eversfield will be sure to meet you on the Kettering platform, and you have Félicité with you. So I think I may tell grandfather not to fidget, seeing that you are about as perfectly safe as it is possible to be."

"Always supposing that there is not a railway accident, you know," said Essie.

"Heaven forbid it!" remarked her sister, with greater solemnity than the unlikely suggestion demanded.

"At any rate," ran on Essie, "if anything does happen to us, it will be all cousin Frank's fault. Won't it, Frank? Because if you had not persuaded grandpapa, and promised him to see us off, grandpapa would never have let us go. So if anything goes wrong it will be your doing, Frank, won't it?"

"We will hope that nothing will go wrong," said Warrington, easily.

"No, but seriously, Frank," returned Essie, in another tone, "we are awfully obliged to you for having persuaded grandpapa, and having managed it all for us; for we should never have done it without you. Grandpapa always gets cross and impatient when we try to bring him to any reason."

Whilst she spoke Violet Chesterfield looked through the side window, an askance look at Frank Warrington, a very strange look. When her sister had done speaking, she added her thanks languidly, a sort of echo only of what the other had said, and asked:

"Is it not almost time for the train to start?"

"In about two minutes." Warrington looked up and down the train, and then went on, "I shall come to meet you this evening."

"Thanks," said Violet, in the same cold tone.

A shadow crossed the man's handsome face, a shadow of pain, but a momentary one only. It was not difficult to understand that shadow. The case between him and the girl was only too plain. The old story, "*En amour il y a toujours un qui aime et un qui se laisse aimer*" And the love was on his side, a man's blunt love, with its unselfish tenderness. On her side existed, perhaps, some admiration for a handsome, accomplished man, certainly nothing more ; and a cruel indifference to his seeing it. Nothing breathes more pitiless than a woman who is loved by a man whom she does not love. All the histories of the worst of tyrants and inquisitors, and of the cruellest tortures to which their victims have been subjected, offer no example of a heartlessness so bitter as that with which a woman will, without hesitation, wound the gentlest feelings of a lover for whom she has no affection.

"Oh, Frank, do you know," recommenced Essie, " we were so awfully amused at something we heard the other night at Mrs. Phillips's. I *must* tell you about it. It tickled our fancy so enormously. It was such an *awfully* funny story, and your coming to see us off has made me think of it. I hope I shall have time to tell you before the train starts. Mrs. Phillips has a niece, or a cousin, or something, I really forget what exactly. And she—I mean the cousin—lived with her great-aunt, or her great-uncle, or her great something. And she was engaged to a man for whom she did not care a bit— you understand."

Frank Warrington nodded assent. From her corner Violet Chesterfield was regarding her sister with a certain degree of curiosity. Apparently this story was new to her.

"Well," went on Essie, " this girl was engaged to this man, a Mr.—really I forget his name—we will say Smith. And she could not for the life of her discover how she was to escape from having to marry him. I can't tell you all about that. It would take too long. Anyhow, the time slipped by, and at last the wedding-day was fixed, and the girl grew positively desperate, when, all of a sudden, she hit upon a plan. It really was so awfully funny I can't help laughing when I think of it."

And she began to laugh.

"Are you crazy, Essie?" interrupted Violet, in a low, cold voice, from her corner.

"Why? Why should I not tell Frank?" demanded Essie. "The story is no secret."

"I am sure Frank does not want to hear it. Don't listen, Frank."

"No. But it is a very funny story," insisted Essie. "Now, Frank, listen. This girl managed to get an invitation from her godmother to come and pay her a visit before her wedding. The godmother had been always awfully kind to her; like Violet's godmother, Mrs. Eversfield, you know. I don't know where the godmother lived. But it was near Dover. The girl's friends refused to let her go. So she appealed to Smith to help her, and he agreed. She got away from home on the sly, and the amorous Smith met her, and accompanied her to Victoria Station, and put her into the Dover train and promised to come and meet her again in the evening. You understand?"

"Yes."

"Well, the train started all right. And—that is the end of the story."

"How so?" asked Warrington.

"Why—can't you see?"

"She never came back?"

"*Never*," said Essie, with a shake of her pretty head, and a look of the drollest solemnity. "But, don't you see, the joke of it was that it was Smith that had assisted her to escape from himself."

The minute hand of the clock had reached the hour. At St. Pancras the trains start with the greatest punctuality, and without the least fuss, and at the same instant a guard's low whistle sounded down the platform, and the train began to move.

Frank Warrington walked a few paces by the side of the train, shaking hands with the girls, wishing them "*Bon voyage,*" and adding:

" Telegraph from Kettering."

The speed quickening slightly, he was just about to turn away from the train, when Violet suddenly leaned forward and looked in his face.

" *Adieu*," she said, in a tone that had a ring of strange significance.

And a moment afterwards, he being left by that time some three or four yards behind, Essie put her head out of the window.

" Good-bye—Mr. Smith," she said, laughing.

Then she drew in her head, and the window-sash went up with a little jerk.

CHAPTER IV

THE train rolled away, winding round the curve out of the station. Frank Warrington stood looking after it. Soon the end of the last carriage disappeared, and there was no more to be seen : only the porters with their trucks, and other railway servants, and the news-boys, and the people who had come to see their friends off, moving away.

Warrington turned, and took six slow steps towards the way out of the station. Then he stopped, and, facing about, looked in the direction of the train that had vanished.

His mind misgave him. Incredible as the thing was, he could not shake off a haunting misgiving that his cousin Essie had been describing to him an impudent hoax of which he was himself at this very moment the victim.

" But this is impossible ! " he said to himself.

Yet he could not make up his mind to leave the station. Lighting a cigar, he began walking up and down the long platform. And he went to look at the time-table. The train was due at Kettering at 11.28 A.M. He might have remembered that.

The train did not stop except at Kentish Town between London and Kettering. It would be very easy to telegraph to Kettering. Only, if really bent on mischief, the girls might easily go on beyond Kettering.

The train stopped next at Sheffield, or they might change at Kettering for Nottingham. Only then Mrs. Eversfield would see them. Well, it would be easy enough to telegraph to all these points : "Two young ladies, sisters—tall, fair, *et cetera*, dressed— that would be rather more difficult to describe— accompanied by a French maid—should alight at Kettering, and be met by a Mrs. Eversfield—suspected of intention of escaping from their guardian. Have train watched. Arrest ladies, if they pass Kettering." Thus Warrington to himself, whilst consulting the time-table. One thing he knew for certain, Mrs. Eversfield would not assist the girls in any mischief. If they alighted at Kettering, and were met by her, all was well. In that case he would only have to pay for the telegrams, and no one need ever know anything about the matter.

He did telegraph to Kentish Town, to know if by any chance the girls had commenced operations at once, by leaving the train there. Answer in the negative.

With a jerk, Frank Warrington brought his cane up under his arm, and, swinging round on his heel, walked away from the telegraph-office, and out of the station.

He was ashamed of himself. He appeared to be forgetting that he was a gentleman and the girls ladies. Ladies and gentlemen do not do things of this kind. A girl who respects herself does not jilt a man without a word of explanation a month before her wedding-day Young ladies do not go on their travels with no more luggage than a lady's-maid and a hand-bag. Well-bred girls have more regard for their own reputations than to vanish in the manner related in the history of Mr. Smith. The story of Mr. Smith was simply a story, and probably not true; it seemed doubtful whether any man could be such an ass as Smith—though some great fool might, perhaps.

And resolving to banish from his thoughts a suspicion which he was ashamed ever to have entertained, he hailed a hansom, and, jumping into it, named to the driver his grandfather's house in Welmore Street.

"Is General Chesterfield down?" he asked of the boy in buttons who opened the door.

"At breakfast, sir."

Laying down his hat and stick on the hall-table, Warrington crossed to the dining-room.

Seated at one end of the table, with his back to a roaring fire, was an old man, very stout, and perfectly bald, with a large and very rubicund face. He was dressed in a hideous flowered dressing-gown, and, with a large table-napkin tucked under his double or treble chin, was commencing with a plate of Julienne soup what was evidently, from the number of things on the table, to be a very long and elaborate *déjeûner*.

"Good-morning, grandfather; how are you this morning?" said Warrington.

"I've got the indigestion," growled the old man crossly. "What's the time?" he asked in the same tone, as Warrington drew a chair to the side of the table.

"About half-past ten."

"And those jades of girls not down yet. They treat me with no more respect than a sweep. Upon my soul, I'll not put up with it!—I'll *not* put up with it."

"Down! They had breakfast at nine," said Warrington, sitting down. "I breakfasted with them. You forget. I have just come back from seeing them off from the station."

"Station! What station?" demanded the old man, holding a spoonful of soup in front of his mouth.

"From St. Pancras."

"What do they want to go to St. Pancras for?"

"Gone down to Kettering, you know, to see Mrs. Eversfield."

"I said they should not go down to Kettering," exclaimed the general, passionately, turning half round in his chair to face his grandson. And he gave the table a great thump with his fist.

"But, you know, last night you gave them leave to go," remarked Warrington, altogether undisturbed at the old man's temper.

"I said they should *not* go. I will not have them go to see Mrs. Eversfield; and they shall not go," replied the old man, still more angrily. "I'll not have them running about the country like a pair of milliners."

"But, you see, as you gave them leave, they are gone."

"I don't care. They shall *not* go," thundered the general. "I say they shall *not* go."

But, bringing down his fist once more to emphasize his determination, the old fellow, whose sight was not so good as it had been, this time just caught his knuckles on the edge of his soup-plate, which thereupon flew spinning into the air, showering its contents all over himself.

"Ugh!" he exclaimed, with disgust, pushing back his chair and holding out his hands as he watched the soup dripping down on the carpet. "Here, get me a napkin; get me something. Here, James! Ugh!"

The man-servant came to his assistance, the soup

was wiped off the carpet, a clean table-napkin provided, and another plate of soup. Meanwhile, Warrington explained how he had seen the two girls and their maid safely off from St. Pancras in a compartment which they would have to themselves all the way, the general growling all the time, and asserting the wilful disobedience of the girls, and declining to hear anything Warrington wished to say in explanation.

"Very well," he concluded at last, passionately, "very well. I wash my hands of the whole affair. I said that the girls should not go. I told them so last night after you left. You choose to assist them to disobey me. I have nothing to do with it. If anything happens, it is all your fault. You understand, sir, all your fault. Not mine. And if you wish your wife and her sister to conduct themselves like milliners—very good. Only not so long as they are in my house, please. You have assisted them to disobey me; and I wash my hands of the whole affair."

And he pushed his plate from him and poured himself out a glass of Chablis.

Cod "*à la Hollandaise*" succeeded the Julienne, and the painful subject of the Misses Chesterfield's conduct was dropped. The old man was still cross, and exceedingly huffy, but by degrees his breakfast and his grandson coaxed him into a better temper, and by one o'clock grandfather and grandson were getting on together capitally. The old man had finished his breakfast, and was sipping a cup of strong coffee and smoking a cigar in which Warrington had joined him, standing leaning against the chimney-piece.

A servant came in with a telegram for the general.

"Now, then, what's this?" exclaimed the old man, pettishly; "why do you bring me telegrams directly

after my meals? Eh? Haven't I trouble enough
to digest my food, without having my stomach loaded
with telegrams. Eh? What's it about? Take it
away."

Warrington stepped forward.

"I told the girls to telegraph as soon as they
reached Kettering," he said, quietly. "No doubt it
is from them."

"Very well," said his grandfather, not too pleasantly
"Then you had better look at it."

Warrington took the telegram from the servant.
and, still leaning against the chimney-piece, tore it
open.

He turned as pale as ashes.

The telegram was not from the girls, but from
Mrs. Eversfield.

*"Misses Chesterfield not come by eleven twenty-eight.
Am I to expect them by a later train, or are their plans
changed? I wait at station for reply."*

Warrington felt the floor giving way under his
feet.

Sitting up in his deep armchair, the general was
sipping his coffee. Putting down his cup, he leaned
back again, and replacing his cigar between his lips,
puffed a slow cloud of smoke.

"I am afraid there is something wrong," said
Warrington, in a cold, even tone, mastering himself
by a strong effort. "Mrs. Eversfield telegraphs that
the girls have not arrived at Kettering."

"Where are they gone then?"

"I don't understand it," answered Warrington, in
the same quiet way "The train did not stop between
London and Kettering, and they must have arrived
there. Only it seems that there is some mistake. I'll
telegraph to Mrs. Eversfield at once," he concluded,
proceeding to leave the room.

In his own mind he had no doubt at all about what

Lad happened. This was the veritable history of the redoubtable Mr. Smith.

He hastily put on his coat in the hall, and snatched up his hat and stick, telling the telegraph boy that he need not wait. Going out, he hailed the first cab he saw, and, promising the cabman a handsome fare, bade him drive for his life to St. Pancras.

For the moment he did not know what he felt most—indignation, anger, mortification, or sheer stupefaction: mortification at the evidently irretrievable loss of his cousin, to whom he was sincerely attached; indignation at the trick that had been played him; anger with his cousin for what she had done, and with himself for proving so easily her dupe; or stupefaction at the sudden occurrence of an incident, so far as he could perceive, utterly unprepared, and perfectly unaccountable.

He already had a theory. The girls had deliberately gone beyond Kettering. Their intention was to leave the train at some station further down the railway. There, some accomplice would be waiting to meet them, some man, or men; all this had not been devised without the assistance of men. Who the men might be was more difficult to conjecture. The girls had an uncle, their mother's brother, and they liked their uncle better than their grandfather. But their uncle was abroad. Other relatives they had none. Presumably, then, the men on whose assistance they were relying belonged to the indefinite class most simply described as "lovers," and these gentlemen were probably to be rewarded with the hands and hearts of the young ladies.

"Only, by Jove, not if I can help it," vowed Warrington, in the corner of his cab.

Another point occurred to him. The girls, if they were well advised, would not go very far beyond Kettering. They could hardly have left out of their calculations that as soon as they were missed they would be pursued by the telegraph.　And they would be missed as soon as they did not appear at Kettering.　Their device would evidently be to quit the train at the next station after Kettering in the hope of getting away before there had been time for Mrs. Eversfield to telegraph to the grandfather, and for their grandfather to telegraph down the railway to stop them.

The next place at which the express stopped after Kettering was Sheffield.　Was that their destination ? or had they gone to Nottingham ?

"I think I have them.　They have been mistaken in their Mr. Smith," quoth Warrington to himself.

The cab drew up with a jerk.　Tossing the driver half-a-crown, Warrington rushed to the telegraph-office.

He telegraphed to Sheffield and to Nottingham, and, at the suggestion of the official, to Chesterfield, where the train might have been stopped by signal.

"Two young ladies, sisters, tall, fair, fashionably dressed, accompanied by a French lady's-maid, have tickets for Kettering, but have gone beyond that station, believed to be attempting to escape from their guardian, perhaps have gone further, please search train and make inquiries."

An answer came back from Nottingham.　No such ladies had alighted there.　Nor at Chesterfield, where the train had stopped.

Warrington went out of the telegraph-office, and took a turn on the platform, considerably lighter of heart.

"You ought to have left the train before this, young ladies," he remarked, in imagination addressing the fugitives.　"I am afraid that you have not been very well advised. We shall have you now at Sheffield."

He had telegraphed to Mrs. Eversfield making some sort of excuse.

Now he was waiting for the train to reach Sheffield.

When it was due there he returned to the telegraph-office.

Telegram from Sheffield: *"No such ladies in the train."*

"But this is impossible," exclaimed Warrington. "I myself saw them leave this station in the train, and if they did not alight at Kentish Town, nor at Kettering, they must have been in the train when it reached Sheffield."

The telegraph clerk asserted that "He couldn't say," with the curtness peculiar to his species.

It appeared to Warrington that it was very easy to say that people who had not left a train must still be in it. The adventure began to resemble magic. If Félicité had had anything bigger than a hand-bag with her he would have begun to believe in diguises.

Another telegram from Sheffield.

"Guard of express says that two young ladies similar to those described, and accompanied by a lady's-maid, alighted at Bedford. One of the ladies was ill, and the train was stopped by signal from the carriage as it was running into Bedford station. Train stopped at Bedford only for a minute. Telegraph to Bedford."

One of the girls taken ill! This was a new aspect of the matter.

And of course Warrington telegraphed to Bedford.

Answer from Bedford: *"The Scotch express stopped here by signal given by passengers. Two young ladies alighted and a maid with them. They had tickets for Nottingham."*

"How on earth did they come to have tickets for Nottingham?" wondered Warrington. Were these his cousins? His head began to turn on his shoulders.

Telegram to Bedford for further particulars, and to inquire what had become of the young ladies and their maid.

Reply: "*One of the young ladies was indisposed, and her sister stopped the train just as it was coming into Bedford. Young ladies and maid left the station shortly after their arrival. Nothing is known of where they went afterwards.*"

A suspicion of the truth rose before Frank Warrington. There was a train in the station shortly to start for Bedford, and he went down by it. He found his suspicion correct. The young ladies who had stopped the express were the Misses Chesterfield. Violet had found herself suddenly indisposed, and Essie had stopped the train. The waiting-room attendant was inclined to think that the young lady had nothing very serious the matter with her. She refused to take anything that was suggested, and, after about ten minutes, said she would walk up and down the platform, believing that the air would do her good. After that the attendant saw and heard no more of them until the telegram arrived.

It was five o'clock by this time, and dark. The girls had had time to go almost anywhere, and further inquiries about them were merely ridiculous. Warrington had nothing left to do but to return to town to inform the general that his grand-daughters had, beyond a doubt, run away, and to see how the old man would like it.

For his own private satisfaction, he had the further knowledge that he had played the part of Mr. Smith to perfection.

CHAPTER V.

On reaching town, Frank Warrington drove straight to General Chesterfield's. He was resolved at once to acquaint the general with the whole truth. To put off facing inevitable mortifications is the foible of those weak characters that seek to gain time with some vague hope of gaining, with time, courage ; and weakness was not among Frank Warrington's faults.

When he reached Welmore Street, the general was just going to dine. Nothing could have been more unfortunate, and Warrington knew it. If he could have reached the general's only a quarter of an hour earlier, the case would not have been so utterly desperate. Now the general would be kept waiting for his dinner. He must hear what Warrington had to say. Then the dinner would be spoiled ; and the general would be furious : and the passion he would put himself into would entirely upset his digestion. And, when once the general's digestion was upset, his self-control became a minus quantity. After which everything was possible, not excluding apoplexy. However, there was nothing for it but to break the fatal news.

Indeed, the general left him no choice. As Warrington came in, the old man was descending the stairs, and, seeing his grandson, at once demanded :

" Eh, Frank, is that you ? But where—where are the girls ? "

Instead of directly answering the question, Warrington asked :

" Grandfather, can I speak to you for a few minutes in private ? "

" Speak to me for a few minutes in private : now : just before dinner ? No—certainly not, sir ! *Where* are those two girls ? "

Receiving no answer, he ran on, angrily, with an oath :

"Not come in yet! Eh? Well, then, I'll not have them out of the house at this time of night. I'll not have it, sir! I tell you, I'll not have it!"

"It is of no use for you to put yourself into a passion, grandfather," remarked Warrington, tolerably coolly. "I'd rather tell you in private, if you could spare a couple of minutes."

"But—I'll not spare a couple of minutes."

"Well, then, I suppose I must tell you here," said Warrington. (They had come into the dining-room, where the men-servants were waiting by the sideboard.) "*The girls have bolted.*"

"What!" demanded the general, stopping suddenly, and facing his grandson.

"The girls have bolted," repeated Warrington.

Going to the hearth, he turned his back to the fire, and stood stroking his moustache, and looking at the general.

For a few minutes the general looked dumfounded, only trembling, and turning crimson with passion. Then he stammered out, in a choking voice :

"What! what! gone away! the hussies! gone : it's—it's—not true!"

"Perfectly true, I assure you," answered Warrington, with very tolerable composure. "The girls have bolted. I saw them into the train at St. Pancras this morning, and got them and their maid their tickets. Three tickets for Kettering. They did not go to Kettering. When they reached Bedford they signalled to the guard to stop the train. Violet said that she was ill, and they were left upon the Bedford platform. They went to the ladies' waiting-room, and remained their a few minutes. After that they must have left the station, for nobody knows any more about them. I have been down to Bedford to make inquiries, and can ascertain nothing."

The serving-men standing by the sideboard looked at each other.

"Here, come with me," said the general.

He led the way to the library, Warrington following him. As soon as the door was closed behind him the general began:

"What the devil, sir, do you mean by telling me a story like this before the servants? And listen, sir. I don't believe a word of it. And I *won't* believe a word of it. Where are these hussies gone?"

Warrington related his history again, with further particulars. And then he told it a third time; the general working himself up into a terrible passion meanwhile, and vowing that he would not believe a word. Howbeit, in time the facts became too strong for him, and then began the real scene.

First the general swore. And then, falling into such a rage that he could scarcely speak, he stammered out, in broken sentences, amidst many very bad words, that the girls were a pair of disreputable hussies, and something else a great deal worse, and that they should never enter his house again—that he would disinherit them, and would alter his will that very evening—that Warrington was every whit as bad as the girls, and an impudent, conceited donkey into the bargain —that it was Warrington's fault and nobody's else that the girls had finally disgraced themselves—that he, the general, did not care a fig what became of any of them—and that he was going to have his dinner.

All that might have been said in a very few minutes. But the old gentleman repeated each particular so many times, and employed so many powerful adjectives and adverbs to emphasize all he said, and stammered so much, that it was past nine o'clock before he and his grandson parted, not very amicably, but less unpleasantly than might have been expected. After all, men understand one another, and make allowances.

Going to the dining-room, the general even said to himself:

"I'm afraid the poor boy is put out about the loss of his sweetheart—the hussy! And confound the young coxcomb! Helping the hussies to disobey me! It's all his doing, confound him! But I'm afraid the boy is put out about the loss of his sweetheart."

Of course the dinner was spoiled. That was a small matter compared with the flight of the girls, but hardly so in the eyes of the general. Anyhow. this last final provocation proved too much for the poor old fellow's already overheated brain. After pushing away a third dish with a savage "Take it away, James. Take it away It's not fit to give to a dog," he got up from the table, vowing he had no appetite. For an hour or two he fretted about the place, sending for the servants, and wanting to know why Warrington had left, scolding in all sorts of unreasonable ways, and grumbling about not being able to eat his dinner. Then he went to bed. The next morning he was complaining of rheumatism in his left shoulder, and looking as yellow as a guinea, and unable to eat his breakfast.

CHAPTER VI.

ABOUT the same time that Warrington left Bedford, a big, broad-shouldered man between fifty and fifty-five years of age, with his large hands thrust into the side pockets of his dark pea-jacket, sauntered into the station at Hunstanton. He was a strongly built man, good-looking for his years, with a bright, clear eye, and a finely moulded face, expressive in a high degree of both energy and good-nature, browned with exposure to the sun and wind, where it was not covered by his heavy moustache and enormous beard that grew high on his cheeks and flowed down on his broad breast. In his air there was something of the man accustomed to command, and something of the easy bearing of a sailor.

" When will the train be in from Lynn ? " he asked of the station-master, who was standing on the platform.

" Six-seventeen, sir."

" It will *not* be late to-night ? "

" No, sir."

" Thanks."

The speaker turned away, and, strolling along the platform, took from his pocket a briar pipe and a pouch of tobacco. He filled his pipe slowly, and then, having lighted it, put his hands again into his pockets, and, walking up and down the end of the platform, smoked his pipe in a leisurely fashion.

When the train was signalled, he had just finished. Knocking out the ashes against a lamp-post, he put away his pipe, and putting his hands again into his pockets, sauntered to the front of the platform with the same leisurely ease that characterized all his movements.

The train rolled in. As it passed, he rapidly scanned the windows of the carriages, and then a smile lighted his face.

At one of the windows were two girls looking out eagerly—Violet and Essie Chesterfield.

" There is Uncle Tony," cried Essie at the same instant, as he turned and came towards them.

A minute later the girls were both on the platform, holding their uncle by his arms, with their little hands on his great shoulders.

" Dear old Uncle Tony !"

" So you got away, then ? " remarked their uncle, smiling.

"Oh, we had such fun !" replied Essie. "Cousin Frank came to see us off; really he did. Last night grandpapa said we should not go, and we were in the most awful fright. But Frank took our part, and at last grandpapa consented. After Frank had gone, grandpapa changed his mind again, and said we should not go after all. But grandpapa never comes down to breakfast till nearly eleven, and so this morning we had an early breakfast. And we told Frank—he came to breakfast with us—nothing about grandpapa having changed his mind. So he took us to the station, and, only fancy, Uncle Tony! he got us our tickets, and *everything !* I could have laughed ! And he told us we were to be sure to telegraph when we got to Kettering. And he said he would come to meet us at St. Pancras in the evening. And, do you know, just before we started, we told him a story about an imaginary Mr. Smith, who was going to be married to a girl who did not care for him, and how the girl got him to see her off by the train, and never came back; just what we were doing, you know. And he never took it in, not a bit. Then all the rest we did just as you told us. Violet pretended that she was ill, and we stopped the train at Bedford. I am sure "—here Miss Essie looked very droll— " that the woman in the ladies' waiting-room at Bedford saw that we were humbugging. However, we got away from her as fast as we could. Then we took the train to Cambridge. And. do you know, we had such an awfully jolly luncheon at Cambridge, we were so hungry! And from Cambridge we came straight on here, and here we are, you see, safe and sound."

"I see," said Uncle Tony. "I'm afraid it's all very wrong, you know. You've no luggage, I imagine, and we may just as well be going." He turned and spoke to the lady's-maid, who was standing a little off. "And how are you, Félicité, quite well ?"

"Quite well, thank you, sir," answered Félicité, with a French accent; "and very glad to get away from the General Chesterfield's house, sir."

"Come along, then," said Uncle Tony to the girls. "The trunk you sent down from town came last night, and was taken on board this afternoon; so we have nothing to wait for."

When they were in the cab, he asked:

"And the general, how did you leave him?"

"The horrid old thing!" exclaimed Essie. "He is killing himself with eating. Fancy! the doctor has told him five times within the last two months that, if he goes on stuffing himself as he does, he will die of it. And yet he eats enough at any meal for three."

"You have been very unhappy with your grandfather?"

"He never said a kind word to us, not once, all the time we were with him," said Violet, passionately. "We have been scolded at, called names, and sworn at for two years."

"Do you mean that he really swore at you?"

"Rather!" said Essie.

"The general's life has been a very rough one," observed Uncle Tony, apologetically; "but in his time he was a fine officer. And your *fiancé*, my dear?" he continued, turning to Violet.

"Oh, I suppose he is all right," replied Violet Chesterfield, indifferently. "You know, he is not at all a bad sort of fellow, uncle. In a way I like him, only——"

"But you must not be changing your mind, my dear. It is too late to begin liking him now."

"You quite misunderstand me," answered Violet Chesterfield, coldly.

"All right, niece."

"I mean, uncle," explained Violet, more confidentially, "that I could like Frank well enough as my cousin—but that I could never wish to marry him. I

should never have dreamed of such a thing, I can
assure you, only we were both of us so utterly wretched
with grandpapa. You can't imagine what we have
endured. Nothing but scold, scold, scold, nag, nag,
nag, all day long, to say nothing of his being in a
perfect fury with us at least twice a week; and
almost mad whenever we said we wished that we
could live with you. We have been nearly beside
ourselves, and there seemed no way out of it except
getting married. And so, when Frank came home
from abroad, and I saw that grandpapa wanted me to
marry him, I accepted him. I know it was wrong;
but—oh, well, I don't want to make excuses, I know
it was wrong."

"Certainly," admitted Uncle Tony.

"Afterwards, you know, when it came to marrying, I began quite to hate him, though I knew he
was not a bad sort of fellow. Still, when I began
to see what it all meant, that I was throwing
myself away for good and all, and should have ever
after to turn round and round in one fatal circle of
Frank, Frank, Frank, nothing but Frank—never to live
anywhere except with Frank, never to go anywhere
except with Frank, never to love any one but Frank,
never have any one to think about but Frank, never
any home but Frank's home, and never any future
but Frank's future, I began to think that I should
go mad. And if you had not come to our assistance
I should have done something desperate, I know,
something awfully wrong, I daresay. However,
thank goodness, it's all over now, like a bad dream ;
and I don't know that I am not a little bit sorry for
Cousin Frank. He has been rather badly used. Still,
I could not help it. I could not have married him "

"I don't think, you know, that you need be afraid
of his wanting you to do so after this," said Tony
Gainsborough, drily.

"Violet," put in Essie, "has been in such an

awful fright all day lest we should be telegraphed after, and caught. I could not help laughing when I thought of it. It would have been such an awful climax."

"Ah, you were not going to be married next month," remarked Violet.

"Well, I think you may consider yourself safe now," said the uncle; "unless we find a policeman with a telegram waiting for us on the pier."

"You wouldn't send us back, uncle?" exclaimed Essie.

"Well, perhaps not," admitted Uncle Tony.

But there was no policeman on the pier. Only a four-oar cutter, waiting, and a man with a lantern.

The girls were soon in the boat.

"Where is the yacht, Uncle Tony?" said Violet.

"Lying off, about a mile and a half out."

He sat down in the stern and took the yoke lines; the girls were on his right and left.

"All ready?" he asked.

"No, uncle, wait a minute," said Essie.

"What is it?"

"Ask the man to hold the light near. I am going to write a line to grandpapa. May I? It will put a stop to his hunting after us all over the country, you know."

"All right—as you please."

Essie drew a little pocket-book from her pocket, and, having opened it on her knees, unfastened a pencil from her watch-chain. The man with the light bent down, holding the lantern at her shoulder. The imperfect light fitfully illumined the boat and the calm water round it, the little group in the stern-sheets, the sailors in their loose shirts resting on their oars, and the iron piles of the pier above them. Whilst the waves sobbed and splashed against the side of the boat, Essie wrote:

"DEAR GRANDPAPA,—I write this on my knees in Uncle Tony Gainsborough's cutter, as we are waiting under the lee of the pier at Hunstanton before putting off to his yacht.

"Violet was quite unable to face marriage with Cousin Frank. She is very sorry for it, and you can tell him so; but she does not care a bit for him, and would never have promised to marry him if we had not wanted so dreadfully to get away from No. 19 Welmore Street, where we were both so miserable, as you must know. However, Uncle Tony has promised us that neither of us shall ever come back to live with you—so we will let bygones be bygones, and say no more about how wretched you have made us every day for two whole long years.

"We have left a lot of things behind us. You can do just what you like with them, and we have paid all our bills.

"It will be of no use for either you or Cousin Frank to hunt after us. But, as you might feel inclined to do so, I am unable to tell you anything about our plans.

"Violet and I hope that you will think of what Dr. Beauchamp told you, and leave off over-eating yourself.—Your affectionate and dutiful granddaughter,
"ESSIE CHESTERFIELD."

She had brought with her an envelope directed to General Chesterfield, and she slipped the paper into it. Tony Gainsborough passed it over to the man who held the lantern, giving him a shilling and telling him to post it. Then he gave the word:

"Give way."

And the cutter left the jetty, cleaving her way, through the calm, gently rippling water, to where the lights of the steam yacht shone out at sea.

CHAPTER VII.

From his grandfather's house Warrington went to his own chambers. It was a relief, after a day of excitements and fatigues of so unpleasant a kind, to find himself once more at last at home, and he put the latch-key into the lock of his own door with a feeling of coming into port, after shipwreck, it is true, but still coming into port.

He passed through the small lobby, and entered the dining-room.

A bright fire blazed on the hearth, and a lamp on the table shed a pleasant light around the comfortable, rather tastefully furnished room. Folding-doors leading into the next room were open, and there the clicking of some machine at work was audible.

A man sitting at a little table was busily at work with a Remington type-writer. As Frank Warrington approached him, he spoke, without looking up :

" Why, Frank, where have you been all day ?"

" Where, indeed ? You may well ask, my dear Eustace," replied Warrington, throwing himself into a big armchair.

The other rose and came towards him.

He was Frank Warrington's brother, and very like him ; nearly of the same height, but fairer and much more slightly built, and with more delicate features : features that presented less of actual masculine handsomeness, but more of sculpturesque refinement ; a finer, more spiritual type—if the term may pass— something almost feminine, that was enhanced by the pensive expression of a face in which, though it had a light of its own, there was a great blank : for the eyes were closed. Eustace Warrington was blind.

" Why, what has happened ?" he asked, sitting down in the chair opposite his brother with that perfect ease of the blind which suggests the idea of sight being a rather superfluous accomplishment.

"In the first place," replied Frank Warrington. "it is all over between me and Violet."

"Finally?"

"Finally, Eustace," answered Warrington, with emphasis.

"And how so?" asked the blind man very quietly

"The girls have bolted from grandfather."

"Where are they gone?"

"That we don't know."

Eustace Warrington leaned forward and seemed to think.

"Grandfather has treated them very badly," he said, meditatively, "and they have been very unhappy with him." Then, raising himself, he said: "Where and how did all this happen?"

Warrington related the history of the day, and made no scruple about expressing his opinion of the Misses Chesterfield's behaviour.

Talking is intoxicating. A man may think much, and feel deeply; but, whilst he only thinks and feels within himself, it is singular how little his passions are moved, either by his feelings or by his speculations. It is when he proceeds to speak, to give his soul utterance in the hearing of other men, that he is carried away. Telling his brother what had occurred, Warrington became very soon bitter beyond measure. And still, harsh as the things were that he said, none of his language seemed to himself sufficiently to express the savage anger against his cousin, and the profound indignation at the way he had been used, that was seething within him.

Eustace heard him attentively, seldom interrupting him. Only, as his brother's language became more passionate, he repeated what he had said before, very quietly:

"The girls have been very unhappy with grandfather, much more so than you have imagined. Of course you did not see it. You people who see are always blind to that sort of thing. But I assure you those two girls have been miserable."

"However grandfather treated them, he treated them better than they deserved, and the event has proved it," returned Warrington.

At the end came the real question, "What was to be done?"

There was no hope of the affair being quietly hushed up. Arrangements for a wedding had gone too far, and the general's servants knew what had happened. And the general himself would not be reticent. As soon as he had got over his first twenty-four hours of rage, the old fellow would cast about him for an explanation of what had occurred that would make the case look best for himself. Both his grandsons knew that. No doubt all the blame would be laid upon Warrington. Rather than marry him, Violet Chesterfield had bolted, and made her sister go with her. And then the assistance that Warrington had lent his betrothed to get away from him : his persuading the general, and seeing his cousins off, and all the rest would make a magnificent story, which the general would know only too well how to relate to his friend Colonel Nysson, and to old Tyler of the War Office, and little Jack Gratton of the Blues. And two hours after that the thing would be all over London.

Only Warrington trusted that he would be before then out of the way of hearing about it. Only the question was, where should he go?

"*La nuit porte conseil*," said Eustace. "Let us leave it till to-morrow. So far as I can see, you have had nothing to eat since breakfast. We will have supper now. Whilst it is being brought up, I'll finish my letters, and we will leave the discussion of our plans until to-morrow."

His advice was good. It is not until after a night's rest that a man learns, in a case like this, justly to appreciate his new situation. On waking, Warrington seemed to himself hardly, on the previous day, to have understood what had taken place, and only now to comprehend that he had lost the girl he had hoped to marry, and all that that implied; the singularly ridiculous figure he himself was likely to cut when the story got abroad; and many other things, unhappily none of them pleasant.

As for the young lady—well, he was well rid of her, and would be a fool if he regretted her. The pretty little escapade of running away from her grandfather was enough of itself to cure any man of judgment from wishing to have Miss Violet Chesterfield for his wife. And unhappily, in addition to that, Frank Warrington could, with truth, lay to her charge other delinquencies still more serious.

When they were first engaged, his cousin had been cold and unresponsive. When a date for the marriage came to be talked about, she only, after considerable delay, consented, with evident reluctance, to name the wedding-day. But a week or so later a gradual change came over her. The marked coolness of her manner disappeared. When Warrington came to see her she received him with smiles, and showed herself amiable and responsive, almost affectionate. That, then, Warrington inferred, was the date when she first laid her plans to escape from him, and began to see her way to carrying them into execution. If so, it was not difficult to find ugly words for the disingenuousness of a girl who began to be indulgent to her lover as soon as she saw her way to deceiving him.

And these considerations rendered more easy the bitterness with which Frank Warrington proceeded next to judge the finishing stroke of his faithless mistress's deceit, and the malice that had found amusement in making him an accomplice in his own humiliation.

It did not occur to him to remember that it was not Violet but her sister who had found so much amusement in his part of the escapade, and had entertained him with the legend of Mr. Smith. Neither did he reflect that it was quite possible that Violet Chesterfield had made use of his assistance with reluctance, and only because her escape was impossible without it. He was far too angry to give really cool thought to anything, and he summed up his verdict on the whole affair in a single little word—" low."

When a woman behaves very badly to a man who is really attached to her, the man does one of two things. Either he forgives her and then loves her ten times better than he did before, or, if he does not forgive her, he sooner or later hates her. A man seldom forgives a woman for being unladylike. A man seldom forgives a woman who wounds his *amour propre*. A man never forgives a woman who wrongs him and then disappears. To pardon, he must at least be able to see her.

And Warrington was beginning to be aware already of a revulsion of feeling that turned against his mistress, and grew sour with hatred. Probably, had he tried, he could not have helped it. And perhaps he would have been a rather poor-spirited mortal if he had tried. Men are not to be asked to retain their esteem for women in spite of anything the women may do.

Having got thus far whilst dressing and shaving, Warrington proceeded to breakfast. Eustace was already waiting for him. Over the breakfast-table the brothers discussed what should be their plans; Warrington a little sulky and very savage, Eustace quiet and cool as he always was, and, as he often was, a little philosophical.

" You have been badly treated by your *fiancée*,

Frank," he admitted. "The best thing you can do is to forget it."

"No doubt. Only how?"

"Let us go down to that place in Dorsetshire, and, instead of selling it, live there. You won't be wanting now to marry for a year or two."

"For a year or two! Never, my dear fellow. I have had a lesson in what women are. You don't find me putting my neck into that noose again."

"That may be, or not. Only, if you are not going immediately to marry, there is no reason why we should not go and live, at any rate for a time, at Lynhurst. You will be able to afford to spend something on the place, and that may very likely in the end pay you well. At any rate, you can hunt, and I will grow roses. To live in the country will be paradise to me. So I propose that we betake ourselves to Lynhurst. But I don't want to be selfish. Take the day to think about it; to see whether you would like it too. And we will talk the matter over again in the evening."

"It is certainly worth thinking of," admitted Warrington.

Rising from the breakfast-table, he lighted a cigar, and asked:

"You see a good deal, Eustace, that most of us do not see. Did you think this affair between me and my cousin would end like this?"

"No, I did not. I thought that she would marry you. May I tell you why?"

"Pray do not hesitate."

"I thought she would marry you to get away from grandfather. Only, you see, she has managed that somehow else."

"Cutting, Eustace."

"The truth, Frank."

Warrington went out to see the general, and left Eustace alone.

"Frank has been shamefully used," said the blind man to himself. "But he was a good deal too ready to believe that the girl admired him and liked him more than she did. And, of course, he was ignorant of how miserable she and her sister were with the general. Though why people should be able to perceive less with five senses than with four is an odd problem. Now, too, of course, Frank will be out of humour with all the sex."

He was right about that. When a man has singled out one amongst women as more worth believing in and loving than all the rest, and found her faithless, it is easier for his vanity to change his opinion of all womankind than to confess his personal incapacity to distinguish a woman worth having.

And, making his way to the general's, Warrington was soliloquizing thus: "One hears it said, that women are a bad lot. But I have never hitherto given my assent to it. Only this is a somewhat staggering experience. I should have said that those two girls were ladies—if there be any such things. Only it seems that 'lady' is far from being the equivalent of 'gentlewoman.'"

He found the general in bed, ill, and very, very cross. The old man was hungry, and had not been able to eat his breakfast. Warrington was rather alarmed at his yellow appearance. But the general was so out of temper, so furious that his granddaughters should have run away from his house, so angry at the failure of his cherished scheme of marrying his eldest grandson to his eldest granddaughter, so put out about the breakfast he had not been able to eat, and so resolved to mix all these subjects together, that no connected conversation of any kind was to be got from him.

While Warrington was with him, Essie's letter arrived. The doctor had just called, and insisted on the general's being kept quiet. Of course the letter put him into a frightful passion; to crown which he declared his intention of having everything that the doctor had forbidden for luncheon.

On Frank Warrington the note had no effect of any kind. He had made up his mind about the Misses Chesterfield, and Essie's letter merely served to confirm him in his opinion.

For the rest, he was thankful enough to find that there would be no occasion to make investigations about what had become of the girls.

When he returned to his brother at dinner-time, he said :

"I have been thinking of your proposal, and I like it. We will go down and live at Lynhurst. And we'll see whether we can't do some good with the place. At any rate we shall be out of the reach of hearing anything about this affair, and out of the way of all these cursed women."

"Lynhurst must be a strange place if there are no women there," thought Eustace to himself; "and Frank must know that as well as I." But aloud he said only, "That is it, then. We'll go down to Lynhurst."

CHAPTER VIII.

So, after all, the new master of Lynhurst did not sell the place, but came to live in it.

The brothers sent down their furniture and Frank Warrington's horses. They put up at the "London Hotel," and had the small suite of rooms, in which the former owner of Lynhurst had lived, refurnished, and a part of the large, long-empty stables made fit for use. And in a very days they had established themselves, comfortably enough for bachelors, in their new home, and began to look about them.

They found that they had a good house, a handsome house it would be if put into repair and properly furnished, and what might be a beautiful place if they could find the judgment, money, and energy to make it so. They had what might be capital preserves; they had what might be beautiful pastures. The point was to make them such. The dilapidations were terrible, and the mortgages very formidable. But the enterprise of redeeming the place was an engaging one, and the young men entered upon it at any rate with zest and spirit, and a resolution to do their best.

They had come to live in a quiet way and they carried out their intention. They breakfasted at an earlier hour than in town, and devoted the mornings to business, to becoming acquainted with the property, to seeing what could be done for it, and to making arrangements to have it done. Together they went about all over the place on foot; and what a treat that was to Eustace, who was fond of walking, and promised himself soon to be so familiar with the whole neighbourhood that he would be able not only to walk about his brother's estate unaccompanied, but to stroll down to the little town, and to manage all his own business there without the assistance of his valet, indispensable in London.

In business matters, meanwhile, in the choice of servants, employment of hands, and other such affairs, he proved of the greatest service to his brother. His delicate ear was so quick to detect in the turn of a voice indications of incapacity or deceit, which people, accustomed to study to deceive the eye only, were negligent to conceal. In the evenings the brothers had the same pastimes as in town. Warrington read aloud, or they sat down together to chess, or Eustace took out his violin, or opened the piano. In the big house, Eustace could enjoy his indoor pleasures better than in town, as well as in the grounds those of the open air. A grand piano would have somewhat crowded the London chambers; but here he had one of the large rooms opening from their little suite for a music-room. Frank Warrington, devoted to his brother, had at least this gratification, if no other, from his country life, to see how enormously Eustace's pleasures had been in an instant enlarged. Even the site for the rose-garden had been already chosen, and the ground partly laid out according to Eustace's design, and some of the rose-trees planted.

Lynham, however, was a little disappointed. Two young bachelors who came to do the best thing they could for their estates, and lived in a rather secluded way, were not what people had expected. They were both in excellent health, and so of no use to Dr. Gregg. They preferred having things from London to paying fifty per cent. more for inferior articles in a small Lynham shop; and so were of no use to the tradespeople. The elder brother, who was "the rich one," was reputed rather morose, and the younger was blind and poor: and so they were of no use to the pining virgins of Lynham. Howbeit, as they came with excellent introductions, and Warrington at once subscribed handsomely to the nearest hunt (though he made, and kept to, a resolution not to follow the hounds more than once a week), they were well received. The rector, and Dr. Gregg, and Brown of the bank, and the local solicitor called, and Eustace received them, and was considered an agreeable and accomplished young fellow. Being at the same time less engaged than his brother, and, like many blind people, a bright conversationalist, fond of talking, and always ready for a chat, he was considered, in a small way, an acquisition. But it was clear that the universally useful, public-spirited, much-desiderated ideal owner of Lynhurst had, after all, not come.

A month soon slipped away. Eustace already began to find his way, unaccompanied, about the parts of the ground nearer the house; and Warrington was deeply engaged in his schemes for doing as much as he could afford for the estate—very much less, alas, than the state of the place required. He and Eustace knew still very little of their neighbours, though they had already received two or three invitations, one only of which had been accepted, and that much more for Eustace's sake than for Warrington's. To Frank Warrington, just at present, the greatest treat in the world was to be left to himself; to indulge himself with a long solitary walk or ride, sometimes in the country, sometimes along the long sands, which presented, when the tide was low, a promenade of several miles, and no bad place for a gallop. The change of scene and of occupation had done much to take him out of himself, and to divert his thoughts from recollections of his cousin's behaviour. But, when he did recollect her, neither change of occupation nor of scene served much to qualify the bitterness with which he judged her perfidy, or, rather, that of all her sex. At such times to saunter by the sea, or to ride slowly in the low evening light across the downs, smoking a good cigar, and letting his anger cook in his breast, afforded him a savage satisfaction of a sort that will perhaps be better understood by men than by women.

It was in this humour that he, one afternoon late in November, strolled down to the beach, after having been into Lynham on business.

At four o'clock the sun was already setting. The short afternoon was closing apace, and the few people remaining on the beach were leaving it. The sky was grey with dull clouds, a breeze, growing chilly, passed over the sands, blowing nearly parallel with the shore. The sea was neither calm nor rough: a restless, choppy sea, that broke coldly in low, curling waves, monotonously, almost mournfully. A good deal of rain had fallen recently, and the cliffs were soaked with moisture. Down their faces trickled little streams, whose ceaseless dropping made a wistful accompaniment to the cold splashing of the sea and to the soughing of the wind. The circumstances were hardly such as any one would have been expected to choose for a walk on the sands, but they assorted with Frank Warrington's humour, and going down to the waterside he strolled on along the beach.

The tide was rising, but had hardly yet reached the half-flood, and there was a broad tract of fine sand, tightly cemented by the water it contained, firm and pleasant for walking. Not at all displeased to see the grey light fading, nor to have the lonely beach to himself, Frank Warrington sauntered on a long way, occupied only with his own thoughts, now and then stopping to look seaward, not at anything in particular, but only at the restless movement of the cold waves ; and then again strolling on, dashing away from time to time a broken shell or a fragment of seaweed that lay in his path—angrily, impatiently. He was very savage this afternoon, savage with that seething, fermenting anger which works in all the male animals when irritated by the caprices of feminine humour. Somehow he believed that he could with satisfaction have taken a woman, any woman not too old, and have wrung her neck, just to convince her what he thought of the whole of her species.

" The miserable lying wretches !" he said in himself, sulkily. " The devil take the whole tribe of them ! I am afraid there is no hope of his doing that. But he may have me if I ever again put myself in the way of being fooled by one of them."

And striking an ancient, fishless shell, he sent it flying into the sea.

CHAPTER IX.

HE strolled on a long way. The tide had yet far to rise before it could inconvenience his return. The twilight began to turn to gloom, and the beach had become quite deserted. But when a man is very angry it is pleasant to wander in solitude by the sea with the shades of night falling, and no light to be seen but the white gleam of the surf.

The beach was not everywhere of the same breadth. At some places the cliffs presented to the sea a long flattish face, at others they advanced a bit, and then fell back again, making small bays, or wound in and out irregularly. There were points where at high water it was not possible to pass in front of them, and there the sands were more level, broad plateaux of rocks, bordered with seaweed, stretched out towards the sea, and the cliffs rose high in tall, perpendicular peaks. Warrington passed several of these headlands, having satisfied himself each time, by a glance at the tide, that he should be easily able to return.

All of a sudden he was surprised to see, only a little way in front of him, a figure loom out of the gloom. It was so dark that any object became indistinguishable at a distance of a few yards. The figure approached, moving very slowly, as slowly as he was walking himself. Was it some other man come to sulk by the sobbing sea, in the dark? No. It was a woman : a girl. She was nearer now. A tall girl, apparently fashionably dressed, wearing a high hat ; with her hands hanging before her tucked into her muff ; walking slowly, her head bent, and her eyes on the ground.

When they were nearer, she saw Warrington. He thought she started. Then they passed quite close to each other. Without turning his head, Warrington stole a hard questioning look at her from the corners of his eyes. And, at the same instant, the girl, without turning her head, stole a precisely similar hard questioning look at him from the corners of her eyes.

For a moment the two keen, searching glances met —her eyes were nearly level with his—and then both quickly looked away.

" He looks handsome. What on earth can he be walking about here in the dark for?" thought the girl—it was Lily Hardwick—as she passed on.

" She looks pretty. What on earth can she be walking about here in the dark for?" thought Warrington, as he walked on.

Stopping, and standing facing the sea, he turned his head, and looked after her.

He could just see her. She was walking very slowly; had she, too, turned? No; her figure was disappearing—had disappeared.

But he was mistaken; Lily had stopped. Her curiosity had been as much exercised as his. And across the murky night the two had looked questioningly into each other's faces, and had seen nothing, and passed on.

Warrington fell back upon his own thoughts, and strolled perhaps as much as half a mile farther.

A noise behind him suddenly arrested his slow steps. It was a singular noise. Was it a squall, a sudden fierce storm coming over the sea, for there was a sound of something rushing, a sound not unlike water pouring heavily? Only there was a distinct rumble. It could hardly be distant thunder. The noise had none of the character of thunder. Perhaps an explosion at a gunpowder magazine a long way off. Only where were there any magazines? The sound lasted a perceptible time, and seemed divided into three intervals, of which the third was the loudest and longest. Then again all was silent. Only the waves plashed on, and the cold night wind moaned under the cliffs.

Wondering what it could be, Warrington walked a few steps farther. Then the same sound reached him again. Only this time it was briefer, and not nearly so loud.

What could it be? He stopped again and then turned back. He could not go much farther. There was another headland not far in front, to round which required lower water. The breakers were already washing against its base. And the noise had awakened his curiosity. So he turned, and strolled back towards Lynham, keeping along by the gleaming surf.

Before long, out of the gloom, came again a figure. This time, too, walking towards him. It was the girl again. Only this time she walked fast. She had her muff, thrust back like a great cuff, upon her arm hanging by her side. Her other hand was raised to her face. She was holding something against her cheek—her handkerchief, and she hurried over the damp sands swiftly.

As Warrington was passing, she stopped.

"I beg your pardon," she said quickly, in a soft, musical voice. "But you cannot pass that way, the cliff has fallen."

"The cliff fallen!"

"A great piece of it. It reaches right into the sea."

As Warrington only looked surprised and said nothing, she continued, pointing with the hand that was thrust through her muff:

"There are steps in the next cove to the top of the cliff."

And she moved to go on.

"But the water, madam, is already up to the cliff that way."

"Oh, no. Not yet. Impossible!" she answered,

incredulously; and with a tiny bend of her head she went on.

Warrington knew that the water was up to the cliff. He had seen it. He waited till the stranger was out of sight, and then he went on to inspect the fallen cliff. It extended in a great landslip many yards into the sea, and through the darkness, that rendered any clear view of what had happened impossible, were plainly audible ominous sounds of the occasional thud of stones still falling or of mud slipping down.

Clearly he was a prisoner till the tide should ebb. And so was the young lady. He turned and walked back in the direction she had taken.

By-and-by he came again to the other end of the bay. And there was the girl. She was looking nervously at the sea, which was getting deep under the cliff.

Warrington passed her and looked at it, too, for several minutes; then, submitting to necessity, he proceeded to light a cigar.

Lily Hardwick looked at him hard. Was he not going to speak to her?

The cigar was lighted, and Warrington threw away the vesta, and, pushing his hands into the pockets of his short coat, proceeded to walk back in the direction of Lynham. Lily had followed every movement intently, and looked after him wistfully as he left her.

But when an instinct of chivalry is innate in a man, a great many women may treat him very ill, and yet, if he finds a young and pretty woman in a predicament, he will not be able to avoid coming to her assistance. So Frank Warrington took only a very few steps, and then turned back to the stranger.

"I am afraid that it is no go," he said, putting down his cigar, and pointing to the deep water under the cliff, and taking their common calamity for an introduction.

"Ah, no! But what is to be done?" asked poor Lily, in a tone that showed her to be much more frightened than Warrington had supposed, and very pleased to be spoken to.

"Nothing ; but to wait for the tide to turn."

"But at high tide the water comes right up to the cliff, all along the bay."

"Indeed! Are you sure? Anyhow it cannot be very deep," said Warrington, encouragingly. "Evidently we are prisoners here. And perhaps it may be as well to reconnoitre whether there is not some place above high-water mark. Suppose," he suggested, "we walk along under the cliff and see?"

"Under the cliff! Oh, no, thank you," exclaimed Lily, drawing back. "These cliffs come down, I've had enough of them for this evening."

"You were near the cliff, then, when it fell ?"

Near! she was all but underneath it. And when she heard the crack, and saw the great black masses come toppling forward in the gloom, one piece after another, and each larger than the last, with stones flying about in the air all around her little head,— she hadn't had a fright either, of course not! She described it all very graphically : but no more going near the cliff for her—no, thank you.

Warrington could not help laughing.

"It is not likely that any more will come down to-night," he said. easily. "Anyhow, I'll walk along under the cliff, and reconnoitre, and come and tell you. Meanwhile, if you will pardon my offering advice, you had better walk up and down. It is cold."

He proceeded to make his inspection. All along packed close under the cliffs he found a heap of broken seaweeds and rack, that proved the tide came up to them. Only here and there a rock cropped out, and offered a little coigne of vantage. If the sea was not rough, the tops of those rocks might remain dry. His investigations being finished, he returned to his companion in misfortune. Keeping the end of his cigar in view, she had come along with him, walking by the edge of the sea.

"You are right," he said. "The water does come to the base of the cliff. But there are a few rocks here and there."

"Close under the cliff only," answered the girl, distrustfully.

"But the only alternative will be to stand in the sea."

"Oh, good gracious——" began Lily, with her breast heaving.

The falling cliffs had given her a fright that had evidently unnerved her. And indeed the occurrence might have unnerved courage made of stouter stuff.

"Come now!" said Warrington, kindly. "Don't be frightened. Our situation is really much more ridiculous than dangerous. At the worst we shall probably be up to our ankles in sea-water for an hour or so, nothing more. As for risks, there are risks everywhere. are there not? And you see, after all, it is best to face them pluckily. And I am sure you have some courage, now, haven't you? And so you must try to be brave, you know. Now, suppose we make the best of it, forget all about the cliffs, and walk up and down, and try to keep ourselves warm : may I offer you my arm?"

The girl hesitated for a moment, and then quickly put her arm within his.

"I'll try to be plucky," she said, stepping out by his side, "but I am awfully frightened."

"You have had a fright, you see—you'll feel all right again presently. There is no real danger. This is, in fact, only a very ridiculous adventure, I assure you."

"I'm sure it's awfully kind of you to take so much trouble to help one to get over one's fears," answered the girl, gratefully. "Light another cigar, do. I don't mind the smoke, and I am sure you will enjoy it, and some one may see the light and come to help us."

He lighted a cigar, and then they walked up and down, up and down, on the beach that presently grew much narrower. He had travelled, and he talked to her about things he had seen ; and he had read a good deal, and told her about things he had read. He was one of the men who had the knack of amusing women ; and, listening to him, Lily began to forget everything else.

But presently she said :

"What a lot you have read. You seem to have read almost everything."

"Oh, dear no. But I have a brother who is blind, poor fellow ; and I read a good deal to him. Often the same book, when he likes it, several times over."

"Ah, then," said the girl, a little archly, "I know. I think, who you are. You are Mr. Warrington of Lynhurst."

"I am."

"And this," thought Lily, "is the man whom every one calls so morose and disagreeable. I only wish there were more men like him." Still, she did not tell him that : but requested only to hear the rest of what he had been relating.

By-and-by, the sands being more level on the top, the tide came in very fast.

"Now we must go to those rocks," said Warrington. "You won't be frightened."

"You'll stay with me."

"Certainly."

It was horribly cold on the rock, though he did his best to shelter her. He offered her his coat, but she refused it.

"No, no—no, no," she said, almost crossly, "you want it yourself. I am not very cold ;" which last was not true.

As Warrington had anticipated, the tide did not reach the top of the rock. They got a little splashed, that was all.

And all the time he still talked on to the girl, keeping her amused out of a mine of reminiscences that was apparently inexhaustible, and which he had the art to make entertaining. The tide turned, the sea gave them back first a little, and soon an ample, tract of sand on which to try to recover their limbs from the stiffness and the cold, and at last, retiring from the base of the cliff, set its prisoners free; the whole affair turning out, as Warrington had predicted, to be a ridiculous adventure and nothing worse. Only the girl, though she showed a good deal of spirit in trying to conceal the fact, was evidently ready to sink with fatigue.

The steps were soon reached. Warrington gave her his arm up then, and then they found themselves in a lane.

" You live at Lynham ? " he asked.

" No, I live quite near here. At Cliff Cottage. Our garden has a gate into the lane only a little way further up. You will come in, will you not ? " she continued, " my cousin is sure to be up, and she will be very glad to see you. You must be very cold, and you will let me offer you something in return for all your kindness ? "

But he declined. He would walk straight back to Lynhurst.

They soon reached the gate, and Lily opened it with a latch-key.

" There is a light in the drawing-room," she said, looking in. " My cousin is up. Won't you come in and take something ? "

But he declined again.

" Then good-night "—she offered her hand, and, with it resting in his, continued—" and thank you so much for being so kind to me."

The door closed behind her, and Frank Warrington
went on up the lane. He half wished now that he
had accepted the girl's invitation. Now that she
was gone, he was oppressed with an odd sense of
loneliness. What had passed between him and this
young girl—who had walked arm and arm with him
for a few hours, who had managed to be brave
because he protected her, who had consented for a
while to rest her shoulder against his—that he should
feel so odd a loneliness when she left him?

CHAPTER X.

LILY HARDWICK followed a little path for a short distance, and then, leaving it, struck across the lawn.

The cottage and the fir-trees around it made a
single black mass in the background, but in two of
the lower windows lights gleamed brightly through
the down-drawn blinds.

"Perhaps your friends, missing you, will send
some one to find you. Did they know that you were
on the beach?" Warrington had asked, as they were
walking together on the sands. And Lily had
answered, "Oh, no, my cousin won't send any one.
She will know that I am somewhere." But now she
said to herself:

"I hope Maud has not been anxious about me."

She need not have distressed herself. In the
drawing-room of Cliff Cottage, prettily lighted by
shaded lamps and warmed by a fire of glowing coals,
Mrs. Gainsborough was bearing very philosophically
any apprehensions to which her cousin's absence
might have given birth.

Seated, or rather reclining upon, a rug on the
drawing-room floor, at a little distance from the warm

fire, with her elbow on a low chair and her head pensively supported on her hand, Maud Gainsborough was idly regarding the glowing coals, listening to the stillness of the country night, unbroken by any sound except the soughing of the wind amongst the pines, and indulging herself in a long reverie.

She was a woman in whose nature reverie and imagination predominated strongly. To-night minutes had passed, quarters of an hour, hours, and still all the time, moving only a little now and then, Mrs. Gainsborough had been there, crouched upon the rug, immersed in her meditations.

Her thoughts were of a young widow, a very young widow, one five-and-twenty only, and in appearance quite a girl, a young girl. The widow was tall and handsome, and had brains, and—in a way—courage. She had a graceful figure, too, and a picturesque face, deep dreaming eyes, and beautiful black hair. Her husband had been dead some years. His death she did not regret. Perhaps she loved him once. Perhaps not. Certainly she did not love him when he died. Their existences had proved very uncongenial. And the widow was well pleased to be freed from him, and to call her own her beauty, and her courage, and—her fifteen-thousand a-year.

This young widow of whom she was thinking naturally interested Mrs. Gainsborough very much: for the young widow was herself. Hers the unregretted husband, who had died some years ago ; hers the dark dreaming eyes, and the other charms (perhaps she flattered them a little to herself) only not hers, unfortunately, the fifteen-thousand a-year.

Mrs. Gainsborough was building air-castles then? No. Not that either exactly. The fifteen-thousand a-year *was.* Only it was not Mrs. Gainsborough's—though it might have been ; that is, if Lily Hardwick had not stood between her and the possession of it. Not that it was Lily Hardwick's either—though it might have been; if Lily had been aware of its existence, and had known how to set to work to get it. This fifteen-thousand a-year which formed so integral a part of Mrs. Gainsborough's day-dreams, was safe in the custody of the Court of Chancery, where for the present, having mentioned its existence, it will suffice to let it rest.

And Mrs. Gainsborough had, instead of this splendid fortune, an income of a much smaller and more precarious sort, a little jointure: one-hundred-and-fifty pounds per annum; and an allowance made her by her brother-in-law, Anthony Gainsborough, two-hundred a-year, on condition that she lived at Cliff Cottage, Lynham, which he let her have rent free. A very, very sore subject with the young widow, was this "wretched two-hundred," and all the conditions that "that Anthony Gainsborough" had attached to it. But when one has no money, you know, how can one help one's-self? It made only three-hundred-and-fifty. And Maud Gainsborough could not live at Cliff Cottage on three-hundred-and-fifty. At least, so she had said to herself. Howbeit, happily her cousin Lily Hardwick, who was an orphan, had wished very much to live with her; and as Lily's guardian had nothing to say to the contrary, Lily came, and with her another two-hundred. Besides which, Lily had a liberal allowance to do as she liked with, so that the two ladies made up between them something nearer seven hundred than six. And on that they *could* live.

Howbeit, although, with the assistance of her cousin, Maud Gainsborough had arrived at those happy figures, so vainly desired by many—the number of pounds on which to live *is* possible—yet the widow's imagination would at times, as to-night, busy itself with that one thing wanting to complete the ideal she had of herself—the fifteen-thousand a-year of her own. And, when Maud Gainsborough fell to thinking about that, her thoughts were generally long and serious.

To-night they were very serious.

When she came in, it was a little before dinner-time. She had asked of her servant :

" Is Miss Hardwick in, Ann ? "

" Miss Hardwick came in and went out again, ma'am."

" Where did she go ? Do you know ? "

" She went into the town, ma'am. She said she thought she should walk along the beach."

They frequently walked into the town along the beach when the tide was low. The road was steep, and often very muddy, and the sands level and clean.

" You don't know whether she did go along the beach, Ann ? " asked Maud.

" No, ma'am."

Maud Gainsborough went upstairs. Before the maidservant she had allowed nothing to escape her that could raise in the girl any suspicion of the serious nature of her information. But, on reaching her room, she sat down, and, with her face paled with excitement, asked herself :

" Is it possible ? "

Just before leaving Lynham she had heard of the fall of the cliffs. The whole of the town was in a fever of excitement at the news, for it was reported that there were men out on the beach.

If Lily Hardwick had gone along the sands to Lynham ?

Dinner-time came, and Lily did not return.

" I'll dine, Ann," said the widow. " I daresay Miss Hardwick has stopped at Dr. Gregg's."

Lily was a favourite at Dr. Gregg's.

" At what time did Miss Hardwick start to go to Lynham, Ann ? " continued the widow.

" About half-past four, ma'am."

Maud Gainsborough thought :

" And the cliff fell a few minutes after five. If Lily walked fast she had passed the place. In that case she is really gone to the Greggs. If she walked slowly—she must have walked very slowly not to have reached that part of the beach by five. Is it possible ? But I shall be very sorry, too, for poor Lily."

The widow dined; and went to the drawing-room; and had her coffee; and still her cousin had not returned.

She took up a book and tried to read. But the words swam before her eyes. If anything should have happened to Lily!

Mrs. Gainsborough slipped gently from her chair to the floor, and surrendered herself to her reverie.

Suppose—not that the widow wished it ; not at all; she would be horribly sorry if anything happened to Lily ; the amusing little puss!—still, suppose that some accident had happened? Then—there was nothing more between her and the fifteen-thousand a-year!

Could it really be true? True, perhaps this very night, that that fifteen-thousand a-year was hers.

It was true, certainly—if anything had happened to Lily

Lily was not aware of the fact, nor had the faintest suspicion of it. No one had any suspicion of it, neither Lily, nor Lily's friends, nor Mrs. Gainsborough's friends, nor any one in the whole wide world. The secret was all the widow's own, and had been so ever since the day when she discovered it.

But—if anything happened to Lily.

Then the money was the widow's : yes, this very night !

And, lying before the fire, Maud Gainsborough repeated to herself, " Can it be? Has my day-dream turned actually into reality ? "

She fell to thinking what she would do, of the steps she would take : of the letter she would write to

Anthony Gainsborough—ah! what a letter that should be! And if the future that should follow—that brilliant fairyland future.

Ten o'clock! If Lily was at Dr. Gregg's she would return soon now.

Half-past ten. And no Lily. Her prolonged absence became strange, unaccountable. Something must have happened.

Maud Gainsborough rose and rang the bell, and gave orders that the groom should go at once into Lynham to Dr. Gregg's and find out if Miss Hardwick was there.

The man returned a little after eleven.

Miss Hardwick had not been at Dr. Gregg's—and the cliff had fallen.

Mrs. Gainsborough asserted at once her disbelief that the cliffs had anything to do with Miss Hardwick's absence. Miss Hardwick must be at Mrs. Brown's, or perhaps at the rectory, they always kept late hours at the rectory. She would sit up for Miss Hardwick. Ann and the cook could go to bed.

And she sat down again on the rug before the fire. Poor Lily!

But the fifteen-thousand! A feverish excitement obtained possession of Mrs. Gainsborough; her pulse became quick, and her cheek flushed. The drawing-room clock struck half-past eleven with a soft, silvery chime; and, overstrung in every nerve, she started almost as if she had received a blow. Then she sank again into her former position.

Lily crushed under the falling cliffs! Fifteen-thousand a-year! Was it possible? Fifteen-thousand a-year! After all: fifteen-thousand a-year!

Any other woman would have been pacing the room unable to remain still, with these torrents of excitement coursing in her veins. But Maud had passed through moments more feverish even than this; and her muscles had been schooled sternly to obey, not her emotions, but her will.

Still at last even she moved as if she would get up.

St! What is that?—a step?—yes—on the lawn.

Yes. It comes nearer. And Maud Gainsborough sits up listening.

A tap at the window and a voice.

" Maud, Maud."

Lily! No fifteen-thousand a-year to-night.

A momentary contraction of Maud Gainsborough's handsome face; an instant of disappointment, disillusion; and then, as she rose, her lips parted in a smile, and she almost laughed a little laugh at her own folly, with an easy toss of her head as she came to the window to open it.

"Good heavens, Lily! Where have you been?"

" Oh, I am half dead, Maud!" said the girl, sinking on a chair. " I'll tell you all about it presently. But, dear, give me something warm to drink. I am perishing with cold."

Maud Gainsborough bustled about the house, and, in fewer minutes than might have been thought possible, she had prepared with her own hands a cup of cocoa, and kneeling before the drawing-room fire, to which she had made her cousin come closer, was warming some ox-tail soup in a little saucepan. And meanwhile Lily related her adventures.

Maud put her to bed, and brought her up a hot-water bottle, and insisted upon her drinking a little hot wine-and-water. If the fifteen-thousand a-year had depended upon her cousin's life, not on her death, she could not have been more careful or more kind.

" I only hope Lily won't have rheumatism, or pleurisy, or anything serious," she said to herself, going to her own room after having shut up the house and put out the lights: " I suppose a bad cold is inevitable."

CHAPTER XI.

APPARENTLY the cold was inevitable. At any rate Lily Hardwick had one; and for the next few days was confined to her room. She even developed a little hacking cough, and complained of pains in her chest. Mrs. Gainsborough began to be a little alarmed, and called in Dr. Gregg.

The quality on which Dr. Gregg most prided himself was his power of intuition. One look at a patient, and Dr. Gregg knew all about what was the matter. The widow had mentioned that her cousin had a nasty little hacking cough and complained of pain in her chest, and the doctor was able to make a good beginning.

"Ah, I see, Miss Hardwick," he commenced. "Now you have a nasty little hacking cough, eh?"

"Yes, Dr. Gregg."

"And a pain in your chest?"

"Yes, a little."

"Ah, you see. I can see it all. And when you cough it hurts you a great deal?"

"N-o."

"No! Ah, well, in some cases a cough of this character is not accompanied by any particular pain, in other cases there is a good deal of pain. But, I see, in your case there is no pain. A tiresome little cough, and a little uncomfortableness about the lungs. And—now—you don't sleep very well?"

"Oh, but, yes, I think I sleep much the same as usual."

"You sleep much the same as usual? Ah, yes, you sleep much the same as usual. Heaviness about the head; eh?"

He was feeling her pulse.

"Yes."

" You see, I know all about it, my dear young lady. Cough, not painful; some uncomfortableness about the chest; sleep well, heaviness: pulse a little feverish. But—appetite, eh? now I am right, am I not?—bad appetite?"

" N-o. I don't think so, doctor."

" No, not bad appetite. Well, sometimes there is no loss of appetite in those cases. I see—appetite good, sleep well. Tiresome little cough—occasional pain in chest. Heaviness about head; pulse a trifle rapid, but appetite good. We shall soon set you up again, Miss Hardwick. I will send you a little prescription which you will take, won't you? We shall soon set you up again."

" What an ass he is !" quoth Mrs. Gainsborough to herself, standing by the fire.

" No occasion for alarm, my dear Mrs. Gainsborough," said the doctor, reassuringly, as he left. " Just as well, though, to have taken it in time. I shall send Miss Hardwick a little draught." And, going along the little drive to the gate, he continued to himself, " Nothing of importance. Send her something quite harmless. Leave it to Nature."

So Lily was left to Dame Nature, and to her cousin's nursing. It was the best thing that Dr. Gregg could do for her. He was seldom dangerous, so long as he did nothing.

Healthy young blood, and the nursing, soon got the better of the cold. After a day or two in bed, Lily was able to sit up in her room, and to amuse herself with writing letters. At the end of the week, though she was still not to go out of the house for some days, she was downstairs again in the drawing-room.

Towards the end of an afternoon—Mrs. Gainsborough had gone into Lynham, and not yet returned —Lily received an answer to one of her letters, written to a schoolfellow in London. She had related briefly her adventure on the beach as the occasion of the cold that had made her a prisoner in her room, and in reply her friend wrote :

" Your adventure, dear, really was very nearly *most romantic*. The tide really ought to have risen a little higher, so that you might have been in some *danger;* only just a little, wee bit, but enough for Mr. Warrington to have *really saved you*. But, even as it was, he was really most *chivalrous*, and, as he is reputed to be so *morose*, you must feel quite *vain*. I am sure you will like to know all about him ; and, as it happens, I can tell you something I heard only last week, and which [*sic*] I believe is *half a secret*—the real reason why he went to live at Lynham. Two months ago he was engaged to his cousin. She is *very beautiful*, but *quite heartless*, and he was *most desperately* in love with her."

And here followed the history of how Warrington was duped into assisting the flight of the Misses Chesterfield, with many embellishments of the facts, and a lavish use of italics. The writer of the letter was responsible for the italics, but not for the embellishments. They were simply the natural accretions the story had gathered in town.

Lily Hardwick read it twice. She had not yet arrived at the age that replies to any history with an incredulous " And how much of that is fact ? " and without hesitation accepted for truth all that her friend had written her. Putting down the letter on her lap, she leaned forward, with her cheek rested on her hand, and thought.

She felt very sorry for Mr. Warrington, rather indignant too. She would have liked to have had it in her power to " pay out " that cousin of his for the way she had treated him. Poor Mr. Warrington ! No wonder he was morose ! And this, then, was why he had come to bury himself in the country.

She read the short concluding portion of the letter,

and, folding it up, placed it in her pocket, and then went to one of the windows.

Cliff Cottage was a pretty little place, cosy, deeply clad in ivy and creeping plants. It was only two storeys high, but with more room inside it than any one, acquainted with the exterior only, might suppose. A thatched verandah, festooned in the summer with creepers, ran round three sides of the cottage, and, above the verandah, low, half-dormer windows with little diamond casements peeped out coyly, amidst the thick ivy, from under the projecting thatch of the roof. On the ground-floor the sitting-room windows opened to the ground. Inside, there was a little hall, rather dark, with quaint narrow windows of coloured glass that gave a peep into the rustic porch with its low seats; a good broad staircase of shallow stairs; and a really wonderful number of fair-sized rooms. A greenhouse flanked one side; at the back were a convenient little stable-yard and stable, and coach-house. The whole lay planted in a sheltered hollow, a little below the level of the country road that ran behind it, and hidden from view among a small plantation of Scotch firs. Some of the firs grew quite close to the cottage, even spreading their broad branches over its roof. Before it the lawn sloped only very gently, and the garden, sometimes wider, sometimes narrower, winding a little with the turns of a natural hollow, sheltered by trees on either side, descended slowly to the brink of the cliff. Where the garden ended at the cliff's edge, there was a ladder of steps, leading down to a little cove, inaccessible otherwise, except by boat, even at the lowest tide. The garden itself was exceedingly nicely kept. The closely-shorn lawns, the tidy beds, in which the many-hued chrysanthemums were just now in all their glory, the neatly clipped shrubs and the handsome forest trees all evinced the most ungrudging care bestowed upon them.

Before Lily's view, as she stood at the window, the view of the long garden wound picturesquely down to the cliff. Beyond, closed in on both sides by the leafless trees, there was a glimpse of the sea. The sun was sinking fast towards the horizon in a ruddy glow, crossed by hard black bars of clouds lightly edged with saffron, and the low light came up the perspective of the autumn garden with a charming effect.

"How pretty it is here!" said Lily to herself, "morning, afternoon, and evening, lovely in every light; and how beautifully the sunset must be glowing now, through the woods at Lynhurst. I wonder whether Mr. Warrington admires the country Whether all these lovely sights go a little way to console him for the way his cousin used him. I do feel sorry for him! Poor Mr. Warrington!"

Nothing appeals to a young girl's heart more strongly than a story of unhappy love, and this story of the ill-usage of a man, who, a perfect stranger, had been kind to her, stung all Lily's feelings of right and of generosity into a keen indignation. She saw no ludicrous side to the story. She saw only the wrong, the falsehood, the cowardice, the cruelty, the worthlessness of the girl who mercilessly duped the man who loved and trusted her. How angry he must have been! And how grieved too. If he really loved his cousin so much, what a blow for him to find that she did not care for him a bit, that she was so worthless, so undeserving of the affection of any man. And they were engaged too! To be married in a few days! (that was what the letter said). And he had felt it all so much that he had come down here in the country to bury himself. She would always think quite differently of him now. He seemed altogether another man since she had learned this about him. How she wondered whether he still cared for his cousin. Surely he could not. Yet men did care for women who behaved very badly to them.

The door opened, and, Maud Gainsborough entering, disturbed Lily's reverie.

In Lynham Maud had met Mrs. Wood, the rector's
wife. Mr. Warrington and his brother had been to
dine at the rectory. Mrs. Wood thought the blind
brother " very interesting, poor fellow," Mr. Warrington rather reserved. Oh, and Mr. Warrington's
name was Frank.

" I thought you would like to hear all about it,
dear, as you take so much interest in the gentleman."

Thus said the widow in conclusion, with a touch of
significance.

But the one word that struck Lily was "reserved."
No wonder, poor fellow ! It would be strange if he
were not reserved, if he ever trusted any one again
as long as he lived, after the way he had been
treated.

Quite easily she asked, sitting down :

" Did you ask Mrs. Wood whether she thought him
good-looking ? "

" Oh, yes, I said I had heard that he was good-
looking, and Mrs. Wood said it was quite true. I am
really becoming quite curious to see him."

She stood before the glass unfastening her brooch.

Lily had taken up her work.

" And so Mr. Warrington is called Frank, is he ? "
she answered. " That is not a very remarkable name."

" Everybody is talking about your romantic
escape," went on the widow. " It has caused, I
assure you, almost as much sensation in Lynham as
the fall of the cliff."

" Has it ? " asked Lily, indifferently.

Turning over her work, she drew out the needle
from the stuff and began to sew, quite unconscious
that her cousin was watching her.

" I have been wrong," said the widow to herself;
" I thought it was a smite. Particularly when she
wondered whether he would call to inquire how she

was. But she takes it all too indifferently. She has not lost her heart this time."

Maud Gainsborough was quite right about that. Lily had not lost her heart at all. She liked the man, and, since she had learned his history, she was very sorry for him. And that was all. She was not in love with him, not the least bit in the world. A young girl very seldom falls in love all in a moment.

By-and-by the ladies went upstairs to dress. In Lily Hardwick's room, a bright fire burned on the hearth. Its leaping flames lighted fitfully the pretty room, with its tasteful satin-wood furniture, and blue silk curtains, and little girlish nick-nacks placed here and there. It was one of the best rooms in the house, and Lily, who had been allowed to furnish it as she pleased, had been a little extravagant. There was a low wicker chair by the fire, and the girl sat down on it, and again drew out her letter.

Once more she read it through. She might have spared herself the trouble, for there was nothing in it of interest but what was already sunk deep into her memory. Then, rising, she crushed the letter in her hand, and threw it into the flames.

"If he comes down here to escape from all this, at any rate his secret shall be safe with me," she said.

And lighting her candles she proceeded to dress.

Maud Gainsborough had said that Lily Hardwick's adventure on the beach had occasioned almost as much sensation as the fall of the cliffs, and that was not far from the truth. Almost every one was talking about it with that eagerness to talk which is indigenous in small places, where there is nothing to talk about. The same afternoon some one mentioned it—with a view to obtaining, if possible, some further information on the topic—to Eustace Warrington. Eustace was a little taken by surprise, for he had not before heard of the incident. But he had more discretion than to betray his ignorance. When, however, he and Warrington were alone after dinner, he said :

"The other day, when you were caught by the tide, and did not get home here till midnight, there was a young lady, I hear, caught at the same time with you."

"Yes ; some girl who lives at Cliff Cottage."

"My dear fellow, I wish you had mentioned the fact to me. Why didn't you ?"

"Why ? I really did not imagine that it was a point of any importance. Why do you wish that I had told you ?"

"Because, you see, every one down here has heard of your adventure ; and is talking about you and the young lady. And I, who had heard nothing, when I was this afternoon asked about it, very nearly looked foolish, I assure you. The man who spoke to me was most desirous to gather up any crumbs of information that were to be had ; and if I had been taken off my guard, and he had gone away in a position to inform the next man he met, 'Do you know, Mr. Warrington's brother had never heard of it at all, till I told him. There is some mystery in it,' he would have been very much delighted. Whether you would have been equally pleased is for you to consider."

"They may say what they like for anything I care," remarked Warrington.

"At any rate, my dear Frank, I should like to hear all about it, if you please," observed Eustace ; "I don't wish again to be taken by surprise, as I was this afternoon."

The request was reasonable, and Warrington could not refuse to comply with it. He made the story very short. The blind man listened with a good deal of attention, and asked at the end :

"And Miss Hardwick—for, of course, you have

learnt her name by this time—a nice girl, rather, is she not ?"

" I am not a judge of girls. I dare say she is well enough," answered Warrington.

He did not deny that he had acquainted himself with her name.

The conversation dropped. But Eustace had already learned, at any rate sufficiently for the present, what he was anxious to know. That was not alone what had happened on the evening that his brother had been imprisoned by the sea, but also why Frank had been reticent about a part of his adventures, and whether his reticence had any connection with an altered humour which he had for the last few days been displaying.

On the evening itself when he came in from the beach about midnight, hungry, cold, and distinctly cross, Eustace had had at once a suspicion of something having taken place beyond what his brother related. At the time Eustace had conjectured some little annoyance about monetary arrangements, for which Warrington was seeking the assistance of the local bank ; and he had purposely abstained from asking questions, seeing the business was not exactly his. Since then, however, Eustace had assisted at six distinct long jeremiads on the cursedness of women, the folly of love, the peculiar nature of feminine disingenuousness, and the perfect impossibility of a man's being sufficiently on his guard against the knavery of young girls. A month since Warrington had declaimed in this way a good deal, as indeed it was very natural that he should. But since he had been in the country, and had interested himself in his estates, he had got the better of this weakness. Now, the sudden recrudescence of his complaint must have had some cause.

Eustace believed that he could now give a shrewd guess at what the cause was. Frank had not returned to Lynhurst quite heart-whole from the five hours spent on the beach in the November night with pretty Lily Hardwick.

And if he had known that Warrington had not only talked to Miss Hardwick (as he said), but had talked to her as kindly and encouragingly as it was possible for a man to do; if he had known that Miss Hardwick and his brother had not only walked up and down (as Warrington said), but had walked up and down arm-in-arm; if he had suspected that they had not only (as Warrington had related) stood upon a rock, but that the young girl had been glad to lean her shoulder against Warrington's, and that he had put his arm round her to shelter her from the wind —if Eustace had suspected anything of all this— which Warrington did not relate— he would have been a good deal more certain of his opinion than he was.

Eustace was a bit of a philosopher in his way, and he was not taken by surprise at this new turn of events. On the contrary, he found it rather natural. A man who has just been badly used by one woman is susceptible in the extreme of a sudden passion for another; and if, at a critical moment, some young girl, bewitching, fresh, uncorrupted, crosses his path, and shows the faintest inclination to like him, he succumbs to her fascinations almost infallibly And, that this might very probably occur in his brother's case, Eustace Warrington had conceived from the first, especially when Warrington began to vow and protest that he would never marry, nor permit himself again to fall a victim to the seductions of a woman. Do not vows always imply a consciousness of weakness ? Could any one be conceived vowing not to do what he knew was impossible ? Briefly, in Eustace's opinion, Frank Warrington was, without having the least suspicion of the fact, on the brink of falling in love. What would ensue depended, unless

Eustace was very much mistaken, upon how much
time elapsed before Frank next saw Miss Hardwick,
and what might occur on the occasion of their meeting.

CHAPTER XII.

THAT meeting the fates had decreed should take place
soon.

In the middle of the next week there was a meet
not far from Lynham at a somewhat popular spot.
where a large field almost always assembled.

The previous week Warrington had, owing to
business, missed his usual outing with the hounds.
and, the morning proving promising, he announced
at breakfast his intention of going to the meet.

A numerous and picturesque gathering was already
assembled when he arrived, forming under the winter
sky an animated scene of men and women, horses.
drags, pony-carriages. dog-carts, scarlet coats, pretty
costumes. well-cut habits. and rich, warm furs.
scattered in many groups. with the grey sky overhead.
and the copse and pine-woods behind for a background.

Warrington rode up to some friends, and was talking to the rector's son, when the master came up.
and, after wishing him good-morning, said :

" Lady Louisa is anxious to introduce you to two
ladies, friends of hers, Mr. Warrington."

" But, really, Sir Robert——" began Warrington.
not looking particularly gratified. and preparing to
offer some convenient excuse.

" Nonsense, Mr. Warrington, you must not refuse."
interrupted Sir Robert. " I believe that, as a fact, one
of the ladies is known to you already. But indeed

you must not disappoint Lady Louisa. She is over
there by the gate."

Evidently Warrington was not left much choice of
action.

Crossing the field to where the master's wife, in a
dark brown habit, was conspicuously mounted on a
thorough-bred bay, Warrington perceived with her a
young girl, a slight, tall figure whom he had no difficulty in recognizing, and a lady in a black habit,
with her low hat coquettishly set forward over a very
striking face.

"There are two ladies, friends of mine, here, Mr.
Warrington," said Lady Louisa, after their first
greeting, " who very much wish that you should be
introduced to them ; " and, turning round, she presented him : " Mr. Warrington, Mrs. Gainsborough,
Miss Hardwick."

Lily was looking charming. Not a trace of her
indisposition was left in her bright young face ; and
in royal spirits, anticipating a good scamper after the
hounds, she was looking as sparkling and gay as
summer morning sunshine.

Warrington addressed himself to her first.

" I hope you are none the worse, Miss Hardwick,
for that very cold evening spent upon the beach ? "

The young girl's lips parted in an arch smile that
displayed her small teeth, white as pearls.

" I had a dreadful cold for a few days, but it is all
over now," she answered.

Maud Gainsborough was regarding Warrington
from under her brows with a fixed gaze of her deep,
dark eyes. The strange intensity of that gaze had a
resemblance to fascination.

And the truth is, Maud was fascinated. The first
moment that she saw Frank Warrington, something in
his appearance, his handsome, aristocratic face, his
carriage, the slightly reserved expression of his
features, or all these together, in an instant attracted

her regard, and held it riveted. When Lady Louisa introduced him, as he raised his hat, and his eyes and Maud's for a moment met, something that passed with the lightning rapidity of an electric shock. troubled the young widow, thrilled into the very core of her being, and even made her, for an instant. change colour.

It seemed to her that she knew this man, had known him for years.

Something about him answered the most familiar impressions of her recollection—or of her imagination. It appeared incredible that she had never seen him before. They must have met somewhere—and she knew him. But she was also sure that they had never met; sure with the most positive assertion of her reason. She could never have met him, and afterwards have forgotten that meeting. Till a moment since, she had never set eyes on him. He had not crossed her path until this instant of their introduction. Her recollection of him, as some one familiar in another world, or known in a previous state of existence, resembled that strange impression of certain recollections which comes upon the imagination in spots never visited before. He was the man that had been at her side unseen these how many years! in her heart, in her dreams. It was his face, his voice, his bearing that she had been looking for, expecting ever since she had been a young girl. Her real other self was before her, the man whose name fate meant her to bear, whom she had sought and not found in her husband; whom she had looked for and not seen among her many admirers; the ideal of her maiden fancy and of her womanhood's yearnings.

It all passed in an instant; that recogniton that was not a recognition; that impression that was a fascination; that conviction that was in its first instant—love.

She sat looking at him timidly, half dazzled, listening to what he was saying to her cousin, with her heart beating.

Lily too, though she was chatting with him merrily, was regarding him with more seriousness in her heart than her laughing lips would have let any one suppose. This pleasant, agreeable man, who was talking with her, was the man who a few weeks ago was so shamefully used, who held at this moment the secret of it all in his breast. Any morsel of the sadness of life looks large and strange when it comes near, and to Lily it seemed well-nigh impossible that this man who was talking with her could really be the hero of a story of a deceit that had made her blood boil with indignation. And yet she knew that it was so.

None the less she was replying playfully to something that he had said.

"I think I might almost be cross with you, Mr. Warrington. You might have had the chivalry to come and inquire after my health. Now, don't make excuses off hand. Take your time to think of some good ones."

Warrington turned to the widow.

"I hope, Mrs. Gainsborough, that you were not very much alarmed about Miss Hardwick that evening."

"A little," replied Maud, lying promptly. "I was dreadfully afraid, you know, that she might have been killed by the fall of the cliffs. I am sure that we are both of us very much obliged to you for all the care you took of her, and very pleased to have found an opportunity of offering you our thanks." Having made this gracious speech very prettily, she went on, "I think, Mr. Warrington, that you must know some of my poor husband's friends. He was Mr. Anthony Gainsborough's brother. You know Anthony Gainsborough?"

" I have met him. Rarely though. You know, of course, that he is almost always in his yacht."

"Ah, the lucky man! yes," said Maud, dreamily. " That yacht! I was to have been invited to go a cruise in it once. But the invitation never came."

" He is a strange man," observed Warrington. Recently he had found Anthony Gainsborough a very strange man : notably in the way in which he had assisted the flight of the Misses Chesterfield.

" Ah, you know that, then," observed Maud.

And she looked at Warrington significantly She and he had found already a secret point of contact.

" You hunt often, Miss Hardwick ? " asked Warrington, turning to Lily.

" Not very often, Mr. Warrington. I like it too much. You see," she explained, laughingly, "to hunt one should be a little bit staid, sure of never becoming over-excited by the chase, always careful to keep on the safe, not to try ticklish jumps, to be content to wait one's turn at the gates, and not to mind coming up when every one else is riding away after the death. For all that one requires to be rather wise."

" And you are not always wise ?" asked Warrington, laughing, and pleased to hear her confessing so real a zest for the sport.

" Alas, no," replied Lily.

" I shall expect to see you ride home with the brush, Miss Hardwick," said Warrington.

" Oh, no, please, don't expect anything of the sort," returned the girl, quickly. " I shall not be in at the death. I shall have a good gallop or two, and enjoy myself thoroughly. But I am not a first-class horsewoman, and you must not expect to see me doing wonders. My cousin here is far more likely to be in at the death than I."

The girl's modest disclaimer was as pretty and natural as her previous confession of keen pleasure in the chase.

" You and I shall very likely, then. have the pleasure of finding ourselves together, Miss Hardwick," observed Warrington ; " I am a regular cockney, you know, and have a great deal to learn."

All of a sudden it occurred to him that he was talking a great deal to Miss Hardwick, and very little to her cousin ; and so, turning to Maud Gainsborough, he began to say something to her about Cliff Cottage. The edge of its garden joined one corner of his estate. In the midst of that the hounds were thrown off, and, a general movement ensuing, Warrington wished the ladies a pleasant scamper, and said, " Good-morning."

It was some time before they got away. One or two coverts were drawn without a whimper, the field, in loose order, moving slowly along the brow of the hill after the dogs. Once for a few minutes—at a spot where a little group were assembled, who conjectured the place likely to be a good one for a start in case they found—Maud discovered herself again near Warrington, and was unable to resist the pleasure of exchanging half a dozen words with him. Then, all of a sudden, a holloa came from the other side of the wood, a little way off, just as the hounds gave tongue.

In a moment there was a scurry and a rush ; the foremost of the field were off, and those around Warrington and the widow wheeled to follow them. From the other points, the others came up helter-skelter, and then in an avalanche they all swept away down the slope, dogs and horses, scarlet coats and dark habits.

In the fore-front was Lady Louisa, Warrington and Maud not very far behind, fairly in the ruck, and Lily amongst those who were bent upon enjoying themselves, with a certain regard to not being a nuisance to the others.

Pug led them first across tolerably open meadowlands, with little brooks and low fences. The fences little by little scattered the more timid part of the field in search of gates and convenient gaps. The hounds ran fast, pointing for some way straight up the valley, and only a pick of the field kept near them. Presently they wheeled a little to the left, and then came a broad brook, and a plantation through which the drives were narrow. There were some catastrophes at the brook, and after the plantation only the best riders had the hounds in view, as they followed close upon the fox. But, after a run of nearly half an hour on the brow of the hill, Reynard got into a copse, and then the thing was to get him out again ; and meanwhile the check allowed a good part of the stragglers to come up. Pug was drawn at last, and a fairish fresh start ensued over the open downs.

Presently the ground dropped and there came a flight of posts and rails, and then an almost impossible blackthorn hedge with a deep ditch behind. One or two very bold hands ventured at the hedge, but the greater part of the field turned to a gate only a little way out of the line, whilst a few, seeing the crush there was there, preferred another farther out of the track, but less crowded.

Chance favoured these last. As the fox, making a wide detour, came round again towards the hill, many of those at first left far behind, striking out a bold line, managed again to nick in with the foremost of the hunt. Crossing a field, Warrington found, amongst a good many others quietly taking their turns to pass, one by one, over a stile in the corner, Maud Gainsborough, keeping back a little to allow others to go before her. Warrington had been over this ground only a little time before, and felt sure that by bearing a little more to the left he could take a line better than that which those in front of him were selecting, and also one not involving waiting for a turn. As he passed Maud Gainsborough, he felt moved to invite her to share the benefit of his knowledge.

He would hardly have done that if it had been Lily. He would have been on his guard. But there is a way of showing a liking for a girl, into which the most cautious of men are easily betrayed, and that is doing little kindnesses to the people who belong to her.

And so Warrington, stopping for a moment by Maud Gainsborough, said :

" Do you feel inclined, Mrs. Gainsborough, to attempt that fence over there at a weak point, say there "—he pointed with his hunting-crop—" we could afterwards cuts across the meadows beyond by a far shorter route."

" I think I would try, if you would go first."

They rode off together, two or three others as so on as they saw their move, turning to follow them.

" Bravo, Mrs. Gainsborough," said Warrington, as the young widow came over after him safely, and very prettily too, her neat figure perfectly balanced, as she sat back, with her little hands well down, setting her horse straight at the fence, a momentary flush of excitement lighting her classical face. He had broken the way a little, and made a very fair jump for her.

Across the fields they rode on together, keeping well in front of the others. The line they were taking should evidently bring them into a good position. But presently, when they came nearer the hounds, they met a rather wide water-jump.

" You can do it," said Warrington. " The taking off is good, and the opposite bank sound."

" There is one man in it already, and those others only just got over."

" But they are lower down—it is wider there. You will try ?"

A nod signified her assent. In her heart she knew she would have put her horse at the English Channel to keep with him.

And they were over—both. But the others had turned aside.

Up the hill. The pace was sharp and the hill steepened. One of the ladies who had been all the way hitherto in the front dropped behind. There were then only two others now besides Maud. The hounds were topping the brow of the hill, and began to disappear. Then the land became less steep and they were on the top. And there are the hounds, tearing along a level glade, with the fox in view, as it seems, but a yard or two before them. Some one goes a purl over a fence that Maud crosses flying, following Warrington's lead, she hardly knows how. The horse of one of the ladies has refused that fence. Maud has loosened her rein and is plying her whip. Will it be really with him at her side that she will get the brush? With only her light nine stone to carry, and comparatively fresh, her horse flies with her as if she was but a feather, and she is neck and neck now with young Mrs. Rivers, the best horse-woman of the hunt.

And, at the death, a neck in front of her.

All except the ladies have jumped off their horses.

As the huntsman comes up with the brush, there seems to be a moment's hesitation.

Maud Gainsborough bows to Mrs. Rivers.

"I think it was a drawn race, Mrs. Rivers," she says.

"Oh, no, Mrs. Gainsborough, the brush is yours."

And, as it is fastened to her saddle, Maud turns and says to Warrington, "I owe this entirely to your kindness, Mr. Warrington," with a blush of such gratification mantling her beautiful face that the man cannot feel other than flattered.

Lily came up, as she said, when the rest were beginning to think of riding away, having, nevertheless, enjoyed herself royally

The cousins rode home together unaccompanied.

"You have made quite an impression upon Mr. Warrington, Maud," said Lily, playfully.

But the young widow made no answer. She had become very pensive. It was not she, she knew, that had made an impression upon Frank Warrington. She saw a great many things too puzzling to be understood by Lily's bright eyes. It was for some one else's sake that Frank Warrington had helped her, Maud, to win that brush at her saddle-bow, or else she knew nothing of men—and she knew something about them.

CHAPTER XIII.

THE new year came, and a cold afternoon early in January found Maud Gainsborough sitting close to the drawing-room fire at Cliff Cottage, with her feet on the fender, taking herself to task very seriously.

That morning she had done a silly thing, a very silly thing. She had met Warrington in the High Street, Lynham, and she had walked the whole length of the street with him. Really it seemed rather a small matter to be distressed about, but the young widow was vexed about it, and she was vexed with reason. First of all, it would give the Lynham people occasion to talk, and Maud Gainsborough could not afford to be cavalier respecting what people said about her. And in the next place— this was far more serious—that little walk up the High Street had been haunting her memory ever since.

She and her cousin had not seen much of Frank

Warrington since the day of the hunt recorded in the last chapter. Once they had bowed on the esplanade, once they had met in the Lynhurst woods —there was a public way through a part of the woods—that day he introduced his brother who was with him, and the two men had walked a little way with them; and once they had exchanged a few words at a small public concert.

But how large a place the owner of Lynhurst had come to occupy in Maud Gainsborough's thoughts!

She was not in love with Mr. Warrington yet—at least, so she said to herself. But if she allowed herself to be always thinking about him, if she got talking with him and walking with him, Maud knew how it would end.

She had been in love before now—more than once. She knew all about all the symptoms of the complaint from its very earliest stages. And she knew, too, that she could make Warrington fall in love with her. Certainly she had no idea of the vows and resolutions he had been making to have nothing more to do with women; but, if she had heard all about them, she would not have attached the faintest importance to them. She would simply have replied that she knew she could make him love her. And that was the most dangerous part of it all.

"And that is just what I am resolved to forbid myself," quoth Mrs. Gainsborough to herself, mechanically plucking at the fringe of the fire-screen she was holding before her face. "He shall not fall in love with me. I am not worth it, and I should do him a very great wrong. I should be drawing him into a match with a woman beneath him, for I *am* beneath him. And I haven't a halfpenny. And he ought to marry money, and to right his estates. I've done some things in my time that I ought not to have done, and I'll not add this to them to wrong that man."

The man himself had taken a fancy to Lily. And Lily was just the girl he ought to marry. A good girl Lily, and with a nice little fortune of her own. It would be a very fair match for Lily, and for Warrington a very good one.

A strange shadow passed in the young widow's deep eyes.

What a match it would be for Mr. Warrington if he only knew! If he knew, or Lily knew, or any one knew, about that fifteen-thousand a-year. But about that no one knew. So that was nothing to do with the case. Apart from that fifteen-thousand a-year, it would be a very fair match.

The only question was, what would Lily do? Mr. Warrington was already far from indifferent to her, hardly suspecting that himself, apparently. But Lily, though she liked him, was taking her time very leisurely indeed to fall in love with him. Still, gently she was going that way.

The little witch was very attractive, and Frank Warrington was handsome and agreeable, and a very little thing might convince the two that they were created for one another. And these things happen so quickly. Two people meet in the autumn, and before the leaves are on the trees they have bound themselves indissolubly together to share all the pleasures and face all the perils of life.

Well, supposing Warrington and Lily did make a match of it, they would probably afterwards be very happy.

And here it must be recorded, to Maud Gainsborough's credit, that the consideration of the income she would lose when her cousin left her, and the evident fact that she would be brought back to the galling monetary difficulties in which she had found herself when she first came to Cliff Cottage, had no weight with her at all to suggest to her that she should stand in the way of her cousin's happiness.

" I'll manage somehow," she said to herself; "no one knows what may happen between this and then."

But her thoughts came back in another way to herself.

"That is all very fine. But if I do fall in love with that man, shall I have the courage to keep myself from making him love me?"

There were two women in Maud Gainsborough, and she had a dim consciousness of the fact. There was the Maud Gainsborough whose imagination was at rest; a not bad kind of young woman, with some faults, but with a good heart and plenty of judgment. And there was the Maud Gainsborough whose imagination had caught fire. That was a young lady capable of a good deal: of a good deal more than Maud herself suspected. And if her imagination were not imagination of the brain alone, but the more subtle, and wilder, passionate romance of the heart——

"It will never, never do to let it come to that," quoth Maud to herself. "I should have him, if I ruined him. Only, how to prevent it?"

In the evening, after dinner, she said to Lily:

"Lily, what should you say to leaving here?"

"Leaving Cliff Cottage, Maud?"

"No, Lynham."

"Leave Lynham!" exclaimed the girl, with surprise.

"I mean," explained Mrs. Gainsborough, taking note of the tone of startled astonishment, and lying diplomatically, "if we were to go abroad, perhaps for a few months; say next month, when the days get a little longer. We might spend the spring in the south of Europe."

"I should like to travel," replied Lily, slowly. "We might think about it, Maud."

Again Maud Gainsborough took notice of the girl's tone, and of the phrase, "We might think about it,"

Miss Hardwick had her tricks, and one of them was to say, " We might think about it," when, in her own mind, she resolved not to assent to what was proposed, but was too polite to say so.

So it was some minutes before Maud offered :

" It is dull here."

" I don't find it so, Maud. I am very happy."

Thought Maud : " And so indeed am I."

A longer silence ensued, whilst she reflected how quietly and peacefully pleasant the life was that they led : an existence that a good many people might have envied. A pretty little house, and a beautiful garden. Breakfast late, and neither of them particularly punctual in appearing at breakfast, if a longer and deeper slumber than usual made them late in rising, or a little beauty-sleep of another half-hour suggested itself as likely to be agreeable. And breakfast itself always rather dainty, as were all the meals ; though they spent a great deal less time over them than men would have done under similar circumstances. Till luncheon there were the cares of the neat little house, and perhaps a little exercise ; after it walking, riding, or driving ; for they could hack good horses, and they had a pony-carriage ; paying or receiving a few calls, tea, and a lazy hour before dressing for dinner ; and the long, careless evening—music, magazines, perhaps a game of cards. And, to conclude, upstairs, where there were fires in the bed rooms, talk, as only women can talk after they have retired.

It would have been strange if they had not been haypy

Still, Lily's was a girlish, restless nature, and Maud had surmised that possibly the prospect of travel, movement, something new, might have distinct attractions for her. If it had not, it seemed to Maud that Lynham must have attractions not publicly admitted by the young lady, or, more plainly, that things between her and Mr. Warrington had advanced further than Maud had supposed.

"After all," she remarked, " it is not of much use to talk about it.   Very likely we should not be able to go, if we wished it. At least, you could always go, of course.   But perhaps not I."

Lily looked at her interrogatively.

" You mean ? " she asked.

" You know what I mean, dear."

" Something to do with that horrid old Anthony Gainsborough ? "

" Yes.   You see, I should have to get his leave."

" His leave, Maud ! "

" Oh, yes," replied the widow, bitterly. "I cannot go away from here without that.   You see, he lets me have the place rent free, and, if I left it without consulting him, he is as likely as anything to turn nasty, and to stop the allowance he makes me.   And then, where should I be, dear? I could not live upon what my husband left me."

And the widow leaned back in her chair, looking dissatisfied enough at the state of her case.

" If I were one-and-twenty, you should live with me," answered the girl, with the natural generosity of youth.   " Never mind, Maud, I shall be one-and-twenty soon, and have all my money.   Then we'll snap our fingers at old Anthony Gainsborough, and do as we like, won't we ? "

To which the young widow said nothing. She had all the will to snap her fingers at her brother-in-law, and afterwards to do as she liked, but not all the necessary courage.

Lily noticed her silence.

" Maud," she said, after a minute, "what was it that happened between you and Anthony Gainsborough? I often feel awfully curious to know " That was very true. " If it is a secret, Maud, you may trust me with it."

" I don't know that it is exactly a secret," answered the widow

"Then tell me, Maud, do!"

Maud Gainsborough seemed to hesitate for a moment. But, really, she was only asking herself why she should hesitate. She had not a sincerer friend in the world than this young girl, nor one more able to be of use to her.

"Well, then, dear, you shall know," she said. "But first, you must understand, darling, that you are a very lucky girl not to be married."

"H'm. It is a species of luck which, if it be of too long duration, I am not sure that I shall appreciate. Still, go on, Maud."

"It is one thing to be married, Lily," explained the young widow, "and another to find marriages turn out as you anticipate. Of the two evils—I will grant you that both are evils—not to be married is a less one than to be married, and to discover that you have made a big mistake. *I* made a mistake. Mr. Gainsborough was in business: you know that. I believe that he worked very hard, and was successful, and all that sort of thing. I have never been able to see how all that could be of the faintest interest to me. I know that I soon discovered that his not having a handsome independent fortune, as his elder brother had, would make a much greater difference to us than I had supposed; that the life we had to lead was hideously dull; and that he and I saw all these things from exactly opposite points of view. He let me have a large house, and, although he said he could not afford it, allowed me this and that that I wished for, and——"

Maud Gainsborough sat up in her chair, and continued, in another tone:

"All that has nothing to do with it, Lily. To come straight to the point. I met a young married woman about my own age, who played—gambled, I mean. And I went to her house, and joined in the gambling. Of course, gambling is wrong, but, people may say what they like, there is no excitement under the sun equal to that of playing with stakes the loss of which might make you uncomfortable. And I. who was very dull, got quite wild about play. and I got up a little party of my own, and we used to play in my boudoir at afternoon tea for ever so much higher stakes than at Mrs. ——'s. I won't mention names. It was soon whispered about that the play at her house was not a patch upon what was going on at mine, and women left her to come to me, and I can tell you we had some scenes sometimes; and some excitement."

"It must have been exciting, of course. Still it was awfully wrong, was not it, Maud?"

"It was, and, of course, we all knew that we should get into fearful scrapes if we got found out; we married women with our husbands, and the girls with their fathers and mothers. And now I am coming to Anthony Gainsborough. Of course, Mr. Gainsborough knew nothing about this play; at least, at first. I had taken good care that he should not. But afterwards he had to know, for I lost a lot of money and could not possibly pay my debts. I had some trouble to get the money from him, but in the end I got it, and then, somehow, his business affairs went wrong. I never understood his horrid business affairs, so I cannot tell you how that was. All I know is that one night he came home and made a frightful scene, declaring that he was a ruined man, and sobbing like a great baby, and saying that he would have to be bankrupt. He fretted a lot about all this and made himself ill. However, in the end, he got some money from somewhere. and his brother Anthony lent him or gave him some more. and I understood that it was all to come right. I was in monstrously bad luck all that time. and then, to crown it all, I had one most desperate afternoon. I won't tell you what I lost, it was something too dreadful."

The widow paused, and remained silent for a minute. Then, leaning back in her chair, she went on :

"Of course, if I had *won* a lot of money, I should have been an angel. Only as I had lost it—I wasn't. And I *had* to pay my debts, or some of them. And Mr. Gainsborough had to let me have some money And so he had to be bankrupt, after all. I suppose it was very disgraceful, and all that. I can't say I understood it : but Mr. Gainsborough upset himself about it most tremendously. In the end he made himself ill, and the end of his being ill was that he died. The fact is that he was a man without a bit of pluck. The only good thing I can say for him was that he kept my secret for me. For you must understand that all this time that he was ill I was worried out of my life with Anthony always about the house, wanting to understand how his brother could have been bankrupt after all, and I don't know what else besides. However, in the end Mr. Gainsborough died. The doctors said of some affection of the heart. It was not of affection for me. After his death I found that I had only the most miserable pittance, and began asking myself what on earth I was to do. Then Anthony called, and offered to make me an allowance of two-hundred a-year, and to let me live here rent free, if I liked to agree to certain conditions. And one of the conditions is that I am not to leave Lynham without his knowledge."

"You mean that you have to get leave to go any-where, Maud ?"

"Yes," answered Maud Gainsborough, in a tone that expressed plainly enough how far she was from liking it.

"Even, say, to go up for a week to London."

" Yes."

" But you really mean that this man actually said to you, 'I'll let you live there, but the condition is that you never go anywhere without my leave.'"

" He did not say it in those words."

That was true. It had been said in words Maud would not forget so long as she lived. But she did not care to repeat them.

" And you assented ? "

" I had to assent, you see."

" I'd rather have swept a crossing ! " exclaimed Lily. " I'll tell you what it is, cousin," she continued, " I think what you did was awfully, awfully wrong. But I don't see what right Anthony Gainsborough had to put you into prison for it. What sort of man is he, Maud ? "

" A man past fifty, tall, and rather handsome; with about as much pity as Herod," answered Maud, quietly.

" I'm sure I hate him ! " remarked Lily. Leaving her chair she knelt on the floor by her cousin's side, and putting her arm round her neck continued, " Maud dear, you are not angry with me because I said just now that what you did was wrong ? Because it was wrong, you know. Still, we were friends at school, Maud, weren't we ? Do you remember how frightened I was the first day I came, and how kind you were to me. And we'll be friends always, won't we ? And as for that old Anthony Gainsborough, by-and-by, when I have all my money, you shall live with me, dear. And we will go where we choose, and do what we please, and not consult Anthony Gainsborough at all, the nasty old thing."

Maud bent her head, and kissed her, and called her " a darling," and it was somehow taken for granted that, until Lily's coming of age put them in a position to set Anthony Gainsborough at defiance, things should go on as at present, and nothing more be said about leaving Lynham.

But when Lily had fallen asleep that night, Maud Gainsborough stole downstairs with her hat and cloak on, and, going to the little writing-table in the drawing-room, wrote a hurried note.

"DEAR MR. GAINSBOROUGH,—When I gave you my word of honour not to leave Cliff Cottage without your knowledge, I received in return a promise from you that, if circumstances made my leaving necessary, you would at once allow me to go. Such circumstances have occurred ; and I write to beg that you will allow me to go abroad for twelve months. I will live in any place you like to name. But please give me leave at once to leave England.—Yours sincerely

"MAUD GAINSBOROUGH."

Folding the letter without reading it through, she put it an envelope, and directed it to Anthony Gainsborough at his bankers.

Carefully opening one of the drawing-room windows, so as to make no noise, she stepped out.

The January night was cold, dark, and cloudy. She only stopped for an instant to look at it, and then drawing the window shutters together, so that the open window should not be noticed from the lawn, she pulled the hood of her cloak over her head, and, stepping on the grass, made her way noiselessly towards the gate that opened upon the high-road.

Half an hour elapsed, and then the same cloaked and hooded figure returned across the grass, stopped before the verandah, looked stealthily around her, pushed open the shutter, and, with a long breath of relief, was once more safely at home.

No one had seen her.

She closed the window, refastened the shutter, and threw back her hood. The room was cold, and the fire had burned low, but she sat down once more beside it.

She had done the best action she had ever done in her life; and her conscience told her so.

Where, she wondered, was Anthony Gainsborough? How long would it be before her letter reached him? How long before she received his reply? Would the reply come in time to be of any use?

The room was horribly cold. She would go to bed.

Eight days elapsed. In the course of those eight days, she met Warrington twice. They seemed to be fated to come together.

At last a telegram arrived from the Mediterranean:

"*Let me know reason why you wish what you ask in letter.*"

How was Maud to answer? Could she wire back, " I am afraid I shall make a man fall in love with me"? Impossible!

She threw the telegram into the fire unanswered.

But she said to herself:

" So it is all up! Things must go their own way, now. What happens will be Anthony's fault. But God knows that this time I tried to do my duty; and that I hate the wrong that I am going to do to that man."

And she dashed two big tears from her great, handsome eyes.

A singular character, Maud! What would prosperity, and a man able to guide her, have made of her?

CHAPTER XIV

LOVE grows of itself, and of itself passes away; in a moment springs unbidden into being, and in a moment is gone like the perishing of a dream. Man has just as much dominion over it as he has over the forces of Nature and the elements of the world, and no more. By knowledge and observation and contrivance and by favour of circumstance, he turns this too, as he turns tide, and the fire, and air, as he turns oxygen, and carbon, and gold, to attendance on his pleasure and to the service of his will: and that is all. Independent of man, the tides roll on, and the great forces of Nature unfold and exhaust their powers, and so love warms and cools, and man must abide it.

For a fortnight the ladies of Cliff Cottage saw nothing of their neighbour. The reason was simple. He did not hunt on the days they hunted, and all the rest of the time he was busy on the farthest part of his estate. Meanwhile came off the Lynham Christmas ball, one of Lynham's few gaieties. Frank Warrington did not go to it, and Maud returned home thankful, and Lily disappointed.

Two days afterwards fifty yards of the boundary wall of the Lynhurst estate fell flat into Mrs. Gainsborough's garden. When the gardener brought in the news at luncheon-time, Maud Gainsborough said to herself, "This is fatality."

"We ought to send and tell Mr. Warrington," opined Lily, as forward to find any good excuse for seeing or saying something to Mr. Warrington as her cousin for avoiding him.

Maud considered any such step unnecessary. Mr. Warrington would be sure to hear all about it from his own people.

In the afternoon, Maud being gone for a walk, Lily suddenly thought she should like to drive into Lynham. So she ordered out the pony-carriage, and drove down.

Once in Lynham, she drove several times up and down the parade, and then up the High Street, where her perseverance was rewarded at last with the sight of Warrington coming down the street.

He was a little surprised when she drew up beside him.

" Mr. Warrington," she said, " about fifty yards of your wall fell this morning into our garden. Perhaps you know all about it."

No. He knew nothing about it at all.

Well, then, the best thing he could do was to come and see. Would he drive up with her?

Warrington accepted the offer; and Lily drove him up to Cliff Cottage. On the way he offered many apologies for the conduct of his wall. There was not a wall on the estate that was not rotten to the core, he asserted. He hoped that this one had not done much damage.

Maud Gainsborough was still out when they arrived at the cottage. So they went to view the fallen wall together.

" What a pretty place you have here," said Warrington, when that was done.

" Is it not?" answered Lily. " Come down the garden, will you? It goes all the way to the cliff."

So they made the tour of the garden, and talked about the flowers. There were a number of rose-trees, and already one or two tea-roses in bloom. Lily mentioned that in this little shaded glade, for such the garden was, her cousin and she were particularly successful with their early and late roses.

" I should much like my brother to come and see them," said Warrington. " I say see, though he

can't see, poor fellow. But he is a great rose-
fancier."

And he went on to talk about the rosary Eustace
had laid out at Lynhurst.

"And Mr. Eustace Warrington can tell all his
roses, and knows whether the plants are in good
condition, and whether the flowers are all they should
be, although he is blind?" asked Lily.

"It is wonderful what he knows, even that we who
can see do not know: and what he sees that we
cannot see," replied Warrington.

That served them for another subject of conversation. Warrington invariably appeared at his best
when talking about his brother, and Lily was so
much interested that it was quite a long time before
they returned from the farther end of the garden to
the cottage. Maud Gainsborough had come back,
and Lily insisted that Warrington must see her: and
Warrington himself was inclined to think that it
might look better if he did. So he consented to come
in, and to accept a cup of afternoon tea, whilst he
repeated his apologies to the widow.

"Did he come to call, Lily?" asked Mrs. Gainsborough, when he was gone.

"No. I met him in the town."

Maud smiled to herself. She knew all about acci-
dental meetings of that kind.

The restoration of the wall commenced on the
morrow with the removal of the débris, and went on
for the next three weeks. Work was not wont to
be very rapidly executed at Lynham.

But the number of casual meetings that took place
between Lily Hardwick and Frank Warrington over
the repairing of that fallen wall were wonderful. Of
course, Warrington, like a prudent man, had to look
after the work to see how it got on, and visited the
spot, at least once, often twice a day, to inspect progress, and to see that the men were not wasting their

time.   And then, if Lily was in the garden, or at the drawing-room windows, there was a bow to be exchanged, a greeting, a smile.   And sometimes Lily would stroll across, and, warmly wrapped in her pretty furs, stand and talk for a few minutes ; or else they strolled up and down together, sometimes on Mrs. Gainsborough's lawn, which was being sadly trodden down, sometimes on Warrington's path on the other side of the wall.   Once, when Warrington had his brother with him, Lily insisted that Eustace should come and see the roses, and with her arm in his led him all round the garden, telling him the history of every one of their plants.

When the wall grew higher, there was no more possibility of stepping backwards and forwards across it, but they could still meet, and stand on each side and talk ; and for Warrington to lean his elbows on the wall, and to talk to Lily, whilst watching the workmen, or for Lily to rest her elbows on the wall and talk to Warrington, was apparently quite sufficient amusement for both of them.

"What a pity Mr. Warrington should look so much after the men building the wall," remarked the widow

She had only spoken to Warrington across it twice.

"Why?" asked Lily.

"They would have been ever so much longer about it if he had left them alone."

"Of course.   That is just why he looks after them. He would be robbed every hour of the day if he did not keep an eye on all those people he is employing."

"Yes.   But won't you and he be very sorry when the wall is done, dear?" asked the widow.

Lily knew what her cousin meant, and made no answer, only said to herself, "I didn't think Maud could be so idiotic."   But the next day she did not visit the scene of operations. Warrington strolled over twice to see how his wall was getting on. But he saw nothing of Miss Hardwick.

On the third day, however, when he again came to look at the workmen, about eleven o'clock, Lily was strolling up and down the wide garden walk in the February sunshine, and crossed over to him at once.

If Maud liked to be idiotic, what did it matter to her? She supposed she could speak to Mr. Warrington if she chose! And, besides, there was something she wanted to ask him.

Warrington was in wonderful spirits at that date. He did not know when he had felt himself so light-hearted, or in such vigorous health, or half so happy, and careless, and free. All the anxieties of the limited capital at his command, and of his mortgages, and of the considerable sum of money he was spending lay on him as light as a feather. He felt sure of himself, sure of his courage proving undaunted, and his patience equal to any demands. Success and good fortune in the future were quite secure. Everything was going right at Lynhurst. All he had done had turned out well. There were contretemps here and there, certainly—that wall which had tumbled into Mrs. Gainsborough's garden, and had had to be rebuilt, just at a moment when he wanted the money for something else, and that dyke that had broken, and turned all the best meadows into a swamp. But everything could not be expected to go on perfectly smoothly in this world. And all he was doing now was getting on royally, and what he would do by-and-by would set all the rest right. That they should come and live in this jolly old place, and rescue it from destruction, was the happiest inspiration his brother had ever had. He never tired of repeating that. Life was become a delightful exhilaration, full of the keenest enjoyment from morning to night. He had never been so happy as he was now, trudging

about the place all day long, working like a nigger,
enjoying his meals with the appetite of a rustic, and
entering into everything with the zest of an enthu-
siast. Never had his brother and he led so merry a
life : never known the days pass so gaily, the evenings
so pleasantly, as since they had been in Dorsetshire.
His good spirits even attained to that superlative
degree which disposes a man to fall in, as far as possible, with the wishes of every one under the sun ;
and when the rector, after much searching of heart.
at last found the courage to approach him on the
subject of his never coming to church, he surrendered
at once with a good-tempered, " I know what you
mean, Dr. Wood." And the next Sunday morning
he came to church.

At which the young ladies of Lynham turned up
their noses, and said that he had come to hear Mrs.
Gainsborough and Miss Hardwick sing in the choir.

He was in excellent spirits with himself about Miss
Hardwick.

" Saw the little Hardwick again to-day," he said
to his brother, one evening at dinner. " She was
walking up and down in the garden, and we had
quite a long talk. A nice girl that, a straightforward girl, with no nonsense about her, and a good
heart, I should say. Deucedly pretty too, and rides
well ; better than she thinks. I enjoyed a chat with
her very much. The fact is, Eustace, there is a lot
to enjoy in the society of women, if a man has only
once made up his mind not to have too much to
do with them. That is the secret of the thing. A
man is not on his guard against consequences, and
then he gets falling in love, and all that sort of nonsense. Or, at least, he knows that walking about
and talking to a girl may end in his marrying her ;
and that spoils it all. When a man has once had the
sense to say to himself that he is not going to go in
for any of that, that he means to keep himself within

bounds, there is a lot to enjoy in the conversation of a straightforward girl."

All of which was very philosophic, only it was a strange thing that there was no part of the estate to which Warrington so seldom invited his brother to accompany him as to that wall bordering Mrs. Gainsborough's garden.

And, whatever Warrington's views might be, his pretty friend on the other side of that wall was beginning rapidly to entertain less and less platonic ideas of the situation, and to open her bright blue eyes very widely on the truth.

A great part of the wall was finished right up to the coping-stones, when she began, in her counsels with herself, to rise rapidly through such degrees of confessed regard as —" I like Mr. Warrington." " I *do* like Mr. Warrington." " I like him awfully." " I like him most awfully." And then came a mild afternoon in February ; one of those soft afternoons which tell that the spring is really coming. Maud was gone to a working-party at the rectory, for the widow much studied all the little things that provide a woman with allies. Lily, who made no pretence of liking working-parties, stayed at home, and that afternoon there was a long talk over the wall ; Lily, leaning against it, with one elbow rested on the top, and the low, westering sun shining softly into her lovely young face, and Warrington talking to her about — why, about nothing. A good part of the time neither of them were saying anything, only the man feasting his eyes on the girl's exquisite face, as she stood with her eyes cast on the ground, and she simply happier than she could tell, merely because she was with him, because she " liked him most awfully."

At last they parted (for the evening shadows began to fall), and laughingly said, " Good-night." Their eyes met as he pressed her little hand in his, and she could not resist the temptation to return the pressure.

"She liked him so awfully," and was so willing that he should know it.

But she did not go in. She only made sure that he was not watching her, and then turned and strolled down the garden towards the cliff slowly, slowly

"I wonder whether I ought to see him so often, to talk to him quite so much?"

That was the question the pretty little head was pondering.

"I do like him so awfully and I do feel so sorry for him, poor fellow. And I don't mind a bit if he knows it. But I should not like him to think me forward. He does not seem as if he did think me so: not a bit. Still——"

Fifty yards further down the garden she had got as far as:

"I should miss talking to him awfully if I had to give it up. Still, I would rather give it up than have him think me forward."

Fifty yards further:

"When the wall is finished, we shall have to give up our little talks. And that was what Maud said."

And then she got to the edge of the cliff, and, leaning over the railing, stood watching the night falling over the sea.

"Why should I make a lot of words about it?" she thinks, slowly: "I know the truth—I am in love with him." And, though the words are unspoken, a hot blush scalds her cheek. "And I am not ashamed to love him. He likes me I am sure. And I'll be a good girl to him, and show him that girls can be honourable and true and I'll make up to him for the way his cousin used him. I'll be good to him even if he should behave badly to me."

There was only one blood-red streak left low down on the horizon, and she turned and went slowly back to the house.

"He has proposed to her," said the widow to herself, the evening of the next day, when she reached her bedroom. And, white as ashes, Maud threw herself down into a chair, and, with an agony in her heart, drove her teeth into her lips. "Oh, my God!"

She put her handkerchief to her lips. There was blood on it.

But Warrington had not proposed. As a matter of fact Lily had not that day seen him. But there was a pride in her face, a dignity in her walk, a firmness in her step, that they had never had before. And her young lips were riper, and the meaning of her eyes deeper and fuller of the consciousness of life. And Maud had seen it.

"I could take him from her if I chose for all that." said the widow to herself, standing before her glass regarding herself and reckoning how easy the young girl's defeat would be.

"And break her heart, poor little puss! And she is happy! No, she shall have him. It will be better for him!"

But she turned away from the glass with a face full of bitter pain.

CHAPTER XV

Two long, happy days Lily proudly kept her secret of golden sunshine locked in her breast. Then, after thinking of the matter for a quarter of an hour, she came to the opinion that the prettiest, frankest, and right thing to do was at once to be open with Maud, and to confide her love to her.

Frankness, and that artlessness which craves at once to communicate whatever has overfilled the heart, were a much larger part of her nature than reticence.

She had, besides, no wish to keep secrets from her cousin. She and Maud were one in heart and soul, one in tastes, in inclinations, in feelings, in everything—both of the same age within a few years; both mere girls, for Maud's stupid marriage had hardly been a marriage at all; and both, in their hearts, ready enough to fall in love with Prince Charming if he would only come and fetch them away.

At least so Lily thought. Some people would have told her that she was a little goose, and that she and her cousin were not alike at all. Only Lily Hardwick would certainly not have understood them.

Having resolved to take her cousin into her confidence, Lily did not wait long to put her purpose into execution. She made her avowal the very same afternoon, in the twilight after afternoon tea. Seated on the sofa with her saucer and empty cup on her knees, she had suddenly dropped into a reverie so profound that she did not hear Maud Gainsborough ask her whether she would take another cup of tea. Maud, who, at the moment she spoke, was inspecting the contents of the teapot, receiving no answer to her question, looked round.

"How awfully pretty she is!" thought the widow to herself. "It would really be a shame to disturb her. What a picture! I am afraid she has caught it very badly, though. Poor girl! I wonder how long she will remain in that exceedingly picturesque attitude?"

Lily appeared prepared to remain impassibly immersed in her dream for any period of time. So presently Maud Gainsborough softly rose from her chair and came to her, sitting down at her side, and gently passing one arm round her, and then drawing her to her.

Lily let her do as she pleased; only once she glanced guiltily into Maud's eyes, and laughed a little nervous laugh.

Then, half-lying in her cousin's arms, with her eyes turned away, she said:

" I had something to tell you, Maud."

" Suppose I have guessed it ? "

Lily started, and disengaging herself from her cousin, and sitting up, looked her hard in the face. Then, bending forward a little, she said, softly :

" Maud, I love him so awfully—so awfully."

An expression of acute pain shot across the widow's face. But, mastering herself, she took one of her cousin's hands, and began caressing it.

" I feel sometimes as if I should go quite mad I love him so," continued Lily.

" And, Maud, isn't he handsome ? " she resumed, after another pause. " I do admire him so. I expect every other girl down here does too. But I don't care. They don't *love* him as I do : they couldn't. And, do you know, Maud "—this in a lower voice— " I believe that he does not dislike me."

Maud Gainsborough started. Hope, brilliant as summer noontide, had burst in an instant upon the blackness of her night. The man had *not* proposed. The girl was only flattering her heart with her own dreams.

" But, darling," she asked, gently, in her soft, rich voice, " he has proposed to you ? "

" Oh ! no, Maud ! Only I love him so that I don't know even whether I want him to propose. To be engaged to him would be such awful happiness that I think I should feel half afraid of it. But I believe that he does not dislike me."

" Yes," thought Maud, " I believe that, too." But what a weight was gone from her heart ! Aloud she asked, rather markedly, " Already ? "

" Why do you say, ' already,' Maud ? " asked Lily, not quite pleased.

" You have not heard anything, then ?   There are people who say there was a cousin of Mr. Warrington's——"

" Well ? " interrupted Lily.   " There was a cousin of Mr. Warrington's.   What of it, if there was ? "

" My dear, I was going to tell you, only you interrupted me.   Some people say that, only a very short time ago, Mr. Warrington was engaged to this cousin of his, a great beauty, to whom he was very much attached.   And that it was only because the match was broken off that he came to live down here."   She looked at Lily, but Lily's face was inscrutable.   " If any of that is true, it seems to me that Mr. Warrington has not been *very long* in changing his mind."

Lily had risen.

" What was his cousin called ? " she asked, shortly.

" I don't know that any one down here knows."

" Well, then, I know," returned Lily, quickly " Mr. Warrington's cousin to whom he was engaged is a Miss Chesterfield ; and she is very pretty, and he was very fond of her, and—I know all about it."

Folding her arms, she stood at a little distance, with her head slightly turned, looking down at Maud Gainsborough as if she would say :

" Now, then !   You did not expect that, did you ? "

Maud did not expect it.   She said to herself, " So, he has been making a confidante of her, has he ? " That looked serious, and the expression of the widow's face changed.

The girl saw it at once, and followed up her advantage without mercy.

" I know all about it," she said, flopping herself down in a little chair by the low tea-table.   " But that is no one's business but mine.   Mr. Warrington was shamefully, shamefully used. And as to his having changed his mind 'already,' as you call it, I don't see that that has anything to do with it. And, anyhow, I don't care. I wished to be frank and nice about it all to you, Maud. If you don't wish it, I can perfectly well hold my tongue. And so we will say no more about the matter."

And, with considerable *sang-froid*, Miss Hardwick proceeded to pour herself out another cup of tea.

The widow knew how to manage her, and said nothing; only took up her needlework. Lily drank her tea in silence, and then sat looking at the fire. So passed half an hour, or more. Then Lily got up and came across to her cousin.

"I beg your pardon, Maud," she said, kneeling on the floor by the widow. "I got into a temper just now. It was all your fault, with that stupid 'already,' but I'm awfully sorry."

"Come then, darling," said Maud Gainsborough, good-temperedly, coaxing her back to her side on the sofa. "Now, let me hear all about."

So, after all, the tender confession was made. But nothing would Lily tell about Miss Chesterfield. That was not her secret, and she would not be persuaded to communicate anything on the subject. It was disappointing, for the young widow was very anxious to be informed.

After all, though Mr. Warrington had not proposed, it seemed to Maud Gainsborough that things had gone pretty far, particularly as she imagined that what Lily knew about Miss Chesterfield she had learned from her lover. But still it would be an easy thing for Maud to do as she pleased with the young girl's pliant, confiding nature, and with her naïve, child-like love.

But Maud was still resolved to let things take their course.

" She will make him a better wife than I," she said to herself. " Or, at any rate, she will bring him some money. I will not come between them."

CHAPTER XVI.

WARRINGTON and his brother went to a dinner-party at the rectory. The dinner was dull, but the brothers met Maud Gainsborough, who, to do her justice, would have refused the invitation, if she had suspected whom she was to meet.

Warrington—now he had discovered how agreeable feminine society can be when a man has once made up his mind not to be in any danger from its fascinating wiles—would much rather have met Miss Hardwick. But she was not of the party. Failing her, he made himself agreeable to her cousin, and with the assistance of Maud's conversation, which was bright and witty enough, got through the dull evening rather more successfully than the majority of the party.

Maud, too, had by this time invented herself a myth. So that now the only one of the three who was not acting a part was Lily Hardwick. Maud Gainsborough's myth was this; that she freely surrendered the man she loved to her cousin, out of regard for the young girl's feelings, and for the man's good. For the rest of her life she would herself be made happy by the reflection of their happiness, and by the consciousness of having, at the supremest moment of her existence, had enough nobility of character to sacrifice the great passion of her life to the welfare of the man she loved. That was, however, no reason why she should not show herself to Warrington in her fairest colours. Rather the contrary. Some day he would hear the truth. These things always come out some day. And the more he admired her the greater the price he would set upon the sacrifice she had made him, and the higher the opinion of her which he would always entertain. Poor Maud! She enjoyed the dull dinner-party at the rectory that evening as she had enjoyed few things in the whole of her life.

A day or two afterwards came a letter to Lynhurst from General Chesterfield. It was an unlucky letter, and it came on an unlucky day, when Warrington was bothered about finding some ready money.

The general was not at all well. And his medical adviser was entirely deceived about the nature of his complaint. With the general's medical adviser this was commonly the case, at least in the general's opinion.

At present the old gentleman had a bad touch of rheumatism, and the doctor did not choose to treat him for it. So the general was going to pay no more attention to anything that the doctor said. And, contrary to the doctor's orders, he had had some friends to a big dinner, and these had amused him very much by wanting to know whether the story of his granddaughter's escape from her betrothed was true. They had all laughed over the story until they had nearly fallen under the table in fits. Also, it was said at the club that Warrington had gone to hide himself in some hole in the country because he was ashamed to be seen after the Miss Chesterfield adventure. The general thought Warrington had better come up to town for a day or two and show himself. Also some one had put a report about the place that Warrington was so awfully cut up about the loss of Miss Chesterfield that he had become as lean as a lath : a report the general was not able to contradict because he did not know whether it was true or not. Thus the general in his letter.

Warrington lighted his pipe with the document. If his acquaintances in town thought he had hidden himself in some hole in the country because he was ashamed to be seen, they might think it. He did not care what they thought. And if they liked to believe that he had become as thin as a lath with fretting for Violet Chesterfield, they might believe it. He did not care what they believed.

Nevertheless, the letter made him cross, and when, to add to it, he failed in the afternoon to obtain some ready money he wanted, for which he had gone into Dorchester, he returned in the evening to dinner at Lynhurst irritable and in low spirits. Eustace did his best to cheer him, but with no success.

"Frank, old man," he said at last as they sat smoking after dinner, "there is nothing that puts a man so much out of humour with himself and with everything about him as attempting impossibilities. And the fact is we are attempting impossibilities here. We cannot afford all that we are doing. We must make up our minds to one of two things ; either to do less for the place, to go in for all these repairs more gradually, or else to live a little less like country gentlemen with plenty of money to spend. The place is costing us a great deal more than we meant it should. In my opinion, we are trying to do too much at once. And certainly we are trying to do more than we can very well afford."

"Every month that things are left undone, the dilapidations become more serious," returned Frank Warrington, rather gloomily. "If I could have got that money this afternoon——"

"But you see you could not. You have already

got as much as is to be had easily. Now, we must either be content to go on as we are, or else to be bothered out of our lives with loans. There is no third course, my dear fellow, you can see it."

Of course Warrington could see it. But he was cross; and loth to admit anything in a reasonable fashion.

So, instead of answering, he only smoked in silence.

Presently taking a pipe, and filling it, he remarked :

"I think I shall look about for a woman with a lot of money, and marry her. There are women enough, no doubt, perhaps not quite of our own caste, with whom it might be possible to live tolerably peacefully, who would not mind the match costing them a little money. Men marry mostly, sooner or later, some woman or another. And, as I am not likely to be troubled with any more sentimentalities on the subject, I might very reasonably look out for some advantage to result from the contract."

"I think the first question is, whether you mean what you are saying."

"Well, yes," replied Warrington, leaning back in his chair, and crossing his legs. "Say, some woman rather older than myself: a middle-aged woman: a widow. I feel distinctly in favour of a widow, she would have got over all the romance and the nonsense. A woman with some sense, of course. I have wondered in my time, like other young donkeys, at men making marriages with women of this kind, but I can see the sense of it now. I really believe that it would be a prudent thing to do."

"And the lady is to agree to leave the tender passion entirely out of the question ?"

"That is very simple."

"I am not sure that you would find it so in practice," commented Eustace, thoughtfully. "However," he continued, "the lady is not discovered yet."

"Now," resumed Warrington, "there is Mrs. Gainsborough. Certainly she is not a middle-aged woman. And she has no money, so she would not do. But, if she had money, she is a sensible woman. And, at any rate, she is a widow. I was distinctly interested by her conversation the other evening at the rectory: and I should say that it would not be difficult to get on with her."

"H'm," said Eustace.

"You don't agree with me?"

"I agree with you that she is a widow: and that she is poor. That she has sense—yes. That you will persuade her to waive the tender passion—most certainly not. That she would not be difficult to get on with—well, I distrust Mrs. Gainsborough."

"Indeed. Why?"

"Difficult to say, my dear Frank. Mrs. Gainsborough puzzles me. I am sure that I do not understand her; and yet I cannot satisfy myself that the prejudice against her, which I know I am contracting, springs merely from my inability to read her character. I won't say that she is insincere. No, I don't think that she is insincere. And yet——" He broke off, and concluded, "I can't understand Mrs. Gainsborough: and that is a fact."

"You don't think she would make a man a good wife?"

"Not one that he could trust."

"Well, if a man wanted a wife whom he could *trust*—he would want what he would simply never find, I suppose."

"There you are wrong. If a man wanted a wife who would prove an invaluable accomplice in something not quite straightforward, then I should say Mrs. Gainsborough was the very woman for him. If

he could make her first of all passionately in love
with him."

"What has love to do with it ?" demanded Frank,
sceptically. "Women don't love as we do, Eustace.
They love themselves and their pleasures, nothing
beyond. We regard them as animals not so very
unlike ourselves, a little bit better in some respects,
and a little bit weaker in others. But that, I assure
you, is altogether a mistake."

To which Eustace answered, very philosophically :

"The sense of mankind is against you, my dear
fellow. Still, respecting Mrs. Gainsborough, I may
be altogether mistaken, for, as I have confessed to
you, I don't understand her. However, she has no
money, and so we need not trouble ourselves about
her."

"That is true," admitted Warrington ; and he
puffed his pipe in silence.

Eustace resumed, after a few minutes' silence :

"Now, if you could do without a widow it might
be easier to find what you want. If a tolerable sort
of girl, with a pretty little fortune, who would not
mind putting her hand to the work of rescuing
Lynhurst from destruction, would do for you ?"

"Thanks. I have had enough of girls. Only
pray who may this very easily discoverable lady be ?"

"You don't know ?" asked Eustace, significantly.

"No. I certainly don't," answered Warrington,
quite honestly.

"A young lady : a very decent sort of girl : an
heiress : with a nice little fortune : distinctly pretty :
and, I assure you, quite ready to be asked to be
mistress of Lynhurst, as soon as you like."

"You speak in enigmas, my dear Eustace. You
mean one of Sir Robert's girls ? They are not
heiresses. Miss Welsley ? She is not pretty. I give
it up."

"Guess again. I am talking of some one of whom

you have seen more than of any of those ; a neighbour of ours ; tall ; recently much interested in the
building of your wall."

" Miss Hardwick ?   My dear Eustace, you are
talking nonsense."

" Not at all.   The girl is in love with you."

" Then I am sorry for her," remarked Warrington,
shortly.

" Why ? "

" And besides, I have told you that women do not
fall in love."

" In that case, then, there seems to be no reason
for being sorry for Miss Hardwick.   Nevertheless, I
should say that she was distinctly smitten.   If you
don't believe me, take some opportunity of judging
for yourself.   If you find that I am right, Miss Hardwick is, by your own admission, a sensible, straightforward sort of girl.   She certainly has a pretty little
fortune as soon as she is one-and-twenty.   You are
not going to be troubled with any sentimentalities ;
so she will do for you as well as any one else.   And
you can't do better than marry her."

" And pray what on earth should she marry me
for ?   For the pleasure of sinking her fortune in
Lynhurst ? "

" Not at all.   For the sake of providing herself
with an agreeable husband."

Warrington laughed, and Eustace joined him, but
went on in another tone.

" You don't know it, of course, my dear Frank, but
you have recently developed an exceedingly ugly
trait."

" Very likely.   Let us hear what it is."

" You are turned into a mysogynist.   But it is still
a fact that, when you are with women, no man could
be more studiously or successfully agreeable to them
than you give yourself the pains to be.   As soon as
you leave them, you abuse them without mercy ; and

I partly believe that you think what you say. But permit me to observe that your conduct is rough on the ladies, who are irresistibly attracted towards you as one of the nicest of men, without the faintest suspicion of the other side of your character. Into this trap Miss Hardwick has walked."

" Then she should have known better."

" Still, it is open to you, who are not troubled with sentimentalities, to take advantage of her mistake if you choose."

" Only, my dear fellow, I don't choose. I certainly am not going to propose to Miss Hardwick—about whom, besides, you are, I believe, mistaken."

There was a little pause, and then Eustace asked :

" Only, seriously, Frank, I am desirous to know one thing. If I am not mistaken, if Miss Hardwick would have you, why would you not have her? There is no sentimental motive at the bottom of all this."

" Certainly not."

" Well then ? "

But Frank Warrington made no reply.

Gradually a little smile began to play around Eustace Warrington's fine lips, and he continued, rather banteringly :

" I suppose it is not necessary to imagine that you have had a smite as well as Miss Hardwick, and are, in consequence, tender about her feelings. Falling in love is a habit like anything else, and when a man once gets into the way of it, he goes on, eh ? *Qui a bu boira.* Now, I remember that your weakness for Violet began very much in the same fashion, a quiet and rather platonic liking, just as you and Miss Hardwick made friends over that wall; and——"

" Eustace, shut up, and don't be a fool," interrupted Warrington, abruptly, but with perfect good humour. " We have had too much of this nonsense. Let us take out the chess-men,"

"By all means," assented Eustace.

He crossed the room to where the chess-table stood, and, bringing it, began putting the men on the board, thinking, meanwhile, in himself:

"Frank is honestly convinced that I have been talking nonsense. He doubts that the girl can care at all for him, and is entirely unsuspecting that he is smitten himself. All in the dark, just as he was the last time. Strange. How blind these people are who see!"

Warrington was in the dark entirely. and honestly convinced that his brother had been talking nonsense. And yet the next morning, strolling out after breakfast, he did think of some of the things Eustace had said. He reflected in himself thus:

"A man does not pass straight from being jilted by one girl to making a fool of himself over the next one he meets. And I think I am honestly cured of the weakness of falling in love. For which reason, I don't mind admitting without hesitation that Miss Hardwick has her good points.

"It is possible that she may have taken a small fancy to me. Probably she does not see too many men. I have the reputation of being a bit of a woman-hater. And to captivate a woman-hater flatters the vanity of a girl. I helped her in a scrape, too, and she is, very likely, a bit romantic."

A matter of entire indifference to him, all of it. Still, he was a trifle curious on the subject. If he wished to know, he had only to take Eustace's advice, to observe the young lady, and to judge for himself.

CHAPTER XVII.

A FEW days later, wending his way homewards from a long solitary walk, he was overtaken —it was in one of the most unromantically muddy of lanes— by Mrs. Gainsborough and Lily Hardwick returning home from an unsuccessful outing with the hounds. They had drawn all the covers blank. The lane led up a steepish hill, and Warrington walked some little way by the side of their horses. The widow, gradually passing in front, left him and Lily to talk together.

Lily, with a little laugh, made some allusion to their being apparently destined to meet always under difficult circumstances.

"The first time it was the tide, Mr. Warrington. To-day it is hopeless mud. Did you ever see such a slough ?"

"I suppose I ought to tell you," replied Warrington, "that the pleasure of meeting Miss Hardwick——"

"Has made you imagine the lane was quite dry," laughed Lily. "That would have all the essential qualities of a real compliment, would it not ?—falsehood, fulsomeness, and utter incredibility. You have been for one of your long walks ?"

"Yes."

"All alone ?"

"Yes."

"What a shame it is, Mr. Warrington, that you are so unsociable. Why do you not hunt oftener ? and why don't you try to help us all to get up some fun in this dull place? Why cannot you even bring your brother to see my cousin and me ? We have expected you every Wednesday."

"You are very kind."

"I think we are, to wish to see any one so very unsociable," said the girl, archly. " Do you know, I shall soon feel tempted to believe what I hear said of you, that you are a regular, morose, crabbed misanthrope."

" Dear me; is that what they say of me ? " asked Warrington.

" It is ; and you look as if you rather liked it. Only, now that I come to think of it," she continued, " I am not sure that it was not that other long word which was used."

" Which ? "

" Oh, I am not going to say it, for you to laugh at me : the word that means that you don't like ladies."

" Mysogynist ? "

Lily nodded mischievously.

" Well, perhaps it is true, you see," remarked Warrington, in a rather quiet way.

He would give her to understand that he did not much care for ladies, and see how she would like it.

" What ? That you are a woman-hater, Mr. Warrington ? I can hardly believe that," answered Lily, on the spot.

" Why ? "

" It is so mean. You don't think so ? But I do. When I hear girls speaking against men, saying they don't care for them, dislike them, hate them, prefer their own sex, and all that, I always think it sounds so cowardly, so poor-spirited, just as if they did not know how to hold their own with men. And if that sort of thing is contemptible in a girl—what must it be in a man ? "

" Well, I have no wish to contradict a lady," answered Warrington, surrendering with ready grace.

" No, no," put in the girl, quickly, " you shall not get out of it in that way. That is just a trick you men have. I would much rather hear you say anything than that you should pretend to give in to me at once, and still all the time think the same as before."

" You wish for the pleasure of defending your sex, Miss Hardwick ? "

" Add at once, ' and of having the last word of the argument like a woman,' " returned the girl. " But I assure you you wrong me. Come now, let us be honest. I promise you, solemnly, that I will not defend my sex. I will hear whatever you may choose to say, and answer nothing. But you, in return, shall tell me what it is that you really think."

" I am afraid it will be too bad."

" Well, say it all the same."

Warrington was fain to comply. Here was an opportunity to see whether she would care what he might think of women, including herself. But to frame the exact things he should say was difficult.

"I am waiting, Mr. Warrington."

"Then, if you must have it, I am afraid, Miss Hardwick, that women, at any rate young women, are not good for much—rather selfish, untrustworthy, cold-hearted creatures, specious enough very often. I will grant you, but very treacherous."

" Well, I don't think you need say any more. You could not make us out much worse than that," said the girl, rather discomposed.

His words had grated on her feelings, and he could see it.

" Those are really your opinions?" she asked, after a moment.

" Well—yes."

It was plain that she would have liked to dispute what he said. But she had given him a promise not to argue with him, and she meant to keep it. She only turned her face away, certainly with an expression of pain, and presently asked :

" You make some exceptions, I trust?"

"Oh, the present company, you know," answered Warrington, lightly.

"Oh, of course," returned Lily, with some acidity "We know that that means nothing. I am sure that I don't wish you at all to except me." Then, quickly resolving not to be guilty of an exhibition of temper, she went on, good-humouredly: "However, I made you tell me, didn't I? So you will justly think me very silly if I am cross about what you have said."

"And, after all, what people say matters very little, does it not, Miss Hardwick?"

"It matters sometimes."

"You mind what people say of you?"

"I mind what people I like say of me very much indeed," answered the girl, simply and unaffectedly "And, Mr. Warrington, I gave you my word that I would not dispute with you; but I am very sorry that you think of us all like that; I am indeed. I may say that without breaking my word, may I not? I think such opinions are unworthy of you. And, if I had the right to ask a favour of you, I would ask you as a great favour to try to think differently."

"Impossible, I am afraid."

"Quite impossible?"—she spoke very prettily. softly, in a tone of the gentlest persuasion.

They had reached the level, and Maud Gainsborough, a little in front, waited for them to come up. As Warrington made no answer to her last question, Lily went on, good-temperedly:

"Still I hope, Mr. Warrington, that you and I are none the less good friends; and I must try to turn out not so bad as you think me."

They came up with Mrs. Gainsborough, and Warrington wished the ladies "good-bye," and they trotted on.

But Warrington caught, as Lily bowed to him. a shadow of pain in her blue eyes,

Turning out of the lane, he strolled slowly homewards across some fields. There was perhaps something in what his brother had said. The girl did evidently care what he thought of womankind, and so of herself. But, after all, he did not see that much could be inferred from that. Perhaps she had taken a little ordinary liking to him, as to a man who had made himself agreeable to her, and perhaps she was a little vexed to see there was not much prospect of her liking being reciprocated; though, for the matter of that, he was quite prepared to admit that, as girls go, she was a good enough sort.

" And, after all," he concluded to himself, " women do not fall in love. Possibly the better sort don't pretend that they do. And, if Eustace knew as much about it all as I do, he would know that."

And Lily meanwhile reached home, and, whilst Warrington was still crossing the meadows, drank a cup of tea, standing in her riding-habit before the drawing-room fire, and answering, rather at random, such remarks as her cousin made to her, so that Maud said to herself :

" Have they had a little tiff, then ? "

Once in her own room, Lily was able to sit down by the fire, and to give herself up entirely to her reveries.

" I did not think he had got so far as that," she said to herself a little sadly.

But if her love could win him to think better thoughts ?

Was it strong enough, that love ; strong enough for a battle with his disbelief in all love ?

At last she gave it up, saying to herself: " I love him, and I know no more. If I love him enough, I shall succeed. If I fail, it will be because I have not loved him enough; and then it will be better for both of us that I should fail."

CHAPTER XVIII.

OF course that Warrington had wanted some money and had been unable to get it became known. Such things always do become known, especially in places like Lynham, though by what agency it is so impossible to say that the ancient myth, "A bird of the air shall carry the voice, and that which hath wings shall tell the matter," appears almost credible, for sheer lack of any possible explanation of the phenomenon.

Amongst other people Maud Gainsborough heard about that money, and was sorry for Warrington ; sorry that he should be in want of money ; and sorry to hear the gossips making ill-natured tattle for themselves out of his embarrassments.

Warrington's want of cash touched the widow, as the contemptibleness of his opinions of women touched Lily Hardwick. Lily would have given years out of her life, or blood from her veins, not to have her hero mean in his thoughts. The widow recked nothing at all of his thoughts. According to Maud's lights, opinions were just opinions, that is intangible nothings. But the want of ready-money that was real. And so while the young girl questioned her heart what self-sacrifice on her part could make the man she loved more noble of disposition, the widow wished that it had been in her power to put into his hands the ready-money he wanted. With what pride she would have given it him !

It made her think of that fifteen-thousand-a-year, which should be hers and was not. If she had had that in her hands !

She was still pursuing the same policy with Warrington : scrupulously, conscientiously avoiding him in every way she could, and letting things between him and her cousin take their course—a very slow course it seemed. In small ways she even abetted their meeting, and left them little *tête-à-têtes* when they met. But one afternoon at this date, being at home alone, she indulged herself in building a big castle in the air founded upon the imagination of what she would do if she had that magical fifteen-thousand.

Lily should not have Mr. Warrington then. Why should she? Maud would then be a better match for him than she. And Maud loved him as this child never would. Given the fifteen-thousand, Maud would step in between their halting, hesitating loves with her great, burning passion. In a month the man should love her; in less than another month Lily should be forgotten ; and the golden future——

What was the use of dreaming of it? She had not the money. Yet she went on with her dreams.

And meanwhile, perhaps, this will be a convenient place to offer some explanation of this phantom fortune ever floating before the imagination of the widow, and of how she became aware of its existence.

It is necessary to go back between two and three years, to Maud Gainsborough's gambling days, and to a date when she was hideously in want of money. Mr. Gainsborough had paid off her debts about three months before, and she had then made several solemn promises to keep from temptation in the future. The promises had gone the way of the proverbial pie-crust ; and now, so far as she could see, there was nothing for it but to confess the fact and again to ask her husband for money. Only, when it came to confessing, Maud's courage failed her.

It was under these circumstances that, one day, her eyes fell upon an advertisement of a certain publication. Somehow, it is always women's eyes that do fall upon advertisements of this kind. The publication was "The A B C Guide to hundreds of thousands of pounds : or a complete alphabetical register of all persons, in all parts of the world, at present entitled to inherit unclaimed fortunes, with complete instructions how to establish successful claims to inheritances, in many cases, of hundreds of thousands of pounds.　Price one shilling."

Mrs. Gainsborough was in the humour to catch at straws, and she caught at this one.　Who could tell that there was not an unclaimed fortune awaiting her.　Heaven only grant there might be one!　So she wrote for the " A B C Guide."

The post soon brought her the great work.　It was a volume in appearance something between a tradesman's catalogue and a cheap watering-place guide-book.　With trembling fingers Mrs. Gainsborough turned hurriedly to seek her own name, which she had at first been simple enough to suppose might appear in the book with the sum awaiting her set against it.　But she found no Maud Gainsborough.　Nor did she find Maud Spencer, her maiden name.　Nor were the fortunes which were to be obtained in any case indicated in connection with the names to which they belonged.　In fact, the promises of the " A B C Guide to hundreds of thousands of pounds " turned out to be somewhat illusory. Certainly the arrangement was alphabetical.　But the fortunate heirs-at-law appeared only as " The heirs-at-law of A. Jones "—" of B. Brown "—" of C. Robinson "—and so forth.　The whole question, which no one had as yet been able to solve, being who were the heirs-at-law of A. Brown, B. Jones, and C. Robinson.　Still it was interesting to know that A. Brown, B. Jones, C. Robinson, and the rest of them very much wanted heirs.　But it appeared that the fortunes in very few cases amounted to the " hundreds of thousands of pounds."　Also, the prodigious number of Browns, Joneses, and Robinsons who wanted heirs was really bewildering to any one who wished to choose from which of them he would like to inherit. Further information, however, respecting any name was to be had from the enterprising publisher of this great work, upon the payment of a guinea. To put the matter plainly: human ingenuity could hardly have devised a publication of which the real object (to obtain guineas from the unwary) was more plainly evident; or the ostensible object (to inform people whether they were heirs to unclaimed fortunes) more ingeniously traversed. After which no more need be said about the "A B C Guide to hundreds of thousands of pounds."

But Maud Gainsborough was desperate. And. clinging with the resolution of despair to her idea of the unclaimed fortune, she was not soon to be baffled. She looked up the names of all her uncles, and aunts, and cousins, and of her great uncles and aunts so far as she knew them, and then of her grandparents and of her great-grandparents; and still, meeting with no success, she set resolutely to work to read the whole formidable index of names throughout, from A to Z, if haply she might have the good fortune to discover herself heir-at-law to some one.

And thus, reading name after name, with a patience and attention that certainly showed character, Mrs. Gainsborough presently came upon one that arrested her attention—Josiah Klop.

That was an uncommon name. It was not probable that there were two Josiah Klops. And about one Maud Gainsborough knew a long story.

Again it is necessary to go back—back to Maud Gainsborough's school-days; to a date when both Lily's parents were living, and also a great-uncle of hers, who one evening invited the school-girls to his house.

The old man was an antiquary, a genealogist, and

a student of everything dry as dust, bygone, and generally uninteresting.

He was very kind, however, to the two girls, and showed them a number of curious things, and finally in the evening, by way of amusing them, undertook to show them that they were, as well as first cousins on their mothers' side, distant cousins also on their fathers' side—fifth, or fifteenth, or fiftieth cousins—the girls did not trouble their heads which.

To prove that, he brought them out an ancient family Bible, and a large, neatly-written manuscript volume, compiled by himself, and lettered " Monumenta Hardwickiana;" also some very ancient faded letters.

And first he called their attention to one of the earliest entries in the family Bible, and made them read under the name of John Hardwick : " He went away from home June 3, 1696, and was never heard of afterwards." And then, having shown them how they were both descended from this John Hardwick, he told the girls with great pride how he had discovered what had become of this lost John Hardwick.

John Hardwick was a sad scapegrace ; and when he left home he left a wife behind him, and a little son James, from whom all the Hardwicks were descended. Nobody ever knew what became of him, until about 1850, when the old antiquary himself purchased in Brussels a bundle of old English letters, that turned out to have been written by this very John Hardwick. From these letters it was evident that John Hardwick lived for many years in Ghent, and followed the calling of an usurer ; and the name he gave himself in Ghent was Josiah Klop. His letters, addressed to some familiar acquaintance, were very unreserved ; and in one of the earlier ones he referred to the fact of his having changed his name from that of John Hardwick to

Josiah Klop. In the last letter of the collection he spoke of his approaching return to England. But whether he ever did return was unknown. None of his family ever saw him.

The attention that Miss Maud Spencer paid to this history was very slight indeed; and all that she remembered of it barely amounted to the leading facts above recorded. Five years afterwards, with the name of Josiah Klop staring at her from the "A B C Guide to Fortune," she regretted sincerely that she had not paid closer attention to the relationships of the Hardwicks and the Spencers and to all the details of the story of John Hardwick, which had been related to her with so much care.

But, anyhow, she resolved to invest a guinea in further information. The information she got for the guinea was this:

In the year 1736 there lived in Bristol an old man named Josiah Klop. He occupied a dilapidated house and led a parsimonious and secluded life, with an ill-looking coloured servant who cooked for him and waited on him. He was a reticent old man, and unsociable; little was known about him, but it was said that he came from the Low Countries, and that he was wealthy; and he passed for a miser. Suddenly both the old man and his servant disappeared. The suspicions of the neighbours were aroused, and after a few days the house was broken open. The old man was found murdered in his bed, and the house ransacked. Whether there had been anything in it to steal or not was never known, but the coloured servant had vanished, and it was generally believed that he had murdered his master, and made off with what money there was in the house, and perhaps with some valuables. However, the old man's securities, and other properties of his which were in the hands of his bankers, remained, of course, intact. He left his property to a son, but no heir appeared, and the whole passed into the custody of the Court of Chancery. The present worth of his property, at the end of a hundred and fifty years, was believed to exceed half-a-million.

The paper trembled in Maud Gainsborough's hands, and the room reeled round her. Half-a-million!

Compelling herself to be calm, she read the whole again carefully, and then set herself to consider what should be her next step.

She wrote to the old antiquary, saying in her letter that some one had asked her about the family, and that she had been able to tell only a very little. But she remembered how kindly he had once told her all about Josiah Klop, and the cousinship of the Spencers and Hardwicks, and the fortune the old man had made by money-lending, and what ought to have become of it. And would he mind sending her the facts in writing.

Mrs. Gainsborough was a good deal pleased with her letter, and with the ingenious manner in which she had put out a feeler respecting Josiah Klop's fortune.

A reply came almost at once, in a letter of five sheets. The old antiquary wrote that he was very pleased to have received Mrs. Gainsborough's letter. Every one ought to know their own family history. And then followed the facts. First, all the history of John Hardwick, alias Josiah Klop; and then that of his descendants, the Hardwicks; and then the history of John Hardwick's sister's descendants, the Spencers. All the other branches of the Hardwicks were extinct, and William Hardwick, and after him his daughter Lily, were the sole representatives. Also, all the other branches of the Spencers were extinct, and Maud Gainsborough herself was the last of her family. And the letter ended thus, "You make a mistake about Josiah Klop's having made a fortune by money-lending. There is no allusion in his letters to his having amassed any property. Had he left a fortune, his present heir-at-law would be Mr. Hardwick, failing him his daughter Lily your cousin, then failing her, yourself."

Mrs. Gainsborough, for one minute, stared straight before her, a blank stare of disillusion, and then she tore the letter into twenty fragments.

She had discovered a fortune of half-a-million—for her cousin.

Presently, however, she got the better of her first frenzy of disappointment, and picked up the pieces of her letter—a valuable one beyond a doubt—and carefully patched them together, with paste and some tracing paper

Several courses were now evidently open for her. She might inform Mr. Hardwick of the discovery she had made. "Make my cousin a present of the fortune *I* have discovered?" quoth Maud Gainsborough to herself. "Never!"

And, being very bitter indeed about her very bitter disappointment, Maud Gainsborough then and there resolved, and vowed that, if *she* could not have the money, at any rate *Lily* should not.

Then there was a middle course: to make terms, big terms for the disclosure of the secret. The plan appeared to Maud Gainsborough difficult to work, dangerous, and uncertain to produce satisfactory results, and she renounced it almost at once. Probably in that she was wise.

Then there remained the third course—to wait. "Something might happen," quoth Maud Gainsborough. Of course she knew that meant that Mr. Hardwick and his daughter might die. She did not wish her cousin to die, but, if she should die, half-a-million was worth waiting for. Maud resolved, after all, for the present to put away carefully the letter she had at first ferociously torn up, and the other documents bearing on the subject, and to wait.

That left her, of course, where she was before with the gaming debts, and her incapacity for paying them. She did, indeed, read through all the rest of the " A B C Guide," but she came upon no more Josiah Klops. And, in the end, she had to tell her husband, and the collapse ensued which ended in his ruin.

But there remained indelibly branded on Maud Gainsborough's memory that fortune of half-a-million; which ought by every right under heaven to be hers, for she had found it ; and respecting which she had vowed that, if it could not be hers, it should not be any one's else.

A year afterwards "something" did happen. Mr. Hardwick and his wife lost their lives on the Matterhorn; and Lily Hardwick became the last representative of the Hardwicks.

But Maud Gainsborough remained still of the same mind. Even when she met the orphan girl, with her pretty eyes disfigured with tears, and her young cheeks pale with mourning, still she said to herself, " I have vowed that the money shall be mine or no one's. And I will not flinch from it."

She showed the girl every kindness, but she held to her resolution. And when Lily came to live with her—by that date the old antiquary was dead too— still she held to her resolution. And this afternoon she held to it still.

" I found the fortune, and it ought to be mine. If anything were to happen to Lily, it would be mine. If not, it shall be no one's. I may die before Lily, and then the secret shall die with me : but I will not surrender what should be mine. I have vowed that I will not, and I will not."

And with that power of self-deception which belongs to all strongly imaginative natures, she was firmly convinced that in holding to her resolution she was bent upon nothing but doing justice to herself.

But, if what was by right her own had only been her own in reality, what a future would have been before her—what a golden future!

CHAPTER XIX.

LILY, meanwhile, was showing herself about as perfect an epitome of all the charming caprices of a pretty little witch of twenty horribly in love, as any one could wish to see.

First and foremost, she was very much in earnest, and liable, if teased (and Maud could not always refuse herself the pleasure of teasing her), to become very cross, and shrewish, and sulky, for about a quarter of an hour. After that, her resentment mostly vanished with a laugh, and a toss of her pretty head, as abruptly as it appeared.

Then next the little wretch was grown as gentle as an angel, tenderer than tenderness itself with every living thing that crossed her passion-charmed path : the great, over-brimming love of her heart flowing out, as it were, in a flood of gentleness to all the world.

Then, of course, she had taken to losing herself in long reveries, and was at times as absent as the dead. And, by way of being consistent, she was, for the remainder of her waking hours, in one perpetual fever of recollection of her last meeting with Warrington, and of anticipation of the next. Though, if accused of thinking of such things, she became exceedingly indignant.

She had also grown a little shy, and not a little reserved about talking of Warrington, and more coy about speaking of her love than might have been anticipated, considering the irresistible penchant she

had to open her heart on most topics. At the same
time, his name was on her lips, in some trivial connection or another, twenty times a day. And she
had certainly improved ; she had grown a distinct
shade prettier, and more dainty in her carriage,
and more graceful.

In conclusion, to pass over the rest, she had
evinced also, all of a sudden, a talent for coquetry
of the most astonishing kind. So that Maud Gainsborough, who looked on, might well say to herself,
as she began to, on the one hand, "I am afraid that
she is most tremendously 'gone on him,'" and on the
other hand, "She would be more difficult to compete
with than I at first anticipated."

In some humours, to watch her amused Maud
Gainsborough very much indeed. In others, it
made her jealous with a terrible jealousy, a monstrous jealousy; the not unnatural consequence of
the way in which she was repressing and suffocating
her own passion.

But as February advanced, and with the length-
ening days came milder weather, another change
was apparent in Lily. She was growing uneasy.

Her heart had begun to trouble her with misgivings. At the outset love is all sunshine, and it
seems impossible that it should prove ill-starred. It
is content, too, with itself, satisfied to be love, and to
ask nothing. But love cannot rest there : nothing
can rest in this world. And Lily began to be aware
that merely to love Frank Warrington was after all
not quite enough.

As Maud had predicted, she very much missed
the restoration of the wall, which had been finished
long ago. It would have been a blessed sight indeed, if she could, some morning, have awakened to
find another fifty yards of Mr. Warrington's wall
conveniently tumbled into the garden.

For she and Warrington now saw very little of

each other. Perhaps Warrington had unconsciously taken a warning from what his brother had said, and perhaps Maud Gainsborough, also unconsciously, afforded the lovers less assistance than she had done. Certainly days passed, whole weeks sometimes, and Lily saw nothing of her hero.

She even began now and then to have a horrible suspicion that she was playing the miserable rôle of a girl who has given her heart to a man who could not care for her. After what he had told her of his opinion of her sex, it seemed more than possible.

When they did meet, occasionally Warrington was cold—so cold, once, that the girl went home and cried; yet Warrington had only been a little bit on his guard that afternoon, because he could see that one of the first scandal-mongers of Lynham was watching them from inside a shop.

But all their rencontres were not chilly. There were times when they met pleasantly enough, when Warrington was agreeable and even attentive, and Lily gratified and responsive. And now and then they both came uncommonly near downright flirtation.

One morning they met at the Lynham Road railway station.

"Ah, Miss Hardwick, how do you do?" said Warrington. "You are going somewhere?"

"No. I have only come to inquire about a parcel for my cousin. I wish I were going somewhere!" confessed Lily, with a little sigh.

"Where would you like to go? This is February. A little trip to the South of Europe. Shall we say Naples?"

"Ah, should not I just like that," answered the girl, opening her eyes.

"Suppose we go together?" suggested Warrington, playfully.

"Ah, shall we? That would be great fun,

wouldn't it?" replied Lily, coquettishly, on the spot.

"Well, let's start then," said Warrington. "Let us see. There is a train to London in ten minutes. Will you go and book?"

"Oh, no, you must go and book, you know," laughed Lily.

"I think," said Warrington, pulling some gold out of his pocket, and regarding it. "that the fare from London is something like twelve pounds. You don't happen to have twenty pounds about you?"

"No, I don't," said Lily.

"I'm afraid we can't go this morning, then."

"How unfortunate! And just when I haven't any luggage. You'll never get such a chance with a lady again, Mr. Warrington," laughed Lily.

He helped her to get her parcel and saw her off in her pony carriage, she saying playfully, as they parted:

"And, next time you are going to offer a lady a tour abroad, consult your exchequer first. It looks very bad, I assure you, not to be able to produce even the railway fare."

That morning she came back to luncheon in great spirits. But it was not very often that Warrington and she managed such merry little episodes as this.

Probably, however, the contretemps did the little puss good. She learned from experience something about what love really is—and there is more to be learned in that direction than is always supposed—and she certainly became, as time passed on, a little more mistress of her passion, more wary, less easy to trifle with, less disposed to wear her heart on her sleeve, and more reticent and dignified. She became, also, a trifle more difficult to approach, a fact that

Warrington observed and found rather an incentive to cultivate her.

But an act of girlish good-nature on her part, about the same date, made an impression upon him much more profound than she suspected.

The hunting season was drawing to a close, when they one morning met at a meet a little distance from Lynham. Lily was in high spirits. A Mr. Barlow, one of the best riders in the hunt, had promised her a lead, and she was looking forward, as she told Warrington with glee, to the best run with the hounds she had ever had.

A quarter of an hour afterwards, whilst Warrington was exchanging a few words with Maud Gainsborough, she came up to them on foot.

" I am going home, Maud," she said, simply ; " Mrs. Forsythe will drive me back with her."

And then followed the explanation of this sudden turn in affairs.

Mr. Forsythe had a niece staying with him for a few days only, who was afterwards going abroad. This niece had been nursing a sick relation, and had not been out with the hounds all the season. When they got to the meet this morning, they found that Mr. Forsythe's groom had railed over only one of the horses ; and it was difficult to say who was more vexed, Mr. Forsythe or his niece.

" So, as I have had ever so many good runs this season, Miss Forsythe is going to take my horse," concluded Lily ; " and Mr. Barlow has been so kind as to promise to look after her instead of me."

" Oh, but this is not at all fair upon you, Miss Hardwick," said Warrington at once. " Do let me see if we cannot manage somehow."

" Mr. Forsythe has tried everything," said Lily, good-temperedly ; " and, after all, I have had ever so many jolly runs this season already."

And so, in the end, she drove home with Mrs. Forsythe.

But Warrington, relating the incident in the evening to his brother, said :

"That is what I call real unselfishness. I feel a respect for that girl."

The impression the incident made on Frank Warrington did not escape the keen observation of Maud Gainsborough, either at the time or afterwards.

There was a public path through one part of the Lynhurst woods, and at the end of the same week Maud and Lily returning home that way came upon Warrington, giving some instructions to one of his men.

Briefly concluding his orders, Warrington turned to walk a little way with them, and at once entered into a conversation with Lily. In his tone, Maud believed she could plainly detect a note of deference and admiration for something more than the girl's pretty face and charming figure. Warrington was talking to her as to a girl whose conduct had won his respect.

Maud left them to talk, dropping behind under the pretence of picking some of the wild periwinkles. Following a little distance behind them, she could see them walking close together, the man's face often turned to the girl's, and hers often to his, as they conversed rapidly, earnestly, apparently engrossed in the subject they were discussing. From time to time, Lily bent her head as she listened, and from time to time, as she spoke, moved it with a charmingly coquettish grace.

As Maud watched them, a horrible jealousy of the young girl awoke in her, and made itself master of every other sentiment. This girl! This baby! Because she had a little money, was she to have everything ?

Warrington and Lily, still talking in the same

animated way, had stopped to wait for her. As Maud came up to them she made a resolution. This time, Warrington, for once, should talk to her, and Lily should walk behind.

She began from an ordinary question about the men to whom they had found him speaking, to ask about his labourers, and then about the improvements on the estate. In a very few minutes she and Warrington were talking of the wisdom and practicability of different schemes of capital and labour, and interest, and money sunk, and returns, and all sorts of things that were Hebrew to Lily Hardwick, but about which Maud seemed to know a great deal, or, at any rate, could talk very sensibly. And, indeed, any one who had listened first to Warrington's conversation with the young girl, and afterwards to that with the widow, would have said on the spot that there was no doubt which of these two young women was gifted with the most sense. Warrington, himself, was aware of the difference, and the tone of his conversation with Maud was of a more real kind than that with the girl, more like the conversation of a man with a man. He even thought of what he had said to his brother, how unfortunate it was that Mrs. Gainsborough had no money, for the woman certainly possessed a head for business, and might have given any man a deal of help. But, in the middle of it all, he broke off, quite naturally to speak again to Lily Hardwick, simply as if he felt it was not polite to leave her out of the conversation.

If he had looked, he might have seen Maud biting her lips for vexation.

After Warrington had left them, the ladies walked a good part of the way home in silence. Maud was out of humour.

At last she remarked, abruptly:

"You don't seem to get on very fast with Mr. Warrington, dear."

“ What do you mean ? ” asked Lily.

“ Nine men out of ten would have proposed before now—if they were going to do so at all.”

“ Do you think so ? ” asked Lily, a little alarmed.

“ Certainly. You don’t manage him a bit, Lily.”

“ Thank you. But I don’t want to manage him,” answered the girl, with some spirit.

As Maud said nothing, she continued :

“ I was so interested to hear all he had to say about his estates. I wish I could talk to him as you do, Maud. But I am not half clever enough for that. I felt so sorry, too, when he spoke of how many things there are to be done that would cost more than he could at once afford. He seemed so vexed about it, poor fellow.”

The widow was silent. Unwittingly, Lily with her allusion to Warrington’s want of money had put the knife straight into Maud Gainsborough’s heart.

Presently a rumour began to circulate in Lynham that Mr. Warrington’s pecuniary embarrassments, which had so recently been affording the gossips something to talk about, were likely to be only of a very temporary nature.

Dr. Gregg first brought that news down from town, whither he had been to pay his annual visit to a brother of his. And Lily Hardwick, taking luncheon with Dr. Gregg, was amongst the first to hear the tidings.

What was said was this. That Mr. Warrington’s grandfather, General Chesterfield, was so angry with his grand-daughters for having run away from his house, that he would disinherit them, and leave all his money to Warrington. And the general was reputed to be very rich and also very ill.

“ Serve those girls right.” said Lily to herself.

Of course, when she got home she told Maud Gainsborough what she had heard.

Maud listened with eager attention.

" Dr. Gregg told you that ? Did he seem to think it true ? " she asked.

" Quite true."

" And the general is rich ? "

" Very rich, they say. And Mr. Warrington is his favourite grandson."

Wrapped in a rose-coloured dressing-gown, Maud Gainsborough sat up late that night, thinking, thinking, thinking.

If what Lily had heard was true, that altered everything. Mr. Warrington would have no particular occasion to marry money. He might marry any one he chose.

His grandfather must surely be a very old man.

So strongly was Maud Gainsborough impressed with the change that had appeared in the situation, that she said to herself :

" If I could do without Lily's money, I would get rid of her. She should go and live somewhere else. He would soon forget her. But I cannot do without Lily. I should cut a miserable figure on my wretched three-hundred-and-fifty."

No. It was necessary to keep Lily, and to risk the consequences.

CHAPTER XX.

MAUD GAINSBOROUGH had been in love before this— more than once.

Falling in love, after a few times, becomes a rather odd experience. The third and fourth passion has none of the freshness of the first, but it is also free from some of its delusions. A great part of the frenzy of first love belongs to the erroneous opinion of the enormous importance of the adored object to the adorer, and of the essential immutability of the passion. That the beginner should feel this is quite reasonable. As yet he or she has had no opportunity to see any farther. But when once a person has passed through all the phases, those at the end as well as those at the beginning, when, after the loss of one or two beloved objects (supposed to be indispensable to existence, to say nothing of happiness), the passionate pilgrim of life himself, or herself, much the same person as before, only a little wiser, and capable still of being smitten with the gentle passion, the delusions give place to experience. After that, with recollection to assist, there is something very queer in gliding once more into an amour, in experiencing over again the first smite, the soft attraction, the little tendernesses, the anticipations, the unrest, the pleasures of the unexpected rencontres, the disappointments, the melting moments, and the final exchange of existence by which lovers come at last to live, not in themselves, but in each other. And not the least odd part of all is being able to say, "Next I shall have such and such feelings; and, if they continue, afterwards such and such others."

Just at present Maud Gainsborough was able to say to herself that she was beginning to lose her head, and that very soon it would be all up with her.

Whilst a human being can say this, there is still hope for escape. So Maud was not yet altogether lost.

But two months had elapsed since the young widow had received that telegram from Anthony Gainsborough, asking what could be her motive for wishing to leave Lynham, which had made her exclaim, "Things must go their own way."

And the widow at the end of those two months was not feeling safer than at the beginning of them: far from it.

The greater part of the time she had fought hard with herself, and with some success. But recently there had been a whole afternoon devoted to thinking what she would have done if she had had that fifteen-thousand a-year: and one, two, three occasions when she made Warrington talk to her instead of to her cousin. And once she had been far more successful than in the wood. Also three hours of the quiet night given to thinking how the death of General Chesterfield, and Warrington's inheritance of a fortune, would make it easy enough for him to marry whom he chose.

And worst of all, for this had been positive madness, she had gone for a country walk, knowing that she would meet Warrington, and had met him, and walked three miles with him, and—heaven help her! —how happy she had been!

And, since that, she had been thinking of him, thinking of him, thinking of nothing else.

At this rate, the date was not far off when she would be deliberately making the man love her. For she could do it. She had no doubt about that.

And then he would marry her, and love her, and worship her.

And she would have brought him nothing: only a wife who was——

No: never! Bad as she was, she had still grace enough to care a little for the peace of the man she loved.

But the case was becoming desperate. And desperate cases must have desperate remedies.

Maud Gainsborough found one desperate enough.

Mr. Warrington should know everything. She would herself tell him the truth.

After that, he would be out of danger of falling in love with her: alas!

When once she had resolved on the expedient, the

idea became a fixed one with her, and she began to strain every nerve to carry her purpose into effect. That absorption in one aim, when it had once obtained possession of her fancy, was a part of her nature ; and had more than once carried her through with her projects—sometimes, indeed, to her own destruction—where other women would have failed. It did so this time.

To find an opportunity of saying to the man such things as she wished to say, to be fairly sure of seizing the opportunity when it presented itself, to manage that the circumstance should be such as should make a confession possible, and that the occasion should leave her some way of parting from Warrington not too humiliating, after her avowal was made ; all that was not easy   But her resolution and perseverance managed it.

Once more she contrived to acquaint herself with Warrington's movements, and to meet him, this time late in the afternoon, as he was returning home alone. The place was a country road, very little frequented, and their ways lay in the same direction only for a short distance.

On the occasion of one of their last meetings, Warrington had been talking about the restoration of a ruined barn, and the construction of a bridge where one was very much needed to cross a wide stream, and Maud had pointed out to him that by building the bridge of the stone of the ruined barn, and constructing a new barn in another place, he would save time, materials, and labour. He had since put her plans into execution, and had found them turn out as she had predicted ; and he now began by saying how much he was obliged to her.

It was very pleasant to Maud to have him speak to her in that strain, but it was not to have her ears gratified that she had met him. She said, modestly :

"I am glad that my suggestions should have been

of any service to you." And she inquired after his brother.

Thus they reached the place where their roads parted. Stopping there, she said :

" Do you know, Mr. Warrington, there is something I want very much to say to you. Would you mind walking round this way with me ? "

He assented, and they proceeded on together.

Maud was conscious of a great weight settling down on her heart, and her eyes wandered restlessly around the scene before her. The road at this point passed through the corner of a wood, with only a low, slight railing on either side, separating it from the trees that rose, tall and leafless, spreading their wide boughs over it, often interlacing them in an arch. From the west the low sun, setting in a cloudless sky, poured its level, glowing light into the tunnel which the arching branches made. The light pierced in amongst the boles of the trees, and threw on the ground, before Maud and Warrington, long, sharply marked shadows. Farther on the road dipped, and then took a turn. It was shady and dusk there, and nothing was visible but the trees. Half unconsciously the young widow took in the whole scene—the quiet deserted road that had been scoured by recent rains, the long shadows, and the dimness of the wood.

This was to be the spot that she would always remember as the scene in which she confessed her crime—her secret that she had supposed she would never surrender. Already, as she approached telling it, her courage began to fail her, and the weight at her heart seemed intolerable.

How cruel to have to tell her guilt to this man ! To this man whom she loved ! Into whose arms she was fain to throw herself with a prayer to him to save her : instead of which she was going to make him fling her from him. He would do that at once when he had heard the truth.　Was the fatality that had brought her to this pass the first punishment of her crime?　God wields arms so terrible.　It is so easy for Him to make the guilty do such miserable penances for their sins!　And yet, if she chose, she could be silent.　She could easily say some trivial thing and still go free.　But if she once spoke, there would be no taking the words back.　One word, and she would have tossed away all hope, all possibilities. But if she was silent, who could tell what might happen?

No.　She was resolved to speak for *his* sake!

Yet some minutes elapsed before she found the courage necessary for beginning.　At last she said, with downcast eyelids:

"Mr. Warrington, I have something difficult to say　Please do not interrupt me.　You will only confuse me.　You must not think me sentimental. I am a woman of the world, and have seen more of it, unhappily, than you would think; but I am going to say things to you that I certainly would not say to any one whom I did not implicitly trust.　And I say them to you because I do not want you to take me for a woman different from what I really am."

Warrington made no answer, and she looked down the road before them.　There was a little descent here, down it the long black shadows stretched out before them so long.　But she had made a commencement, and it was now more easy to continue.

"I wonder," she asked, without raising her eyes, "whether it has ever occurred to you to wonder why I live here at Lynham?"

"I cannot say that it has.　That is rather your business than mine, Mrs. Gainsborough."

His tone was not very sympathetic.　Really, he was asking himself, what on earth the woman could be aiming at.

" You see, your nature is unsuspicious," said Maud, with a smile. " But there are reasons ; I mean, serious reasons."

Her voice had dropped, and she stopped, and it was a minute before she resumed :

" I think when you hear what they are you will see that you rather overrate me. And I—I should not wish you to be deceived."

That was not how she intended to conclude the sentence when she began it. But her brain was becoming troubled. To confess what no human being had suspected was so difficult. And the man listening with respect, with an evident admixture of surprise at her apparently uncalled-for frankness, was not assisting her.

However, she struggled on :

" In any case, Mr. Warrington, I am going to tell you the truth. I am living here, not of my own choice, but in accordance with a promise which Mr. Anthony Gainsborough exacted from me, after Mr. Gainsborough's death : a promise that I would live in any place he chose, quietly, and——"

She broke off, and in herself continued, " Oh, my God ! how am I ever going to tell him ? "

To tell him ! She was young, handsome, strong, fond of her pleasure, full of healthy, rosy life ; in lack of nothing but money. Just because she had not that, to wilfully wake the dead past out of its grave, and to turn all her future with one word into one long haunted misery ! Was it not madness ?

But her better self prevailed, and she came back to her story.

" That promise my brother-in-law exacted," she went on, dropping her eyes, " as the condition of— of——"

" I cannot tell him. I cannot," she protested in herself. " It is too horrible. I must have been mad when I began this."

And then again, with a sudden determination, she resolved, "I *will* tell him!"   And she resumed:

"The fact was, I was guilty of a great crime. I——"

Her breast heaved heavily, and her lips were quivering with agitation.

"Mr. Gainsborough was not wealthy," she said, hurriedly, at last. "And—I—I gambled and ruined him; and—" ("I cannot tell him," she said in herself. "It is of no use to try")—"and I am afraid his ruin occasioned his death. In fact, I behaved very badly to him. And I am here really in disgrace, living upon an allowance made me by my brother-in-law, on the condition that I behave well, and that I keep out of temptation."

She finished quickly in a low voice, but without embarrassment. When she had done, she once more repeated to herself, but now, in the form of an excuse, "I could not have told him. The thing was impossible." And aloud she added, by way of conclusion:

"And now, Mr. Warrington, you must think what you please of me."

It was not at once that Warrington spoke. To himself he was thinking, "What the deuce should this woman have told me all this for?"

At last he observed:

"I suppose you lived in town, Mrs. Gainsborough. There are great temptations in town. But I imagine that these are questions rather for your own conscience."

And that he said only because he saw that he must say something, and did not know what to say.

Maud Gainsborough hardly heard him. What did it matter to her what remark he made? She had broken down, utterly. She had far better have said nothing at all, than what she had said. For once in her life she had blundered idiotically.

Happily it was not far to Cliff Cottage. A great part of the way they walked in silence, each of them wondering which was feeling the more embarrassed.

At the gate, Maud, saying good-evening, added :

" I shall be at home next Wednesday, as usual, and very pleased to see you and Mr. Eustace Warrington, if you like to come."

That, of course, was equivalent to, " If after having heard of my conduct you prefer to know a little less of me, don't bring your brother on my next 'at home' day."

And so they parted.

" Of course the woman has her faults," mused Warrington to himself, going on his way. " Gambles if she can get the chance, does she ? I dare say. But I don't see what business it is of mine. And what she can have told me for I can't imagine. There is no accounting for women.'

In her own room Maud was crying, with her head buried in the sofa cushions.

" I wish I were dead ! " she sobbed, in a passion of misery ; " I wish that I were dead! I hate it, I hate it, and I cannot help myself ! The miserable coward that I am ! I might have told him and have saved him ; and instead I have made it impossible for myself to tell him the truth ever. I wish that I were dead ! "

Would he call on the next Wednesday ?

CHAPTER XXI.

That was the question which was perplexing Warrington. He did not want to call with his brother at Cliff Cottage on the following Wednesday. But he could see how his non-appearance must be interpreted.

But, as it happened, before Wednesday both Warrington and his brother were in town.

General Chesterfield was seriously ill.

The old gentleman had made many jokes with his friends about the trick his granddaughters had played his grandson ; but, for all that, he had been incredibly put out about the way in which the girls had run away from his house, and, since, had gradually subsided into a state of uninterrupted bad temper. Any reasonable being might have supposed that, seeing the girls were gone, the wisest course was to submit to the irremediable, and to permit time quietly to efface the remembrance of the momentary extreme annoyance. But not so the general. He preferred to make himself ill; and, by putting himself day and night into passions about his granddaughters, brought himself into a state of cerebral irritation that ended by completely undermining his constitution.

So serious did his condition become, that his valet ventured more than once to ask whether he would not like to see his grandsons. But the old man had, on each occasion, answered in his passionate way :

" Confound you, sir ! can't you mind your own business ? Don't I write every week to my grandson myself, sir ? And can't I tell him when I want to see him ? "

But for some weeks past his letters had led Warrington to suspect that the old man was not making the progress he wished to represent; and a day or two after his meeting with Maud a letter arrived from the general—an almost incomprehensible scrawl—that caused him the gravest misgivings.

" I am afraid that grandfather is far from getting on as he says, Eustace," he remarked, as they sat at breakfast, reading the letter that had come by the morning post.

"What does he write?" asked Eustace.

"The same old story, so far as it is possible to make anything of it. Beauchamp does not understand his complaint, and won't let him have anything he likes to eat. And he is evidently in a very bad temper. But he is again confined to his room, and apparently with very little prospect of leaving it. I think I ought to run up to town and see the old man."

"You'll not be able to do him any good. You'll not make him listen to Beauchamp," observed Eustace, in his quiet, discouraging tone.

That was true. Nevertheless Warrington telegraphed to the general's valet, asking him to let him know at once how the old man was.

The reply was exactly what he feared. The general was in a very dangerous condition, and entirely unmanageable.

The brothers held a short consultation, and went up to town the same morning.

The news of their departure was not long in reaching Cliff Cottage. Some gossip brought the information to Mrs. Gainsborough in the afternoon.

"General Chesterfield must be ill," said the widow to Lily.

On reaching their hotel, Warrington and his brother found the general's valet already there, waiting for them.

The general was about as bad as he could be with the jaundice; in all probability dying.

"The jaundice, Saunders!" exclaimed Warrington, with amazement.

"Yes, the jaundice, sir," replied the man. "The general would not admit that it was the jaundice. The merest hint of such a thing put him at once into a furious passion, which was very bad for him.

He insisted that it was nothing but a little touch of rheumatism in his right shoulder."

" Yes; that is what he has been writing to me all along," interrupted Warrington. " A touch of rheumatism in the right shoulder, and his heart a little weak."

" That's it, sir. That's what he says to every one, sir. Colonel Nysson and some of the others sided with him at first, and that made him the more obstinate. But of course afterwards any one could see what it was. But it is no good to say anything to him about it, sir; he only gets into one of his passions—you know, sir—and makes himself ever so much worse."

Warrington took a turn across the room and back again.

" Tell us all about it, Saunders," he said; " when and how this began. Tell us all you can."

The valet commenced. The beginning of it all was the young ladies' going away. After they had gone, the general seemed not to be able to get over the way in which they had left him. He kept on talking about it, fretting, and grumbling, and scolding, until he had fretted himself ill. His temper became worse than ever, and his appetite grew uncertain. He could not enjoy his breakfast in the morning; and then sometimes he would be looking forward to his dinner all day, and, when it was on the table, could not touch it. And he was always complaining about the rheumatism in his right shoulder. It was a long time before he would see the doctor; and then, when the doctor told him he had the jaundice, he went into a great passion, and swore that the doctor knew nothing about what was the matter with him, and that he would not see him again. Colonel Nysson came in the same evening, and set him still more against the doctor. And so, the next time the doctor called, the general would not have him come upstairs.

However, after some days, the pain continuing, the general became frightened about himself, and began to fancy that his heart was out of order. Then he was troubled with pain in his legs, and could not sleep at night, and so he had the doctor again, after all. But still he would not give in about the jaundice. And his temper was something awful. About the end of January he seemed to pick up a little, though he was still very cross, and querulous about himself. He had become, too, as yellow as a guinea. He did not seem to be able to see that himself, and, if any one said anything about the jaundice, it made him perfectly mad. He had by that time taken to always having his breakfast in bed; and, when he was up, he only got about a very little, because his legs were swollen, and pained him. At the end of February he took altogether to his bed. He wanted nothing but game and fancy dishes, and all that the doctor would give him was thin beef-tea, and rice puddings, and milk. So there were rows all day long about his meals, and sometimes, when he had an appetite, he would have what he liked in spite of the doctor. If he could not get it anyhow else, he would have it sent in from an hotel, and then he would eat enough for three, and after that he was worse again. Sometimes he would take a little more stimulant than usual, and, as he had never been a heavy drinker, that would pick him up for a time, and he would believe that he was getting well, and would tell the doctor so. But, on the whole, he grew slowly worse and worse. The doctor made him have a nurse in February, and she had been with him ever since. The only wonder seemed to be how he had held out so long. Now, in these last few days, there had certainly been a change. He slept more, and, though he was still irritable and excitable, his strength seemed to fail him, and his fits of passion were neither so violent nor lasted so long. In fact, the old man appeared to be sinking.

"And all this time, why has no one written?" demanded Warrington.

Because the general would not have it. No proposition made him more angry. He always asserted that he had himself told his grandson all that the doctor said, "lies and all." And so every one supposed that Warrington knew.

The valet left.

"And so we have come up to town, Frank, just in time to see the end," observed Eustace.

It seemed so.

The next morning Warrington called at Welmore Street. He was shocked at the condition in which he found the general. The old man did not indeed present the canary colour he had anticipated; he was rather of a greenish pallor. But his cheeks were hollow, and his appearance that of an utter wreck.

"And pray. sir, what the devil have you come for?" he at once demanded, angrily. "Come to see whether I've got the jaundice, haven't you? Don't believe what I write in my letters? Eh? Or what the devil does it all mean, sir?"

Warrington answered, very quietly:

"What it means, grandfather, is simply that Eustace and I are in town for a few days. But I am sorry to see you so far from well."

"Yes, I'm out of sorts, my boy," answered the general, somewhat conciliated. "My heart is all wrong, and I'm queer all over. But these confounded doctors don't seem to know what is the matter. To cover his own ignorance, Beauchamp wants to make out that I've got the jaundice. The idiots have brought me to death's-door between them. First they destroy my appetite with their filthy drugs, and now they won't let me have anything to eat. And I can't get a wink of sleep either. If I only doze off for ten minutes, this woman they have put here to look after me wakes me up to take some of their beastly medicine. And they won't let me see any one. Nysson came last night, and she knew that I wanted to see him, and still she sent him away. Laid up like this, of course, I can't make any of them do what I wish. But I'd have been up long ago, and quite well before now, if it had not been for their blundering and bad nursing." The old man had been working up his impatience during these last few sentences to a very considerable pitch, and here followed some very ugly words, after which he concluded savagely: "And I don't want any one coming here to look after me—to see how I am and how I am not. You understand me, don't you? When I want you, I'll send for you."

The nurse came in with some beef-tea on a tray.

"Now, what's that you've got there?" demanded the general.

"It's what Dr. Beauchamp ordered, sir."

"I didn't ask you what Beauchamp ordered; I asked you what it was," said the general, savagely.

"It's beef-tea, sir."

"Then I shan't take it," said the old man. "Take it away. I shan't take it. Take it away. Now Will you do as I tell you?"

He had got up on his elbow, trembling with anger.

"Take it away," he repeated, passionately. "I said I'd have a little game-pie. Do you hear? Game-pie. I'll not have that."

Bending forward, he made a grab at the tray as if he would throw it on the floor, and then, exhausted with the effort, fell back on his pillow, mumbling, in a faltering voice, something scarcely audible.

The nurse simply put the food down on the table, and moved towards the fire.

Warrington leaned back in his chair by the bedside and silently bit his lips.

The poor old general! How pitiful an end to the brave old fellow's long, honourable life and many years of distinguished service. It all flashed through Warrington's brain; all the story that he knew so well; of which they were all so proud. And he thought, too, of the poor old man's sorrows; of disappointments of long ago, of which he had only heard; of how he himself a boy—too young to understand—had looked with awe at the erect, military figure standing by the grave of his mother, the general's youngest daughter, and had seen the tears well up in the old soldier's eyes; and of how the old man used to feel the dropping off of all his old friends one by one. For the general had a great heart. His temper was really awful, and had apparently always been the same; but that had nothing to do with his great, warm heart. How kind he had been to Warrington and to his brother! How good to them both when they were left orphans, a second father, and a wiser one than their own.

How kind he had meant to be to the Chesterfield girls—the thankless hussies! There was no end of tender-heartedness in the rough old fellow; any one who knew him could witness to it, his fellow-officers, his friends, the men who had been under him, his men-servants, his beasts, his enemies : only no women, not even his daughters. Of all the animals upon the earth, the one that the general had never been able to understand, nor to make understand him, was a woman. A phenomenon in which Warrington, at any rate, saw nothing strange. And now this was the end of the fine old officer, the tender-hearted, rough old soldier, the brave old man, who had fought his way through five campaigns, and through life's long battle of seven-and-seventy years—to die without dignity, a peevish dotard, in the charge of a woman.

The poor old general!

It was with reluctance that Warrington left him and went downstairs. He would have liked, if it were possible, not to have gone away at all, but himself to have nursed the old man; gently to have curtained from vulgar eyes the old soldier's last defeat, and to have felt that, doing so, he was giving back a little of the love the old man had lavished on his orphanhood.

In the library he sent for the nurse.

"General Chesterfield passed a very bad night?" he asked.

"Oh, no, sir," answered the nurse. "He slept from about nine o'clock till nearly eight this morning. He does not know when he has been sleeping and when he has not, sir, you know," she added, in explanation, with a little smile, seeing that Warrington looked surprised.

"Is that so? Then I presume that is why you sent Colonel Nysson away?"

"Colonel Nysson did not call yesterday, sir, and I should not presume to send any one away except by the doctor's orders."

"The general told me——"

"Oh, he makes mistakes, sir. You must not pay any attention to what he says."

"Indeed?" said Warrington, rather incredulously.

But in the evening, when he called again with his brother, he found that the nurse was right. The doctor was there, and the general was telling him that in the morning he had wished for some beef-tea and the nurse had refused to get it for him.

On the whole, however, he was in a better temper. He was short and cross with the doctor, but he received Eustace with a good deal of affection, and thanked him for coming. For one thing, he could not suspect that Eustace Warrington had come with any intention of seeing whether he had the jaundice or not. Still, he told both the brothers rather gruffly that he did not wish for a repetition of their visit on the morrow. To the medical man Warrington expressed some surprise respecting the beef-tea.

"My grandfather was the last man to be guilty of falsehood," he remarked, with an accent of sorrow.

"And he is not guilty of it," answered the doctor, quickly. "He has the jaundice, and it is the jaundice, not he." He continued, "Come and see him as much as you can, both of you. He will tell you he does not wish it, but he will be hurt if you neglect him." And in a lower tone he concluded, "He will not live long."

But the general sank very slowly. Even now his wonderful constitution continued to bear him up; and from day to day little difference was perceptible. The brothers were assiduous in their visits. The old man continued to tell them that he did not want to see them, and, two times out of three, either scolded them for disturbing him, or accused them of coming to see whether he had the jaundice. However, after a few days, when they happened both to be with him, he said:

"Why don't you two boys come and stay with me, instead of wasting your money at an hotel. I can't do anything to make you comfortable; they have mismanaged me so, and made me so ill; but you can do what you can for yourselves, and I'm sure you are both welcome: only don't come bothering me in my room."

So the brothers brought their things over from heir hotel.

After that they were with him, one or other, almost incessantly, all the day, and often a part of the night.

" I told you when you came to stay with me, *not* to
be bothering me by coming in here," was the welcome
they generally received ; but, on the other hand, if
they left him for five minutes, the old man said to the
nurse :

" Where are those boys gone ? They never come
to sit with me now "

Now and then the old man had a few minutes during
which his reason got the better of his malady. During
one of these he said to Warrington :

" I am a bad-tempered old fool, Frank. I've been
a passionate man all my life ; and being laid up here
a prisoner day after day, and full of pain, isn't the
sort of thing to mend a man's temper. But you must
not mind me, my boy, I can't help it."

Afterwards, he began to sink more rapidly. Every
day he was visibly weaker, and each succeeding
twenty-four hours took from him a little of his small
remaining strength. Only his irritability continued
undiminished. But he was no longer able to rave
and storm at his nurse, and the doctor, and every one
else that came near him. He had sunk into a mere
feeble querulousness — a ceaseless whining complaint
that was interrupted only by his dozing off to sleep,
or by his actual physical incapacity to maunder on.
Then, all of a sudden, one day he was much better.
He complained, indeed, a great deal of cold, and of
the " rheumatism " in his knees and in his right
shoulder ; but he sat up, propped by pillows, and
seemed brighter than he had been for a long time.

In the afternoon the colonel came in to see him.
The general was a little tired, but he kept his old
friend talking for a long time, speaking of one
reminiscence after another of times gone by : not
recollections of his active middle life, nor of his
young manhood, but of the first years the colonel and
he had spent together at Winchester, and of the still
more remote days of his earliest childhood.

L

It was nearly seven o'clock when Colonel Nysson left.

But the next day the general was very much worse, feebler than ever before, and all the day long drowsy and lethargic, only waking from time to time to fret and to complain in a faint voice, and then to doze off again.

And he did not afterwards rally. As the days passed, the heavy lethargy grew upon him, and his conscious moments became rarer and rarer. And still it seemed to take a long time to bring the end.

The brothers had been in town a fortnight. Four days had passed since the afternoon that the old man had talked for three hours of his childhood. To-day he had lain all day like a log—motionless almost, and unconscious. When the night came, Warrington announced his intention of remaining with him. The watch was a gentle service now that the bitterness of the struggle was passed, and death could not be far off. But the general lived through the night. Only in the morning the angel of the dawn gathered up the old soldier's soul as he passed, and when the sun rose the general had entered into his rest.

Warrington himself called on the doctor and the solicitor.

"We shall not open the will," he said, "until after the funeral. The Misses Chesterfield ought to be informed, but I don't know where they are."

"I believe that they are still with Mr. Anthony Gainsborough," replied the solicitor. "We can easily find them. And I may as well tell you at once that General Chesterfield has disinherited his granddaughters."

CHAPTER XXII.

THE same day, at sunset, an English steam-yacht lay off in the Bay of Naples.

On the deck two girls walked up and down, enjoying the cool of the evening.

The yacht was Anthony Gainsborough's, and the girls were Violet and Essie Chesterfield. Now and again the sisters stopped, and, standing side by side, spent a few minutes in admiration of the beauty of the scene, and then resumed their walk and their conversation.

Any one who had known the sisters in London would have found a considerable alteration in their appearance. They looked stronger and healthier. Four months' cruising in the Mediterranean had put brighter roses into their cheeks, kindled a clearer light in their eyes, and given fresh elasticity to their step. But a change more material than that had passed in the expression of the two fair young faces. The shade of disingenuousness they had both had in London had vanished, and, free and happy instead of miserable, the girls had got back the frankness and gentleness natural to their years.

They were talking of their uncle—the same Anthony Gainsborough of whom Maud was wont to give so unsatisfactory an account.

"Uncle Tony is perfection," Essie was saying. "I loved him always: but it is only since we have lived with him that I have understood how good and kind he is."

"I don't believe there is a man in the world like him," chimed in Violet; "he is all goodness. really believe Uncle Tony has never done an ill-natured thing nor said an unkind word in the whole of his life."

"He makes me feel awfully ashamed of myself," continued Essie. "Many times I have positively hated myself when I have been listening to him or watching him, and have thought of what I should have done in his place."

"I know," assented her sister. "I am sure, among other things, now, that we behaved very badly to grandpapa. Uncle Tony took our part and was very kind. I believe he would take any one's part who he thought was ill-used. But hasn't he made us feel, Essie. that we behaved badly to grandpapa?"

"He has," admitted Essie. She continued, "And I know, Violet, that he thinks you behaved badly to Frank."

"That is another thing," observed Violet, coldly.

"Ah. but he will make you think that, too, before he has done. Violet. There is something in Uncle Tony that is too strong for all one's pride and obstinacy. But to return to grandpapa: I wish we could somehow beg his pardon, Violet."

"Yes. I wish we could."

"Uncle Tony has a great admiration for grandpapa," observed Essie, thoughtfully. "Somehow he seems to see all his merits, and to be indulgent to all his faults."

"That is just like Uncle Tony, is it not?"

One of the yacht's boats that had been to the shore for letters came out in a straight line towards the steamer. As it drew nearer the girls stopped at the gangway to watch it come up, and as the mate stepped on board they asked:

"Anything for us, Wallace?"

"Nothing, Miss," answered the mate, and passed on to take the letters he had brought into the cabin.

The girls resumed their promenade, and some minutes passed, time enough for them to walk the length of the deck and back.

Then Anthony Gainsborough came up on deck. The sisters had passed aft, and he followed them. In his hand he held a thin piece of coloured paper.

Essie looked round, and the two stopped for him to come up to them.

"I don't know whether I ought to prepare you for the news," said Anthony Gainsborough. "General Chesterfield died this morning. Wallace found a telegram for me at the hotel."

And he gave them the telegram to read.

Both the sisters read the telegram, and then Essie gave it back. Neither of them said a word, but they were both a little pale.

"I came to tell you that you might know at once," said Anthony Gainsborough. "But I must go now to get ready to go ashore. I must try to be in London for the funeral."

And he left them.

The sisters moved to where two deck chairs stood side by side, and sat down. The first to speak was Violet. Looking up, she said:

"What are you thinking of, Essie?"

"I was thinking that I wish we had begged grandpapa's pardon."

"Do you know, I was thinking the same thing."

"It is too late now," said Essie.

Rising she went to the bulwark and looked at the blue water.

Presently her sister joined her.

"We shall be able to go back to England," said Essie.

"Yes. And I am glad of that. Uncle Tony wished to spend this summer at Twickenham."

The gig was being got ready to go ashore again, and presently Anthony Gainsborough came on deck with a small valise. The sisters went up to him.

"Uncle Tony," said Violet. "Essie and I are

very sorry for the way we behaved to grandpapa; we wish that we could have begged his
pardon."

"Yes, uncle. I wish we had," added Essie, with
the tears coming up into her eyes. " But now—it
is too late."

" Not for the wish, Essie," said Anthony Gainsborough, laying his hand on the girl's shoulder.

Violet took some gold from her purse.

" If you have time, uncle, when you get to London,
buy for us some wreaths for grandpapa's funeral—
the best that you can get."

The boat put off, and the girls stood by the bulwark watching it make its way towards shore.
Only when it had faded from sight in the coming
darkness they went below.

Anthony Gainsborough arrived in time to be present at the general's funeral, and to send the flowers
the girls had commissioned him to buy; and the old
soldier was carried to his grave shrouded in the
white blossoms that betokened his granddaughters'
repentance.

The general's will was a curiosity. After a few
small legacies, it divided his fortune, which was
considerable, into four equal portions, and bequeathed one to each of his grandchildren—Violet
Chesterfield, Essie Chesterfield, Frank Warrington,
Eustace Warrington. But then came a codicil,
dated early in the previous December. and by this
codicil, the general, after reciting his granddaughters' misconduct in running away from his house,
revoked his legacy to Violet Chesterfield, and gave
the whole of it to Frank Warrington, and revoked
his legacy to Essie Chesterfield, and gave the whole
of that to Frank Warrington too.

As the solicitor remarked, it would have been a
simpler thing to make a new will, but the old

gentleman was resolved, not only to make his displeasure felt, but to put it upon record, and had insisted upon the codicil, worded as he chose; and a very ill-natured and vindictive document it proved to be, but—unluckily for the Misses Chesterfield—very good in law.

In the evening Eustace went to bed early. The dreary day had fatigued him, and given him a headache. Warrington and Anthony Gainsborough sat up late smoking almost in silence by the library fire.

But when Anthony rose to say "good-night," Warrington said to him:

"I have one thing to say to you before you go, Mr. Gainsborough. My grandfather added that codicil to his will when his displeasure at my cousins' leaving his home was fresh, and at its height, whilst he was smarting under a great provocation, and at the same time falling into failing health. But I know that grandfather always meant to be kind to the girls, and, had he lived, he might have thought better of what he had done. Anyhow, out of respect to his memory, as soon as the property is in my possession, I shall send my cousins their fortunes. I shall leave it to you, to tell them that as soon as you see them, or to let them learn it when the money arrives, as you may think best."

And, as Anthony Gainsborough was about to say something respecting the generosity of this conduct, he concluded:

"I beg your pardon, but I had rather that you said nothing about that."

CHAPTER XXIII.

WARRINGTON and his brother returned to the country as soon as they conveniently could. Many things required Warrington's attention at Lynhurst, and he was loth to be absent longer than was necessary.

Lily and he met in the High Street, not many days after his return, and their meeting was a bright one. It was with a pleasure quite unexpected that Warrington found himself once more shaking hands with pretty Lily Hardwick, whilst looking into her bright blue eyes. Really, he confessed to himself at the moment, he had a liking for the girl. And, as for Lily, all her uncomfortable fears, that she was wasting her love on a man who did not want it, were charmed away in an instant by the smile on Warrington's face, and the cordial manner in which he shook hands with her and inquired how she had been. They walked home together as far as their roads continued in the same direction, and before they parted stood a full quarter of an hour talking. Lily returned to Cliff Cottage as happy as a queen, saying to herself:

" He likes me. I am sure he does. I am sure he does."

It was May now, and every landscape was robing itself in tender green. The tall elms and the beeches were in leaf already, and it was shady in the woods. The thrift was in flower on the cliffs, painting them with broad dashes of pink; the wild orchids and the tiny bright-eyed forget-me-nots in the marsh meadows; and, in the hedges, the blue-bells and the dog-violets and the yellow broom, with here and there crab apples opening their pale pink blossoms, and the sweet may filling the air with its perfume.

Cliff Cottage was a picture. About the porch the

pirus japonica, with its wide-opened scarlet blossoms and its quaint, gnarled, black stems, was in full flower, and the verandah all around was gay with the hanging blossoms of the pale purple westaria. The ivies were grown very dark, but the young leaves began to peep boldly among the old ones, and the other creepers were in their freshest spring hues. Against the supporting pillars the roses were in flower. Down the winding garden there were everywhere gay beds of tulips, and great, gaudy peonies, and guelder roses, and bright anemones and narcissi, and the chestnuts that bordered one part of the lawn had decked their beautiful domes of foilage with crowded spikes of white and pink blossoms, pointing upwards like tapers to the sky. There were garden seats under the chestnuts in a pleasant, sheltered spot, and already on the warm afternoons Lily had begun to take her book there to read after luncheon. Now, when she got home, she strolled across the lawn to the trees, and sat there for quite half an hour, and afterwards strolled down to the bottom of the garden before going in. Her heart was too full to be able at once to speak to any one.

Even when she came in at last, she said nothing to Maud about having met Warrington. But Maud made a pretty shrewd guess at what had happened.

The terms of General Chesterfield's will had already become known in Lynham, and there had been a good deal of speculation respecting how rich Mr. Warrington would be. Maud had been listening to it all in silence, looking about her meanwhile for some plan by which she might, for a time at least, get her dangerous rival Lily out of her way. It would be no jest if Warrington, now in a position to marry easily, were on the spot to use his liberty to propose to Lily.

His return at a date earlier than the young widow had anticipated found her with her plans immatured;

and Lily's tell-tale eyes that evening distinctly disconcerted her.

Maud had given up resisting her passion. What was the use of it? The love was stronger than she, and she could not wish it otherwise. And, perhaps, she had done all that she could.

But presently another rumour became current in the little country town. There would be no very great difference at Lynhurst. After all, Mr. Warrington would not be so much more wealthy. He intended to share his fortune with his disinherited cousins.

"The man must be mad!" said Maud to herself when she heard it.

One afternoon she and Lily met Eustace Warrington about half a mile from the gates of Lynhurst on the road to the town. He was alone.

"You see, I am getting on," he said, with some pride. "I know my way all about Frank's place now, and I am learning the road to the town. One of these days you will meet me in Lynham alone, doing my own shopping."

He insisted that the ladies should come back with him to see his roses.

"You will be quite surprised to see what a show I have already," he said.

He walked back with them, just flicking the hedge from time to time with his cane, so carelessly that it seemed barely credible that he was assuring himself of his way. When he reached the gate he opened it, and held it for them to pass through.

"You see we have already done something for the place," he remarked, pointing with his stick to the even, newly laid, gravel path on which they were walking: "and now we turn this way."

The rosary proved to be a rather formal, rectangular enclosure laid out somewhat in the fashion of a Dutch garden. Eustace took them from plat to plat, calling their attention to his various flowers. The thing of which he was proudest of all was his knowledge of their colours. Once only he made a mistake. Lily and the widow were too polite to say anything, but he detected it, nevertheless.

"I made a mistake then about those white roses, did I not?" he asked. "They are not exactly white."

"No: cream colour," said Lily

"Cream colour: thank you," he answered; but added, "But you should have told me at once. These colours, you see, are things I cannot get at at all unless some one will tell me. And I was sure from your silence that I had made a mistake"

Then he began to cut them some of the flowers, insisting that they must accept them.

Whilst he was so occupied, Lily standing near him, and Maud a little way off, he asked, with a smile:

"And, Miss Hardwick, what is it that you are wishing to ask me?"

"Dear me, Mr. Warrington, how do you know that I am wishing to ask you something?"

"Why, I can hear in your voice. That is very simple, is it not? Come now, Miss Hardwick, what is it?" he added, good-naturedly, at the same time neatly cutting off a rose with his pocket-knife and putting it into her hand.

Encouraged by his tone, Lily asked, straight-forwardly:

"Mr. Warrington, is it true that your brother has divided the fortune General Chesterfield left him with his cousins?"

"Quite true," answered Eustace, promptly "The thing is not done yet, but it will be done in a few days now. My brother has given his cousins two-thirds of his inheritance. He would like his gene-rosity in the matter to be a secret, but I have taken good care that it should be known. There are too many people who underrate Frank, and have no suspicion of the splendid fellow he is. So what I have told you. Miss Hardwick, you will do me a kindness by repeating. If people were aware how the Misses Chesterfield behaved to Frank, they would know that Frank has done a thing of which not many men would be capable."

"I have heard about the Misses Chesterfield," said Lily, quietly. "And I think," she added, with enthusiasm, "what Mr. Warrington has done is most noble."

That was not what Maud Gainsborough thought when Lily told her on the way home what she had learned from Eustace.

In the first crushing moment of conviction that the miserable rumour was true, Maud exclaimed in herself:

"The fool! The miserable fool! What has he done?"

Then. less passionately. but with a sickly despair, the young widow revolved with herself all that this last act of Warrington entailed. Again he was poor, or only somewhat richer than before. All that was possible if he were wealthy was lost again ; had slipped from her eager hands ready to grasp it, and left her where she was before, with her poverty, and her miseries, and her forlorn, hopeless love.

And she had just lighted on a plan for disembarrassing herself, at least for a time, of the dangerous presence of her cousin ; at any rate, for long enough, in her opinion, to allow her sensibly to supplant what influence the girl had over the man she loved.

And now ?

Now she might spare herself the trouble of carrying out her plans, of doing anything.

It was all over.

Certainly the turn in affairs was cruel for her. Warrington's generous conduct towards his cousins cost her—everything she loved or cared for. She felt so sure of the man, if she once used her arts to bewitch him. And hers was no common love. Maud Gainsborough was not commonplace. She as often behaved ill as well; as often—more often—did wrong than right; but whether she did right or wrong, whether she behaved ill or well, she did not do things in common ways. And she was not cheaply, vulgarly in love with Warrington. She was in love with him with all the energy of her intense, nervous nature, with all the fervour of her vivid, passionate imagination.

The revulsion from the flattery of hope to a new despair made her very bitter. She had ceased to regard a marriage between Warrington and Lily as the legitimate end of their acquaintance; and she was not now disposed to go back to that view of their future. Rather, if she, Maud, was not to have the man she loved, because he was poor, at least it was fair that neither should Lily have him either. He was not for sale, for Lily to buy him with her fortune! If the flirtation grew more serious, Lily should go away after all.

But the flirtation did not become serious. The days and weeks passed, and Lily Hardwick and Frank Warrington got no nearer to each other at all. They met often in a casual way, and Warrington was always pleased to see Lily, and sometimes kind. But his liking for her appeared to be of a very platonic sort.

Lily felt it herself, and asked her heart, with misgiving :

"If he does not love me, why is he always so pleased to see me, so nice, so kind ? He is not so to any one else. But, if he does love me, why does he remain so dispassionate, so cold ? "

One by one, all the sweet hopes that, on Warrington's return, had come back to her in a flock, like the swallows in the spring, began to take their flight, and to leave the poor little heart once more dreary, pensive, and sad. Soon Warrington's cold kindness began to seem more cruel even than neglect. It resembled trifling with her : and how could she suffer that ?

Women deceive themselves less about their love affairs than men ; happily for them, seeing how much less the event is in their own control. Lily was soon saying to herself :

" He likes to talk to me, and to be nice to me, because I am pretty. But he does not care for me really, and I am only being a little fool."

But then what days of heart-ache followed : what a dull, vacant pain ! It made her indifferent to everything. The splendid days of a glorious summer passed in their golden beauty, the royal sunshine filled the laughing air, the flowers bloomed ; and the great earth put on all her pomp and majesty. But Lily heeded nothing. She was trying to learn to live through a great disappointment, and that was enough. It was all over between her and Mr. Warrington. She kept at home and tried to avoid seeing him.

What an opportunity for Maud, if Warrington had not chosen to be poor ! The widow saw it, and, in secret, wrung her hands over her wretchedness.

Lily got no help from her now, and no compassion. Certainly she asked for none. Mrs. Gainsborough's view of the situation was that her cousin was behaving like a little fool, and getting her deserts.

Once she said to the girl :

" You and Mr. Warrington are not getting on very brightly, it seems."

" He does not care for me, Maud," replied the girl, sadly.

Maud knew better than that, but she only said :

" Why don't you make him ? You mismanage him."

" Thank you : you have told me that before."

" If I have, is it not true ? You may have him if you like. You don't like. Then don't have him."

" Look here, Maud," suddenly exclaimed the girl, catching her cousin's arm with a passion that was rare in her. " Do you know what you can be, sometimes ? You can be heartlessly cruel ! "

And she flung the widow's arm away from her, angrily.

And that time she did not come afterwards, as usual, to beg for pardon.

At last Maud Gainsborough got tired of the girl's pale cheeks and low spirits.

" Lily," she said one morning, " what do you say to a month with your guardian Mr. Tanner in London ? You will come in for the end of the season. And you seem so miserable here."

Lily thought. This was going away from *him*. And, heart-sick as she was, she disliked that.

" I know why you want me to go, Maud," she said, " and you mean it kindly. You think I shall be amused, and forget *him*. Well, then, Maud, I *shan't*. I love him too much. And—*I don't want to go*."

" Besides," she ran on, for her cousin, a little nonplussed by the directness of her answer, remained silent, " I don't know that Mr. and Mrs. Tanner want to have me. And I shan't enjoy myself, and I shall only be a nuisance to them."

" Well, dear, if you will not be advised," said Maud, yieldingly.

" No, Maud, it is not that. I am miserable enough, goodness knows. And it seems to me that I always shall be now. But I don't want to be sent away because of Mr. Warrington."

" My dear girl," replied Maud, quietly, " you will

come back again.   And Mr. Warrington will still be here."

Simple and obvious as the remark was, it was a masterpiece of an answer, because it replied, not to the girl's words, but to her thoughts.   And its effect was immediate.

The widow saw that, and continued :

"Please understand, dear, that Mr. Warrington has no weight at all with me one way or the other. The thing I am thinking of is your health.   I promised your guardian that I would take every care of you.   At present I am convinced that you ought to have change of air.   And, if I don't try to make you take it, I don't *think* I am keeping my promise to Mr. Tanner.   If you come back to me no better, I have made a mistake.   Of course that is possible.   But, if you ask me what I *wish*, I believe you do want change of air, and I do wish, dear, that you would take it."

" I'll go, Maud," said the girl.

"There is a dear, good, sensible girl," said Maud, kissing her.   "I wish that I could go with you, dear.   We would have a charming little trip to town together.   But as it would take me six months' correspondence with my precious brother-in-law to get leave, and then he would very likely revoke it at the last minute, that is not possible."

It was arranged that Maud should write and make all the necessary arrangements.   Accordingly, the same evening the widow wrote a letter to Mrs. Tanner.

It will be sufficient to quote only a part of it.

"A Mr. Warrington, who has recently come into an estate in the neighbourhood, came to live here some few months since.   He is a good-looking sort of man, agreeable, and exceedingly gentlemanly.   I began, shortly after his arrival, to suspect that Lily had conceived a little tenderness for him, and it appears that I was right. However, recently, he and Lily have quarrelled. The affair has made poor Lily rather unhappy, and she has been moping a good deal, and is pale and low-spirited. There is nothing serious amiss; and I think that a little change of scene and some amusement would set our young friend right. Under these circumstances, I have thought it best to write to you, if you could have Lily to stay with you for a few weeks in town," &c.

Only, a little further on, Maud remarked casually:

"As you may be curious to know something about the gentleman, I may tell you that Mr. Warrington is a man with whom any girl might naturally fall in love. His place near here, Lynhurst, is a very pretty place, but not large. It is reputed to be heavily mortgaged, and is in a great state of dilapidation, and I believe that Mr. Warrington is far from being able to spend upon it as much as is required. So possibly the little quarrel that has occurred is not to be regretted."

Sealing the letter, Maud said to herself:

"There, they cannot refuse, I think. And I am really growing tired of Lily's dumps."

Two answers came almost by return of post. One for Maud from Mrs. Tanner, one for Lily from her guardian, Mr. Tanner. Mrs. Tanner thanked Maud for her sensible, straightforward letter, and Mr. Tanner sent Lily a very pretty invitation to come and spend some weeks with them in town.

Of course the invitation was accepted, and the date of Lily's departure was fixed for the next week.

Now that it was all arranged, Lily herself was rather pleased with the prospect of her visit. After all, she had her measure of pride, and was disposed to show a little spirit about the way in which Warrington was slighting her.

It chanced that a day or two later she met Warrington on the esplanade. He had been walking, and she had been to morning service at the church.

Warrington was, as always, agreeable, almost deferential; but cool, dispassionate entirely.

Lily cut their conversation short; for his manner hurt her. She had, she said, to hurry home.

"And," she added, "I may as well say good-bye. I am going to London next week, for the end of the season. And we may very probably not meet again before then."

Warrington looked surprised.

"I hope you will enjoy yourself, Miss Hardwick," he said. "but I am sorry to hear that you are going away."

A hundred possibilities had flashed in a moment through his mind; the London season, with its fascinations, its opportunities. its flirtations; and this pretty girl, charming, ingenuous; a dozen men might be ready to make love to her, to marry her.

"Why should you be sorry that I am going away? It will make no difference to you," remarked Lily

Well, really, why was he sorry? He knew he was sorry, but hardly why. And, as he hesitated for a reply, Lily went on, looking down:

"Mr. Warrington, I wish you would tell me what I have done that you should be unkind to me."

"Unkind! Miss Hardwick!"

"I call it unkind to let a girl know that you feel no respect for her. And I am sure you can feel no respect for a girl to whom you say things that you know are not true—as that my going away matters to you. I don't know what you can have seen in me that makes you think I should like to be spoken to in that way." And holding out her hand she concluded, briefly, " Good-bye."

CHAPTER XXIV.

THE return of the Chesterfield girls to England was a very simple affair. One fine morning Anthony Gainsborough's yacht steamed into the mouth of the Thames and up to Gravesend. There a little screw-launch was waiting to meet her. The transference of some necessary luggage occupied a very few minutes, and then the launch took the two sisters with their lady's-maid and their uncle on the flood tide straight up to Twickenham, and landed them in easy time for dinner. The old housekeeper, with new black silk ribbons in her cap, received them with a curtsey in the hall, and so they were at home, and at once, without any further ado, went to dress for dinner, much as if they had returned only from a walk, or had come in from an afternoon spent in town.

Their new home was a large, ugly old-fashioned house, beautifully furnished, and standing in pretty and rather extensive grounds. The girls were not quite strangers to the place. Once they had visited it when their grandmother was alive, and then it had seemed to them a sort of palace in the midst of a fairyland in which grandmamma lived in a kind of royal state. Now, on renewing their acquaintance with it, they found both the fairyland and the palace a good deal smaller than they seemed to recollect them. But they found also many things, which they had not, when little lassies, noticed at all, valuable furniture, and rare books, and priceless pictures.

Anthony Gainsborough was at home and away from home irregularly. Amongst other things he was attending to the repairs of his yacht at present laid up in dock. When at home he wandered about the house and grounds smoking his big pipe, sat in the sun, looked at the flowers, and occasionally talked to the girls. He had the screw-launch on the river, and often took them out with him in it, and he indulged them frequently in the amusements of town.

Left to do very much as they liked, the sisters amused themselves in their own way, and contracted a liking for the housekeeper, Mrs. Simpson, a personable old woman, who had been in service in the family for a great number of years, and knew all the family histories, and on her side took a fancy to the two girls.

One day when they were talking to the old dame, hearing what she had to say about the childhood of their mother and of their uncle, Violet observed that she did not believe her Uncle Tony could be angry if he tried.

"You take care never to make him angry, Miss. If you do, you'll not forget it," remarked the old woman.

"Why?" asked Essie, "has he ever been angry with you, Mrs. Simpson?"

"No, Miss. I never gave him reason: and I hope I never shall."

"But you have seen him angry with some one?"

"I have, Miss," replied Mrs. Simpson.

"Who was it, Mrs. Simpson?" asked Essie, whose curiosity was aroused.

"Not any one you know, Miss," answered the old woman, in a tone that meant she was not going to say any more.

"Then it seems that Uncle Tony can be angry," observed Essie to her sister afterwards, when they were alone.

" And there is some history connected with that," added Violet. " You could see that from the way Mrs. Simpson spoke."

" I should vastly like to know what it is," observed Essie.

But though Anthony Gainsborough was indulgent, he was not a person easy to question ; and Essie's curiosity had to remain ungratified.

One afternoon, when they had been in England about a fortnight, they had taken their needlework out on the lawn and sat sewing and talking under the trees. Whilst they were so occupied, their uncle came across the lawn to them, thrusting a letter into his breast-pocket as he approached.

" Well, young ladies," he asked, " what is it that I find you discussing so earnestly ? If it is permitted to inquire ? "

" We were talking, Uncle Tony, of how much happier we have been with you than we were with grandpapa," said Violet, putting down her work. " How kindly you have treated us, and how ill he did."

" And you might add how ill you behaved to grandpapa, eh ? " suggested Anthony Gainsborough.

" Well, yes. We did not behave very well to him," admitted Essie.

" But," put in Violet, " grandpapa has had his revenge, and disinherited us."

Anthony Gainsborough put his arm within hers, and led her for a stroll around the lawn, Essie coming with them.

" Which is what you might have expected, as you knew what sort of man your grandfather was," said Anthony Gainsborough, continuing the conversation. " Still you would have preferred to have been for-given ? "

" Certainly," said Essie.

Anthony Gainsborough took out his big pipe and

slowly filled it. Then, having lighted it, he remarked :

"There was some one else rather badly used beside the general, was there not ? "

"Mr. Warrington," said Violet. "H'm, yes. He *was* rather badly treated."

"Mr. Warrington is——" began Essie, and broke off.

"Mr. Warrington is what ? " asked her uncle.

"I won't say what I was going to say, Uncle Tony. Perhaps it is not true."

"Good. But now, respecting your cousin. You would prefer to be forgiven by him too ? "

The girls were silent.

"You find that a little humiliating, eh ? "

They came to a garden seat, and he sat down, the girls standing before him, Essie with her arm about her sister's waist.

"Come now, girls," he went on. "Let us look at the matter reasonably. You behaved ill to your grandfather ; yet you think he might have forgiven you. Your Cousin Frank's behaviour was unimpeachable, and you overreached him. If he condones the way you behaved to him, his behaviour is so much the better, and yours so much the worst. If he cherishes resentment, you are defenceless. Anyhow, when you and he meet you have before you an inevitable *mauvais quart-d'heure*, unless you have sufficient spirit and courage to——"

"To do what ? " asked Violet.

"To beg his pardon."

"What—for not marrying him ? " exclaimed Violet.

"Not for not marrying him, but for—I don't want to use hard words, my dear. You did me no wrong, and I have nothing to say to it. I am willing enough to believe that you fell into a mistake. If you have the spirit and courage to beg your cousin's pardon at the first opportunity, you will have proved that a single mistake does not derogate from a fine character."

"Uncle Tony, I have not a fine character," said Violet, promptly.

"And, Uncle Tony, is Mr. Warrington's conduct unimpeachable? Mr. Warrington has coolly enough accepted our fortunes," offered Essie.

"And you would permit a man, whom you have treated as you and your sister have treated your cousin, to share his fortune with you?" asked Anthony Gainsborough. "For remember, after the will the general left, it is his fortune."

The girls were silent.

Anthony Gainsborough drew out the letter he had in his pocket.

"Well, to cut it short, girls," he said, offering them two cheques, "here are your fortunes. Frank Warrington has sent them to you."

"But, uncle," said Violet, regarding the big cheque in her hand with misgiving, "can we accept them, from Mr. Warrington?"

"If you don't, you can't stay with me," said Anthony Gainsborough, with a quiet emphasis that made both the sisters open their eyes. Rising, he concluded, "Try to write and thank your cousin, as he deserves to be thanked, and bring your letters to me."

And with that he left them.

When an hour later the girls came into the library with their notes, Violet said :

"We have written, Uncle Tony, but we should like it if Cousin Frank would see us, and make it all up. We would beg his pardon. Would you go and see him for us: and ask him to meet us?"

Anthony Gainsborough went down to Lynham. But Warrington was inexorable. He would not see his cousins.

" Now it is the girls who are behaving well, and
you who are behaving badly, you know," said Tony
Gainsborough.

Warrington admitted that might be so. But he
would not see his cousins.

Being at Lynham, Anthony Gainsborough went to
call at Cliff Cottage. Lily was out. Maud Gainsborough was at home, and received him, asking herself, in an agony of fear, what on earth could have
brought him down.

It did not appear that anything particular had
brought him. He was down on business, and had
simply come to pay a call.

But he alluded to the telegram Maud had sent
him.

" You wanted to go abroad ? " he asked.

" Why—yes," stammered Maud.

" You still wish it ? "

" No. I would rather stay here now."

Anthony Gainsborough inquired no further.

He only stayed a quarter of an hour, asking no
questions except whether the house was in satisfactory repair, and then left, to Maud's ineffable
relief.

When Lily, who passed him in the road, came in,
Maud said nothing to her about the visit she had
received. Which was a mistake on Maud's part.

<hr>

CHAPTER XXV

THE announcement of Lily Hardwick's early departure
for town, and the sudden disquietude the words had
occasioned him, opened Frank Warrington's eyes,
at last, to the truth which he had been so long

singularly unable to see. As his brother had fore-
told, he had fallen in love with Miss Hardwick.
The little chance meetings with her, and the sound of
her voice, the sight of her bright eyes, and the touch
of her small hand had become somehow necessary to
him, and he shrank from the prospect of foregoing
them. Or, plainly, he was falling in love. And the
more Warrington questioned himself on the subject
the more sure he was of it.

It was his opinion, too, that Lily was not indifferent about him. If she had been indifferent, she
would not have cared what he said.

The wisest thing he could have done would have
been to have talked over these discoveries with his
brother. But such tender little affairs are not the
things men discuss with one another: and Frank
Warrington took counsel only with himself.

He had not the faintest idea of marrying Miss
Hardwick. If he married at all, he meant to marry
a woman a good deal older, and with money. In
consequence, as a man of honourable feelings, he
found that his conduct with Miss Hardwick had
been not altogether free from blame. " Girls," he
argued, " are naturally and instinctively on the look-
out for husbands. A very little attention paid them,
or anything that can be construed into attention, is
at once interpreted by them to signify a great deal."
Miss Hardwick might, from her point of view,
possibly feel that, if his intentions were not serious,
his conduct was hardly gentlemanly. He certainly
did not intend to marry her: and it would be his
duty to be more circumspect for the future.

But he was sorry, too, for the girl. If there was a
girl in the world whom he would have gone a little
out of his way to humour, that girl was Lily Hardwick. He admired her character. He respected it.
He was sorry to be the occasion of giving her any
pain. Still, there was no help for it. The notion of

seriously wooing her was not to be entertained for an instant. If she had taken a fancy to him, perhaps partly by his fault, she must get over it.

As for his own foolishness and susceptibility, that proved only that he was a weaker man than he supposed, and he would have simply to cure himself of his folly

The best thing that could happen for both Miss Hardwick and himself would be that their good-bye on the esplanade should prove a real farewell, that they should not meet again before Miss Hardwick went to town, and that, in town, she should become engaged before she returned to Lynham.

But his thoughts returned very often to Lily and to what possibly her feelings would be if she had really been unlucky enough to form an attachment to him. And so it came about that he formed a resolution, if an opportunity should offer, to let her see plainly the state of the case, and to spare her at least the pain of deceiving herself any further. To do that much appeared to him nothing more than an act of common humanity

Circumstances favoured his plan. After all, Lily's visit to town was unavoidably postponed, and, some days after their meeting on the esplanade, they met again just outside the big, iron gates of the rectory, where Lily had been to pay the rector's wife a visit.

She would have bowed and let Warrington pass, but he stopped. And for the first time he noticed that Lily was paler, and, he thought, a little thinner than she used to be. It was an additional inducement to him to carry out his intention of acquainting her with the truth.

" I am glad we have met again, Miss Hardwick," he said. " There was something I wished to say to you."

" Yes ? "

She was looking into his face wistfully ; thinking

in herself how happy she could have been if he could
have cared for her as she cared for him.

"You know, Miss Hardwick," he went on, "that
last time we met I said something that displeased
you."

Lily nodded. What on earth was he going to
say?

"Well, I know I ought not to have said it; that it
was a foolish, rather sentimental speech. And I
hope you have forgiven it. I forgot I fear, at the
moment, what I really am. I mean, you know," he
continued, in a frank, straightforward way that
appealed at once to the girl's heart, "that I am a
much poorer man than I pass for. I am not badly
off, perhaps, but I have taken on my shoulders the
redemption of a big estate, which means heavy
expenses, you see, and debts, and long responsibili-
ties; and—well, I ought not to be saying pretty
things and paying compliments to young ladies."

Lily stood leaning against the big, iron gate that
stood half-open, with her hand lightly closed around
one of its bars. The sun, piercing through the leaf-
age of the tall trees planted on either side of the gate,
fell in broken light upon her shoulders, and her
pretty hair, and her young cheeks, and made her a
charming picture.

"No one would object to your paying compliments
that you meant," she let fall, in a rather embarrassed
way, looking down coyly

For the moment a suspicion was beginning to present itself that he was going to propose.

But he answered, quietly:

"That is not it, Miss Hardwick. A man in my
position has no right to mean these things, and I am
much obliged to you for having reminded me of it.
That is what I had to say to you. The fact is, Miss
Hardwick, that I fear we have both been deceiving
ourselves; and so, just at present, it is a good thing,

perhaps, that we are going to see less of each other."

The girl looked up, and a sudden light flashed in the depths of her large blue eyes. Then her eye-lids fell, as a hot blush covered her face, and she clenched her hand tightly, in an effort to conceal her agitation. This man was telling her, in other words, that he could see that she was in love with him, but that he had no intention of proposing to her.

But, as he had stopped, stifling as she was, she had to speak.

"That is what you wished to say to me?" she asked.

"And that I hope you have forgiven my silly speech."

For answer, she only asked, "Which way are you going?"

"Homewards. And you?"

"I am going the other way. So I will wish you good-morning."

She just touched his hand with hers, barely that; and so they parted.

"I am afraid she didn't quite like it," mused Warrington, walking on towards Lynhurst. "Still it was only fair to her."

Lily walked a little way towards the town, and then, when she was sure she would not overtake Warrington, turned back.

"I have had a lesson that people who cannot take slight hints get broad ones," she said to herself.

She was quite mistress of herself, singularly little hurt, considering how passionately she loved the man; but indignant, furiously indignant, and already asking herself what she was going to do after an affront of such a nature as this.

Dinner and the evening passed as usual, and she had the skill to manage that Maud should suspect nothing. But, in her own room, she sat up late, brooding over the scene that had passed at the rectory gates, and, when she retired to rest at last, found it difficult to sleep.

The birds and the summer morning sun woke her early, and, finding that slumber would not be courted whilst her brain was in its present fever of indignation, she got up.

For a little while she sat in her peignoir at her open window, wistfully regarding the beauty of the summer morning. Then, a sudden idea occurring to her, she made a hasty toilet, and slipped downstairs.

Leaving the house, she went down the garden; and, reaching the cliff, descended the steps to the beach, and there sat down on the sand facing the sea.

A little breeze blew on shore, just enough to make the sea crisp with ripples. The breeze was fresh, but not cold, laden with the sweetness of the morning and the sharp saltness of the sea. It seemed to nerve her spirits, and to cool the fever of her brain; and by-and-by she ceased to watch the curling of the ripples, and to amuse herself with tossing pebbles into the water, and set herself to reflect seriously.

"I almost vowed to be his good angel," she reflected; "to bring him to believe that we are not all bad. And I love him. I do love him. But that was insufferable."

She stayed a long time on the beach, but when she returned at length to Cliff Cottage her mind was made up.

It was a Sunday morning, and, on fine Sunday mornings, the small fashionable world of Lynham promenaded the little esplanade after morning service. The esplanade lay right before them as they came out of church, and a turn by the sea naturally suggested itself as an agreeable way of spending the half-hour or so between service and the hour of midday dinners.

This Sunday morning promenade was one of the things that Eustace Warrington, with his naturally sociable turn of mind, particularly enjoyed. This morning, he and his brother proceeded as usual after church to the esplanade.

They walked as far as one end of it and then turned back, walking slowly and stopping from time to time to speak to different acquaintances. Presently Warrington said to his brother:

"Here is Miss Hardwick coming."

"Is her cousin with her?" asked Eustace.

"No: she is alone."

Lily had seen them. Her moment was come. She was nearer now; quite close; only a few steps from them.

Warrington was already about to raise his hat, and to give his brother the little pressure of his arm, which was the sign to him to do the same, when something in the expression of Lily's features arrested his attention.

Her face was rigidly set, and she seemed to have no intention of bowing. Instead, she looked for a moment at Warrington and his brother, a hard look from the corners of her eyes, a regard like a stranger's regard of momentary curiosity.

And then she had passed.

Before she had gone a step further, she heard Eustace ask:

"Was that Miss Hardwick who passed us?"

What Warrington replied Lily did not hear.

Warrington's answer was a rather confused "Yes." He had been taken a good deal by surprise.

"But you should not have let me pass her without bowing," said Eustace, annoyed.

"Why," answered Warrington, "the fact is she cut us dead."

"Cut us!"

An acquaintance of Warrington's, one of the hunt, came up. He had seen what had passed.

"You and Miss Hardwick are cuts, then," he remarked to Warrington.

"Yes," said Warrington, easily, "you saw just now."

A good many people had seen: and went home with something to talk about.

Lily left the parade, and went home.

It was all over! for ever, and ever, and ever. The young love-dream and the dear hopes: the proud mission of winning *him* back to believe in womanhood's nobility: all over, vanished, lost! for ever, and ever, and ever.

She said nothing to her cousin. Maud, in the course of the afternoon, remarked that she was pale, and inquired the cause, but she answered, with truth, that she had a headache.

But on Monday afternoon Mrs. Gainsborough heard all about the affair in Lynham, and at once returned home.

Lily was in the dining-room making up some bouquets. She had the advantage of the widow, for she had foreseen that Maud must hear the news in the town, and had guessed that she would at once come back to ask what it meant.

The widow came into the room quickly, without shutting the door behind her, and putting her sunshade on the table, with her hands resting upon it, said hurriedly:

"You cut the Warringtons yesterday on the parade after church."

"Yes," answered Lily, slowly putting a flower into the middle of a bouquet.

"But—what on earth did you do that for?"

"For reasons of my own."

"But it seems to me that you put me in a very awkward position. You might, at least, have told

me what you were going to do. Am I expected to
second you ? Do you want me to cut them too ? ”

“ You can do as you like.”

“ But——” began the widow

“ Oh, my goodness, Maud, don’t bother me about
it ! ” exclaimed the girl.

And, putting down her flowers, she rested her
arms on the table. Then, suddenly bowing her head
upon them, she burst into tears.

The widow came to her.

“ Let me alone, Maud, let me alone ! ” she suppli-
cated between her sobs. “ I am so miserable ; I
wish that I were dead ! I wish that I were dead ! ”

“ Ah ! if you were ! ” thought the widow in herself.
But, as nothing else was to be got from the girl, she
left her with a shrug of her shoulders, and went into
the garden, and sat down under the shade of the
trees to think.

———

CHAPTER XXVI.

Maud’s reflections were somewhat thus :

Plainly something had passed between Lily and
Mr. Warrington. It might be very much her interest to know what it was. But it seemed unlikely
that she would be able to learn.

The thing that disquieted her was that Lily should
thus unexpectedly have played so bold and daring a
stroke. Not that Lily herself perceived that it was
a bold, daring stroke. But she, Maud, saw it. In
this game of cross-purposes, in which every one had
hitherto been waiting for some one else, the girl had,
after all, been the first to venture on a decisive move.
To Mrs. Gainsborough it appeared a very clever
move. And she felt anything but easy about the

consequences. Lily, in all probability, would herself be made very unhappy. And there is no calculating what young, headstrong people will do when they are unhappy. The man was not indifferent to her, and he would not like being cut. It might even open his eyes to his real feelings for the girl. That would be serious indeed. For Maud's own quiet, waiting policy, this sort of thing was fatal.

Still, so far as she could see, her policy for the present must still be to wait. It would not do for her to cut Mr. Warrington. Certainly not. *She* had nothing to gain by that.

" I love the man ; how much more than that chit does or could !" she soliloquized. " And yet he will feel her having cut him. And if I had cut him—he would have laughed at it. My God ! Why do we love these men ? I suppose because we cannot help it."

Her thoughts returned to Lily.

The girl had a sensitive, nervous nature. She had of course no idea, yet, of what she had done : of what cutting the man she loved would cost her. Warrington might possibly take the matter very coolly. In that case Lily would feel his indifference a good deal. It was not at all unlikely that in the end she would be really ill.

Maud was right. In sternly cutting the man she loved, Lily had shown courage and spirit. But she had torn away a piece of her own heart, and the rude operation left behind it a cruel wound, one whose horrible pain made her soul faint. Her spirit had triumphed. She had not bent her head to a humiliation a girl should be ashamed to remember. But her heart bled cruelly. And she was sunk in her own estimation. She had undertaken so proud, so fascinating a rôle : to reclaim a man hostile to her sex, and to make him return her love. And she had broken down. The part she had wished to play had turned out to be beyond her strength, and her faith in herself was shaken to the ground.

Twenty-four hours sufficed to show that she was simply miserable.

She loved this man she had cast from her, tenderly, nobly, devotedly. Only so short a time since she had sunned herself in the belief that that love of hers was not altogether unreciprocated; that he had begun to care for her; and, ravished with the thought, she had spread the wings of her hopes into a very heaven of joy. And now she had thrust him clean away, with the living love still warm in her heart. If that is living love which is mortified by the conviction that the person to whom it is offered regards it with indifference, ennui, disdain.

Her pride held her up for a little while. But afterwards heart and spirit seemed to give way together. The smile faded from her lips, the elasticity from her step, the light from her eyes: and a fixed melancholy possessed itself of her.

For a day or two she struggled against the depression, though with small success. Then the struggle ceased. The melancholy that had invaded her was more powerful than herself, and she had no weapons to combat it. Everything had lost interest for her. A dull lethargy crept over her whole life. The music of her laugh had died out of the house long ago, and it seemed that the very sound of her voice was to follow it.

"She was awfully fond of him," said Maud Gainsborough. "Why on earth did she cut him?"

She was sorry for the girl. It was a pitiful thing to see her so wretched, poor child, and the widow was not without a heart. In her fashion she was even kind. She was very gentle with the girl, with that superlative gentleness which women can show one another when they choose.

Lily made no pretence of concealing how miserable she was. Rather, the thing that seemed to afford her some relief was to confess her wretchedness, to come to her cousin and to throw herself into her arms with a broken cry of—

"Oh, Maud! I loved him so! I loved him so!"

And on these occasions the widow was very patient with her, put her arms around her and let her cry her fill, and chided her never.

Then, as fortune would have it, on two successive occasions when Lily went out she met Warrington. She bore herself admirably, with the most perfect ease and external indifference, but each of these rencontres cost her a stab of pain in her heart, and after them she refused to go any more outside the grounds.

"I wish, with all my heart, the day was here when she will leave for town," said Maud to herself.

She, too, had seen Warrington. That was one afternoon when she was riding. He was on foot. She bowed demonstratively, and then drew up to speak to him.

"I hear, Mr. Warrington," she said, a little seriously, "that my cousin has cut you. I hope you will do me the honour to believe me that I had nothing to do with it."

"Certainly, Mrs. Gainsborough."

"I am very sorry that this should have occurred, Mr. Warrington," continued the widow. "I think I may tell you that. Of course my cousin lives with me, but I have no authority over her. So she must do as she pleases. But I hope this will not make any difference between you and Mr. Eustace Warrington and myself."

"Certainly not," said Warrington.

And so they parted.

"I don't think I committed myself to anything outside the strictest politeness," said the widow to herself, as she rode on. "No, I am sure I did not.

I wonder what it was passed between those two.　He took all I said very coolly."

Yes, he did take it very coolly.　At dinner he said to Eustace:

" I met Mrs. Gainsborough this afternoon and she bowed most cordially.　She also gave herself the trouble to explain that she had nothing to do with Miss Hardwick's having cut us."

He took the cut very coolly too.　At least he never made any allusion to it.

Lily's distress soon told on her health.　With her nervous nature nothing else was to be expected.　By the end of the week her cheeks had lost every morsel of colour. her appetite had become capricious, and she was complaining of being always tired.

Maud Gainsborough became alarmed, and called in Dr. Gregg.　She confided to him that there had been a little *affaire de cœur* which had terminated not very happily. and that her cousin had been fretting.　The doctor looked very wise and began to ask questions in his usual fashion.

" A little low-spirited, young lady, they tell me. But now. let me see, your appetite keeps good ? "

" No. Dr. Gregg, I have no appetite at all."

" No ?　Well, sometimes in these cases the appetite does fail. sometimes it does not. Well. So you are rather low-spirited.　And you have, I can see, a good deal of headache."

" No. Dr. Gregg.　No headache."

" No headache ?　No, perhaps not.　But loss of appetite.　I can see it all.　A little tonic.　We shall soon set you up."

" What was the good of sending for him, Maud ? " asked Lily, when he was gone.　" You know what is the matter."

" How do you really feel, dear ? "

" Tired."

" Not ill ?　You look ill."

" Do I ? "

She got up and walked away. How languidly !
Was this really the same girl who a month ago had
the step of a gazelle ?

<hr>

CHAPTER XXVII.

PEOPLE began to talk of how ill Miss Hardwick
looked.

Maud was taking every care she could of her.
She made her attend to what the doctor said, and,
so far as she could, kept her from moping under the
trees, strolling about in the twilight, sitting at open
windows at night, and all the other foolish things
she wished to do. Lily was not altogether tractable
or manageable, and would sometimes say, pettishly,
" I am miserable : for heaven's sake let me be ; " and
then take her own way after all.

One day, rising from the dinner-table, she suddenly stopped, and, catching at the table with one
hand, laid the other on her heart with a little cry
of pain.

" My dear ! " exclaimed Maud.

" Oh, such a horrid pain in my heart, Maud," said
the girl, presently, with an expression of dismay.

But in a minute the pain had passed, and she
went with her cousin into the drawing-room, and
they had coffee as usual.

" Are you all right now, darling ? Your heart does
not hurt you any more ? " asked Maud, presently.

" No, thanks."

But suddenly she slipped off the sofa on which she
was sitting, and, dropping on her knees on the floor
by Maud, buried her head in her lap.

"Oh, Maud! I shall die," she sobbed, passionately "I am so miserable. I am so miserable. I thought I could bear it, but I cannot, Maud, I cannot! I love him so. I love him so. He might have loved me a little." After a moment she continued, "It is a shame to trouble you, Maud, with my foolish tears. You have always been so kind to me: so good to me. But I don't know how to bear it, Maud. Indeed I don't. If I had a father, or a mother, a brother, or a sister, or any one—any one to go to. But I have no one. I am all—all alone. I have no one but you, Maud, and my heart is breaking. It is indeed, Maud. I love him so. I love him so. You don't know, Maud, what he was to me. It will kill me, I know it will. I wish I were dead. He would be sorry, perhaps, a little bit. I wish I were not going away from you next week to town."

Suddenly she drew herself up with a sharp cry of pain.

Mrs. Gainsborough caught her in her arms.

"My darling!"

"It is that pain at my heart again," gasped the girl, as soon as she could speak. "Oh, Maud, I shall die."

Maud did her best to calm her, and then sent her to bed. Happily there were only five more days now before her departure to town.

Left alone the widow sat herself down to think.

That afternoon, returning home from a walk in the woods, she had met Warrington. He was strolling slowly, smoking a pipe, with his hands in his pockets, when she overtook him.

"Please go on smoking, Mr. Warrington," she said, pleasantly, as they walked on together. "I am sure the society of a woman would be too dearly purchased by the loss of a pipe. Oh, you are too gallant to admit it, of course. Still, smoke, please."

How handsome he was looking in a rough brown

suit, with knickerbockers! How furiously she admired him! What she would have given to throw her arms round his neck, and to kiss him!

Warrington had complied with her request, and continued to smoke. And he politely inquired after Miss Hardwick.

" Just the same. She makes me anxious," said the widow.

How she wished she could ask him what he and Lily had quarrelled about?

" I am very glad to have met you, Mrs. Gainsborough," said Warrington. " My brother and I are the victims of a domestic tragedy. And we were both thinking of calling upon you to solicit your aid."

" I should have been most pleased to see you."

" Well, I'll tell you all about it," said Warrington, as he stuffed down the tobacco in the bowl of his pipe.

He was quite at his ease. He always was with Maud Gainsborough. Maud was a widow. Widows did not pursue men without money. Maud knew how safe he felt, and reckoned a good deal on that imprudent security of his to assist her some day.

The domestic tragedy was only a rebellion on the part of the cook. The brothers, in consequence, wanted a new cook, and Mrs. Gainsborough was fortunate enough to be able to recommend them one.

Meanwhile, they had come in their walk to a point of the wood where the path passed through an open spot on high ground, and offered a view of a corner of the woods and of a part of the property.

Warrington stopped, and called the widow's attention to the view.

" Did you ever see anything more miserable, Mrs. Gainsborough," he said; "more ragged, more wretched? Look at those dead trees. Look at those hedges. Look at that wall. Look at the weediness of

the whole place. Look at that copse. Enough to
make one's eyes sore, is it not? And it is the same
all over the estate. Everywhere nothing but ragged-
ness and dilapidations ; the fruit of years of shameful
neglect."

The widow stood by his side, following with her
eyes the direction of his hand as he pointed out one
feature after another of the dilapidated estate. How
astonished he would have been, if he could have
known how happy he was making her.

" It will cost fortunes to set the place in order,"
he continued, gloomily, as he turned to walk on.

" Well, Mr. Warrington, spend the fortunes," said
the widow, quietly.

" To spend one must have," observed Warrington,
phlegmatically; " and unfortunately I don't possess
fortunes. I suppose that I shall get the place straight
little by little, but I really do not know that I should
not have done better to sell it, as I first intended.
Still, then I should have got nothing for it, and it is
a pretty place."

" Well, Mr. Warrington, you must marry some
charming heiress, you know," suggested the widow,
laughing.

" H'm. And what do you think, Mrs. Gainsborough, of a man who marries a woman with more
money than himself ? "

" Oh, I think, of course, that it is all a question of
love ; that the money is nothing," replied Maud, sar-
castically.

And she and Warrington laughed.

" Still, you are too much a man of the world, Mr.
Warrington, not to concede the sensibleness of a
mariage de convenance," observed the widow.

" I entirely agree with you," answered Warrington,
readily " A real *mariage de convenance* is a very
good thing. There is no bosh about love in it. The
man and the woman each bring something to the

contract, the position of both is better by what each has received from the other; and their common interests form a solid bond of union. I think if I could meet with the combination of a sufficient fortune and a moderately insupportable old maid, anxious to be married—so that I could feel that the obligation was reciprocal—I should think it almost my duty to venture."

The widow laughed and suggested :

" Or what do you say to the daughter of a wealthy butcher ? "

" No : I must have a lady."

" Ah, then, I don't think you are quite fair. You ask for two things, you see, birth and money ; and you offer only one, marriage."

" Your remark, Mrs. Gainsborough, shall have my serious consideration," rejoined Warrington, playfully.

By-and-by their roads parted, and they said " Good-bye," and Warrington went on his way with his hands again in his pockets, saying to himself :

" Sensible woman, that widow."

When Mrs. Gainsborough reached home she found Dr. Gregg in the hall. He was just leaving. He had called to see Miss Hardwick.

" How is Lily to-day ?" asked the widow.

Well—to be plain—the doctor evidently did not know He talked a good deal, but he said nothing. Miss Hardwick had been suffering again from a pain in her heart. She was weak, a little low. Perhaps there was a little weakness in the action of the heart: there sometimes was in those cases. But sometimes there was not. He would make a little change in his prescriptions. Probably the change of air and scene in town would set her up again.

CHAPTER XXVIII.

IT was the evening of the same day.

Lily had retired. and Maud sat alone in the drawing-room thinking. Something recalled to her mind Dr. Gregg's visit of the afternoon, and then she began to estimate what, in her judgment, was the real worth of that great luminary of medical science, when presently an odd idea flitted through her brain.

"What an opportunity a man such as Dr. Gregg presented for the commission of a great crime."

Presently Maud had forgotten all about Lily. Leaning back in her chair, she was lost in imaginations, pursuing the strange suggestion that had presented itself to her fancy.

This stupid little quiet place, Lynham, dull, gossiping, full of scandal, but simple withal, and unsuspecting of anything out of the common. The very place for the execution of a deed of darkness. And this idiot, Dr. Gregg : a man really incapable of dealing with anything more serious than a loose tooth. or a mild attack of the measles; with his consequential airs, and his blabbing tongue, and his belief in his own powers of intuition, and his vanity, and his gross ignorance, the very accomplice the doer of the deed of darkness should have! What a place and what an assistant—say for an *empoisonneuse*.

Maud Gainsborough began to elaborate. Of course the *empoisonneuse* would come down from London and bring the victim with her; the husband, stepson, aunt, aged guardian, or whosoever it might be. And then she would take a house. Where ? Not on the Marine Parade, nor in Church Street. It is only in London that people. who want to be hidden, live in the most crowded places. Some little house just outside Lynham. That lone house near the ruined mill. Or, better still, Cliff Cottage. Cliff Cottage was more secluded than the house by the old mill. And then the victim could walk unseen in the long garden, and the *empoisonneuse* could descend the steps to the little, lonely beach, and cool her fevered brain with the fresh breeze from the sea.

Then the victim would be ill, and Dr. Gregg would be sent for at once. " Ah ! a little indigestion, I see. Ah, you need not tell me. I know. You have a pain in the pit of the stomach."—" No, not at all."—" Not at all. No ! No pain in the pit of the stomach. Ah, well, sometimes in these cases there is not any pain in the pit of the stomach. At other times there is a good deal. Well, I see, a little indigestion, but no pain."—" Oh, yes, doctor, I have a great deal of pain."—" Oh, a great deal of pain. Ah, I understand. Indigestion, and a great deal of pain, but not in the pit of the stomach. You see, my dear sir " (or " madam," according to the sex of the victim), " I know all about it. And now, tell me, I am right, am I not, nausea after meals ? "—" No, doctor No nausea."—" No, no nausea ? Well, sometimes in these cases there is a great deal of nausea ; at other times, as in your case, you see, none." And so on. Meanwhile, the patient somehow grows worse, slowly, very slowly. " Well, doctor, what do you really think ? "—" A rather protracted case. But nothing out of the common, I assure you. A derangement of the digestive system. You must take care of him—or her. I shall make a slight alteration in the prescription. Possibly, in a day or two, we may see an alteration for the better." By-and-by it is " Tabes. Heart slightly affected." A little indisposition to believe the doctor, and he becomes obdurate on that last point. Would stake his professional reputation on it. So now it is " severe affection of the heart " and " tabes." Patient grows worse. Patient dies—and Dr. Gregg signs the certificate without an instant's hesitation. That is the man for your *empoisonneuse*—the man who signs the certificate without hesitation.

Maud Gainsborough runs the story through her head again. If the gods had only given her the literary faculty? She fills in little points of detail, and makes improvements and modifications. The *empoisonneuse* is very clever. She has the sagacity not to commence operations at once. but to wait until her " victim " happens quite accidentally to be a little out of health. There is nothing really serious the matter when Dr. Gregg is first called in ; no occasion for secrecy. Every one knows all about it, and so no suspicion is ever aroused. Also she has a previous acquaintance with Dr. Gregg and his peculiar characteristics. It was the knowledge of them that made her select Lynham for the scene of her crime. She is a clever woman, too, a little chic. and knows how to flatter the doctor and to turn him round with her little finger. Also she cultivates the simple folk of Lynham. She goes regularly to church, and is respectful to the aristocracy, and sends the rector flowers for his altar. And so all the story over again up to the *dénoûment*, " the doctor signs the certificate."

And it might all be true ! Every word of it. What an opportunity !

Suddenly Maud started from her idle posture of repose and sat upright in her chair.

Something had struck her that made her turn pale. She bent forward. and, with her elbow on her knees, rested her cheek upon her hand.

" My God ! But—if I had wanted to do it ! "

A light had broken upon her of an unexpected sort The *empoisonneuse* who had remarked Dr. Gregg's weaknesses ; who could turn him round with her little finger ; the tenant of Cliff Cottage, a little fashionable, well-established in the opinion of the rector, and a subscriber to his favourite charities; it was—herself. And the victim, already in uncertain health, suffering from some affection of the heart: that was Lily. And if she, Maud Gainsborough, chose—if she chose—*hers* the horrible opportunity

The doctor would sign the certificate. And no one would ever suspect anything.

"If I chose," said Maud to herself, "I could do it; as easily as I can walk across this room; more easily than I shall succeed in getting Lily cured of fretting about Mr. Warrington, poor child!"

Again she ran over the whole story in her mind. Only the *dramatis personæ* were real now, the earlier incidents facts, and the whole sharply defined with exact details of place, and circumstance, and date.

"How horribly simple!" said the widow to herself.

And if it were really to happen?

She had no intention of taking in hand any such thing. But the imagination of it fascinated her with a hideous fascination.

Fifteen-thousand a-year!

Fifteen-thousand a-year, and liberty!

Mrs. Gainsborough's thoughts became again more connected. Mr. Warrington was a man of the world. And a widow with fifteen-thousand a-year; a good-looking woman, phlegmatic, a little cynical, agreeable, provided with some common sense, ready for a marriage of convenience, that widow might have Mr. Warrington in a month. If she, Maud, had that fortune, with the art that she would know how to use, to make him believe her motives as mercenary as his own, Frank Warrington would marry her without twice thinking of the matter.

And Maud said to herself, "In some ten months, seven perhaps—wealthy—free—and Frank Warrington's wife. Instead of having to wait slow years and years to draw him to me; and then both of us poor. In some seven months his wife! And so easily."

She began to calculate. Could it really be done in seven months?

First—H'm— : for *that* say two months.

Then to claim the property. There were the documents to get somehow. They were in Mr. Tanner's hands. Those once obtained, the application to the Court of Chancery and the substantiation of the claim should be matters of but little time. But there might be some delay necessary to get the documents from Mr. Tanner without awakening suspicions.

How to get them? How to get them quickly? How to get them without causing dangerous surmises?

If Lily only had them, how simple it would all be! Lily ought to have them.

Lily might get them.

Maud rose, and began pacing the room.

Thus now Lily is going to London. And she, Maud, asks her before she leaves to get Mr. Tanner to show her the family papers: and to ask that Maud may have a copy of any of them that referred to her family. That was reasonable enough.

Lily returns with the papers. She is not much better for her change of air. And after her return to Lynham she has a relapse. And—" and so on and so on." (That is how the young widow expresses it to herself.) Lily grows worse. And Dr. Gregg says *tabes* and *heart complaint*. And—well—Lily dies. And Dr. Gregg—signs the certificate.

Afterwards she, Maud, looking over her cousin s things, finds amongst them those papers which her cousin had brought from town. And reading those papers Maud suddenly discovers to her unspeakable surprise that she is entitled to fifteen-thousand a-year!

And the Court of Chancery gives it her.

The people at Lynham talk, and wonder what she will do. But she only stays where she is. Somehow

she and Frank Warrington manage to understand
each other : and she becomes his wife.

All quite possible : easy even ; hideously easy.

" If I did ?" says Maud to herself.

And she answers herself, " The girl is miserable,
poor child ! She says she wishes she were dead."

" Shall I ?"

A shudder ran through her whole body, and a
sudden sensation of cold struck her heart. Of what
is she thinking ? With a quick movement of her
head she looked around her in dismay, as if some one
was watching her who could read her thoughts.

Unexpectedly a reflection in one of the mirrors
caught her attention. Her eyes fixed themselves on
it. Slowly she walked towards it as if drawn by
some supernatural force.

A woman dressed like herself : handsome—yes—no
—yes—a handsome fiend, and with eyes of fire !
How pale and haggard ! What lips, livid as death !

Maud Gainsborough turned away with a shudder.
It was too horrible. Throwing herself on the sofa,
she buried her face in the cushions, as if afraid of
seeing some other hideous reflection of herself.

She could not lie like that : she was suffocating,
she must have air !

The suffocation passed. She was better. And
she sat up on the sofa, wiping her lips.

She had been making herself delirious with her
own imaginations. Bah ! it was very stupid.

She began to fan herself. And then she rose and
rang the bell. She would not risk letting the servant see her face, but opened the window, and looked
out at the summer night. The cool air was refresh-
ing. And how quiet the place was ! When the
maid came, she said, without turning round :

" Jenny, bring me some cold water, and the
brandy."

The girl came back with the things, and Maud

poured herself out a weak glass of brandy-and-water, and sitting down in a low easy-chair by the table, drank it at her leisure.

When calmer, she ventured to think again.

" Now, what is all this that I have been frightening myself about ?—Why, nothing ! "

" Possibly Lily will die. Poor girl ' And, if so, I shall come into fifteen-thousand a-year."

" And if Lily does not die : that is, in the course of nature ? " That was the real point.

" Then I must choose between my duty and my love. For it just depends on a turn of my hand. Nothing else ! "

" I wonder how most women would choose ? "

" At any rate, I have not to choose to-night."

And with that she seemed satisfied.

But presently she rose.

It would be curious to try an experiment. Not an experiment on Lily, but on the doctor

The widow proceeded to do a very strange thing.

First she locked the door. At one end of the drawing-room was a handsome, rather old-fashioned escritoire, with a revolving lid. It was a rather heavy piece of furniture for a drawing-room, but she had found it in the room when she came to the cottage, and had let it remain there. Its numerous drawers were very convenient for storing a number of little things. She went now to this escritoire, and opened it. Out of a drawer which she unlocked she took a key, and with that key unlocked another drawer.

The drawer contained things not usually to be found in a writing-desk.

A pair of apothecary's scales in a little box : some measuring-glasses : some phials apparently empty : and a bottle of some stuff like minute, white scales, much resembling powdered talc, and of the same unbleached hue.

Maud Gainsborough looked at those things. and said to herself, " When I brought all these things here, I meant to destroy them. I wonder why I never did so ? "   And she thought of the evening at Dr. Gregg's, when the Cambridge man told the story of the stolen poison. That man little thought that the thief was sitting at the table.

Bringing the drawer with all its contents to the table, she sat down.   In one of the bottles there was a little liquid.   She looked at it, and, seeming to mistrust it, put it back again.

Taking one of the empty phials, she carefully washed it, using some of the water the maid had brought her.   Next with the scales she weighed, taking great care, one grain of the scaly-looking stuff.   And next she measured an ounce of water. She had no distilled water, but again used that the maid had brought her.   She did it all very neatly ; like a surgeon's daughter who had often watched, and sometimes assisted, in such processes.   And finally she dissolved the white stuff in the ounce of water and put it into the clean bottle.

That done, she quickly corked the bottle, and then put everything away, relocked the drawer, and locked up the key, too.   Then, with the mixture she had prepared in ner hand, she came back to the other end of the room.

She did not at once put it down, but stood with the phial in her hand thinking.

Her face was pale, but no longer haggard.   Its expression of horrible wickedness had entirely passed away.   For the moment she was looking singularly handsome.   A dim light burned still in her dark eyes, but her face was tender and sad.

By-and-by. taking the phial with her, she went upstairs.

CHAPTER XXIX.

LILY was worse, much worse. All the previous day she had been unusually lethargic, and, on rising, she had turned suddenly giddy, and with difficulty saved herself from a fall. All the day she had been languid to a degree, disinclined even to move, and quite unable to eat anything.

Dr. Gregg called in the afternoon. He looked very wise, and asked a number of questions. Whether anything had happened on the previous day that had upset Miss Hardwick; whether she had fatigued herself with over-exertion; whether she had possibly eaten anything that had disagreed with her.

To all Lily replied in the negative. She had on the previous day done nothing different from what she did every day. She had not been out of the house. She had taken the medicine he prescribed and attended strictly to his injunctions.

Still here was certainly a most serious change for the worse in her condition.

There had been, during the last two days, a change in the weather also, which had become very sultry. In the end Dr. Gregg attributed his patient's extreme prostration to the heat. "In these cases," he asserted, " any sudden sultriness in the weather sometimes has this effect : though not always."

Lily denied that she had felt the heat oppressive but that only made Dr. Gregg more decided in his opinion.

Mrs. Gainsborough followed the doctor out of the drawing-room, in which the consultation had taken place, and invited him into the dining-room.

" I am very anxious about my cousin, Dr. Gregg," she said, in a tone of well-acted alarm. " I trust that you will tell me the truth about her. This sudden collapse seems to me very ominous. I quite understand your not wishing to say anything before my cousin that might alarm her. But this giddiness on first arising ; that is a bad symptom, is it not ? "

The doctor did not think so.

" At least, you see," he explained, " Miss Hardwick has been for some weeks in a rather low condition, and there is a slight affection of the heart ; and then, this sudden change in the weather. These cases are sometimes accompanied by a dizziness at first awaking, though not always. The heat has affected her more than she supposes."

" You think that is all ? You think the change in the weather could have this effect ? "

" But, you see, my dear Mrs. Gainsborough, that it has had this effect. Miss Hardwick is in a delicate condition. You must take care of her."

" I don't know what to think, I am sure, Dr. Gregg," said Maud, walking up and down the room. " You, of course, know best, but I can hardly believe that this sudden collapse is due merely to the sultriness of the weather. If so, my cousin must be in a much more delicate state than I have supposed." The doctor offered no remark, and she went on—" You don't think it possible—that—perhaps—something in your prescription may have disagreed with her. You altered it four days ago."

" Impossible, quite."

" And you really believe this due merely to the heat ? "

" I am sure of it."

Maud had been all the time walking up and down the room in an anxious, agitated way.

Suddenly she stopped.

" There would be no danger in her travelling ? "

" Oh, let her go, by all means. The change is the very thing she wants. If the day after to-morrow she is no worse, certainly send her."

Maud accompanied the doctor to the door.

" As I expected," she said to herself, looking after his departing brougham. " Only I never thought of his putting it down to the weather. Well, I have tried my experiment, and with the result I expected. And—why, there is the end of it. Lily will be all right the day after to-morrow, It soon passes off."

And the day after the morrow Lily was a good deal better, and quite able to go up to town.

The afternoon before she left, Mrs. Gainsborough had, as yet, said nothing to her about the family documents. But in the evening she took counsel with herself about what she was going to do. Perhaps it would be more correct to say what she was doing.

The meditations of that evening, when she had been so much overcome by her own imaginations, had not been forgotten. On the contrary, they had been ever since more or less present in her memory : especially the discovery that it depended on little else than an act of her own volition whether her cousin should recover, or she herself become the fortunate and happy wife of the man she loved.

Which it was to be she had not yet decided. There was no occasion at present to decide.

But it was necessary to decide whether she would now take any steps to obtain copies of the family documents in the possession of Mr. Tanner. Should she ask Lily to procure copies of the documents she required ?

And why on earth not ?

If she did not ; if she was so singularly senseless as to let slip the opportunity that now offered itself for obtaining documents that might be some day of priceless importance to her : what would that benefit any one ?

And yet some plaguy little voice did murmur faintly :

" But you are taking, one by one, every preliminary step necessary for the accomplishment of a horrible crime. You have tested the effect of your drugs upon your cousin. You have made proof of the stupidity of the medical man. And now you are about to possess yourself of the documents you will want after the girl's death."

To which small timid voice, Maud replied, not timidly, but boldly :

" What I have done, and am doing, may happen to coincide with what I should do, if I wished to proceed to a crime. But I have at present no such intention. These coincidences are merely coincidences. The documents contain interesting records of my family, of which I am the last representative. That I should wish for copies of them is only natural. That they might, under other circumstances, be of service to me is beside the question. As for the two drops I gave Lily—that was a silly gratification of a silly curiosity. It did no harm, and now, at any rate, I am sending Lily to town, which is the most hopeful way of getting her really cured."

And, having thus satisfied herself, she said to Lily, on the morning of her departure :

" By the way, Lily, Mr. Tanner has in his care all the memoranda of the family history that your uncle made. Do you remember his showing them to us girls, and pointing out the connection of my father's family with yours? Whilst you are in town, I wish you would do me a favour. If your guardian would permit it, I should very much like to have copies of those of the memoranda which refer to my family as well as to yours. Will you speak to him about it ? "

" With pleasure, Maud."

Lily went up to town by the afternoon express and arrived at Waterloo in time to reach her guardian's house an hour before dinner.

CHAPTER XXX.

THERE are people whose lives are an absolute monotony. Nothing has happened to disturb their tenor
since a date almost forgotten; and it appears inconceivable that anything should happen to disturb
it until death puts a period to both monotony and
life. Of this number were Mr. and Mrs. Tanner.
They had been married more than thirty years, and
nothing that could be called an event, or that had
made the smallest difference in their condition, had
happened to them since the date of their marriage.
They had never had any children. They had lived
all the time in the same house, which they had no
intention of ever leaving; a house of colourless
bricks, with round arches over the square windows,
in a terrace in Paddington. Here every morning Mr.
Tanner came down at precisely the same minute to
breakfast: after breakfast departed at the same
minute for his bank: and was seen no more until he
returned home half an hour before dinner. He dined,
and after dinner smoked two cigars, doing meanwhile absolutely nothing. At half-past ten went to
bed. Every morning Mrs. Tanner came down to
breakfast five minutes earlier than her husband, and
after breakfast returned to her room. At half-past
eleven she went out of the house somewhither, and
at half an hour before dinner returned to it. After
dinner she knitted, and at a quarter-past ten went to
her room. Every day Mr. Tanner went to the same
places; to his bank, and to his club, and nowhere
else. And every day Mrs. Tanner went to different
places; shopping first, always at different shops, and
afterwards sight-seeing. There was not a sight to
be seen in London, provided it was to be seen in the
daytime, that she missed. A week afterwards she

had no more recollection of it than Mr. Tanner, who had not seen it at all; and could no more have told what shows she had seen, nor at what shops she had purchased than he could. And that was the whole of their existence. The only difference was on Sundays and Bank-holidays, and when they went to the seaside, in the autumn. On Sundays Mr. Tanner went to church and to his club, instead of to his club and the bank. And Mrs. Tanner went to different churches instead of to different sights. On Bank-holidays Mr. Tanner spent all the day at his club, but Mrs. Tanner still went to see whatever there was to be seen. And when they went to the seaside in the autumn they went always to the same lodgings at Hastings in which they had spent their honey-moon. One day only in the month Mrs. Tanner was "at home," and sacrificed her inclinations to her visitors. In the course of years the profound monotony of their lives impressed itself upon everything about them, their house, their manner of thinking and speaking, and their plain, perfectly meaningless features, so that nothing could be conceived more dull, more stolid, more insipid than themselves and the atmosphere of everything that surrounded them. And yet these were excellent people, kindly, charitable, sterling souls, the husband the personification of uprightness, and the wife of motherly goodness.

Such were the people to whose charge Lily Hardwick was committed for the next few weeks.

Some time had passed since Mr. Tanner and his wife had last seen her, and they found her much altered and not a little improved, grown from a lanky, rather troublesome hoyden into a tall, ladylike, and charmingly pretty girl. But they were shocked and startled to see how delicate and ailing the girl looked; so pale and thin and fragile, with a faint blue shade under her large eyes, whose lids seemed to confess secret tears. When, after the fatigues of

her journey might well be supposed to be worn off.
she was no less pale and weary than on the evening
of her arrival, they began to be alarmed, and Mrs.
Tanner inquired, with a good deal of circumstance,
whether Lynham and the sea-air agreed with Lily?
whether she was happy at Cliff Cottage? and
whether Mrs. Gainsborough was kind? To all of
which Lily replied in the affirmative. Finally Mrs.
Tanner asked whether she had been for any time
past in declining health.

"I thought Cousin Maud had written and told you
all about it," answered Lily, to this last question,
rather reservedly and with a little effort.

"Well, my dear, yes," answered Mrs. Tanner.
"But I don't like, dear, to see you so pale and
delicate."

To which Lily said nothing.

"Are you very unhappy, dear?" said the good-
hearted woman, coming close to her and coaxing her
with her arms.

"Oh, yes! Mrs. Tanner." And, laying down her
head on the good dame's fat shoulder, she fairly
burst into tears.

Mrs. Tanner comforted her as well as she could,
and Lily apologized for being a baby. But as the
days passed and she grew no brighter, though Mrs.
Tanner took her about and did her best to amuse
her, the good woman and her husband held a consultation.

"The poor girl is more unhappy than she has any
right to be, Tom," said Mrs. Tanner. "It seems to
me that she is breaking her heart about this young
man, and fretting herself into a regular decline. I
think I should like to take her to see a physician."

So Lily was taken to see a certain celebrated
physician.

It was necessary first to give the physician a few
hints. That Mrs. Tanner did in her plain, motherly

way, and then Lily herself was introduced. The physician asked a good many questions, and seemed to regard the case more seriously than Dr. Gregg had done. Especially he was unable to understand the sudden loss of strength and dizziness at first awaking produced by the change in the weather. He questioned Lily about that at considerable length. Also he examined her heart, and assured her that that organ was perfectly sound. Finally he gave her a little simple advice, and wrote her a prescription. After she was gone he said to Mrs. Tanner:

"There is nothing the matter at present, but she is nervous and overwrought. Let her have as much variety and amusement as you can without fatiguing her. If she should again complain of dizziness in the morning I should advise you at once to take advice about it. But I don't think that you have any reason to be anxious. A little time and change of scene should set her up."

"I'm sure I am very glad I took her, Tom," said Mrs. Tanner to her husband. "It's a weight off my mind well worth the money. I'd never have forgiven myself if anything had happened to John Hardwick's girl through our neglect."

As for the change of scene and amusement the physician had recommended, that was no doubt excellent advice, but, with the best will in the world to follow it, Mrs. Tanner, dear soul, had only elementary ideas of how to entertain a young girl, and to keep her from brooding over her heart-troubles. All day she honestly dragged Lily about from one sight to another, and then, in the evening, in the silence of the dull drawing-room, Lily, tired to death with what she had seen, was at liberty to be as miserable and disconsolate as she chose.

She wrote to her cousin, telling her at some length of the visit to the physician. And Maud Gainsborough said to herself, "Ah, if we had the physician

here at Lynham, that would be very dangerous.
However, I am glad that Lily has been to see him.
What he has said confirms Dr. Gregg's opinion. I
shall take care to make that known."

And she did so. The next time she saw the
rector's wife, she said :

"My cousin is still in town with her guardian.
He has taken her to see a celebrated physician ; and
he says just the same as Dr. Gregg ; that there is
nothing actually wrong with Lily at present, but that
she is in a delicate, rather critical state of health. I
am very glad to have Dr. Gregg's opinion confirmed.
I think Dr. Gregg is a very clever man."

Maud Gainsborough was spending a good deal of
her time alone. And lately she had taken to often
going down the steps to the little, secluded beach to
have a solitary stroll on the sands. She had forgotten
that she had pictured her *empoisonneuse* doing that.
She did it herself because her brain grew so heated,
and the sea-breeze cooled it.

Meanwhile, Lily proffered the request with which
her cousin had entrusted her for a copy of the family
papers. Mr. Tanner assented at once, as to a
natural and reasonable wish of Mrs. Gainsborough's.
He himself showed Lily the old Bible and all the
manuscripts, and was at some trouble to assist her
to understand them ; and he promised her that,
before she left, he would have copies of all made for
her by a competent person, that she might take
them back with her as a present to her cousin.

Mrs. Gainsborough had come to stand very high
both in his estimation and in that of Mrs. Tanner ;
partly on account of the sincere affection with which
Lily always spoke of her ; and more still for the
sensible way in which she had behaved about this
unlucky little love-affair of Miss Lily's.

One day at dinner it happened that Lily, speaking

of her cousin, let drop something about Anthony Gainsborough.

"Maud's hateful brother-in-law," she called him, and added. "That horrid man!"

"Do you mean Mr. Anthony Gainsborough?" said Mr. Tanner, rather surprised. "Do you know him?"

Not Lily! nor had she any wish to know him, "the wretch."

Quoth Mrs. Tanner, "I don't think that you would speak of him in that tone, my dear, if you knew him."

"Did Mr. Tanner know him?" asked Lily.

Both Mr. and Mrs. Tanner had known him for many years, and they respected him very much. He was a good man, with a kind, good heart.

"He was very cruel to Maud," remarked Lily.

Mr. and Mrs. Tanner did not think that possible.

"I think, my dear, you must be making some mistake," said Mrs. Tanner, a little in the tone of a rebuke.

Lily felt sure that she was making no mistake. However, she had better manners than to dispute with her hostess. But what had been said acted as a stimulant to her curiosity. She would have liked very much to have asked to be introduced to Mr. Anthony Gainsborough, and to have an opportunity given her to judge for herself of a man about whom she had heard opinions so strongly and so diametrically opposed.

After all, what she was wishing for came about of itself.

Mrs. Tanner's "at home" day arrived, and, for once, instead of going sight-seeing, Lily and her hostess remained at home to receive visitors. Several came and went, and then Lily was suddenly surprised to hear the servant announce:

" Miss Chesterfield and Miss Essie Chesterfield."

And Violet and Essie came into the room.

For one minute Lily hardly knew whether she was to credit her senses. The next a host of questions crowded her brain. Were these really the Misses Chesterfield? Was that taller girl who entered first the cousin with whom Mr. Warrington had fallen so much in love? who had treated him so shamefully? And how on earth came they to be here?

The two had shaken hands with Mrs. Tanner and Lily was introduced. Violet sat down to talk to Mrs. Tanner, Essie attached herself to Lily, and began to chat about the weather.

Conversation with Mrs. Tanner was fairly hard work. Lily had already observed that in the case of other visitors. After a very few minutes there came a pause. Violet used it to say :

" And, Mrs. Tanner, Uncle Tony told us that we were to apologize to you for his not having come to-day to see you himself. He was very sorry not to be able to come, because he has not seen you for so long. But he was detained by business."

Lily, talking to Essie, overheard the speech. Then these really were *the* Misses Chesterfield.

Well, she would not have thought it. Surreptitiously she stole searching glances at the sisters' faces, trying to read something more of their characters than at first appeared. She did not succeed in deciphering much. Violet was the handsomer, a quiet, rather reserved girl : Essie the prettier.

" And have you been yachting with your uncle lately ? " asked Mrs. Tanner.

" Not since we returned from the Mediterranean," replied Violet. " Uncle Tony's yacht is laid up at present. But we hope to go for another cruise early in the autumn. Uncle Tony has his steam-launch, and we make the most delightful little voyages on the river."

And Essie proposed :

" And Uncle Tony would be so pleased if you and Mr. Tanner would some day come with us, Mrs. Tanner. Perhaps you could come some evening. It is so beautiful on the river in the evenings. And " —turning to Lily—" perhaps Miss Hardwick will come too."

Mrs. Tanner declined for Mr. Tanner and herself. They never went on the water. But she added, that she made no doubt that a cruise on the river would be a treat to Lily, who assented on the spot.

So before the girls left it was arranged that she should some day go with them.

After they were gone Mrs. Tanner said :

" And you will be able to judge for yourself about Mr. Gainsborough."

That was just what Lily was thinking.

The promised invitation soon came. Mrs. Tanner drove Lily to Twickenham after luncheon, and left her in charge of the girls and of a friend who was going with them, who promised to see Lily safely home in the evening, and then they all walked together to the river, and Lily was introduced to Anthony Gainsborough.

She was a good deal surprised by his personal appearance, his frank, open, kind-hearted face, and his good-natured manner. And she certainly could not say that his behaviour to herself was anything but most kind. His nieces evidently worshipped him, and appeared to have every reason for doing so. Indeed, Lily could not conceal from herself that there was something about the man, particularly in his speech, and his good-natured way of regarding things, that would make it natural for people to be attracted to him. And certainly he did not appear to be the sort of man who could be cruel to any one. Still, Lily *knew*. And she was not disposed to let a mere first impression, and words, and manners weigh with her more than solid facts. Incredible as it might seem, this was the man who had treated her Cousin Maud shamefully, and who did all in his power to make her life miserable; and Lily listened to every word he spoke, and studied every movement of his face, with a strange curiosity to understand this apparently kind and really heartless man.

However, she spent a delightful evening. Anthony Gainsborough took the greatest care of her, and gave himself a good deal of trouble to amuse her and to point out to her every object of interest by the river-side. He seemed to her to know everything, to have been everywhere, and to have the knack of making everything that he said entertaining. Also, to her great surprise, he inquired after Mrs. Gainsborough.

"I left her very well, thank you," replied Lily, feeling very indignant, and wishing that she could add, "Why are you so unjust and tyrannical with my cousin?"

"I was down at Lynham about a fortnight ago, but you were not at home. Of course your cousin told you I had called."

"No," said Lily, a little surprised, and wondering in herself what he had called for, and why Maud had said nothing about it.

Was he, she speculated, going to bully Maud in some new way?

But when she at last bade him "Good-bye," and thanked him for the delightful evening she had spent, there was a spell in his voice and a cordial kindness in the shake of his big, strong hand that Lily found irresistible, in spite of her prejudices; so that she was very pleased when he said:

"I am glad that you have been amused. You must come with us again, Miss Hardwick."

"Oh, yes, do," said Essie.

" I shall be most happy to come, if you will be so kind as to have me," replied Lily.

When Lily reached home, she was looking brighter than she had done any day since she reached town. It was strange; for Anthony Gainsborough and his nieces were about the last persons in whose society Lily Hardwick would have supposed that she could find any pleasure. But we are no more masters of our impressions than of our affections; and somehow, whilst she had been with these people, she had felt that there is, after all, sunshine in the world—that things which are amiss may come right in the end, and that altogether to despair is weakness. And she looked forward with pleasure to meeting her new friends again.

That, and Mrs. Tanner's gratification at the bright humour in which she had come home, and an inclination on Essie Chesterfield's part to cultivate a little friendship with Miss Hardwick, resulted soon in another invitation sent and accepted ; and after this second followed several more. And, as it appeared that something at last had been discovered that was really a diversion for Lily, Mrs. Tanner schemed for her to see as much as possible of the Chesterfield girls and of their uncle.

About the latter Lily changed her opinion.

But only by degrees. As long as she could, she clung to her prejudices. But her natural honesty would not permit her to hold out against facts ; and at last she admitted frankly that her bias against the man had been unjust. After that she began to believe that her cousin must have fallen into some mistake. For certainly there was a misunderstanding somewhere. It was impossible that Anthony Gainsborough should have behaved as Maud represented.

She had written nothing to Maud about her new friends. She had purposely abstained from so doing when she first made their acquaintance, because she wished to take time to form her own opinions. Afterwards, when she was about to say something, she found some awkwardness in not having named them before. Finally, she put off mentioning them until her return to Lynham.

CHAPTER XXXI.

THAT was about the end of July. She was certainly stronger than when she came up to town. The mere change of scene had not been without effect. Possibly even her somewhat fatiguing daily sight-seeing expeditions with Mrs. Tanner had done something towards distracting her thoughts; and the kindness of her guardian and his wife had undoubtedly cheered her; whilst the hours spent on the river and with the Chesterfield girls had been productive of a great deal of good. But for all that she had gained more morally than physically. Her face was brighter and happier, but she was still pale and thin and her appetite was poor. And there were still hours when she was unhappy enough. She told Maud that she should not forget Frank Warrington, and she had not forgotten him. On the morning of her departure from London she was far from looking her brightest. She could not without a little regret part from the kind hearts she was leaving.

However, Maud, who met her at the railway-station, was at once struck with the marked improvement in her appearance. and said to herself, " I had no idea she would come back looking so much better."

A feeling of uneasiness came over her; a misgiving that the "opportunity" might have passed. All this time that her cousin had been in London, Maud Gainsborough had not been thinking of nothing; and the "opportunity" had become a far more definite idea to her than when Lily left.

As for Lily, she thought the welcome the widow gave her a little awkward and strange.

She had brought down with her the copies of the family papers which Maud desired to possess. Little suspecting that she was presenting her own death-warrant, she, after dinner, brought them into the drawing-room, and gave them to Maud with a little speech, saying how kind Mr. Tanner had been in having them copied properly by some competent person, for which he had insisted on paying.

"So you ought to thank him for them, not me, Maud," she concluded, putting the papers into her cousin's hands: "I only asked for them."

Maud had already opened the packet, and the first thing that caught her eyes was a formally attested certificate of the agreement of the copies with the original. But that was more even than she had hoped for!

She had here evidence in her hands hardly second to the documents themselves. Her pulse quickened with excitement, and a sudden glow of eagerness brightened her features.

Putting down the papers, she caught Lily in her arms.

"Oh, but you darling! This is more than I asked for," she exclaimed, kissing the girl effusively. "And it is to you that I owe them, dear. If you had not asked for them I should not have had them. But I will write to Mr. Tanner too."

There was nothing constrained or artificial about her thanks, as there had been in her welcome. Her

P

pleasure at receiving these documents was most sincere.

Maud sat down at the table on which the lamp stood, and, putting her coffee by her side, began to peruse the papers. Here and there she recognized names and particulars, pointed out to her by Lily's uncle on that dimly remembered evening of her school-girl days. How many things had happened since then! The family tree, with the dates of births, marriages, and deaths, accompanied by many references to old registers and deeds, and wills and monuments, was made out much more fully and clearly than she, resting upon her own recollections, had supposed. Absorbed in her papers, an accurate study of which she was nevertheless postponing for another time, she hardly noticed Lily. Only now and then she said, " Dear me, these are very interesting;" or " My dear, I don't know how I am to thank you enough."

To which Lily would reply, " I am very glad that you are so pleased with them, dear."

And once she asked, " Did Mr. Tanner show you the papers ? "

" Some of them. I am afraid that I did not altogether understand them."

So the evening passed almost in silence, very quietly.

Lily rose at last and said :

" I think I am tired, Maud. I'll go to bed."

" I am afraid that I have been awfully unsociable, dear, to be absorbed like this in these papers, and on the first evening of your return, too," said the widow, frankly looking up with a smile at the girl standing over her chair. " But you will forgive me, won't you ? What you have brought is what I have been wishing for for years."

" There is nothing to forgive, Maud. It is pleasant

to be at home again : to spend an evening again as we have spent so many."

Maud had risen, and stood with her hands on the girl's shoulders, looking straight into her eyes.

"You look tired, dear," she said. "To-morrow we will have a long talk about everything. You must have so much to tell me, I am sure. Good-night, darling." She put her arms round the girl and kissed her tenderly. "I hope you are not sorry to come back to me, after all your gaiety."

"I was sorry to leave town. But now that I have got home again I am glad," said the girl, frankly.

Yes. After all, she was glad to be once more at home, to be with Maud in the little cottage, and to have returned to her own quiet life. And when she got upstairs into her own room, and sat down on her favourite window-seat, at the little window looking out over the long garden and the trees, and the distant sea, grey in the dim moonlight, a gentle spell fell upon her senses, the weird of the old life, half restful, half melancholy, but very, very dear. There had been an unreality in her life in town, an artificial restlessness that had made her all the time not quite herself. But now again everything was real, the little cottage, and the shadowed garden, and the moaning sea, and the quiet stillness of the country night ; and she was herself again.

Downstairs, Maud had abruptly thrust the papers away from her, all in a heap ; and, after that, had risen from the lamp-lit table, and gone to the window, and sat down with her back to the light in the chair Lily had left.

"And now ?" she said to herself.

It was time to come to a decision.

Yes : to-night : at once.

Lily had come back from town distinctly better. The change had done her good. In a day or two Dr. Gregg would call. Indeed, she had asked him to do so. If he found Lily so much better, and then, a fortnight hence, all the old symptoms made their reappearance, would that not arouse the suspicions even of the most unsuspicious? It ought to do so. Whereas. if the doctor found Lily very much the same as before she left—a little brighter, perhaps, but not really any better—then he would, without doubt. say :

" Well, Mrs. Gainsborough, you see, sometimes in these cases, change of air is beneficial, and at other times not."

" It seems, then. that it must begin now or never," soliloquized Mrs. Gainsborough.

Happily. there had been hardly any one at the station. It might be said that no one had yet seen Lily

That was opportune, too. In fact, not to begin now was to let slip the last opportunity.

" Only I don't want to begin now," meditated Mrs. Gainsborough. " Not the very moment that the poor child has come home."

And she thought of the girl with real pity.

After which she fell back into long meditations about herself.

She was not a woman of action. That was the fact. Reveries, imaginations, retrospections, and speculations—those were her element, not action. When it came to action, she always wanted a little more time to think. That was a part of her character. There was only one way in which she could act, and that was by acting at once.

Who was it said, " What you are loth to do, do at once ?" The man who coined that maxim must have been a dreamer like herself.

It was an excellent maxim for a dreamer—" What you are loth to do, do at once."

At last she arrived at a decision.

" I'll give Lily one drop to-morrow and on the next day. There will be nothing in that. The doctor will find her much as he expected to find her, and that will please him. Afterwards, if this must be done, I shall have taken precautions against arousing suspicions, and, if not, things will take their course just as if I had done nothing."

Morning seldom brings us back the impressions with which we fell asleep, and when Lily awoke early, it was with a consciousness of depression. Somehow, the charm of the return home was gone, and the keen regret for the kind hearts left in London had come back. So Lily was out of spirits.

Maud came in about eight, bringing her a morning cup of tea. She found her looking less bright than on the previous day.

And Lily drank the tea.

All the day Maud watched her closely. The drug she was using was of a horrible virulence, and she knew that she must observe the exact effect of every dose.

Lily's appetite was very poor. She apologized for it, saying that it had been often so in town. Towards evening she appeared a little languid. And so ended the first day.

CHAPTER XXXII.

THE next day Lily's languor was more distinctly marked. She had no appetite at all, and a disinclination to do anything. She had talked of a ride, but the ride was put off, and she only strolled for a little while in the garden. In the evening she complained of a slight headache.

The doctor called in the afternoon, and remarked on the fact that the change of air appeared to have done Miss Hardwick little real good, much in the terms Maud Gainsborough had anticipated. He agreed entirely with the opinions expressed by the London physician, excepting only about Miss Hardwick's heart. He was convinced that the heart was slightly affected—very slightly. There was no occasion for any alarm. A little care necessary, that was all. So the doctor's visit was over. However, Lily nevertheless had yet another drop out of the widow's phial the next morning.

And the next day, and the next.

On one of these evenings, Lily, beginning with, " By the way, Maud, I have a surprise for you. I have not yet told you of all the people I met in town," related her acquaintance with the Chesterfield girls and with Anthony Gainsborough.

Maud said easily :

" Oh, yes, I know that the Tanners know them."

She evinced a good deal of curiosity regarding Violet Chesterfield, and asked Lily several questions about her. Respecting Anthony Gainsborough she said very little.

" You liked him ? Very likely, my dear," she remarked. " Permit me only to observe that you don't know him as well as I do. But, dear, by all means have your own opinion about your own friends."

She was showing herself exceeding kind ; devoting herself to Lily with unremitting attention, remaining with her all day long, and doing her utmost to cheer and to amuse her ; seemingly having just at present no thought of anything besides the girl and her recovery.

"If no one else can cheer you up, and endeavour to make you well, you must see whether I cannot. darling," she said, affectionately.

" You are awfully kind, Maud," answered Lily.

Lily had been home about a week when Mrs. Gainsborough one morning had to go into Lynham to do some shopping. She invited Lily to go with her, but the latter declined.

Maud went alone, despatched her business as fast as she could, and returned home at once.

On entering the drawing-room, she found Lily on the floor, with her face buried on the seat of a chair, crying.

"My dear child!" she exclaimed, flying to her. " What has happened ? "

" Nothing, Maud. I am a baby. I don't know why I am crying. Only after you went out I felt so miserable. I wanted to cry so ; I could not help it. And so I sat down here, and cried. That is all." But presently she went on : " I was so glad to come home, to come back to you, Maud. And now, I don't seem to be glad about anything. I don't know why it is, but I am miserable, utterly miserable. It seems awfully ungrateful, I know, dear, when you are so kind. But I am not ungrateful, dear "— Maud had knelt down beside her, and, putting her arms round the young widow's neck, Lily laid her pretty head on her bosom and reiterated—" I am not

ungrateful, dear. I love you, Maud, I love you. I
love you with all my heart ! "

Maud Gainsborough was as pale as marble.

As quickly as she could she persuaded the girl to
get up, and to rest a little on the sofa. Then, saying that she would take her things off and be back
in a minute. she ran to her room and locked the
door.

" I cannot go on with it—I cannot ! It is too
horrible ! " she cried to herself, wringing her hands.
" It seemed all so simple. But I cannot do it. I
haven't the courage. I can't do it. I *must* give
it up."

The next day she brought Lily her morning cup
of tea, as usual. But this morning there was no
drop in it out of the phial.

" I am throwing away fifteen-thousand a-year, I
know," said Maud to herself, as she left the room.
" But I haven't the nerve to go through with it."

The drug she was using was one whose effect
is very transient. In two or three days Lily,
though still pale, had begun to recover her appetite, and to emerge from her languor and despondency.

But Mrs. Gainsborough thought with a good deal
of chagrin of her lost fortune. She had given up
fifteen-thousand a-year very precipitately.

All this time Lily had seen nothing of Warrington.
She had been out but seldom, and their paths had
not happened to cross. But a day or two afterwards
she met him on the parade.

She had been sitting on the sands with Maud,
and had left her to take a turn with the rector's wife
and her daughters. Just as they drew near the end
of the parade, Warrington came out of the London
Hotel through the gardens, and then, turning
sharply, came right upon them.

If he had seen them he might, very possibly, have avoided the encounter.

Had the weeks which had elapsed since Lily had last seen him done anything at all towards effacing his image from her heart? Lily could not herself have said. But certain it is, that now that she suddenly found herself, in an unexpected moment, face to face with this man, all the love she had for him welled up in her heart in an instant.

She was aware that she had changed colour, and was probably deadly pale. However, she had enough self-possession to turn a little aside, and to leave the rector's wife and daughters to speak to him, and herself took a few steps that brought her to the edge of the parade overlooking the sands, and there waited, standing with her back turned to Warrington and her friends. She did not listen, but she could hear every word of their conversation; a commonplace conversation about things of no interest. How the man's voice thrilled her! How vividly she could, in imagination, see every expression of his handsome, manly face! And how her heart, disobedient to her judgment, yearned, and yearned, and yearned towards him!

Warrington, talking to the rector's wife, stole a glance at her where she stood alone by the edge of the parade. The light breeze toyed with her ribbons and laces, and her sunshade made a delicate shade about her head and shoulders. He could only see her quarter face, but he noticed how thin she had grown and how pale. There was a little droop in the corner of her lips too, and the lids fell over her eyes, as if they were weary "The girl looks ill and unhappy. Little better for her change," thought Warrington, listening to what the rector's wife was saying about the Sunday-school children having a treat in one of the fields at Lynhurst. Presently he stole a second glance at the troubled lips and heavy eyelids, and thought to himself, "Yes, ill and unhappy: there is no doubt about it."

The rector's wife said, "Good-bye," and he went on his way and Lily rejoined her friends. Then they, too, left the parade and she returned to Maud on the sands.

"Well?" asked Maud, looking up from her book.

"We met Mr. Warrington," said Lily, half absently.

Resting her cheek on her hand, she sat silent, wistfully regarding the sea. But presently a nervous movement of hers made Maud look round quickly.

"Are you crying, dear?" she asked.

"Crying? No. What is the use of crying? Besides, I have made up my mind to cry no more about what can't be helped. But I wish that I was dead."

"Yes," she ran on, in a cold, dogged way, "I wish that I was dead. What is the good of living on and on, without a bit of happiness, or a bit of hope? He will never love me, and I shall never cease to love him. I love him to-day just the same as I loved him when you sent me to town, just the same as (if I live so long) I shall love him fifty years hence—dearly, passionately. And to be so miserable as I am for long years and years, is it worth living for? I don't think it is. If any one were any the better, I would not so much mind. But to be just merely wretched, to have the heartache, and to know it is to to go on for ever and ever and ever, and that all the pain is mere useless pain—*that* is wretchedness not worth enduring. It is wrong to kill oneself, or I would do it. I don't believe that you, Maud, have ever loved as I love that man. So of course you can't understand."

After which, she would say no more on the subject.

But all the rest of the day she was taciturn and low-spirited, and the same on the morrow.

"My dear, I think you might have some spirit," remarked Maud. "The man does not care for you. It is rather weak, is it not, to be so abjectly attached to him. If a man did not care for me, I should soon cure myself of liking him."

A pretty audacious statement, seeing that the widow knew that Warrington did not care a pin for her, and was herself over head and ears in love with him.

"I don't want to cure myself of loving him," retorted Lily, rather sharply. "I am proud of loving him. I would rather love him, and be miserable all the days of my life, than love any other man and be happy."

"Very well, dear," said the widow.

But she began to lose patience. To herself she said, "What a fool that girl is making of herself. It is really wonderful, only it is also very stupid. The man is in love with her. Only she has neither the sense to see it, nor the ingenuity to make him declare himself. And so she goes about the place sighing. Such an existence is quite a misfortune."

Really her hasty determination not to accelerate the demise of her unfortunate cousin began to seem to deserve serious reconsideration. At a pinch her courage had failed her, and she had at once thrown up her enterprise, without much reflection about what she was doing. But on second thoughts she believed she had been too precipitate. The case had so many different aspects. And they ought all to be taken carefully into consideration one by one.

Of course, there was that fifteen-thousand a-year between which and herself stood nothing but this

girl's frail life. Fifteen-thousand a-year by right of
discovery Maud's own. But about that she would not
think. She was not a miserable wretch that would
poison a helpless girl for her money. But there
were other and graver points to be considered. The
girl was miserable. So miserable that she openly
asserted that she wished herself dead. So miserable
that it might be an act of mercy to let her have her
wish. She was ill, too. The disappointment with
which she had met was so enormously beyond her
power to support it, that there seemed to be every
probability of her health entirely breaking down, of
her slowly wasting, and sinking into an early grave.
And what a horrible, slow torture it would be! To
shorten such suffering would be a charity.

It was a mere question of euthanasia. And seriously, Mrs. Gainsborough approved of the theory
of an euthanasia. If she were herself dying miserably of some horrible, protracted torment, she
would be exceedingly grateful to any one who would
mercifully give her her quietus, and put her out of
her pain. And so too. if she could foresee all, very
probably. would Lily.

There were also other considerations of an entirely
different stamp. And these Maud had certainly
rather forgotten when she faltered in her purpose.
Poor, handsome Frank Warrington, and his encum-
bered estate ; and the use the money would be to
him. And that passionate love which Maud bore
him. That love which was not fain to wait for long,
long years.

Lily had said, " I don't believe that you have ever
loved as I do." Ah, much she knew! A poor,
feeble passion, hers, put side by side with Maud's.
And if Maud chose to make her know it ? It was a
sort of challenge that Lily had thrown her. Suppose
she accepted the challenge ? Lily might sigh for

the man, fret for him, pine for him. Suppose she, Maud, were to commit a great crime for him.

Yes, for him: not for herself. She would not have done it for herself. But for him she would do it.

For him she would do anything. For him—and because the girl had challenged her.

And if the deed was a great sin—did not love atone for, hallow everything?

And yet Maud Gainsborough hesitated still. She was always unready when the moment for action came. All that day, and all the next, and all the next after that she wavered in uncertainty of purpose, undecided whether or not to put her hand to the crime lying, so easy of accomplishment, within her reach. Not that those thoughts were restraining her which might naturally be supposed, at such a juncture, to have forced themselves upon her consideration—the vulgar one of the risk she would run, or the serious ones of the gravity, in the sight of Heaven, of the sin she meditated, and the monstrous inhumanity of its merciless cruelty.

Such thoughts had little weight with her. A certain pitifulness for the helplessness of her victim she did feel; and a distaste for the lying, and the duplicity, and the hypocrisy without which her cousin's destruction could not be accomplished; and she did wish that the life she had to take could have been one which had not been so closely, so gently united with her own. But the thing that really held her back was the disinclination to *do*, to act. If she could have dreamed Lily's life away, if she could have managed that, by some mysterious spell, her own reveries could be translated into reality, so that, as she mused on, the girl should droop and sink, softly lulled into the eternal sleep; then Maud would not have hesitated at all.

But, insufficiently nerved for action as she was, Maud, all through those three days, was drifting towards it. For power to corrupt the soul, nothing is to be compared to the dalliance of the hungry will pleasing itself with the imagination of an act it as yet lacks courage enough to take in hand. And in this woman there was not so very much corruption of heart to be accomplished. That which she had not been able to tell Warrington, if it had been spoken, would have made him shudder. And the remembrance of it was with her often in these days. Only this that she meditated now would be worse— the destruction of this poor child.

But, ever dwelling upon it, ever desiring it, ever wishing that it was only more easy still, the woman was moving towards it, rapidly growing willingly blinded to every horror, to every consideration of right and mercy and trust, and giving herself over entirely to the guidance of a passion that deepened suddenly with an awful intensity as it found its imperious demands, that not even crime should stand in its way, met with a hearing, whilst her heart (at least as far as concerned her cousin) turned to stone, and her conscience staggered, drowsy and drunk with dreams and sophistries.

One of those evenings, after dinner, she and Lily had their coffee beneath the verandah. Lily had brought her book and laid it open upon her knees, but the work had not enough of charm to enchain her thoughts, and, with her cheek rested on her hand, she fell into a reverie: one so deep that she did not notice her cousin's rising and leaving her.

Alone, Maud strolled down the garden. When out of sight of the cottage she sat down on a garden seat. A rose tree grew above it, and, putting up her hand, she plucked one of the roses, and then, leaning back in the corner of the seat, fell to smelling the flower and mechanically brushing her lips with its soft petals, whilst she once more resumed her now ever-recurring train of thought.

The evening was calm and still, delicious with the gentle coolness that concludes a summer day. Already the light was fading, and the outlines of the black-green trees stood out boldly against the softly deepening sky. Scarcely a breath stirred their leaves. Down on the beach the sea slumbered, hushed and motionless. Not a sound even of rippling wavelets rose to the ears. From inland came only now and then broken whispers of sound of the sort that seem to accentuate the stillness. The peace and silence of the moment was intense.

The spell of it entered into Maud's soul. Listening motionlessly, she pressed the soft, fragrant rose to her lips. What should her future be? Such as this moment—calm and rest unspeakable? After one bitter moment of a dark struggle, calm and rest unspeakable?—or for ever and ever disappointment, disquiet, want, weariness, war with the pitiless world?

But who that was not mad would doubt?

CHAPTER XXXIII.

It was towards seven o'clock in the evening, about a fortnight later.

Eustace Warrington sat alone in the large, barely furnished drawing-room, that he had taken for his music-room, playing the violin.

Outside the westering sun shone brightly. But the Spanish blinds were lowered before all the windows, and the room was both dim and cool. A vague scent of the mignonette, in the beds on the lawn, stole in at the windows.

Absorbed in the liquid strains that flowed from the eloquent edge of his bow, the blind man sat on a music-stool playing adagio, adagio, rapt in his music. His fine, sculpturesque face wore a strange expression of melancholy, and the pensive strains seemed to fill the room with a charmed atmosphere of exquisite sadness.

The concluding chord floated out at the open windows into the sunlit air, and died into silence. The player removed his instrument from his shoulder.

"I do not know what is the matter with me this afternoon," he said, half aloud, rising and walking up and down the room. "It is not usual for me to be oppressed with a melancholy I cannot overcome. I wonder what time it is?"

He took out his gold repeater and made it strike. One, two, three, four, five, six; one, two, three.

"Past a quarter to seven," he said. "I'll go and dress for dinner. How this impression haunts me!"

He rose from the music-stool, and, going to a table, put his fiddle into its case; and then crossed the room to the door. A stranger would hardly have believed he was blind. He was becoming very familiar with the place.

At dinner he asked:

"Is there any news, Frank?"

"Not much. I hear that Miss Hardwick is worse."

"So I am sorry to hear. The rector was here for a few minutes this afternoon."

"I saw her this afternoon, but only for an instant. She passed me in the High Street driving in the pony-carriage. I thought her looking shockingly ill, poor girl."

"I am very sorry to hear it," replied Eustace. "And that is all?" he added, as if expecting to hear more.

Warrington had nothing else to relate of any interest. All through dinner Eustace seemed *distrait*. After dinner, when they were smoking, Warrington reverted again to the subject of Miss Hardwick's ill health.

"That is a very sad thing about Miss Hardwick."

"What is the matter with her?" asked Eustace. "You saw her yourself. What impression did she give you?"

"I thought her looking miserably ill. Pale, and with leaden shadows under her eyes."

"All of which means nothing to me, my dear fellow," remarked Eustace, with a smile.

"No. I beg your pardon. Well, she has grown very thin: seems dull, lifeless almost: tired, exhausted. I should say that she was in some sort of decline."

"You did not hear her speak?"

"No."

"What do they call it?"

"Nothing that I can understand. Atony: great prostration. A slight affection of the heart, accompanied by great nervous debility, I hear Gregg says."

"Who is an ass," remarked Eustace. "Poor girl! It is all very sad. She is a nice girl. She has a charming little hand, too, shapely and soft, with a nervous touch; and a pretty, playful voice, with unexpected tones in it, light, laughing notes, and deeper modulations full of meaning. She should have a heart as sweet as a rose. I am very sorry that she is ill. Of course you know what is being said about it all?"

"What?"

" Different things, according as the speakers are
by nature cautious or given to exaggerations ; parti-
sans of yours or of Mrs. Gainsborough's ; disposed to
think that Miss Hardwick has been a little silly, or
that you have been very unkind to her ; in fact,
according to all the different shades of character and
veracity of all the gossips of Lynhurst. Brutally—
that you have treated her shamefully : encouraged
her, and then jilted her ; and finally broken her
heart. Or, more mildly—that there has been an
unfortunate little love affair between yourself and
the lady, and that she has felt what has happened
exceedingly deeply. Or, simply—that she has fallen
head over ears in love with you, and is very unhappy
because you do not reciprocate her passion. These
are the things, at least, that reach my ears, from
various people. And I suppose there is some truth
in it, is there not ?"

" In the way you put it in the last case, Eustace, I
believe there is some truth in it."

" The girl has taken a fancy to you ?"

" I believe she has : or really, I think I might say
I know it."

" And you ?"

" Miss Hardwick is no more to me than to
you."

Eustace was awhile silent. He was weighing not
his brother's words only, but also their intonation.
Presently he asked :

" Do you remember a conversation that you and I
had about Miss Hardwick a day or two after you first
became acquainted with her ?"

" I am afraid that it has left a stronger impression
upon your memory than on mine."

Said Eustace to himself, " Ah, he does remember
it." Aloud he continued, " I took the liberty on that
occasion to say that you would fall in love with Miss

Hardwick, or something to that effect. Possibly you remember that?"

"I remember. Only it seems that instead she has fallen in love with me. Your intuition was right in the main, and wrong in particulars. Eh?"

"And you replied?"

"That I certainly should not."

"For reasons: you remember them?"

"I remember that you gave yourself a good deal of trouble to dispute my reasons."

"Because your reasoning was false."

"It seems not—I think," replied Warrington, good-temperedly

Eustace rose and went to the open window, and standing there, with his shoulder against the wall, continued to smoke in silence.

Warrington, who had all along remained at the table, regarded him. The expression of his brother's face struck him. It was a most unusual thing for any shade of melancholy to display itself in Eustace's features; but there was one there this evening.

"What is the matter, old fellow?" asked Warrington. "You look out of spirits."

"I am so, rather," admitted Eustace. "A melancholy mood is an unusual thing with me; and when it comes depresses me a good deal. To-night I am not quite myself. This poor girl's fate weighs somehow on my mind. We came down here, you and I," he went on, pensively, "to make ourselves a home in this dull place: a little to husband our fortunes: a little to lead a country life: a little to be quiet. We formed acquaintances, of course; and amongst them was this young girl. They say she is pretty. I know she is charming, a brighter, gentler, finer soul than any of the rest down here. And now she is wasting, perishing away I regret it. Something about it seems to me piteously sad. I am romantic to-night;

sentimental, what not.   Laugh at me, my dear fellow,
by all means."

"No.   I do not know that it is any laughing
matter.   Report gives the girl out to be in a dangerous way;   and death is not a laughing matter for
any one."

"I'll tell you what it is, Frank," said Eustace,
presently moving to the other side of the window, so
that he had his back towards his brother.   "You
might have done worse than marry that girl."

"I am not a marrying man, and you know it."

"I know what you say about it.   But the girl is a
good girl.   And she will have money   And—" this
with a little more of his air of good-humour—"your
place here wants the money, if you don't want the
girl."

"Only at such a price, my dear brother, I prefer
to be without the money. '*Les femmes ont trois
tours de plus que le diable.*'"

"Miss Hardwick, too?"

"I suppose so.   At any rate I have no wish to
try."

"I don't believe it, Frank.   And," he added, in a
low tone, "I am not convinced that you do."

And he came back to the table.

"Are you convinced in your own mind, Frank,"
he asked, sitting down, "that this girl is suffering
through no fault of yours : through no fault at all of
yours?   The girl has taken a fancy to you.   That is
on all hands conceded.   You know that you have
taken it into your head to have a nasty opinion of
women, and sometimes you say things that are tolerably bitter—things that might perhaps wound a girl
a good deal, a girl that was fond of you."

"I have a nasty opinion of women," admitted
Warrington.   "And, as it happens, Miss Hardwick
knows I have it.   But that is all beside the question.

I never behaved to a woman otherwise than I would have behaved when I thought differently of them, and you know it."

"I know that you don't intend to behave differently," said Eustace.

"Why all these questions to-night, my dear fellow?" asked Warrington, not a little surprised at Eustace's persistency in the topic of conversation. "What has put all this into your mind?"

"I don't know," replied Eustace thoughtfully, as if unable to explain what was passing within him, even to himself. "Somehow, I have it weighing on my mind to-night that we two came down here and broke this girl's peace. But I don't know what is the matter with me this evening."

"Are you sure, Frank," he resumed after a pause, "that you are in no way the occasion of this girl's illness?"

"No, Eustace. I am *not* sure."

"I do not know what you may have done, Frank. But I take it, a woman does not break her heart about nothing. And it seems that this girl is breaking her heart about you."

"You are going too fast, Eustace," interrupted Warrington. "Nothing has passed between us of the sort you might imagine. I have never knowingly given Miss Hardwick the least occasion to suppose that I cared for her. I assure you of it on my honour. And the reason is simple—because I am not in love with her: and have no intention of being in love with any woman. There have never been any reticences between you and me; and I hope there never may be. You are a shrewd reader of character. I am not, and you may know me better than I know myself. But I have never concealed from you what I have believed to be my real sentiments. I am resolved not to have anything to do with love affairs. I made a solemn

vow to myself to that effect the night after I learned
Violet's flight, and I mean to keep it. I don't say I
will never marry. A man may marry for so many
reasons. But I have done with love. Tender relations with a woman are not my *métier*. There may
be men whom women love and treat them well. I
believe there are. I am not one of that sort. And I
prefer to have nothing to do with people who, as I
foresee, will treat me ill. Justly angry as I have been
at the way my cousin behaved to me, I am able to
see that what happened was, in reality, a happy escape
at any rate for me; and that, had not the affair terminated as it did, both my cousin and I might have had
afterwards to go through things of which I should not
like to think. Having then once escaped from a life
of misery, I have no wish to expose myself again to
the risk of falling into it. I have vowed to have done
with love affairs. I think you know me well enough,
Eustace, to be sure that I am not the man either to
have encouraged a woman to love me, or to have pretended that I was in love with her when I had no
feeling for her beyond that of singularly agreeable
but indifferent acquaintanceship. That Miss Hardwick may have taken a greater fancy to me than pru-
dence warranted, seems to be generally believed. That
I have not been careful enough to prevent her liking
me, is I allow possible. I sincerely regret it. That
I have in any way encouraged her to like me, is not
true."

"Then I should say——" began Eustace, and broke
off.

"I know what you would say, Eustace: and I say
the same to myself. The mere fact that the girl may
have conceived a liking for me, and have been disappointed not to find her affection reciprocated, is not
enough to account for her breaking her heart about
the matter. And the people who believe she is break-

ing her heart about it are, as it seems to me, justified in suspecting that there is something unknown in the background—or, plainly, that I have been trifling with the girl. But I have not. I have had my lesson about women, at least, as far as I am concerned. I don't grumble about it: I accept it. Life cannot give everything to every one of us. It has given you many things, and not sight. It has given me many things, and not to be able to get on with women."

"That theory is tenable. Life has its disappointments and also its compensations," observed the blind man, philosophically. "It may have in store a compensation for you."

"Let us hope so."

"If you did find yourself some day in love with a girl, Frank?" proposed Eustace.

"I should do my best to cure myself of it, and certainly get out of her way."

"But supposing that you had reason to know that she was in love with you?"

"I should still do the same."

"We are accustomed to be plain with each other, Frank," pursued Eustace, after a moment's thought. "Suppose it was evident that this girl Miss Hardwick was in love with you: and suppose conviction was forced upon you that you were in love with her: and taking further into consideration that the girl has a pretty fortune, that she is a charming girl, and that she is possibly making herself very unhappy about you: then?"

"I should still do the same," replied Warrington, firmly.

A shade of disappointment crossed Eustace's face, but he said no more. He left the table, and sat down on an arm-chair by the hearth, and a long silence followed. Eustace's cigar went out, and he threw the

end away, and sat musing with his brow rested on his
hand.

Frank Warrington still remained where he had the
whole time been, at the table.

"You seem really to have the dumps very badly
to-night," he remarked at last.

"I have. I am uncomfortable, and I do not know
why. At least, that is not quite true. The fact is—
Well: it is foolish to talk about dreams, and it is
more foolish still to believe in presentiments. And
yet I have had a dream that has had upon me all the
effect of a presentiment; and I cannot shake it off."

"Well. Let us hear all about it. I am a little
curious to know what sort of thing a blind man's
dream can be."

Eustace smiled, and rousing himself a little said :

"As foolish as any other man's. But, if you wish it.
You must know then that I fell asleep after luncheon,
on the sofa in the music-room, and I had a singular
dream. I dreamed that you and I went to see Miss
Hardwick; to see her, not to inquire after her.
Well, when we got to Cliff Cottage, we found the
place neglected and ruinous. It was years since
anything had been done to the place, or since any one
had entered it. I felt with my cane that the mosses
and weeds had grown thick upon the walls, and the
paint on the gates was many years old, and blistered
off by the sun. The gates opened with difficulty,
and squeaked on their rusty hinges. However, we
went in. Inside, the place was all overgrown. The
vegetation was rank and wild, and smelt coarse and
unwholesome. The paths were covered with mosses
and long grasses. The shrubs, and the brambles that
had grown amongst the shrubs, had encroached upon
the walks, and caught our feet as we advanced. Big
boughs, too, had fallen, and even trees; and you had
to lead me round them. So we made our way towards

the house as we could. When we reached it we found
it in the same condition as the grounds, the steps of
the porch had fallen out of the level, and the weeds
had pushed their way up through the tiles, making
them uneven. In the hall, the floor-cloth was in
holes, and ragged. I caught my foot in it and nearly
fell. In the drawing-room the carpet was worn
through to the boards, and I noticed that several
panes of glass in the windows were broken.'

"How the deuce did you find out that the glass
was broken?"

"The wind came into the room in little puffy
draughts as it does through a broken window, and I
could smell the rank vegetation outside. When we
sat down the furniture seemed rickety, and it was
very much worn and damaged, and the upholstery
was threadbare and at places torn. A thick covering
of dust, too, was on almost everything, and came off
on my fingers. In fact we were in a ruinous.
deserted house, untenanted for years. But the odd
thing was that there was a large party assembled. I
recognized the voices of almost every one we knew in
Lynham. And of other people too. A great number came in turn to speak to me, and, whilst they
were doing so, I was surprised to find myself in
evening dress. I was, at the moment, speaking to
one of the rector's sons, and took the opportunity of
laying my hand on his breast. He was also in
evening dress. In fact we were all so. Soon I heard
that there was to be a ball. But it appeared that
there was no room in which they could dance, all the
floors were so uneven, and most of them so rotten.
And there were no lights, except some dip-candles,
which flared in the draught from the broken windows,
and stank horribly. But—this is the real point of
my dream—everybody was doing their best to appear
in excellent spirits, and to seem not to remark all the

contretemps and unpleasantnesses. Some ignored them entirely, others whilst partly admitting them, with a light laugh, turned them into easy jokes. All were talking, and laughing, and jesting as gaily as possible. Only in the voice of every individual without exception, howsoever cleverly they were labouring to disguise their real feelings, I detected an undertone of misgiving which assured me that they all felt exactly what I did, a horrible oppression, occasioned by the assurance of something sinister around us, which we, each of us, were too terrified to confess. In the midst of this I simply awoke, but I found myself still under the influence of the same indefinite fear or misgiving which had oppressed me in my dream. And I have not since been able to shake it off. But I can guess that you are smiling at me."

"No. I am wondering what you eat for luncheon."

Eustace laughed.

"That is the same thing, is it not?" he said. "Only I had nothing for luncheon different from what I usually take, a few buscuits and a glass of claret. Your question is the very one I first asked myself. Seriously, however, this stupid dream has left a strong impression on me."

After a minute he continued :

"It is puerile to believe in presentiments in the way in which the superstitious, the ignorant, and the silly believe in them ; and yet I am disposed to think that in some ways cur instincts are not without a real prescience of danger, the more because that would be easy to explain. First there might be a dim consciousness of something amiss in ourselves, weakness, timidity, or misapprehension ; all which are dangerous things. And secondly, seeing how roughly we reason, it would be quite possible for our instincts to be affected by a number of trifling things, all of which had individually escaped the observation of our reason, though taken in the aggregate they might form a serious whole. And that is just what I feel to be passing in myself at present, a dim apprehension of instinct that gives me a presentiment of something sinister very near."

"You have been sitting in a draught, old man, and dreaming at the same time of our tumble-down place here, and of Miss Hardwick's being ill," said Warrington. "Come now, suppose we have a game of chess."

"By all means," said Eustace, rousing himself.

So they went to the library, and sat down to play.

"What are you going to give me?" said Warrington.

"Only a bishop to-night."

The play then began, and Frank Warrington checkmated three times running.

"I'll only give you two pawns," said Eustace.

But he still lost the game.

"It is of no use," he said, gently pushing the board aside. "I am under some influence from which I cannot free myself."

"Odd!" remarked Warrington to himself. "For the first time in his life, Eustace's imagination has got the better of his reason."

CHAPTER XXXIV

WHETHER there was any truth in Eustace Warrington's ingenious theories respecting the possible causes of his sinister presentiments; or whether his mental disquietude was simply a case—rare with him—of that apparently spontaneous depression of spirits to which almost every one is from time to time subject (for to conceive of any occult or supernatural agency miraculously warning Eustace Warrington of dangers in the future would be absurd), this, at any rate, is certain, that the realities which were going on at Cliff Cottage surpassed in horror all the quaint imaginations of Eustace Warrington's postprandial dreams.

Maud Gainsborough was carrying out her resolution.

Every day Lily drank in one way or another her tiny fraction of a grain of aconite; and the drug did its work slowly and steadily. Gently it reduced her to a condition of so profound a prostration that any consequence began to appear possible, a fatal decay, perhaps a slow recovery, or even a sudden collapse.

The widow, meanwhile, watched with anxiety the effect of every dose.

Within the last few days, a new fear had presented itself. If she proceeded too rapidly she might awaken suspicion: and she had never had any intention of proceeding rapidly. But it occurred to her now, that if she undermined the girl's life very slowly it was possible that some one would be found to declare that the climate of Lynham was killing Lily, and to propose her immediate removal. By-and-by any one who pleased might recommend removal. Lily would die before she could be removed. But just at present it would be too early to hazard a fatal dose. So the widow, haunted with a perpetual misgiving as to what might any day occur, was doing her best to steer a middle course, to undermine the girl's life as rapidly as she dared, and yet not too fast, for fear of attracting attention.

There were moments, and not moments only, long hours, when the task that she had set herself revolted her, made her blood run cold to her heart, and turned her face to the colour of ashes.

After she had given her cousin a dose in the morning she would go back to her own room, and, dropping into a chair, sit motionless with her head thrown down on her arms folded on the table, morally stunned. Left alone in the evening after Lily had gone to bed, she found it impossible to remain still, and tired of pacing the room went out into the garden, and thence, afraid of being noticed by the servants, down to the little, lonely beach, where, assured of not being watched, she would walk up and down, up and down, up and down by the hour, grateful for the darkness and the coolness of the sea air. And when she returned to the house how haggard she was! So haggard that she shrank from seeing herself in the glass. At night, in spite of all the fatigue she gave herself, sleep became difficult. The tension of her nerves, constantly over-strung, refusing to relax itself in natural repose.

It was a grim, ghastly task that she had set herself in the destruction of this girl, and it taxed and overtaxed all the will and energy she possessed. But she persevered.

Externally she was still very kind to Lily; devoted to her. There had been, for a few days, a slight break in the affectionateness with which she had treated the girl on her first return from town. When her courage proved for a moment insufficient for the perpetration of the crime she meditated, her temper became uneven and disturbed, and her way with Lily uncertain, at times even brusque. But, now that she had once more resolutely embarked on her crime, her manner recovered all its exceeding gentleness. Her attention, her kindness, and her lavish expenditure on the girl of the tenderest signs of affection were untiring.

"Poor girl," she would say to herself. "It is hard upon her, and I do feel for her, having to die so young. And I wish the stuff did not affect her spirits. If I knew of anything that would keep her bright and happy, I would infinitely rather use it. It makes me miserable to see her struggling with herself, to keep back the tears that come without any cause to her eyes. Poor Lily! It seems hard to believe that I am doing her a kindness, and saving her from years of pain and misery But, after all, what must be, must be."

That was Maud Gainsborough's motto now : "What must be, must be."

Dr. Gregg had resumed his daily visits. Marasmus was the last long word he had found out for what was going on at Cliff Cottage. Marasmus and a considerable affection of the heart. Maud amused herself with pretending to think he might be mistaken, and she quoted what the London physician had said. But all that only confirmed the doctor in his own opinion.

However, he began to shake his head, and to look exceedingly serious.

And well he might. Lily wasted, wasted like wax before the fire. The actual loss of vital force was slow : from one day to another there was scarcely a perceptible difference. But the girl was utterly indisposed to make the least struggle for existence, and was sinking with indifference into her grave. So far as Dr. Gregg could see, there was nothing to be done but to go on calling, putting down his visits, and giving her things that could do her no harm. She had come to have no appetite, and ate nothing to speak of; and so, for one thing, was in reality starving.

The languor and indifference that had got possession of her was astonishing. Her will seemed to be more feeble even than her strength. Now and then she was capricious, wilful even, and intractable, and would then insist upon doing or attempting to do what she chose; but, for the most part, she was merely reluctant to exert herself to make the smallest movement. Mrs. Gainsborough took her for easy drives in the pony-carriage, but the drives only tired her and made her head ache. And once she crawled as far as Lynham and back. Later, only to stand for a few minutes appeared to be a fatigue to her, and the instant she could she dropped into a chair. If left to herself, she hardly moved for hours together; and would sit a whole afternoon, almost motionless, reclining on a low lounging chair in the fresh air by the open drawing-room window. She had again, on rising, been seized with a sudden vertigo, and had fallen twice on the floor. She began to take her breakfast in bed, and her cousin assisted her to rise, standing ready to catch her in her arms if she should be giddy.

"I don't like this giddiness on rising," said Maud Gainsborough to the doctor, after it had occurred once or twice. "Do you really think that that can be occasioned merely by general debility, and a slight affection of the heart?"

"Certainly In these cases there is very often a certain degree of giddiness on first awaking; not always. And, as for the affection of the heart, feel for yourself; see how abnormal and irregular her pulse is."

It was so certainly. a rapid pulse, small and soft and irregular.

Some days she appeared much worse. Then the widow the next morning diminished even the small fraction of a grain she usually gave her. When Lily recovered a little, she returned to the usual dose, but never exceeded it.

At the end of about ten days an incident occurred of a graver character. Lily was in miserable spirits. and had been crying in the morning. Now in the afternoon she was sitting under the verandah, a piteous picture of exhaustion. Maud was doing some fancy work, and presently put it down to look for her embroidery scissors which she had mislaid.

"I know where they are, Maud. I saw them upstairs. I'll go and get them for you," said Lily. And she made a movement to rise.

"No. You stay where you are, dear. I'll get them." replied the widow

But Lily wished to go, and when her cousin would have insisted, became cross. At times the depression from which she was suffering reacted a good deal on her temper and judgment, and made her unmanageable and petulant.

"I'm not so ill that I cannot go upstairs," she said now. "Goodness knows I am weak enough without your wanting to make me out still worse?"

And with that she rose and went to fetch the scissors, her cousin not caring to thwart her.

The widow waited three minutes, five minutes; and Lily did not come with the scissors! Maud Gainsborough rose and went upstairs after her.

She found her lying on the floor of the landing. supporting her head on her hand, and panting for breath.

She had run upstairs, not quickly, and on reaching the top her breath suddenly failed her; she could not

say whether she felt exactly dizzy or faint, but she
had sunk on the floor, just as she was. She explained
it all, drawing her breath with some difficulty

Maud put her to bed. And the next day gave her
no dose, and the next day only half a dose. She had
not relented, but she believed that she had reached a
point where, if she did not mean to cut the matter short,
she must allow her patient an interval of repose.

So for a few days Lily grew no worse. She even
improved a little. Too little for Dr. Gregg to perceive, but not too little for Maud's watchful eyes to
notice.

One of these days Maud would have had her take
a drive, but Lily declined. She would rather walk in
the garden. The widow, feeling tolerably secure
about her for the present, left her therefore. and went
out to pay some calls. When she was gone, Lily
changed her mind and took it into her head after all
to go for a drive. Why not? She would have the
pony-carriage and drive into Lynham. So she gave
the order and went to dress.

When the carriage came round, she set off gaily
enough. The tiny excitement had given a fillip to
her spirits. She drove into the town and did some
shopping, and then turned towards the parade.

In the street she passed Warrington, walking
slowly in the direction of Lynhurst. A sudden flush
suffused her face, followed by an equally sudden
pallor. The most trifling emotion now made her
flush or pale. She reached the parade and drove
twice up and down, and then turned the ponies' heads
homeward again. The encounter with Warrington
had put her out of humour with her drive.

R

CHAPTER XXXV

EUSTACE WARRINGTON was in the town that afternoon.
He had walked in with his brother, but remained
behind him to attend to some affairs of his own.   He
had grown quite familiar with the whole place, and
rather liked to be left to go about like the rest of the
world.   There was something indeed a little strange
in the spectacle of this man of educated appearance
and gentlemanly dress occasionally feeling his way
with his cane along the kerb, like a blind beggar.
But it was only here and there that Eustace was
reduced to this expedient and he took a pride in
being independent.

Only presently, crossing a street which he had
assured himself by his ear was clear, he was suddenly
startled by the sound of some vehicle approaching
at a very rapid pace.   The vehicle was, in reality, a
butcher's cart without any driver.   Some boys had
entertained themselves with scaring the horse, whilst
it was waiting at a gate, and the brute had bolted.
Now it was coming down the street in a zig-zag way
with the empty cart rattling noisily behind.   The
sound, coming first from one side of the street and
then from the other, perplexed Eustace, who was
near the middle of the road, and he stopped, aware
that the driver, keeping on the left of the street,
should pass behind him.   The next instant the noisy
vehicle was upon him and, at the same instant that
some one called out to him in words he could not
understand, he sprang back, just in time to escape
being run over, but not in time to escape being
knocked down.

The box of the wheel struck his knee.   His leg
gave way under him, and he fell, and the horse and
cart passed on.

A little crowd gathered round him; the chemist from over the way, and several other shopkeepers, and the man who had called out, and some passers-by.

Eustace's knee gave him great pain; and he was unable to rise. Three men took him up gently, to carry him into the chemist's shop.

"Send word as quickly as you can to my brother," he said. "He has gone home to Lynhurst."

At the same instant Lily drove up, and, seeing the crowd, stopped to inquire what had happened.

"Blind gentleman run over, Miss."

A sudden horrible fear smote Lily's heart. Mr. Warrington was so attached to his brother.

"Is he hurt?" she asked, breathlessly.

"It's Mr. Eustace Warrington, Miss," answered another man standing near. "He was not run over; only knocked down; but he has hurt his knee."

And, whilst he spoke, Eustace, carried in the arms of the men, in her hearing repeated his request.

"Send at once to Mr. Warrington at Lynhurst."

"Tell Mr. Eustace Warrington that I just now passed Mr. Warrington, and that I will drive after him and send him back," said Lily to the man who had spoken to her. And, giving her ponies a flick, she drove off at a sharp trot in the direction of Lynhurst.

Warrington had walked on slowly. He was not a mile out of Lynham when he heard a trap coming along the road behind him.

A minute later Lily suddenly drew up short at his side, almost throwing her ponies on their haunches.

Warrington stopped, regarding her with surprise.

"Mr. Warrington: I beg your pardon," she said, hurriedly: "but Mr. Eustace Warrington has met with an accident; not a serious one: and he is asking for you: he is at Campbell's the chemist in New Street."

How it made her heart leap to be again speaking to this man! The blood had rushed into her face and scalded her cheeks, but she could not help it. All the way she had been in a flutter of agitation, thinking of what she should say, wondering whether she would overtake Warrington, and really once more speak to him face to face, assuredly for the last time; and for once be able to do him a tiny service. Now that the moment was come, and that he was here listening, with his dark eyes fixed on hers, the reality surpassed her anticipation.

He had raised his hat to her as she spoke. Now he asked, anxiously:

"What has happened?"

"Mr. Eustace Warrington was crossing the road, and was knocked down by a cart. I came up immediately afterwards. He was asking for you, and I drove on at once. I believe there is no occasion for any serious alarm, but I heard that he had hurt one of his knees."

"I am extremely obliged to you; I really am extremely obliged to you."

He spoke hurriedly, a little embarrassed as it seemed, and again raising his hat, turned to go back to Lynham.

"But, Mr. Warrington," exclaimed Lily, turning on her seat, for he was already striding away, "won't you—won't you take the ponies and drive in? You will get there so much sooner; and I fear that your brother is in pain."

"Your brother"—she ought to have said "Mr. Eustace Warrington"—but a little touch of nature brought the more familiar term to her lips, and she did not herself notice it.

She rose to leave the carriage.

"But you?" asked Warrington.

"I'll wait over there under the trees."

She pointed to a seat a little way down the road, under the shade of some elms.

"You can send me the pony-carriage back."

"Really, but this very kind of you," said Warrington, half hesitating to accept her offer.

She had her foot on the step of the carriage, but was half afraid to trust herself to step out unaided. Warrington saw her embarrassment, and held out his hand to assist her, and she placed her hand in his—his touch thrilling every nerve in her.

He took the opportunity the moment gave him to look closely at her. The piteous sight! This pretty girl! A great pang of pity wrung his heart. What a wreck the poor little thing was! How wan! how pale! how thin! Her cheeks as white as lilies; the little bones cutting sharp angles in her young face; her eyelids so heavy; her great eyes full of a desolate languor; the small hand that lay in his a mere handful of poor little bones; and her arm so powerless that it was a wonder how she could have managed the ponies.

What Eustace had said a few nights before came into his mind. And he asked himself:

"Did I really come down here and destroy this poor girl's peace?"

Not willingly would he have done such a thing. There was a natural chivalry in him that would rather that he should have loved her, and have been jilted again, than have broken the poor girl's heart like this.

What was it that made him feel that now, at this moment, if he might have done it, he would have liked to draw the little broken thing into his own strong arms and to have held her there against his breast, and to have said to her something—what could it be?—that should have again given her life and courage, as he had given her courage that day of their first meeting on the beach.

But she was safely on the ground. All that both of them had felt had occupied less time by far than it has taken to relate. And she had said "Thanks," and he had let her hand go. And now she stood aside to leave him to step into the pony-carriage.

He did so at once. He was anxious about his brother, and yet he was loth to leave her to wait alone by the roadside.

"Are you sure that I ought to leave you here?" he asked.

"Pray do not apologize."

"I am more obliged to you than I can say."

For all answer a little bow—a cold, formal little bow.

Wheeling the ponies round, Warrington drove away. He was soon in Lynham, thanks to the nimble little beasts. Eustace's knee-cap had been displaced by the blow from the wheel. Warrington quickly made arrangements for his being taken to Lynhurst, in the way that would give him the least pain, and then hurried to the pony-carriage to drive back to Lily. He might, indeed, have sent the carriage to her by some one else a quarter of an hour sooner, and he chided himself for selfishness for not having done so. But he wished himself to take her back her carriage. He could not have exactly said why

He was anxious about his brother, and yet, somehow, all the way he was thinking of Lily Hardwick.

He found her waiting under the trees at the place she had named. During his absence she had been saying to herself: "Now, if he brings the ponies back himself, that will be acknowledging that he appreciates what I did. If he sends them back by some one else, that will be because he does not care." Only as the delay grew longer she became sure that he would himself come back with them. And here he was at last.

Not that their meeting had any meaning now. That was all over.

As he drew near she rose, and came a few steps to meet him.

" I have arranged everything for my brother. And I do not know how I am to thank you," ho said.

" You are very welcome. I hope Mr. Eustace Warrington is not seriously hurt."

The tone was perfectly polite, but a perfect stranger might have used it.

" We fear that his knee-cap has been dislocated— that it may prove a long and rather painful affair."

"I am very sorry to hear it." Still the same reserved tone.

And she moved to step into the carriage.

" May I assist you ? " said Warrington.

" Thanks."

And she accepted the support of his arm.

Then taking her seat she gathered up the reins.

And then with a little inclination of her head, whilst Warrington raised his hat, she spoke a word to the ponies, turned them round, and drove away

Half a minute Warrington stood looking after her. Then he walked on toward Lynhurst.

He was disappointed. He had fancied that, after he had brought her back her pony-carriage, what had occurred might furnish an opportunity for a reconciliation. He had hoped it, too. She had behaved very prettily, very kindly, in coming to tell him of his brother's misfortune, and in lending him her little trap. After that he thought that she might accept some sort of apology, and then they would be friends again. But evidently her intention was nothing of the kind.

He was sorry for it. He would have liked to be able to show her that he had deeply felt her kindness.

And, poor girl ! How ill she seemed to be !

He would not have believed that a mere disappointment in love could have so utterly broken a girl's life. And certainly he himself was not worth what she was suffering. She must have been very much attached to him—very much more than he had ever suspected.

He began to think with himself that if, instead of making her understand that he had not the least capacity for caring for her, he had proposed to her and made her his wife, he would at least have done a good action. And he would have had a charming little wife, charmingly pretty, and charmingly bright, and with a good heart, too.

If he could have foreseen all that would ensue, he really did not know that he would not rather have married her, than have let the poor little thing go and break her heart in this way for a man not worth it.

<hr>

CHAPTER XXXVI.

" Mrs. Gainsborough's compliments, sir, and she would like to know how Mr. Eustace Warrington is this morning."

Thus the servant coming into the room where Frank Warrington was sitting by his brother's bedside.

It was the second day after Eustace's accident. The injury he had received had turned out after

all to be more serious than was at first supposed.
There was even some danger of Eustace's being
lame; and Warrington was contemplating with
disquietude the prospect of his brother's being
perhaps deprived of the pedestrian exercise, which,
as well as being good for his health, was one of his
principal pleasures. Dr. Gregg had been sent for at
once, and had done what he could. Whether he
had done what he should was another question, and
one about which neither of the brothers felt altogether satisfied. In any case, there was no doubt
that Eustace would have to remain for a long time
in bed, and to bear a good deal of pain. Warrington
had had a bed made up for him in one of the large
unoccupied rooms. The place was bare and comfort-
less in appearance, the few pieces of furniture dis-
consolately scattered at wide distances from one
another, and the paper partly torn off the blank
walls. But none of these things mattered to Eustace; and the room was large and cool and airy, and
filled in this summer-tide with the fresh fragrance of
the trees outside.

Eustace was in great pain, and had hardly slept
at all during the night. On the previous day he
had been better. Warrington had read to him for
several hours, and, though suffering a good deal,
Eustace had been able to give his attention to what
was read, and had been amused. But this morning the pain was too acute for him to be able to
listen.

He was bearing it all very patiently; with his
usual good spirits making a jest even of his suffer-
ings, jokingly expressing a hope that a series of
sinister accidents might not be about to make him,
as well as blind, lame, deaf, dumb, and insensible;
and laughing at his brother for blaming himself—as
he had done severely—for having left him alone in

Lynham, and so having been indirectly the cause of what had ensued. " As if, my dear Frank," he said, laughing, " it was not all my own fault ; seeing that I infinitely prefer having my own way, and taking the consequences. to being always dependent either upon you or upon any one else. A weakness on my part, I know, but one of which this little contretemps is not going to cure me, I assure you."

At the same time, though not in any way alarmed about himself, the pain he was suffering strongly disposed him to agree with his brother that they should seek some advice more trustworthy than that of Dr. Gregg.

" What am I to say to Mrs. Gainsborough, Eustace ?" asked Warrington. " I suppose it must be that you are in more pain this morning ? "

" Yes. Unluckily you may say that with a good deal of truth."

" Who has come ? " asked Warrington.

" The man-servant, sir."

" I'll go down and speak to him myself," said Warrington. And he added, in explanation to Eustace, " I want to know how Miss Hardwick is."

" Ah, he wants to know how Miss Hardwick is." said Eustace to himself, as soon as the other had left the room. " I wonder whether Frank's eyes will ever be opened respecting Miss Hardwick. He is a deal blinder than I. These people who can see are all alike in that respect. It is a most extraordinary thing. And they have no sense of touch or hearing to compensate for it. I really sometimes think that we are the better off, after all."

Meanwhile Warrington went to the hall to speak to Mrs. Gainsborough's servant.

The momentary rencontre between himself and Lily Hardwick, of which his brother's accident had been the occasion, had left an impression upon

Frank Warrington altogether disproportionate to its brevity and the simple nature of all that had passed. The girl's behaviour; her driving off to find him the moment she had learned what had happened; the crimson that flushed her face as she addressed him; the loan of her carriage; her wan features; the wasted little hand she had laid in his; her reserve, and the air of an utter stranger with which she parted from him; every one of these had furnished him with matter for reflection that had since occupied his mind every moment that it was released from his immediate anxiety about his brother.

Really, without in the least suspecting it, Lily Hardwick had again played a master-stroke. She had compelled a man, who was not indifferent to her, to notice and admire her, and at the same time had refused him any opportunity to express what he felt. The skill of the most accomplished of coquettes could not have gone much farther.

And her master-stroke was producing its effect.

There is no surer way of parting love than to part the lovers. The expedient is almost infallible. It is almost as difficult for men and women to continue to love those whom they never see, as to fall in love with those whom they have never seen. Young people who value each other's affections ought to be warned of this, to take it to heart, and to remember that howsoever highly they may rate their own powers of constancy, they will be very foolish to trust to the sincerest passion to withstand what is really a law of Nature: that those who are parted cease to love.

After all, that is a gentle, tender law of the great mother's, made to spare many hearts, and a law, too, with a mighty reason. For that the young should love is the most important thing in the whole great world. Everything else, politics, law, order, science,

art, literature, philosophy, virtue, and truth are in
importance, all of them taken together, just a mere
bagatelle compared with the love of the young.
Humanity got along without any of these things for
many thousand years, the greater part of humanity
gets along without most of them still. But without
love, plain, unsophisticated passionate love, the whole
future of the race would not be worth sixty years.
And so if young people are thwarted in their love,
parted and kept out of the way of bringing their
passion for each other to happiness, Nature (who is
not to be thwarted) gives them oblivion, mostly very
promptly (she does not stand upon ceremony, Nature),
and a new love. If she did not, how many people
would have children? In how many cases is a marriage the wedding of two first loves? So, seeing
that this is Nature's way, let all whom it may concern
take the fact to heart, and keep in sight of those
whose love they prize.

But, to resume; when, on the other hand, young
people who are attached to each other, after having
been parted only for a little time, insufficient seriously to affect their passion, unexpectedly find
themselves again thrown into each other's society,
then the converse takes place: there is a sharp re-
action, a few minutes suffice to repair, and more than
to repair, any coolness time and separation may have
produced in their mutual attachment.

This was exactly what had happened to Warrington. The chagrin he had at first felt, when Lily Hardwick cut him, had to some extent worn off with time.
But now that he had again exchanged half a dozen
sentences with her, felt the touch of her hand, looked
into her wistful eyes, and then seen her turn away,
relentlessly determined to be for ever a stranger to
him, he discovered that there was something between
her and him stronger than he had suspected.

He found Mrs. Gainsborough's servant waiting in the hall.

" Will you please," said Warrington. "give my compliments to Mrs. Gainsborough and tell her that Mr. Eustace Warrington has spent a bad night, and is this morning in great pain ; but that we hope that everything is going on satisfactorily. And, by the way. how is Miss Hardwick this morning ? "

"Not so well, sir."

Warrington returned to his brother.

" Miss Hardwick is worse," he said, briefly.

That was all. but the cadence of his voice was grave.

And Eustace heard him cross the room and sit down by the window.

Later the doctor called. and had nothing very definite to say : " Sometimes in these cases there is very acute pain, in fact generally." After luncheon Eustace slept a little and Warrington went out to take a turn in the avenue.

When a man is for ever thinking of one little face ; when he is for ever dreaming of the touch of one small hand ; when nothing can divert his mind from five minutes spent the day before yesterday with a girl with weary eyes ; when the pain of one little heart is more to him than the pain of all the world ; when the sadness of one little breast seems sadder to him than all the sadness he himself has ever known ; when he begins to think to himself what he would not gladly do, or suffer, to bring the smiles back into that little face, to drive the pain from that little heart, to restore the light to the once bright eyes— what is then the matter with the man ?

What is the matter with him ? The question must be a very difficult one to answer, for Frank Warrington walked up and down in the avenue, and could come to no conclusion.

But in the evening, after dinner, smoking alone under the shaky old verandah, he confessed the truth to himself at last.

"I have been in love with that girl for the last six months or more—that is the fact."

There are moments in the life of a man, when he receives the impression of a curtain being suddenly drawn aside, displaying an unexpected panorama. All that he sees has been there for a long time, only the curtain has hid it. The effect upon him is a shock of sharp surprise, heightened by the fact that he knows what has suddenly been revealed to him is already of long standing.

It was such an impression that Frank Warrington received this evening, and a long time he walked up and down on the uneven flags, reviewing in the new light suddenly thrown upon it his own history of the last eight months.

He summed it all up for himself very briefly at last.

"Eustace told me how it would be with me, and I would not believe him. The girl, too, fell straight in love with me, and I have given myself the trouble to break her heart. Because my cousin, who did not love me, and with whom I should most probably not have been happy, jilted me, I have, of my own free will, coolly flung away a charming girl who does love me, as charming a girl as any man could ask for as his wife: and, having been duped by one woman, I have behaved like a brute to another. Certainly I am a fool."

And now?

That is always the great question. The past, nothing can be done with that. In the present something is always possible.

Leaning against the pillar of the verandah, Warrington was half disposed to go straight to Cliff

Cottage. even without going upstairs to see his brother. and to ask to see Miss Hardwick, to tell her that he had been a blind idiot, but that he had found his senses at last, and that he was come to ask her to remember that they had been friends.

Only this did not seem to be a very hopeful speech to make to a young lady. And the more he pondered what he really should say for himself, the more difficult it appeared to find anything reasonable. He could not go point-blank to the girl and tell her, " I love you."

And he began to think of the other side of the question : " How would Miss Hardwick reply ? "

Suppose she were to reply that she had no desire to be loved out of compassion.

That decided him. Lily Hardwick would refuse any advances he might make. He had found out the truth too late. He might have had her only a few weeks ago, and the girl would not have broken her heart. Now—she would refuse him.

He was quite right. If he had gone to see her that evening, supposing that he had managed to see her, which was unlikely, Lily would have told him that their acquaintance was at an end.

In addition to which she would not have lived another forty-eight hours.

Mrs. Gainsborough had heard of the adventure of driving after Warrington to tell him of his brother's accident. She found in the proceeding a significance quite different from any that either Lily or Warrington had given it, and had already taken counsel with herself what she would do if this last move of her cousin's should have consequences.

So it was well that Warrington did not act upon his first impulse. Instead, he returned to his brother.

Eustace was in a little less pain. Warrington sat down by his bed, and they began to talk of the advisability of consulting some one more experienced than Dr. Gregg. If the thing could be managed Warrington would have had Eustace go up to town and have the best advice procurable. It turned out that Eustace himself had thought of the same thing. The only question was how he would bear the journey. Warrington proposed to bring over a well-known surgeon from the neighbouring county town, and to take his advice on the subject. If he thought Eustace could be moved, they would go up to town together, and remain there until Eustace was well.

"Only," objected Eustace, "if this is going to be an affair of some months, you will want to come down here to look after the place."

"The place must look after itself," said Warrington. He moved restlessly, and Eustace heard it. Then he added, "The truth is, I shall be glad to get away. I don't know that I won't sell the place, after all."

Again he stopped, but resumed after a minute:

"You may as well know all about it. I don't want to make secrets. You remember possibly a conversation that we had a few days ago; on the day of your ominous dream?"

"We talked about Miss Hardwick?"

"Yes."

"My dear fellow, do not say any more. I perfectly understand what you mean. You have discovered that, after all, I was right about you and Miss Hardwick."

"Yes," bluntly

"Well, I can't tell you how glad I am to hear it."

"Only, unfortunately, you see I have recovered my senses a little too late," remarked Warrington, sombrely.

" How so ?   What do you mean? "

Warrington explained what he meant, with which the reader is already acquainted.

But Eustace interrupted him.

" Look here, Frank, you have been blinder than a mole.   You have found that out at last.   For once, just believe that I can see some things.   Go, the first thing to-morrow morning, to Miss Hardwick.   Think nothing about what you will say to her till you are with her, and then say the first thing that comes to the tip of your tongue."

In a way, the advice was good advice.   Warrington could see that.   But he told his brother frankly that he did not believe he should follow it.

And he did not : fortunately for poor Lily, whose immediate fate, as has been said, was just at this juncture hanging upon a thread.

CHAPTER XXXVII.

INSTEAD of going to Cliff Cottage, Warrington, on the following morning, directly after Dr. Gregg's visit, which was early, went off by rail to try to find the medical man of whom he and his brother had spoken on the previous day.   He was fortunate enough to bring him back with him in the afternoon. A consultation followed, with the result that it was decided that Eustace should at once be taken to town, the medical man being of opinion that the journey ought not, with proper precautions, to do him any harm.

By noon the next day, the brothers had both left Lynham.

S

The news of their departure reached Cliff Cottage the same evening.

Maud Gainsborough at first hardly believed her ears ; and then drew, secretly, a long breath of relief. For the last three days she had been apprehending the new complications which she believed must inevitably arise now that her cousin had chosen to renew her acquaintance with Frank Warrington. But once more chance had proved her ally. Warrington was gone away. If Eustace's case proved only half as slow as the medical men predicted, long before the brothers returned the day of anxieties about Lily would be over.

She herself took the news to Lily.

"Mr. Warrington and his brother have gone away to town. They left at noon to-day quite suddenly. Mr. Eustace Warrington is to be under the care of some celebrated surgeon."

Lily was lying on the drawing-room sofa, to all appearance only half conscious, in reality prostrated with a maddening headache. She made no answer, but she said to herself:

"So, then, it is all over !"

She was in too much pain to think, but some vague, straggling impressions passed across her aching brain. She would liked to have seen Warrington once more, just once more : perhaps to have put her hand in his, and to have said, "Good-bye." This morning—was it this morning, or yesterday ?— when she was a little better, she had been resolving that the accident which had occurred should not become the ground of a reconciliation. But, what had that to do with it ? Why, that perhaps it would have been better if she had relented a little : only because she would never see him again. Never ! never ! never ! seemed to beat upon her aching brain like the strokes of a hammer Before he came back she would be dead. She was sinking every day. They tried to persuade her that she was not, but she knew better. She would die. And she would never see Frank Warrington again. If, instead of only bowing to him that afternoon, she had said " Good-bye," that would have been better.

But what was the use of wishing that she had done differently? The opportunity was past. And she could not think: her head gave her too much pain.

Maud had sat down by her side.

" Perhaps it is just as well that they are gone, dear. I mean, darling, that perhaps you will feel it all less, now that Mr. Warrington is gone away."

But the girl still said nothing.

" Are you very ill to-night, dear? " asked Mrs. Gainsborough, bending over her.

" Oh, for goodness sake, Maud, do not speak to me. You put me to torture," exclaimed the girl, impatiently. " I am mad with headache."

" Where is the pain, dear? "

" At the back of my head."

Maud rose and glided away from her, saying to herself:

" Yes, I know it does bring a headache at the back of the head. I am sure I wish that it did not. It is no pleasure to me to make the poor girl suffer so."

By the window she paused and looked out.

" Three months," she reflected in herself. " It would be something about that time, the doctor said, before Mr. Eustace Warrington will be well. Three months—August, September, October. The trees will be in all their glorious autumn tints, but the days will have become shorter, and we shall have fires. There will be chrysanthemums in the garden,

some dahlias, and the last of the roses. And Lily
will have been buried weeks before that. People
will be beginning to forget all about her. Perhaps
the little marble cross will be already standing above
her grave. *He* and I might meet by it some day;
that will be worth remembering. The hunting season
will be beginning. And I shall have found those
papers. We shall have all the winter before us, the
days of thick furs, and of afternoons that turn soon
into twilight, and of confidences by the bright fire-
side. And I shall be in black. Black always becomes
me. And I shall be able to talk to him touchingly
about poor Lily, so touchingly. I shall soon make
him come to me. The magnetism will be stronger
than he will be able to resist."

And, with her pulse heightened with pleasurable
anticipation, the young widow turned from the
window, and took up her fancy work.

It turned out to be a good thing that Eustace had
come to London. Dr. Gregg had not gone to work
in the right way at all, and his patient would, in all
probability, have become permanently lame under
his treatment. After a little consideration, Eustace
preferred, rather than to be nursed in lodgings, to
become a paying patient in one of the larger hos-
pitals. He got more attention and better advice in
that way than was procurable in any other manner.
and, besides, he was amused with the idea of spending his enforced imprisonment in the study of a
hitherto unknown phase of life. His brother took
rooms near the hospital, and every day spent a number of hours with him : and, though Eustace suffered
a good deal of pain, the cure of his knee, under the
careful watching and nursing of the hospital, pro-
gressed surely and satisfactorily.

More than once he broached to his brother the
subject of Miss Hardwick. But he found that War-

rington was disinclined to talk about her, and invariably at once changed the conversation to some other topic. Warrington had thought a good deal about her since he had been in town. That goes without saying. But he was unwilling to converse on a subject about which he still remained very undecided. He had not, in fact, been able to make up his mind how a man in his position ought to behave.

Two courses were open to him. One course was, seeing that he had had the stupidity to reject the affection of a girl for whom he had formed a sincere attachment, to cure himself of his passion for her as best he could ; to call time and circumstances to his aid to efface a love he had forfeited the right to plead. The other course was simply to wait and see what the future might bring forth ; perhaps some day to return to Lynham to earn the right to press his suit, and then to see if, after all, Miss Hardwick would perhaps pardon and accept him.

Of the two courses his inclination was, on the whole, towards the former. There is a disposition on the part of every man of really honourable feelings to forbid himself the love of a woman, though he may be sincerely attached to her, the instant he detects anything to blame in the history of his passion.

But for the present, at any rate, the course he was pursuing was the latter, a mere waiting upon uncertainty.

He was in no particular good humour with himself, a trifle dull and out of spirits, and disposed to smoke a great deal, and to say little, as he had done after his cousin jilted him.

Eustace formed his own opinion about his brother's despondency He believed that Warrington, having found out that he was in love with Lily Hardwick, had come to London with the deliberate intention of curing himself of his liking, in accordance with the resolution he had so often expressed never again to fall under the influence of a woman.

Eustace regretted the resolution. He could have given more good reasons than one for honestly wishing that his brother would marry Lily Hardwick. She was a good girl, and would make an excellent wife. If he was at all a judge of character, she was just the wife Frank should have. Her gentle companionship would do Frank a world of good, and with their two fortunes, which were fairly equal, they would be comfortably off, and Warrington in a position to complete the redemption of his estate. For his own part, Eustace would gain a sister-in-law whom he could sincerely like, and the girl would marry a man she loved.

But Eustace said nothing about all these things to Warrington. He knew his brother's temperament. Warrington was a man to whom it was useless, under certain circumstances, to say anything. So Eustace held his peace, and patiently left events to go their own way.

Meanwhile day succeeded day, and in a manner that was eventless and a trifle dull, more so for Warrington than for Eustace, who had a knack of being always amused at what was going on around him, a fortnight passed by.

Then one afternoon, quite unexpectedly, Warrington ran up against Anthony Gainsborough in Pall Mall.

" My dear Warrington ; you in town ! " exclaimed Mr. Gainsborough.

" Well, I was just going to say the same thing to you." replied Warrington. " I imagined that in this month of August you must be either on the Norwegian coast, or up in the Baltic, or on some other voyage or another."

" No. We are all at Twickenham."

Warrington noticed the "we," and knew what it meant.

"Can you come over and dine with us?" continued Anthony Gainsborough.

"Well, you know that I had rather not," replied Warrington, frankly.

To change the subject he began to explain what had brought him to town.

"Have you had luncheon?" said Anthony Gainsborough. "No? Well, come and have luncheon with me at the 'Travellers,' and we will have a talk."

So the two men went to the club together. After luncheon Anthony Gainsborough again tried the strength of his persuasive powers in a pressing appeal to Warrington to come to dinner.

"What you are doing, Warrington, is not right," he said at last. "Your cousins are asking—begging to be permitted to make you *l'amende honorable*, and you refuse them—two young girls. It is not right, my boy. But if you won't, you won't."

Howbeit, Frank Warrington was obdurate.

"Whom do you think I met in town this morning?" asked Anthony Gainsborough of his nieces at dinner.

Neither of the girls could guess.

"Frank Warrington."

"Uncle Tony!" exclaimed both the girls simultaneously And Essie went on: "But why did you not bring him back with you to dinner?"

"I did my best to persuade him, I assure you," answered Anthony Gainsborough, "but he is uncommonly shy of you two young ladies, and I could do nothing with him."

"I wish I could see him," remarked Essie.

"You think you could persuade him?" asked her uncle.

Essie's only answer was to repeat :

" I wish I could see him."

If it had depended upon Warrington, that she would certainly never have done. Howbeit, very few things depend upon a man's own will, happily for men, and she and Warrington met before the end of the next week.

Warrington went in the evening to the theatre. He had a taste for the drama, and, having had no opportunity for indulging his taste at Lynham, had several times lately, when the hospital regulations precluded him from being with his brother in the evenings, dropped in at such houses as were open.

He was in the stalls. When the piece began, the three stalls nearest to him in the same row were unoccupied. Towards the end of the first act, a movement on his left aroused his attention to the fact that some one was coming down the row, probably the occupants of the empty stalls. He looked round casually.

Anthony Gainsborough and the two Misses Chesterfield.

So what he had refused to accord, in spite of all the justest and most kindly persuasions, chance compelled him to submit to without consulting his tastes at all. A thing that in this world very often happens.

Anthony Gainsborough was the first of the three, and at once sat down in the stall nearest Warrington. The girls, who had changed colour, bowed as they passed, Violet first, Essie after her. And Warrington, of necessity, returned their bows. By that time Anthony Gainsborough was offering his hand, and shook hands with him with a very cordial " How do you do, very glad to see you." Essie was next to her uncle, and bent forward to see if there was any possibility of shaking hands

with Warrington across him. But Warrington had
already resolutely fixed his eyes on the stage.

The drop-scene fell. As it came down Warrington bent over to Anthony Gainsborough, and
indistinctly said something in the form of an excuse. Anthony Gainsborough could not understand
it, and it was not Warrington's intention that he
should understand it. And then Warrington rose
and left his stall.

He had foreseen what would ensue if he remained in the theatre, and he meant quietly to
slip away.

But before he had reached the end of the row
Essie had risen too.

" Where are you going, my dear?" asked her
uncle.

" Don't you see that Cousin Frank is leaving?"

" He will come back."

" That is what I am not so sure of."

And she followed Warrington out. He had his
crush hat in his hand, and made straight for the exit
of the theatre.

" Ah! I thought so," quoth Essie to herself.

The people coming out to promenade in the corri-
dor during the entre-act impeded Warrington a little,
or she would hardly have overtaken him. As it was,
however, just as he reached the glass-doors that led
into the vestibule, a tall, slim figure slipped suddenly
before him, and a girl held out her hand.

" Cousin Frank."

And as he hesitated, though it was only for an
instant, she added, looking into his face:

" What! you won't shake hands?"

Of course there were already half a dozen people
looking on. And Warrington had to shake hands.

Essie Chesterfield drew him a little aside from the
doors.

“You know, Frank, that you are being awfully unkind,” she said, confidentially, in a slight tone of reproach. And then, looking him right in the face, she added, with intention, “Will you come to luncheon at Twickenham to-morrow?”

“I am very sorry——” began Warrington.

“Then, listen. No!” He had made a step towards the exit, and she put herself in front of him. “Frank, you are awfully unkind. When will you come?”

Warrington simply looked down on the ground.

“You mean that you won’t come at all?” said the girl. “It is awfully unkind. Vi and I want to beg your pardon, and to thank you; and you know it. And, Frank ”—she dropped her voice—“you *must come.*”

“But really, Miss Chesterfield,” protested Frank Warrington, and he looked around him.

He was exceedingly uncomfortable. He could not exactly say how many people were admiring this small *intermezzo* of a domestic drama between herself and her cousin which Miss Essie Chesterfield was providing for their entertainment, nor how many were listening to the subdued schooling which the tall girl was administering. But, to judge from the smiles and side glances of which he just caught a glimpse, they must be a good many.

“Listen,” went on Essie, in a lower voice. “You *must* come. If you won’t, Frank, I’ll kneel down ”— she pointed to the floor at her feet—“and beg your pardon here, before every one. I will! Shall I, or will you come to luncheon to-morrow?”

A pretty dilemma for a man to find himself in! With a girl who was about to go down on her knees in a nice open place, close to the exit of a theatre, with a score of men and women standing around to see.

" If you cannot make up your mind, you leave me
no choice," continued Essie, seeing Warrington delayed reply, as much because she had clean taken
his breath away with surprise as for any other
reason.

And resting one hand against the wall, she actually
bent her knee.

" No, no, Miss Chesterfield," exclaimed Warrington, stepping forward and arresting her movement.
" I'll come to luncheon."

He had positively turned pale.

" To-morrow ? " looking straight into his eyes.

" To-morrow."

" To-morrow at two, then.   You *will* come ? On
your honour as a gentleman ? " laying her hand on
his shoulder to emphasize her words.

" Yes."

" No ; say ' on your honour.' "

" Well "—he could not help laughing—" ' on my
honour,' then."

" Then that is all right," said Essie, removing her
hand.   " Are you going back to see the rest of the
piece ? "

" No ; I am going home."

" Then good-night, and *au revoir.*"

They shook hands, and Warrington went out of
the theatre, and she back to her stall.

She had had the best of the encounter by a good
deal, as she had had the last time she and her cousin
parted—in the Midland Railway Station.   But the
truth is that in every single combat of this sort
between a man and a girl, the sentiments natural to
the man, and the courtesies that education and the
usage of the world have added to them, and the
absolute liberty of attack the woman enjoys, and the
very narrow bounds within which the man is compelled to limit his defence, give the girl a crushing

advantage, against which no man can hold his own, unless he is a boor or a lover.

When Essie got back to her uncle, she said:

"Frank is coming to luncheon with us to-morrow, at two."

"You persuaded him, then?" asked Anthony Gainsborough, with surprise.

"No; I forced him."

On the morrow Warrington kept his promise, and went down to Twickenham.

When he returned home in the evening, he had been at Anthony Gainsborough's house, not some three hours, as he anticipated, but more nearly ten.

And when Eustace inquired about all that had happened, there really was nothing to tell. Warrington, on his arrival, had found his cousins alone: and their apologies for the way they had behaved to him were made before their uncle came into the room—a few words gracefully spoken, and very sincerely: that was really all, and it was all over. The only thing that had astonished him was that Essie, in the midst of her little speech, burst into tears. Afterwards, Anthony Gainsborough came in, and they had luncheon. And Warrington remained till late in the evening, talking to him and to the girls about their cruise and about his estate at Lynham.

CHAPTER XXXVIII.

So the whole quarrel had come to an end. And, on retrospect, there did not seem to have been very much in it. An escapade of two girls who ought to have known better, but whose lives were being made a burden to them, and a breach between two young people going to be married, who had had the extreme good fortune to quarrel before the wedding-day instead of afterwards. It appeared that it would have been rather to be regretted if things had fallen out anyhow else. Warrington began to fancy that he had shown himself more resentful than wise.

And the next day the girls went to see Eustace.

At any rate the reconciliation was a boon to Eustace. His knee was progressing, and he suffered much less pain ; but he was still unable to leave his bed, and was permitted little change of position, and the hours (though he never complained) were sometimes very long. His visitors, too, were few. Most of his friends were out of town, and so to have his cousins come to see him, and to receive an occasional visit from Anthony Gainsborough, were very welcome treats to the blind man. The girls came often. They brought him flowers and fruit, and stayed with him a long time, sometimes reading to him, more often telling him of all the gossip they knew, and talking to him (frequently both at once) with all the careless gaiety of two light hearts without a chagrin in the world. There was a talk of Eustace's going to Twickenham for a few weeks as soon as he was well enough to become an out-patient, and Eustace himself evidently looked forward to the plan with pleasure.

As for Warrington, now that there was nothing to keep him away from Twickenham, he went there somewhat often. It was a good deal more pleasant to have Anthony Gainsborough's agreeable house to go to when he pleased than to wander backwards and forwards only from his chambers to the hospital, and from the hospital to the club, and from the club back to his chambers.

One evening, Anthony Gainsborough, coming home rather late after dining at his club, asked :

“ Have either of you girls ever heard the name of
any young lady at Lynham mentioned in connection
with your Cousin Frank ? ”

Neither of them ever had.

“ My informant said something about a young
widow. But it appeared to me to be mere gossip,”
said Anthony Gainsborough.

The following day, when Warrington was having
luncheon at Twickenham, Violet asked quite casually,
in the course of the meal :

“ Essie, is it not a long time since you heard from
Lily Hardwick ? ”

“ Yes, more than three weeks.”

“ You answered her last letter ? ”

“ Long ago. I think I must write to her again.
I am afraid that she is ill. In her last letter she
spoke of herself as being far from well.” Looking
across the table at Warrington, she continued :
“ Did you know that we knew Miss Hardwick who
lives with Mrs. Gainsborough at Lynham ? ”

“ I think I have heard something to that effect,”
said Warrington.

A few days later he asked Essie :

“ Have you heard from your friend Miss Hardwick ? ”

“ Why, no,” answered Essie. “ I wrote, but I have
had no answer. It makes me think that she must
be really ill—too ill, perhaps, to write. I wish I
knew.”

After a short pause, Essie went on : “ I believe
that you do not know her, do you ? She was here
with us a good deal in the summer, and when we
asked her about you she told us that she did not know
you. But ”—Essie looked at him archly—“ she told
us that report gave you an uneviable character.”

“ Indeed ? ” said Warrington.

“ Yes,” answered Essie. “ I forget now exactly what

it was that she said—'mysogynist.' I think. Some
sort of rather morose animal." She went on, looking
at him a little significantly : "I don't know that she
was not a wee bit right. You are a good deal altered,
Frank, from what you used to be."

"You think so?"

Essie did not answer the question, which perhaps
wanted no answer, but smoothing out her dress
remarked :

"I never quite understood how it was, Frank, that
you managed not to know Lily Hardwick. You
know Mrs. Gainsborough quite well, do you not?
And Lily Hardwick lives with her."

"Yes, I know Mrs. Gainsborough," answered Warrington.

And there was a shade of embarrassment in his
tone.

"I am afraid Lily Hardwick must be very ill,"
resumed Essie, speaking rather to herself than to
Warrington. "If you don't know her, I suppose it
is of no use asking you how she was when you left
Lynham."

"But I happen to know. The day before we left,
Mrs. Gainsborough sent to inquire after Eustace.
And I took the opportunity to ask the servant how
Miss Hardwick was that morning, for we knew she
was not well. And that morning she was worse."

"Let me see," said Essie, "that was a month ago.
Ah, but I have heard since then. She was not well
when she came up to town, and she had a relapse
after her return home. I did not understand exactly
what was the matter with her."

"I was told great lassitude, and some slight
affection of the heart."

"Do you know how it began?" asked Essie.

That was a difficult question. But Warrington
managed to extricate himself.

" I was told that she had been very much upset
about something, and that it had affected her health.
I do not know how far it is true "

" Upset about what ? "

" Well, really, you see, I am only repeating hear-
say. I am afraid that I cannot tell you much more."

And he began to talk of something else.

But, guarded as he had been, his manner had
awakened in Essie a suspicion of something concealed. And she was not long in forming plans to
discover if her suspicions had any substantial grounds.
After a very brief reflection, she resolved to see
whether anything was to be learned from Eustace.
And on the occasion of her next visit with her sister
to the hospital she acted upon her resolution. And
very surprised were both she and Violet when they
found out what there was to hear.

" Good gracious. Eustace," exclaimed Violet, before
Eustace had said a dozen words. " What are you
saying ? Frank is in love with her. You don't
mean it ? "

" Tell us everything about it, everything, everything," cried Essie, without waiting for her sister to
finish what she was saying.

Eustace did tell them everything, from the evening
on the beach to their leaving Lynham. He was
under no promise of secrecy. And he had some
hope that by speaking he might do good. And in
that he was more right than he suspected.

"You see," he concluded, in his philosophic way,
" when a man has been shamefully treated by one
woman—that is you, Vi——"

" Yes. I plead guilty. Eustace," admitted Violet
Chesterfield.

" Well, then, that is just the time when he is most
likely to fall straight in love with another woman.
And that, you see, is what Frank did. Only—as

you had used him so badly—he had unluckily made some sort of vow to himself never to have anything to do with young ladies. He is exceedingly fond of this girl, and she is simply breaking her heart about him. But he will have nothing to do with her. Now, you two made the mischief, and put it into his head to make this vow. You had better see if you can't mend it by making him break his vow."

"And, meanwhile," put in Essie, "what is the matter with poor Lily is that she is simply breaking her heart?"

"Yes."

"Well," said Essie, when she and her sister were again in the carriage to drive home, "what do you say to what we have heard this afternoon?"

"I didn't think Frank would have changed his mind so soon," answered Violet, evidently not quite pleased.

Essie burst out laughing.

———— —

CHAPTER XXXIX.

IT was a day or two later. The two sisters, walking slowly up and down a shaded path in their uncle's garden, were engaged in discussing the revelation Eustace Warrington had made to them, and Essie was describing a plan of action upon which she had determined.

"But, Essie!" cried Violet, a good deal surprised at the boldness of the measures her sister was describing, "you don't mean that you are really going to talk to Frank about his being in love with Lily Hardwick?"

T

"Certainly, that is just what I *do* mean," replied Essie, stopping to select a tea-rose from a bush. "Lily is my friend. Frank has behaved badly to her, and I am going to interfere."

"But——"

"Well, but what?" demanded Essie, fastening the rose in her bosom.

"How can you? How will you manage it? How will you begin? You'll make him awfully angry "

"He can be as angry as ever he likes," remarked Essie, looking down at the rose to see how it matched her dress. "I shall attack him quite directly, and the very next time I see him. *A propos*, that is well thought of. He is coming down to-morrow to dine. He is sure to come early. He likes sitting on the lawn here better than sitting in his chambers, and he knows that we are going on the water. You and Uncle Tony shall go on the water; I shall stay at home and get Frank to walk down with me to meet you, and on the way I will make him understand what he has to do."

"And you will see that he won't do it," answered Violet, in her careless way.

Essie made no answer. She had resolved on her part. It was some one's place to interfere, to put a stop to Lily Hardwick's breaking her heart, and to Frank's being a goose, and refusing himself a charming girl to whom he was sincerely attached. And if no one else would do anything, she, Essie, would. And she would succeed, too. She had turned her Cousin Frank round with her little finger already on two occasions, and she could do it again on a third. At least she herself entertained no doubt on the point.

The following afternoon Warrington did come down, as Essie had predicted. He was rather surprised to find her at home.

"Vi and uncle are gone on the water," she said. "I am going down presently to meet them. Will you come down with me?"

Warrington assented, suspecting nothing. His brother had not informed him of what he had told the girls.

So, half an hour later, Essie and he set out together.

As soon as they were fairly out of the grounds, Essie commenced,

"I have a bone to pick with you, Frank."

"What about?"

"About my friend, Lily Hardwick. Why did not you tell me that you knew her; and liked her; and had quarrelled with her; and all about it?"

And, turning her head, she looked straight at his face for his reply.

Warrington had changed colour, and looked anything but pleased.

"Well, you don't say anything," remarked Essie, as he did not answer.

"Who told you anything about this?" demanded Warrington.

"Your brother. He told Violet and me the other day. He was under no promise of secrecy, he said, and he told us everything. You have been behaving badly, Frank, to Lily Hardwick."

"Possibly," admitted Warrington, with a considerable degree of coolness. "Suppose we change the subject."

"No, Frank," replied Essie, firmly. "Now we have begun it, we will go on with it."

"To be plain, then, I had much rather not," objected Warrington.

"Why?" demanded Essie, flatly. And as he made no answer she went on: "Look here, Frank, be reasonable now. Give me your arm. There"—

she came close to him and slipped her arm within
his—"now, listen to me, Frank, and don't get
cross. You are awfully put out about this affair.
Don't say that you are not. Remember every one
can *see* that you are not yourself a bit. Every one
who knows you is saying, 'What is the matter
with Warrington?' and meanwhile you are upset
altogether, taciturn, and out of spirits, and vexed,
and grave, and dissatisfied. I've seen it these three
weeks, and Eustace is quite unhappy about it. And
you are miserable yourself, Frank. And you don't
know what to do. You are ashamed to go to Lily,
and to tell her the truth. And you can't make up
your mind not to love her. And you'd be a dreadful
goose if you could, for she is the dearest girl in the
whole world. And so you're in a regular hobble, you
see. And now, won't it be much wiser, seeing you
have a knowing little cousin—that is I, you know—
who can help you and will help you in any way I
can, won't it be much wiser to accept my assistance,
than to be cross with me, and to behave just like a
self-willed man—that is to say, an obstinate bear—
and to refuse my assistance, when you know very
well that if I don't do you any good I can't do you
any harm?"

Warrington was silent. He knew the girl meant
to be kind, and he had to admit a great deal of truth
in what she was saying; certainly in her last remark,
that if she did him no good she could do him no
harm.

"Well, now then," resumed Essie, "Frank, you
are very fond of Lily."

"I suppose so," granted Warrington, vaguely.

"You *suppose* so! Oh, you men! I wonder how
any girl can waste her affections on you. You
suppose so! And Lily, she is fond of you?"

"They say so."

" You know nothing about it, then ? "

" Oh, yes ; I take it it is true. But I thought you heard all about this," added Warrington, who was not enjoying being catechized.

" Well, then : and now, pray, how came you two, you and Lily, to quarrel ? "

" She cut me, you see."

" What for, Frank ? Come now."

" Look here, Essie, I'd rather not talk about all this."

" But, you goose, you must talk about it, if I am to help you. Now, sir, what did Lily cut you for ? "

It was useless to try to put her off, and so Warrington, seeing he had no alternative, replied :

" Well, you see. I knew she was getting rather fond of me," he explained, somewhat sheepishly ; " and I believed I had had enough of the amenities of young ladies. I mean——"

" Oh, I know what you mean," interrupted Essie. " That refers to Violet and me. We shall never hear the last of it, I know. Never mind. Go on."

" Well, then. I didn't want the girl to care for me, when I couldn't care for her, you see," explained Warrington, becoming a little more at his ease. " And so, I tried to make her understand that. Well, I meant it kindly, I assure you."

" You tried to make her understand that it was no use to fall in love with you."

" Yes—exactly so."

" And then she cut you." She walked on a few steps in silence, and, looking on the ground, continued, " Of course you were surprised at her cutting you ? "

" Well, I was."

" Just like a man ! " commented Essie. " He

says something to a girl that makes her fit to drop
for shame and mortification ; and then, if she lets
him understand that there really are limits to her
patience, he is taken entirely by surprise. Well,
now, Frank, it is useless to talk about the past, is it
not ?   We cannot alter that."

" Certainly not," conceded Warrington.

" But do you know what you have got to do ?"

" No, I don't," replied Warrington, rather blankly,
and beginning to think the assistance he was supposed to be going to receive was very problematical.

" Well, then. Look here, Frank. If you had a
sister—first of all—this would never have happened :
but next, she would, long ago, have told you what I
am going to tell you now. You have no sister, you
see, so you must be content, for the nonce, to take
me for one. You remember you were quite ready
for that once upon a time ;" this with a mischievous
little look from the corners of her eyes.

" Ah, but I escaped from that," said Warrington,
with a laugh.

" Thanks to me. Still now, cousin, you'll think
the advice I am going to give you is nonsensical,
and all that, I daresay, but remember that in some
things women understand women better than men
do. And what you must do is this : you must go
down to Lynham at once ; and you must see Lily
Hardwick. You must not think beforehand anything about what you are going to say to her, but
when you do see her you must tell her that you have
been a donkey ; that you didn't know your own
mind ; and that you want her to let bygones be
bygones ; and after that you can say anything else
you like ; and she will listen to you. Now, will you
go down to Lynham to-morrow ?"

" I may as well tell you at once that I won't,"
replied Warrington, after a pause   " Your advice is,

I daresay, good advice. But it is advice I have heard before. That is unluckily just what Eustace recommended me to do."

"And why did you not do it?"

"Because I don't believe Miss Hardwick would listen to me."

"Frank, you know nothing about it," said Essie, with all the importance of an authority. "She *would* listen to you. You go down and take her by surprise, and say what I have told you. And she will listen to you. I am sure of it; because if I liked a man, and he had behaved to me as you have behaved to Lily, and then he were to come to me and say what I have told you to say, I know *I* should listen to him and forgive him."

That was certainly a strong argument.

Still, however, Warrington repeated, a little doggedly,

"Possibly. Still, I tell you fairly, I am not going."

Essie drew her arm out of his, and said,

"Look here, Frank, do you know that you are very tiresome?"

Warrington lighted a cigarette, and they walked on together a little way in silence. After all, it was Essie, not Warrington, that had come near to losing her temper.

In his heart Warrington felt a little for her, although she had certainly taken upon herself to interfere in what was not her business. She had meant kindly, and she had given what was possibly good advice. If it had only happened not to be the one thing he was resolved not to do.

But suddenly Essie stopped short.

"Frank," she said, turning and facing him, "I'll not be humbugged. You ought to go to Lynham, and you shall!"

"I'm afraid not, Essie."

"Yes—you *shall* go. I'll make you. I've spoken to you kindly and nicely"—she walked on as she continued—"I have told you that I would be your friend and help you. I have said to you just what your own sister would have said. And you ought to do as I have told you. But if you won't, do you know what you are?—a nasty, selfish, ill-natured wretch! Oh, yes, I mean it," she continued, coming nearer him, and giving him a positively savage little slap on his shoulder. "If you don't go down to Lynham and see Lily, you are a nasty, selfish, hard-hearted wretch. Listen, Frank: I don't want to think you are the sort of man to be cruel to a girl—cruel! you hear what I say, don't you?—cruel! nor that you have a mean, contemptible pride that can't confess itself to have been in the wrong. But, cousin, do you know how you are behaving to the girl you say you love?"

It was not the sort of speech a man would be likely to answer, and Warrington did not answer it. He simply went on smoking his cigarette.

"Do you remember, Frank, when I helped Vi to get away from you?"

"I do," said Warrington.

"Perhaps you remember how you felt that day, and what you thought of Vi—and of how she had behaved to you?"

"Perhaps I do," admitted Warrington.

"And it does not occur to you that *you* are behaving far worse to Lily Hardwick than Vi behaved to you? Vi was a girl, and kept the truth from you, a man; and you, a man, are keeping the truth from Lily Vi did not love you, but you say that you love Lily. All that came of Vi's deception was that you escaped from marrying a woman who would never have made your life happy. The consequence of *your* deception is that Lily Hardwick is breaking her heart. Vi had a motive, bad enough; that she was ready to do anything to escape from grandpapa. But you have no motive, Frank, but your own pride. And if Vi was mean to let you believe she loved you when she didn't, and to encourage you to love her and then to jilt you; what, pray, are you, who will neither let a girl you love know that you love her, nor undeceive her in her belief that her love is returned with indifference, but coolly look on, and see her break her heart? If you suffered, what do you think Lily is suffering? We women love more than you do."

Warrington dropped his eyes, and looked down.

In an instant Essie had stepped up to him, and put her hand on his shoulder.

" Frank ! "

" I will think of what you have said, Essie. I will, really."

" I knew you would," said the girl.

Late in the evening, after dinner, he came across the drawing-room to her, when she was playing the piano.

As she saw him approach, she leaned a little towards him, without ceasing to play.

Bending to her ear, he said :

" You will not tell any one ? "

" No."

" I'll go down to Lynham to-morrow."

CHAPTER XL.

WARRINGTON was a little surprised the next morning to find on his breakfast-table a note from Essie, enclosing one of her cards.

" Use my name without hesitation, if it can be of any use to you," ran the note. " Say that I sent you to inquire after Lily, because I could get no answer to my letters, or anything else of that kind that may prove of service to you. And *bon voyage.*"

He set out by an early train, arrived at Lynham about noon, and had luncheon at the " London Hotel."

It was with mixed feelings of apprehension and anticipation that he, after luncheon, lighted a cigar, and directed his steps towards Cliff Cottage. Could it be really true that he was on his way to make a proposal of marriage to Miss Hardwick? The thing seemed impossible. But a thousand reminiscences of her filled his brain.

Would he, as his cousin predicted, succeed in rectifying the consequence of his mistakes? How would he find Miss Hardwick? The better for his absence? Disposed to pardon him? Or already fairly advanced with the task of forgetting him? He answered himself in conjectures of all kinds. But, of the things men say to themselves, they believe the good and disbelieve the bad, and so are, after all, very little wiser for their reflections.

The familiar gate of Cliff Cottage came in view, the pines, and the little thatched cottage, covered with creepers, nestling among them. It seemed to Warrington a long time since he had last been at the spot. He entered, and passed down the short drive, recalling casually Eustace's queer dream of the place being turned to desolation. The reality was a contrast to the dream. The garden was bright as ever with flowers, and in a condition of the most exquisite neatness.

But, when he reached the porch, he found a little card fastened to the handle of the bell, with the request, "Please do not ring." And the knocker was wrapped in wash-leather.

Warrington stood looking blankly at the muffled knocker. For the moment, the shock of the surprise had paralysed his thoughts.

"Miss Hardwick must be very ill," he said to himself, with misgiving. Then he knocked gently.

After all, it might not be Miss Hardwick. Mrs. Gainsborough might be ill, or some one staying in the house.

He knocked lightly, and waited. Some time elapsed, and no one came. He began to doubt whether he had been heard. At last, however, the door was opened by a maidservant of Mrs. Gainsborough's whom he recognized.

"Is Mrs. Gainsborough at home?" he asked.

"Yes, sir."

"You have some one ill in the house."

"Miss Hardwick, sir."

It was as he feared, then!

"Indeed. I have been away in town. She was not well when I left. There has been no improvement in her health?" He hardly knew what he was saying.

"Oh, no, sir. Miss Hardwick has been sinking for many weeks," said the girl.

"Is she in danger?"

"Oh, yes, sir. The doctor gives no hopes, sir."

The girl made her answers as if she was quite tired of repeating the same thing to different people.

"Mrs. Gainsborough is at home?" asked Warrington.

"Oh, yes, sir."

"Do you suppose I could see her?"

"If you will come in, sir, I'll see. Mis'ss sees very few visitors."

Still the same tone of an oft-repeated answer.

Warrington entered, and was shown into the drawing-room. He kept the servant waiting a few minutes whilst he made some more inquiries respecting Miss Hardwick: how long it was since she had been able to go out? whether Dr. Gregg was still attending her? and so forth. Then the girl leaving him went to seek her mistress.

Warrington stood with his back to the hearth, and thought. How familiar the room seemed! The old escritoire, the little writing-table with its ormolu ornaments, the cosy low chairs, the feminine trifles, the round table strewn with books, the fresh sweet flowers.

And so the doctor gave no hopes. Was it possible? In this very house Lily Hardwick lay dying. Could it be possible? Did women, when they really loved, break their hearts for a man in this way, and lie down and die? Had he really wrecked this girl's life? He would never forgive himself.

A miserable load of disquiet, a species of moral and mental suffocation oppressed him, and made his thought slow and laboured.

He waited a long time, half an hour or more, moving restlessly about the room, unable to sit still, continually revolving, painfully, anxiously, the same train of thoughts.

Had he come too late? Would they let him see her? Was the girl really dying? Had he really broken her heart?

The servant returned.

Mrs. Gainsborough sent him her compliments and hoped that he would excuse her not seeing him. Miss Hardwick was so very ill this afternoon.

A reasonable request enough of Mrs. Gainsborough's.

But he was loth to go.

He sent the servant back with another message. Would she kindly tell Mrs. Gainsborough that he was sorry to seem importunate. But he had come down from London on purpose to hear how Miss Hardwick was. Friends of Miss Hardwick's had sent him. They were most anxious to know all they could about her. In fact, he had promised them to see Miss Hardwick. If that was impossible, he begged that Mrs. Gainsborough would see him ; would herself let him hear what he was to say to Miss Hardwick's friends. He did not mind how long he waited, or, if Mrs. Gainsborough would name any time when it would be more convenient for her to see him, he would call again.

So the servant went to see.

She returned in a few minutes.

Mrs. Gainsborough was very sorry, but she hoped he would excuse her. Miss Hardwick was so very ill.

It seemed there was nothing to be done but to leave.

He laid two cards of his own on the table ; and the one of Essie Chesterfield's.

" I wish I had brought Essie with me," he said to himself as he put the cards down. " I don't feel at all sure I am doing right to leave without seeing any one."

And he walked to the door slowly, as if waiting for some idea to occur to him before he reached it.

" Will you, please, give my compliments to Mrs. Gainsborough," he said, stopping, and speaking slowly: "and tell her how exceedingly sorry I am to learn that Miss Hardwick is so very ill; and that I regret that Mrs. Gainsborough could not see me. I suppose there is no hope of her seeing me if I wait, is there?"

"Mrs. Gainsborough is very sorry, sir, but I was to beg you to excuse her, because Miss Hardwick is so very ill."

"You will, please, give her my message," said Warrington.

And he passed into the hall.

"That girl is well trained to repeat what she is told," he said to himself: "but it seems that I must go back to town having effected nothing. I wish I had had Essie with me?"

In the drive he paused, and looked back at the cottage. Which was *her* window? In which room of the house was it that she lay dying. He had no means of guessing. He turned and went back to Lynham.

Was it possible that this girl was really dying? Did girls break their hearts, and die like this?

The pretty girl she was! And a nice girl, too. A good-hearted girl, and a spirited little thing. The pluck with which she would go at a fence, or a brook, or anything if she was once persuaded that she could manage it. And now dying!

What would he not give to see her and to tell her—even if she were dying—that he had loved her all the time.

He had never known it as he knew now: now that he was to lose her; now that he was never to see her face again. His darling dying. Yes: it was *his darling* that was dying.

There was a dull pain in his breast; of the sort that comes to strong men when forced to face the impending of a great, inevitable grief.

He was sure that he ought not to have let himself be turned out of the house by the maidservant, without insisting on seeing Mrs. Gainsborough at least. But what could he do?

He went into Lynham and called on Dr. Gregg. The doctor was out. Warrington waited to see him, and had the grim satisfaction of hearing from the surgeon's own lips that there was no hope of Miss Hardwick's recovery. She had been slowly sinking for weeks. The wonder was that she was still alive.

From the doctor's house Warrington went straight to the station, and returned to town and to Twickenham.

As he crossed the hall, Essie rushed out of the drawing-room to meet him.

" Well?" she exclaimed, with a bright smile on her face that faded as her eyes met his.

" Miss Hardwick is dying."

" Dying!" exclaimed Essie, with consternation. " You have seen her?"

" No."

" You have *not* seen her! But——"

" Come into the library, and I will tell you all about it," said Warrington.

When he had concluded, he said,

" I wish you had been with me, Essie."

" Yes. I would have seen her," remarked Essie, with a certain determination. " But, if she is dying, Frank, it could not have done much good."

CHAPTER XLI.

THE doctor, as he had told Warrington, could hold out no hopes.

Indeed, every one at Lynham was only waiting from day to day to hear of the anticipated end. Lily herself, an emaciated wreck, prostrate, pallid, and almost lifeless, for hours together unable to lift her head from her pillow, was almost weary enough to wish that the end might come.

After Warrington and his brother went away to town, Maud Gainsborough had taken, morally speaking, a look around her. The result of her survey of the situation was an assurance that no further impediment lay in her way; and that she might proceed to the destruction of her cousin with that quiet deliberation which she had always regarded as the safest and surest way of accomplishing her end.

For a fortnight Lily still went out of doors. She even went twice into the town. But on the second occasion she was taken faint, and had to be brought home. After that she did not go farther than the garden. Soon her walks in the garden became shortened. She could no longer get so far as the top of the cliff; soon only half-way down the garden, and back; then no further than the chestnuts, and the tennis lawn.

The decline of her forces was slow and extremely irregular. One day she would walk three or four times as far as on the preceding. The next day she was scarcely able to crawl a few yards. Getting up in the morning was always a terrible task. She was invariably dizzy on rising, and during dressing would lie down two or three times to rest.

Even on her best days—that was when the widow had given her a smaller dose of the drug, or suppressed one dose, or even both—she would lie for hours on the sofa, or recline in a lounging-chair, indisposed for the least exertion, often complaining of headache, and almost invariably a prey to an indescribable dejection. The least thing made her cry, and the most trivial emotion brought into her face either a sudden flush or an equally sudden deadly pallor.

By-and-by there was no more walking in the garden. Only all the long summer afternoons her chair was put by the open drawing-room window, and she lay there still, and with wistful, hollow eyes looked at the sunshine and the slowly moving shadows, and the trees and the flowers, and the dappled lawn—all so near and yet all gone out of reach of her failing strength.

Sometimes, when she went upstairs, on reaching her room she dropped on her bed breathless and exhausted. The headaches, too, became worse—terrible headaches, day after day, intolerable, maddening.

"Oh, Maud," she would wail, "this is insufferable. I shall go mad. I would rather die than this. It is harder to live in such awful pain than to die any death."

Quoth Mrs. Gainsborough to herself on these occasions :

"I am putting her out of her pain as fast as I can. How impatient she grows."

Now and then the widow gave her a larger dose. Then she lay for hours perfectly motionless, unable to raise her head from her pillow.

And all the time, day by day, she became paler and thinner, more disheartened and more fatally prostrated.

U

Every one was very kind. She had plenty of visitors. Indeed, she had too many visitors. But it was not Mrs. Gainsborough's aim to exclude visitors. Mrs. Gainsborough invited the greatest publicity for her cousin's slow decline. So Lily's girl-friends came to see her, to chat with her, and to try to cheer her. The rector's wife and other good souls of the neighbourhood came, and brought her presents of all sorts of little dainties to tempt her appetite. Sometimes she was equal to seeing them, and sometimes not. If she could see them, she exerted herself to be at her best, at any rate to keep in subjection the senseless tears that were always ready to flow for nothing ; and she would thank them for the presents, and for coming to see her, and promise to eat what they brought—if she could. But it was seldom that anything got eaten. Food in any shape had become an impossibility to her. Among other people, Sir Robert called with his wife. Saying good-bye to him, Lily fairly broke down.

" I shall never ride to hounds again, Sir Robert," she said, with her hand in his, and then, quickly turning away, burst into a flood of tears. The bluff baronet was scarcely master of himself when parting with Mrs. Gainsborough in the hall.

Then one day Maud Gainsborough had a fright.

Lily ran rather rapidly upstairs and fell down in a dead faint.

For an hour or two Mrs. Gainsborough believed this was the end. And she did not want the end just yet. She had one or two things to do before the end came. However, after about an hour and a half the girl revived a little. And the widow, for a day or two, diminished her dose.

But she took warning from the alarm, and delayed her last precautions no longer.

She insisted on a consultation.

So Dr. Gregg brought a friend with him, and they spent more than an hour with Lily. Lily was a trifle better that day. Dr. Gregg insisted on the affection of the heart, and the stethoscope, on being used, revealed a distinct murmur. That was no great wonder, considering the girl's anæmic condition. So the murmur passed for a valvular murmur, and the doctor's colleague corroborated his opinion of heart complaint. In fact, the two medical men were much agreed about the whole case. It mattered little to Maud Gainsborough whether they were so or not. She had had her consultation, and she would take care to talk about it.

The doctors were perfectly welcome to try any new treatment and prescriptions. She felt no anxiety about their ability to neutralize the effect of judiciously administered aconite.

When she went upstairs to Lily, after they had left, the girl asked eagerly :

" What did the doctors say, Maud ? "

" They give us no hope, dear."

" Oh ! Maud," exclaimed the girl, with despair.

After a few seconds she added, " It is an awful thing to have to die, Maud."

" Well, you must be resigned, dear," replied the widow, in a mechanical sort of tone.

" I do try to be resigned," said the girl, gently. " But it is not so easy as you seem to think. And, do you know, Maud, you say things to one awfully cruelly sometimes."

In the evening Maud Gainsborough said to herself :

" Now we have done with the consultation, the next thing is to write to Mr. Tanner."

So she wrote to Mr. Tanner, a long rambling letter, that contained an enormous number of words, and yet said very little : a letter full of harrowing descriptions of Maud's own heart-broken consternation and dismay at the discovery of the terribly serious condition of her " poor darling," and at the impossibility of hoping any longer "even against hope." Cleverly mingled with all these lamentations were scraps of what the doctors had said, and many confused explanations of why Maud had not written sooner, " all along she had been believing, trusting, praying that the case might not be really so very serious "—and ever so much more of the same sort. About the only thing really clear in this beautiful epistle was, that if either Mr. or Mrs. Tanner wished to see Lily Hardwick alive, they must come down to Lynham at once.

Upon Lily Hardwick's guardian and his wife the letter fell like a thunderbolt.

" I can't go to see her, Tom," said Mrs. Tanner, when her husband read the widow's letter aloud. " I'm sure it would break my heart. But do you go."

Yes. Mr. Tanner would go. There was no doubt about that. And he would make Mrs. Gainsborough know what he thought. Very angry indeed was Mr. Tanner.

And the next day Mr. Tanner came down to Lynham. Lily was much worse than she had been when the medical men had seen her; in fact, she was worse than Mrs. Gainsborough meant her to be on the occasion of Mr. Tanner's visit. And Mr. Tanner was immensely shocked, as well he might be. Lily seemed scarcely to know what was going on and bade her guardian good-bye in a sort of semi-conscious dream, but she sent her love to Mrs. Tanner, and begged him to thank her for all her kindness.

Altogether a very unpleasant business was this visit of Mr. Tanner's. Mr. Tanner asked no end of questions, and was disposed to be terribly angry. He told Mrs. Gainsborough point-blank that it was a disgraceful thing that his ward had been suffered to become so ill without his having known anything at all about it ; and he was very imperfectly pacified by the widow's assurance that she had had no suspicion of the seriousness of her cousin's condition until after the consultation that took place a few days before. Also Mrs. Gainsborough asserted that she had employed the best medical skill available in the neighbourhood. And she had the courage to suggest that, if Mr. Tanner was dissatisfied, he should himself send down some celebrated man from London. Her heart flinched as she made the proposition, for she could see that Mr. Tanner was half inclined to act upon it. But in the end he left, dissatisfied enough, but satisfied that everything that could be done for the girl had been done, and insisting only on hearing from Mrs. Gainsborough every day.

Very thankful was Maud Gainsborough to see him depart.

" If I had let him know that Lily was ill as soon as he would have liked, I should never have been able to finish this at all," she said to herself. " Now I have done with everything but the finale."

Already Lily was confined to her room : in a day or two more, to her bed.

She lay now for hours together, like a log, motionless, and apparently incapable of moving. Existence seemed to have reached the lowest point at which its continuation was possible : and her life hung by a thread. The widow had reduced her doses, one of those which the girl had not so long before been taking twice a day would have proved fatal now. Visitors still came to see her, and Mrs. Gainsborough from time to time admitted one of them, that people might see for themselves what was going on, but more often excused even herself from seeing them.

Lily seemed scarcely to notice them, and was often apparently unconscious of their presence. Now and then she rallied a little, generally only to complain piteously of insufferable pain or exhaustion. But at other times she would have Maud Gainsborough summoned, and—utterly unsuspecting of the truth —throw herself into her arms, clinging to her with wild yearning, and clasping with weak arms the last thing left within her reach, in a world fast slipping away from her grasp.

Maud Gainsborough endured the embraces and endearments, and responded with kisses to the feeble, fondling words. To do so was politic. She no longer shrank from such scenes, though they bored her enormously. The long weeks employed in the merciless murder of the girl had hardened her, and made her completely callous to what she was doing. She suffered no longer from shocks and revulsions. She had no need now to go down on the beach, and to walk up and down, up and down, by the sea because she could not rest. If she went out, it was simply because being in the house with her sick cousin bored her.

Unexpectedly one afternoon Lily began to talk about Warrington. She had been asking questions about all the people who had recently been to see her or to inquire after her, and then she said:

"And Mr. Warrington, he has never been?"

"He is in town, you know."

"I know. But he has never sent any message?"

"No."

Lily heaved a sigh.

"Maud," she said, "I should like to see Mr. Warrington. Now that I am going to die, it cannot much matter what passed between us. And perhaps I was too hard on him. I wish I could see him. I should like to tell him that I am still his friend.

Last time I parted from him, I only bowed and would not speak. I should like it better if we could part friends."

Maud Gainsborough made some remark about the exceeding unlikelihood of a visit from Warrington, who, in the first place, was in town, and whom, in the second place, Lily had herself chosen to cut.

"I know, Maud," said the girl. "But if he knew how ill I am; and if he knew that I wished to see him, I think he would come."

And presently she went on:

"He might come even yet, Maud. If he does, you will let him see me, won't you, however ill I am? Even if he has to wait a whole day, you will make him wait. Maud, I loved him so! If he comes, you *will* let me see him—you will keep him here till I can see him? You promise me, Maud."

"Yes, I promise it, if you wish it."

The girl lifted up her pale lips and kissed her.

If Mrs. Gainsborough had been superstitious, she might have imagined the sick girl inspired with some presentiment of coming events, for it was the very day after this that Warrington called. But how Maud kept her promise is known.

CHAPTER XLII.

Maud Gainsborough sat musing.

She had reached a point where she might now any day destroy her cousin without raising a shadow of a suspicion. And Dr. Gregg would sign the certificate without a moment's hesitation.

And she was going to do it.

Would a day ever come when, with her head resting on Frank Warrington's breast, she would be able proudly to confide to him what she had gone through, what she had dared, to win him? Would he understand her, appreciate the measurelessness of her passion, the infatuation of her devotion?

The widow feared he would not. It was an unsatisfactory confession to make to herself that the man for whom a woman could have dared all this was a man from whom she could never venture to ask the meed of her measureless love. But—men have no poetry. They are so simple-minded. They never see how circumstances modify acts, and hastily call everything by the first name that comes to hand.

Of course, at present Frank Warrington was in love with the little fool upstairs, and would call what Maud had done—murder.

But, perhaps, by-and-by——

No. Maud would not deceive herself. It would never do to tell Frank Warrington. She had gauged his character, and there was not poetry enough in it to understand a tragedy. All the perils she had boldly faced, all the horrors she had waded through, all the courage she had found, all the nerve and skill and intelligence she had displayed, they must all be for ever buried in the depth of her own breast—never confessed to the man for whom she had staked everything.

"And these men are the things we love, and cannot help ourselves," quoth Maud.

But she took a resolution. To-morrow Lily should be much worse, and to-morrow night should die.

To-morrow! And the game was lost already.

For that same morning Warrington received a letter. Eustace had left the hospital, and the brothers were both of them at Twickenham. Coming down to breakfast, Warrington found amongst the letters awaiting him one from Lynham, directed in a lady's handwriting entirely unknown to him.

Within it was a short note in another hand, written with a pencil.

"DEAR MR. WARRINGTON,—You must forgive this scrawl, which I write in bed with a pencil, because my cousin would not like me to write. But Miss Barrington kindly promises to post this for me. I am very ill, and they tell me I must die, and I should so like to see you, to beg your pardon, if I have not always behaved to you as I should, and to part friends. I spoke to Maud only the day before yesterday about your coming, and she promised me solemnly that, if by any chance you called, you should certainly see me. Do please come.

"Ever your faithful friend,
"LILY HARDWICK.

"Wednesday afternoon."

The letter was indeed a scrawl, a sad scrawl, written with a trembling hand that seemed to have found a difficulty in holding the pencil.

Warrington read it twice: and then his eyes fixed on the date: "Wednesday afternoon."

Presumably Miss Barrington—he had met her in the hunting-field—had in the course of Thursday gone to Lynhurst, and got his address from the housekeeper, and posted the letter in Lynham for the London evening post. The postmarks agreed with that.

But it was on Tuesday that he went down to Lynham, and Lily Hardwick, writing on Wednesday, spoke of a promise given her "the day before yesterday." That was on Monday. Then, on Monday Mrs. Gainsborough gave her a solemn promise, that if by any chance Warrington came to call, he should certainly see her. On Tuesday Warrington did call, and certainly did not see her. And on Wednesday she wrote, plainly ignorant of his having called, "Do come."

That he would certainly do. But the dates seemed to be all contradictions.

While he still stood with the letter in his hand, Essie came into the breakfast-room.

"Good-morning, Frank," she said; and then, in another tone, "Why! what is the matter?"

"Read," said Warrington, handing her the letter.

"But when was this written?" asked Essie, turning the letter about. "Wednesday. Then— then, the day before yesterday—that is Monday."

She looked up at Warrington, and their eyes met in a look of recipocral interrogation.

"You will go, Frank?"

"Certainly."

At breakfast, Warrington mentioned that unanticipated business would take him away for the day. He was taciturn and preoccupied.

When breakfast was over, Essie seized an opportunity to speak to him.

"I have been thinking of nothing but that letter, Frank," she said. "It is most mysterious. Did Mrs. Gainsborough, on Monday, promise Lily that she should see you, but, when you came, change her mind?"

"After her promise? And what for?"

"Well, Frank, I have misgivings," observed Essie. "Suppose Mrs. Gainsborough has not chosen that you should see Lily? Then you go down again today. And she has given orders, perhaps, that you are not to be admitted. What are you going to do then?"

" But all this is most unlikely," retorted Warrington.

" But—if it happens," insisted Essie. " Listen,
Frank. Last time you went down you wished that
you had taken me with you. This time will you
take my advice ?—show that letter to Uncle Tony."

" To Mr. Gainsborough ? What for ? " demanded
Warrington, who saw no reason for the proposition.

" Uncle Tony knows Mrs. Gainsborough better
than you do, and he will read between the lines."

Warrington demurred.

" It would be necessary to tell him all that history,
you see," he objected.

" I will tell him that, or as much as he will need
to know. You can have no reason for hesitating to
put every confidence in Uncle Tony. Frank, be persuaded."

" But this is probably merely some mistake, you
know. You see "—he spoke with pain—" how ill
Miss Hardwick is."

" That is a mere presumption of yours. Think,
Frank, if I should be right, what that means : Lily
will never see you."

" And what difference will showing the letter to
Mr. Gainsborough make ? "

" You show him the letter and see."

Warrington yielded to her persuasion at last, saying :

" Go and speak to Mr. Gainsborough then, while I
see my brother."

When he returned downstairs, Essie and Anthony
Gainsborough were in the library.

" Where is this letter of yours, Warrington ? "
asked Anthony Gainsborough. " May I see it ? "

He had, as usual, his pipe in his mouth, which he
always smoked after breakfast ; but there was a
shadow on his face—an expression of cloudy dis-

pleasure and of profound mistrust that contrasted so strangely with his invariably genial, open mien that Warrington regarded him with unconcealed surprise.

"Read, by all means," he said, offering the letter.

And at the same time he looked interrogatively at Essie, who sat by the table, as if he would say, "What does this mean?"

Essie, for answer, only shook her head, which explained nothing.

As Anthony Gainsborough read the letter the shadow on his face deepened.

"What is your explanation of this letter, Warrington?" he asked, in a short, hard voice, still holding the note in his hand.

"Essie has told you the facts, I believe. I imagine that the letter simply contains some mistake. Miss Hardwick is evidently very ill, and I conceive that she has confused the days."

"It is possible," said Anthony Gainsborough in a sceptical tone, and continued: "Only, why should Mrs. Gainsborough not like Miss Hardwick to write to you?"

"I don't know, unless it was because she was afraid of Miss Hardwick's over-exerting herself."

"That does not explain her having recourse to the assistance of a friend to post her letter," remarked Anthony Gainsborough, coolly.

Then suddenly turning, he said, angrily:

"Mark you, Warrington, if that woman promised the girl, on Monday, that you should see her if you came, and when you came on Tuesday, broke her word—broke a promise solemnly given to a dying girl that she should see her lover, that was a wickedly cruel thing; and I shall know what she meant by it."

How strange the words sounded, and how strange their harsh, almost savage tone from the lips of this quiet, good-natured, easy-tempered man! Warrington and Essie exchanged a look of surprise, as well they might, and each of them secretly asked themselves what all this could mean.

"I think it more likely that there has been some mistake," said Warrington.

"Let us hope so. Only, if that woman has broken a promise solemnly given to a dying girl that she should see her lover, that is a wickedly cruel thing ; and I shall know what she means by it."

He spoke very quietly this time, in his ordinary even voice, but with a certain firm determination that had a most ominous ring.

Essie sat silent, her eyes going from one of the men to another.

"I don't think that Mrs. Gainsborough is the sort of woman to do a thing like that, you know," observed Warrington.

"What have you seen of her character?" asked Mr. Gainsborough.

"Well—something."

"What she has chosen to show you," said Anthony Gainsborough, in a brusque, harsh voice, most unlike his ordinary tone. "The woman's a liar. Oh! I know her. She's a liar."

He was walking up and down the room slowly, as he often did whilst he was smoking. Presently he asked :

"Of course you are going down?"

"At once."

"And you will insist upon seeing Miss Hardwick ?"

"I shall attempt to do so."

"Yes," said Anthony Gainsborough. "And if Mrs. Gainsborough refuses to let you see her "—he stopped in his walk and turned towards Warrington —"you telegraph on the spot to me. *I'll* make her let you see Miss Hardwick."

He went on to the end of the room, and there stopped again.

"I know this woman better than you do, Warrington," he said, quietly. "But I don't want to prejudice any one. I shall be very happy to learn that your explanation is the right one ; that there is simply some mistake. It is just possible. But if Mrs. Gainsborough refuses to let you see Miss Hardwick—you telegraph to me. Don't insist. Don't waste your time. Don't do anything. Turn straight from the door and go to the telegraph-office. Telegraph to me, 'Refused,' and I'll *make* Mrs. Gainsborough let you see the girl. And I'll know what she means by refusing you, too. Now, don't let me keep you. Be off. And I hope you'll find your lady-love better than you anticipate. If you do, give her my kind regards. She is a charming girl."

And he gave Warrington his great hand, and shook hands with him heartily.

In the hall Warrington said to Essie :

" You were right, Essie."

" I mostly am, Frank," replied Essie.

When he was gone, Essie returned to her uncle. He was still smoking in the library.

" It is my opinion, Uncle Tony, that you would have done better if you had gone down with Frank. I don't believe that there is any mistake at all. Lily very seldom made mistakes. Mrs. Gainsborough simply does not want Frank to see her."

" On what do you ground that ?" asked her uncle.

" On the fact that Lily was evidently not allowed to write to him. That must mean something, and may mean anything."

" You are quite right."

He was filling another pipe. That was unusual. After his one pipe after breakfast he generally went about his day's work.

"That woman has had too much money to spend lately," he remarked, lighting the pipe. "And I dare say she has been getting too much of her own way. I know her. Still I don't wish to prejudge the matter. We will hope for the best. It may be a mistake."

The hours of the morning passed quietly.

Anthony Gainsborough had been going into town, but did not go. All the forenoon he strolled about the house, and the lawn in front of the house.

About twelve, Essie found that an order had been given for the dog-cart to be got out, and to be kept standing in readiness to start at any minute. Violet was in the drawing-room, playing to Eustace. Essie went out in the garden to get some flowers.

Presently her uncle came to her.

"How long will it take you to get ready to go out?" he asked.

"To go where?"

"To go anywhere."

"A few minutes only. I have only to put on my hat and gloves."

"Get ready, then."

Essie went in and put on her hat, and put her gloves in her pocket, and returned to her flowers. When she came in again from the garden, Anthony Gainsborough was in the hall.

"Ah! you have your hat on. That is right," he said. "I have been thinking. And, if I have to go to Lynham, I may take you with me. I may want you there."

"As you wish, uncle."

What could he want her for?

She went into the breakfast-room to arrange her flowers. In the midst of her task, the housekeeper came in.

"Can I speak to you, Miss?"

“ Certainly, Mrs. Simpson.”

“ What has happened, Miss, if I may be so bold as to ask ? ”

“ Why ? ”

“ Mr. Warrington (I don’t know whether you know it) is gone down to Lynham. John, who went with him to the railway-station, heard him ask for his ticket. I suppose he’s going to see Mrs. Gainsborough. Miss, isn’t he ? ”

“ Well, you see, you know, Mrs. Simpson,” observed Essie, evasively.

“ But has anything happened down there, Miss ? ”

“ Nothing that I know of.”

“ But ”—in a lower voice—“ is Mr. Gainsborough going down, Miss ? ”

“ Perhaps.”

“ You are going with him, Miss ? ”

“ Perhaps, if he goes. Why ? ”

“ Well, Miss, if there’s anything wrong down there, this time you’ll see.”

“ See what ? ”

“ What you will see, Miss.”

And the old woman left with a knowing nod.

What did she mean ?

A quarter to two.

Anthony Gainsborough, still strolling about the place, crossed Essie coming out of the breakfast-room.

“ Keep about ; be in the hall, or in the drawing-room,” he said.

And he went out to walk up and down before the house. The dog-cart had been brought round, and stood by the front-door.

Suddenly a shout like a clap of thunder echoed through the hall into the drawing-room.

“ Essie ! ”

Essie rushed into the hall. Anthony Gainsborough

was already in the dog-cart. He had met the boy
with the telegram in the drive. Essie ran down the
steps, and sprang up beside him. She was hardly in
her seat before he put the horse into a gallop with a
sharp cut of his whip.

The dog-cart swung out of the gate, and then
dashed along the road towards Surbiton.

" If we are lucky, we shall catch the express," said
Anthony Gainsborough, at the same time pushing a
telegram into her hands.

It contained one word only—" Refused."

Essie thought of the old housekeeper. and her remark, " You'll see, Miss—what you will see."

The old woman was right. She was going to see
what sort of thing is " the wrath of the dove," the
awful anger of a tender-hearted man.

CHAPTER XLIII.

THE windows of Lily's room stood open. A soft
breeze from seawards stole in through them, cool and
fresh, with the scent of the waves. Outside there
was brilliant sunshine. The September day was hot.
But this side of the cottage stood in the shade.

In her bed the poisoned girl lay motionless, with
her eyelids closed, to all appearance unconscious.
Only her breast heaved irregularly as she laboured
for breath. Her thin arms were drawn away from
her body a little to the right and left. The doctor
had put them so, to make her breathing more easy.
Her head was bent on one side. The sheets were
hardly more white than her wasted face and cheeks,

but her beautiful hair lay tumbled in disorder on her pillow, and the long fringes of her eyelashes, and the two rows of perfectly even pearly teeth between her colourless lips, contrasted with her death-like appearance—young womanhood's sweetest freshness, with the last stage of decay.

The simple, tasteful room was a little in disorder, and unlike what it used to be. It was a long time since she was able to attend to it, and all that Maud Gainsborough or the servants had done wanted the grace of her touch. There were a few flowers on the table by the bed. She loved the flowers, and had asked for them only this morning ; but before they came she was too ill to see them—or they would not have remained so ill-assorted as they were. Beside them lay a little book of devotions.

Dr. Gregg stood by the bed looking on. Looking on was the only thing left that could be done.

And a little behind him, pretending to be watching, but really with averted eyes, looking at the sunshine out of doors, was Maud Gainsborough, sitting sideways in her chair, with her handkerchief pressed against her lips. She was pale, and her face bore an expression of weariness, but there was a strange gleam of living light in the depths of her eyes, and her handsome face, haggard as it was, had a weird, unnatural beauty, such as might have served for the portrait of a sorceress of antiquity, broken by the exhaustion of some ghastly rite. In the pocket of her dress she had in a tiny phial a few last drops of poison, enough, in fact, to destroy three or four stalwart lives. All the rest she had this morning thrown away, saving the contents of the bottle in the old escritoire downstairs.

" She is sinking," said the doctor.

Maud Gainsborough wonders whether that is really so. It might be. This morning's dose might, in the girl's weak condition, be final, without the other one she proposes to give in the evening.

"You can do nothing, doctor?" she asked.

"Nothing. She is sinking. You should telegraph for her friends, Mrs. Gainsborough, if there are any whom you wish her to see."

"There would be no one to telegraph to but her guardian: he came to see her last week, and bade her good-bye."

Rising, she came to the bed, and, bending over the girl, kissed her on her forehead.

"My poor darling! So young, doctor! She is only twenty. This is very terrible."

There were real tears in her eyes. The last drop— it would be an awesome deed to give that! And the hours were speeding towards it, and she was a little unnerved. Now, too, in the last extremity of the poor, shattered life, some of the pity for the girl which she had felt at first had returned.

The doctor left, and Maud Gainsborough moved to the window-seat. It would have been a relief to her to leave the room, but appearances had to be considered. So she sat by the window, where she could not see the pale girl in her bed, and where she could not herself be seen by any one coming to the house.

Downstairs the housemaid Ann was turning away all visitors and messages of inquiry with the same answer,

"Mrs. Gainsborough cannot see any one. Miss Hardwick is dying."

Ann had been crying.

Towards one, Mrs. Gainsborough came downstairs. The cook took her place for a time, with instructions immediately to summon her mistress if Miss Hardwick should be any worse. She would not be any worse, Maud knew very well. Already, on the contrary, she was breathing a trifle more easily.

The first fierce effects of the virulent but transitory poison were passing off. By-and-by, towards the end of the afternoon, Lily would open her eyes, and become conscious. In the evening she would be able to take something—and, an hour or two after that, she would be out of the reach of everything in this world for evermore.

"Well! What must be, must be!"

So Maud went downstairs and sat in the dining-room, and watched Ann laying luncheon.

Another knock. Ann went to answer it, leaving the dining-room door open behind her.

Mrs. Gainsborough bent her ear to catch, if she could, the voice of the visitor.

Suddenly she started. The voice was Warring-ton's!

"Is Mrs. Gainsborough at home?" he asked.

"Mrs. Gainsborough cannot see any one, sir—Miss Hardwick is dying."

"I *must* see Mrs. Gainsborough."

He spoke with authority, and the words reached Maud in the dining-room clearly.

"Mrs. Gainsborough has given orders that she cannot see any one, sir," replied the servant.

"Take her my card. Tell her that I must see her. She knows that it is important. I will wait here."

"What can he have come again for?" thought Maud to herself. "And what does he mean by saying *I* know?"

Then the servant came in with the message, and at a sign from Maud closed the door behind her.

"I can see no one, Ann. You must tell Mr. Warrington that Miss Hardwick is dying, and that I can see no one."

The servant left. Would she succeed in getting rid of Warrington?

Ann returned.

" Is he gone, Ann ? "

" Yes, ma'am."

" What did he say ? "

" Nothing, ma'am. He just turned and walked away."

Mrs. Gainsborough drew a long breath of relief. The widow was not the first woman who has drawn a sigh of relief on having finally succeeded in compassing her own destruction, nor will she be the last.

After luncheon, she again went upstairs, and released the cook. When the cook was gone, she went to the bedside, and regarded Lily closely. She was not so much better as Mrs. Gainsborough had expected to find her at the end of the hour and a half that she had been downstairs. The effect of her morning dose was passing off very slowly. The widow felt her pulse, and listened attentively to her breathing. That last dose must have come very near being fatal. Well, the next would be more certainly so : a good thing. It had been a horrible business, and had lasted a terrible time.

Downstairs the inquiries still continued. About half-past four Lily began to be a little restless. The doctor was to call again about five, or as soon as he could afterwards. How would Lily be when he came? Then the cook came up, and urged her mistress to go downstairs and to have a cup of tea quietly.

" Do, ma'am, now ; you're looking quite worn out."

So Maud went downstairs, and had tea brought her in the dining-room. Afterwards she opened her work-basket, and began sorting out some silks for a piece of fancy work.

To-morrow ! only to-morrow, all her dreams would be realized : the fifteen-thousand a-year, and everything! She could not help thinking of it. To-morrow—only to-morrow! This had been a gruesome business with her cousin, and she had run some awful risks. But the prize! And now she had only to wait till to-morrow.

Another knock. More inquiries. With the silk in her hand, the widow suddenly looks up and listens. Surely that is a man's step in the hall.

Ah, the doctor, of course. He has come a little before his time. That is a very good thing. Every half-hour Lily will be better just at present. And the sooner the doctor sees her the less difference he will find in her condition since the morning.

The door opened and Ann came in.

" Miss Essie Chesterfield, if you please, ma'am, and Mr. Anthony Gainsborough."

Every drop of blood in Maud Gainsborough's body rushed to her heart.

" Who? " she gasped, catching her breath and staggering up from her seat as if she would fall.

" Miss Essie Chesterfield and Mr. Anthony Gainsborough."

" Anthony Gainsborough! Anthony Gainsborough! " replied Maud, in herself utterly unnerved, and instantly seized with some inconceivable alarm. " What can Anthony be come about? What on earth is this? What can have brought him here, and of all days to-day? "

" You must tell them that I cannot see them, Ann," she answered, nervously turning her back to the servant.

" I've told them so, ma'am," said Ann.

" Then tell them again. I cannot see any one. Where are they? At the door? "

" They are in the drawing-room, ma'am."

" In the drawing-room! But I told you to let no one in."

"I didn't let them in, ma'am. The gentleman asked, ' Is Mrs. Gainsborough at home ? ' and I said, ' Yes, sir.' And then, before I had time to say any more, he walked straight in and went into the drawing-room, and the young lady after him. And then, when I followed him and said you could not see anyone, ma'am, all he said was, 'Go and tell your mistress that Miss Essie Chesterfield and Mr. Anthony Gainsborough are here.' "

" Well, then, you must go and tell them again that I cannot see them."

The servant left.

The instant the door closed behind her, Maud Gainsborough, leaning back against the table, pressed both her hands on her heart.

What on earth was it that was the matter with her ? Fear. Yes ; abject, horrible fear ! It was cowardly, miserable ; but it was so. She was faint with ghastly, deadly fear. The one man in the whole wide world whose very name made her shudder. What was he come for to-day ? What could have brought him at this moment ? She believed she saw it all. Something had transpired ; somebody had suspected her, and somehow the thing had reached Anthony Gainsborough. If so, there was not a hope left for her. Oh, God in heaven !

CHAPTER XLIV

MEANWHILE the housemaid went to the drawing-room.

Anthony Gainsborough had sat down. He had his elbow on the table at his side, and had crossed his legs. Essie stood by the window, looking at the lawn.

"If you please, sir, Mrs. Gainsborough is very sorry, but she cannot see any one."

"You tell your mistress, my girl, that if she does not come at once to see me, I shall come to see her," replied Anthony Gainsborough, looking at the maid without the least concern.

And Ann departed to take the message to her mistress.

Faint with terror, and pallid as death, Maud heard it and told the girl to leave her. Then she dropped into the nearest chair and laid her head down on the table, but only to start up again the next minute.

What on earth was she to do?

In vain she cast about her for some loophole of escape. She could find none. Must she really go and face this awful man? And he, perhaps, had discovered what she had been doing. The tears came into her eyes for very terror.

Well, at any rate, the tears might help her.

And putting her handkerchief to her eyes, she went to the drawing-room.

What must be, must be!

Anthony Gainsborough had risen and stood by the hearth. Essie was still at the window. Making her a slight bow, Maud Gainsborough went at once towards her brother-in-law, and feigned to take no notice of the fact that he did not offer his hand.

"Oh, Anthony," she began, sinking into a chair, with a sob, "I—I am in such trouble. My poor cousin is dying."

One look in Anthony Gainsborough's face had sufficed to assure her that her very worst suspicions might, in all likelihood, be true. She was quivering from head to foot with abject terror, and sobbing like a child. It looked altogether very like wild grief, and it was wild fear.

"Miss Hardwick is dying?" demanded Anthony Gainsborough, in a cold, hard voice.

"Oh, yes," sobbed the widow; "so the doctor says."

"Do you know why I have come?" asked Anthony Gainsborough.

He spoke coldly, calmly; only in his voice there was an undertone, ominous, menacing, of terrific determination. Even Essie, standing by the window, but no longer regarding the flowers, looked round.

For an instant the widow raised her eyes, but only to cover her face again in her handkerchief. The room was turning round her. She could think distinctly of nothing.

"When you came to live here," said Anthony Gainsborough, in the same tone, "I told you not to use the liberty I left you, to be guilty of any more heartlessness. Do you remember?"

Maud answered nothing. She had buried her face on the back of the chair. To herself she was saying, "He knows everything! He knows everything! Oh, my God!"

"A few days ago," continued Anthony Gainsborough, "you solemnly promised your cousin that, if Mr. Warrington came to see her, she should see him."

Maud started. How on earth had he discovered that? There had been no one with herself and Lily when the promise had been given. And she had only yesterday asked Lily whether she had talked to any one about it, and Lily had said, "No." And Lily spoke the truth. Had the man second-sight? And what was he coming to from this beginning?

"You promised your cousin that, if Mr. Warrington called, she certainly should see him," he repeated, in the same even, calm voice.

"But who told you?" asked the widow, beginning to think that she must be losing her wits.

Instead of answering, Anthony Gainsborough demanded,

"When Mr. Warrington called on Tuesday, why did you break the promise you had given?"

"She was not well enough to see him."

"She saw other people; she saw Miss Barrington."

There was no change in his voice; it was the same with which he had spoken throughout, soft, calm, perfectly undisturbed, but with a ring of quiet resolution that was most disconcerting.

As for the widow, she seemed to herself to have drifted into a world of sorcery This man knew everything. If the next thing he asked for was the bottle of aconite in her pocket, she would not be much more surprised than she was already.

Once more he was simply repeating his question, in the same quietly inexorable voice,

"You solemnly promised this dying girl that she should see her lover if he came. He came, and you broke your word. What did you mean by it?"

Slowly the truth was dawning on Maud. Anthony Gainsborough had come down furiously angry because she had not let her cousin see her lover. How he had found it out, God knew. But of all the rest he had no suspicion.

And she ventured to answer.

She meant nothing by it. Only Lily was so ill. The promise was not a *solemn* promise. The promise had only been given the girl because she was so ill: to calm her. To keep her from exciting her-

self. She could not have borne to see Mr. Warrington. It would have been too much for her.
True, she had seen Miss Barrington: that did not
excite her. What had been done, had been done
only out of kindness and consideration for the girl's
health.

All this, and much more of the same sort, Maud
said; growing a little voluble as she ran on, and
perceived how plausible what she was saying
sounded.

Only, at the end, Anthony Gainsborough answered,

"Very good. You know I know you do not
speak the truth. So, now that you have finished
with all you wish to say, will you please to answer
me what you meant by breaking your promise?"

"I have told you the truth, and I don't know
what more you want to know," answered the widow,
a little shortly.

She might have said, with more truth, that she
did not care what he wanted to know. She certainly
was not going to tell him that she was herself in love
with Warrington, and resolved that he and Lily
should not meet. Anthony Gainsborough would be
in a passion, of course. He would turn her out of
the cottage, and refuse to make her any farther
allowance. And he might. A deal all that would
matter to her to-morrow! And to-morrow Lily
should be dead. Dead without a doubt; dead,
without a shadow of pity; now that she had been
bothered about her like this. She, Maud, would
have her revenge for it. It was easy enough. And
as for Anthony Gainsborough, since he knew nothing
at all of all she feared, he might stay and scold her
as long as he pleased. He might stay all night;
and, if he liked, take Lily the glass of milk with the
fatal drop in it, and poison her off himself. He
should, if he stayed long enough.

It was all very fine in thought to hector it in this fashion. But before the hearth stood Anthony Gainsborough, repeating in his inexorable voice :

"You will, however, let me know why you broke your promise to this girl, that she should see her lover."

Maud tried repeating word for word the same answer she had given before. In vain.

Maud tried putting the same answers into other words. In vain.

Maud tried framing other answers of different clever kinds. In vain.

Still the cold, inexorable voice insisted in the same words,

"Why did you break the promise you gave the girl that she should see her lover ?"

And the widow who, when she was groundlessly frightened, was on her guard, now that she had emerged from her fears, did not remark the peril into which the cold, insisting voice was pushing her.

At last Anthony Gainsborough seemed to tire, and the widow was glad of it. This ceaselessly reiterated demand hammering at her ears was beginning to make her stupid.

Anthony Gainsborough walked from the hearth to the window, and looked out at the lawn and the sky. Then he came back.

"You do not choose," he said, "to answer my question with anything but excuses. When I came down here, I imagined that you had been simply very cruel. You have made me suspect that the case is graver by far. There is only one explanation of your conduct left. You have some reason for keeping people from seeing Miss Hardwick. I am going to know what it is."

Maud Gainsborough winced. This was a sudden turn of affairs which she had not contemplated, whilst framing excuse after excuse. But though the situation had, in an instant, taken a much more serious aspect, she could face the accusation, and she did.

" I have no reason for keeping people from seeing my cousin," she said quietly, and cautiously too. After all, this was not a man to trifle with. " Numbers of people have seen her. The doctor will be here in a few minutes, and will tell you so. If she should recover consciousness, she will tell you so herself."

" You have let whom you chose see her, and whom you chose you have kept away, that is to say," replied Anthony Gainsborough.

After a pause he added,

" I shall see her myself."

And after another pause,

" And, after I have seen her, I shall have the house searched."

For a minute the widow believed everything lost. Anthony Gainsborough's first statement, that he would himself see her cousin, filled her with inordinate misgiving of what the consequences might be ; his second, that he would search the house, gave her a sensation of the earth opening under her feet, and she turned to the colour of ashes—and Essie noticed it. But it was for a moment only. The next instant, a revulsion, more sudden even than her dismay, gave her a little new assurance. The extremity of the situation had inspired her imagination with a device. Want of imaginative inventiveness was not among her failings. Now, after all, she believed she might save herself.

Looking up, she said, firmly :

" You have no authority to search my house,

Anthony; and I shall not permit it. There is a limit to the insults that even I can endure." And she rose from her seat and confronted him. "I will not have my house searched."

"The house is not your house, but my house," answered Anthony Gainsborough. "You pay me no rent, and I pay the rates and taxes. The house is my house, and the furniture is my furniture; and I shall search my house, and smash anything you do not choose to unlock."

"Search then!" said Maud, sitting down again. Looking round, she asked in a petulant voice, "Do you want to see Miss Hardwick?"

"I am going to see her."

"Am I to come with you?"

"No. I prefer to go alone. Where is she?"

"In the best bedroom."

He turned to Essie,

"You will stay with Mrs. Gainsborough. Ah, by the way, I have not introduced you. My niece, Miss Essie Chesterfield—Mrs. George Gainsborough."

The two women bent their heads to each other without moving from their seats, and Anthony Gainsborough left the room.

CHAPTER XLV

THAT was what Maud Gainsborough had reckoned on.

It was a feeble chance. But within the last half-hour she had passed through a variety of mental phases so numerous, so opposite, so rapid, and often so unexpected that she appeared to herself to be moving in a dream. Only half an hour since in the dining-room she was tasting the quiet security of a certain triumph, of a safe release, and, since then, there had succeeded fear, fear so abject, hope, desperation, relief, stupefaction, agony, security, desperation, courage, new fears, new desperation, and sudden reassurance, revulsion upon revulsion, till she hardly knew whether her judgment was speaking her the truth or not ; only that she believed she saw a chance of evasion, and was going to avail herself of it.

The plan had burst upon her in a moment, at the very instant when she cowered under the conviction that everything was lost, after Anthony Gainsborough said that he would search the house.

What had suddenly struck her at that instant was this. That should he go to see Lily first, and commence his search afterwards, there would be the moment of his absence, during which she might contrive an opportunity to abstract the bottle of aconite from the drawer of the escritoire.

How easily, she reflected, she might have done that an hour earlier. How easily have taken the bottle from its hiding-place, have carried it down the garden and flung it into the sea. But half an hour ago and now were different times. Then the absoluteness of her security and of her successfulness almost transcended belief. Now it was a question whether a perilous expedient, whether the events of a few critical seconds, would allow her to snatch the only chance of escape from certain ruin.

She was resolved to risk the attempt.

As soon as the door had fairly closed behind her brother-in-law, she rose from her seat. It was not possible to say how soon Anthony Gainsborough might return, and only prompt action could save her.

"You will excuse my writing a note, Miss Chesterfield," she said.

"Oh, certainly "

The widow went across the room, and taking her keys from her pocket, opened the old escritoire and sat down to write.

Essie's eyes followed her.

Unlocking a drawer Maud took out some note-paper. Then she rose, and going to the writing-table fetched the ink.

Essie observed the act. Evidently letters were usually written at the writing-table, and the widow's choosing to write at the escritoire had attracted her attention. Maud, too, had thought of this. But she had to risk it.

Sitting down, she began to write. When she had done she asked, with a curl of her lip:

"Do you wish, Miss Chesterfield, to see what I have written?"

"As I am left here to watch you I may as well," replied Essie, with a coolness of effrontery for which Maud could willingly have boxed her ears.

Instead, however, leaning back in her chair, she offered the note for perusal.

Essie rose and took it. It was simply a request to the rector to pay her a ministerial visit.

"There can be no objection to your sending that," said Essie, returning it.

And now for the critical moment.

Mrs. Gainsborough put her handkerchief down on her right, beside the note she had just written, and unlocked another drawer. She was keeping her head cool, and her hands steady. She wished to prevent Essie from attaching any importance to the unlocking of the drawers. From the drawer she took out some envelopes. Then she lighted a little taper. Next to find the sealing-wax. There was none on the writing-table. She unlocked a drawer and rummaged it all over. Not there. The widow rose and opened another drawer. As she now stood, Essie Chesterfield could not see what she took out of the drawers, nor indeed whether she took anything out or not. And now. This was the drawer containing the bottle. She rummaged it over as she had done the others. Now she had the bottle in the hollow of her hand. Now it was under her handkerchief. And she locked the drawer, and unlocked and rummaged another, the one in which she knew the sealing-wax to be.

"Ah : here's the sealing-wax," she said, aloud, and sat down.

The bottle lay still under her handkerchief. Quite casually the widow looked round her. Essie was not regarding her. As a fact Essie had not seen what she had done.

Maud gave a sob, and took up her handkerchief, pretending to wipe her eyes, bending down over the table of the escritoire. She had the handkerchief in her left hand now, and the bottle in it. As she hung her head down, she unfastened the bosom of her dress with her right hand, and, as she again passed her hand before her face, let the bottle slip into the bosom of her dress.

A full minute elapsed before she ceased sobbing, with her head bent low, and her hands busy with her handkerchief, in such a way that she believed no one could see what she had been doing.

Then once more she wiped her eyes and raised herself, and proceeded to seal her letters. They might search the house now, if they liked.

She was saved!　After all, saved!　Essie had not turned nor spoken.

How cold the little bottle was against her breast! And how her heart throbbed!　The strain of the moment of peril had almost overtaxed her.　It was with an effort that she was keeping her hand steady whilst she proceeded to warm the wax, holding it in the flame of the taper.

"Ah!"　A sudden start—the widow drew her hands back—too late!—bang down came the revolving cover of the escritoire on her wrists.

With her step of a cat, Essie had come behind her whilst she was holding the wax in the flame, and, at the same instant that the widow saw her, slammed down the revolving lid.

It caught the widow's wrists in its wooden jaws like the teeth of a gin, making her give a scream of pain, in spite of herself.

"Scream! that is right, scream!" said Essie, holding down the lid by its two handles with all her might; "they will come all the sooner."　And, raising her own voice, she called, "Uncle Tony, Uncle Tony!"

For an explanation of her conduct, she said to the widow:

"I am certain that I saw you hiding something in your bosom."

Quivering from head to foot, Maud Gainsborough sat breathing heavily, scarcely conscious in her mental agony, of the pain in her wrists.

Essie, still leaning with all her might, held the lid down mercilessly, and, as Anthony Gainsborough did did not come, called again:

"Uncle Tony, Uncle Tony!"

The next instant the door opened, and Anthony Gainsborough strode into the room.

"Mrs. Gainsborough has something hidden in

her bosom," said Essie. "You hold that handle, Uncle Tony, on that side, and I will take it out."

With an "Oh!" of desperation that rent the air of the room in a wail of agony, the widow dropped her forehead on the lid of the escritoire.

And Essie, putting her hand into the bosom of her dress, drew out the bottle and handed it to her uncle, and took her other hand off the lid of the escritoire.

Anthony Gainsborough held up the bottle and read the label aloud: "Aconite." Above was in letters half an inch long, "POISON."

Essie saw them.

"Have you any more elsewhere?" demanded Anthony Gainsborough.

"No," asserted the widow.

She had not forgotten the little phial in her pocket, but she trusted to his now searching no further.

Anthony Gainsborough removed his hands from the handle of the escritoire.

For a few seconds the widow remained motionless. Then, releasing her arms, she turned, and faced her foes. The edge of the escritoire had cut her wrists, and the blood trickled down on her hands. Turning away, she staggered to the sofa, and threw herself upon it with a wild cry:

"Oh, my God!"

Essie had stepped back to the escritoire, and stood leaning against it, pale and speechless, looking from her uncle to the widow, quivering with mental agony on the sofa—from the widow to her uncle.

Anthony Gainsborough crossed the room, and rang the bell.

"Is there a man-servant in the house?" he demanded of the housemaid.

"Yes, sir," answered the girl, regarding with astonishment her mistress lying on the sofa.

"Send him to me."

When the man came, he said, quietly:

"I want you to go at once to the police-station. I will give you a note to take with you. You can take my trap, which is waiting at the gate, and bring back the policeman with you in it."

And he made a step to go towards the little writing-table.

But the widow had sprung from the sofa, and threw herself before him on her knees on the floor at his feet.

"No, Anthony, no, no!" she screamed. "No, for God's sake, no! Not the police! I'll confess, I'll confess, Anthony. I'll confess everything. Don't send for the police! for pity's sake."

And she literally grovelled on the ground before him.

"Why not?"

"No, Anthony! no! no!"

And, catching his arm, she held him with her blood-stained hands, her little wrists showing already discoloured and swollen.

"Anthony! Anthony!"

Anthony Gainsborough turned to the man.

"Go into the hall, and wait till I call you," he said.

"No, Anthony, you must not send John! Not for the police!" cried the widow, as the door closed behind the man-servant. "I'll confess, Anthony. I'll tell you everything. Indeed I will. Only don't give me to the police. Listen Anthony," she continued, still kneeling and clinging to his hand, as if she feared lest he should go to the table and write. "I was tempted, I was tempted cruelly. I'll tell you everything. I will indeed, Anthony."

She let his hand go; and he folded his arms, saying nothing, but looking down at her with a face of stone.

With her breast heaving convulsively, and her eyes anxiously watching his unmoved, impenetrable face, the widow went on, wildly, hurriedly:

"If I tell you everything, Anthony, you will spare me, won't you? I was tempted. Listen. I will tell you. I will confess everything—everything truly. Only, for God's sake, don't send for the police. Listen—Anthony. I found out—it was quite by an accident—that there is a great unclaimed fortune to which I am entitled. I am telling you the truth, indeed I am. I will show you all the proofs, if you like. And there is only Lily Hardwick who has a claim to that fortune before me. And she knows nothing about it. Only Lily, Anthony, was between me and wealth, wealth such as I had never, till I found this out, dreamed of. I have known all about it ever so long: ever since I have had Lily with me, and before that. You understand me, Anthony, that I have known, all the time that Lily has been here, that she stood between me and a great fortune, and that if she died I should be rich, enormously rich. And I could easily have killed her, Anthony. But I never attempted it. I never thought of it. And you made dependence very bitter for me, Anthony; indeed you did. Many a woman in my place would have poisoned Lily long ago. And I could have done it easily, I assure you I could. Only I did not: not until I was tempted. As I breathe, I am telling the truth.

"But I—I——"

She stopped short, but only for a few seconds.

"I will tell you everything—truly—I will indeed," she went on, in an agonized voice, hanging her head, as a hot blush flushed her cheek. "I

met a man I will not name. I could not help it,
Anthony. He came here—I mean to Lynham.
And, the moment I saw him, I knew what would
happen. I knew that I should love him. One
cannot help loving. But I wrote to you to let me
go away from here, because I did not want to love
him. And you would not let me go. It is all as
much your fault as mine, Anthony. If you would
have let me go, none of this would have happened.
But you would not let me go. And then it all
turned out as I knew it would, and I loved him—I
love him now—passionately, passionately !

" And, Anthony, I did it for his sake !

" Listen to what I tell you : I did it for his
sake ! "

She looked into his face to see if she had touched
him at all. But his face was impassive.

" I swear to you, Anthony, that I did this thing
for that man's sake. I swear it to you, by God in
heaven ! Not for my sake, but for his sake. I
would not have done it for my own sake. I would
have remained poor. I did it for his sake. Not
that he knew of it. I should never have told him of
it. He would not have understood me.

" He is poor. Do you see ? Too poor to marry
me—and I too poor to marry him. I do not tell
you who he is. It makes no difference who he
is. But I tell you I loved him passionately, passionately : and if I had that fortune—he would
come to me—and love me as I love him.

" And then, listen. This was what tempted me.
It was so easy.

" Lily was ill. You know she was ill.

" And she was unhappy, too.

" Mr. Warrington came here, and she fell in love
with him. And he would not notice her ; and she
fretted and pined for him, and fell ill.

"And I loved the man I tell you of so; and I wanted the money so much to offer him, and sometimes I thought Lily would die. I did think it. And I thought it would be only a little sooner, or a little later.

"And she was so unhappy, too, so miserable. She fretted and pined so : and said that she wished she was dead. And, Anthony, could I help thinking, if she were dead, how happy, how happy, I and the man I loved would be?

"Anthony, was I not tempted? You won't send for the police? Don't you see how I was tempted? And that is not all. You have not heard all. There were other things that made it easier. Ah! Anthony, you don't know what the temptation is when the thing is easy. Lily was ill, and I knew that she would only seem to get a little worse, and a little worse. And I happened to have the aconite—by an accident : quite by an accident. It lay in my way, you see. And I knew that Dr. Gregg was ignorant, and would not suspect anything. Do you see how I was tempted? Was it strange that I yielded? Anthony, would it not have been stranger if I had been able to resist—when it was so easy? And then, when I began giving her the aconite, she was only a little worse and a little worse ; and nobody thought anything of it. They all made it easy for me to poison her. They did indeed, Anthony. If they had not, I should not have dared to go on. It was as much their fault as mine, because they all made it easy for me.

"Do you see how I was tempted? You won't send for the police? Don't you see, I had only to give Lily just one little drop once or twice a day. It was so simple. And I knew that she trusted me, that she loved me, and would never suspect anything. If she had suspected me, Anthony, I could not have done it.　But, like all the rest, she made it easy for me, and tempted me.　It was as much her fault as mine.　If she had not trusted me, I would not have attempted it.

" And, Anthony, I was not heartless, as you said. I hated to see her suffer, as she did.　Indeed I did. But how could I help it ?　If I had had anything else that I could have used, anything that would have distressed her less, I would gladly have used it, but I had nothing.　It was not my wish that the stuff should make her suffer.　I swear to you, Anthony, that it went to my heart to see how the aconite tortured her.　And I had to steel myself to give it her, and not to give way to my feelings, or I could not have gone on.　I have not been heartless, Anthony.

" And, after all, I have done nothing.　Lily has had some pain, but even now she will probably recover.　And if she recovers, as she probably will, what have I done that you should want to be cruel, and to have me punished ?

" And there is another thing.　It was not only so easy, but, you see, it seemed to matter so little.　Lily had no father, nor mother, nor sisters, nor brothers, nor relations of any kind ; no one but me belonging to her in all the whole world.　If she had had friends and relations, I would not have done it ; Anthony, I vow to you I would not.　I would have hesitated to pain them by her death.　But, you see, she was all alone, without any friends ; quite alone.　And, when I thought of my great love, it seemed so little to take one life, only one—one little, lonely life that nobody cared about.　Anthony, see how I was tempted !　You won't send for the police ? "

She had done, and, with her hands clasped, she bent towards him, looking into his immovable face as he stood with his hands folded before him.

" You devil ! "

That was all he said.

Only, after about a minute, whilst she waited, watching him with agony in her eyes, he demanded:

" You poisoned your husband ? "

" If I tell you—will you let me go?" gasped Maud Gainsborough.

That was half a confession. Anthony Gainsborough made no reply to it, but only repeated his question.

" You poisoned him, with aconite, as you have tried to poison this girl ? "

The widow hung her head. Of what use to deny it ? Perhaps confession might earn her some mercy. Almost inaudibly, she answered:

" Yes."

Anthony Gainsborough turned to the writing-table.

The widow started up from the floor, and rushed to him, catching his arm.

" Anthony! you are not going to write for the police, after all ? Not after what I have told you— Anthony ! "

" What do you suppose I am going to do then ? "

And, scribbling off a few lines, he shouted:

" John ! "

The man came in, and Anthony tossed him the note, saying:

" To the police-station, and quick."

A moment Maud Gainsborough stood still, whilst her eyes swept round the room, and an inarticulate cry came from her lips parted in horror, and then she staggered to the sofa and flung herself down on her face with a wild shriek of despair.

Anthony Gainsborough rose from the table, perfectly unmoved, and went towards Essie, who stood leaning against the wall horror-struck and shuddering.

" Oh, Uncle Tony ! " she exclaimed, in a tone of consternation.

Her uncle put his hand on her shoulder and took her to the open window.

" You will not forget what you have heard ? " he said.

" Forget ! Would it be possible to forget ! " said the girl.

Sinking into a chair, she gasped :

" Uncle Tony, I feel faint."

" Come outside."

Assisting her to rise, he led her into the fresh air.

" Are you better ? " he asked presently.

" Yes. But, oh, uncle, how dreadful ! Mrs. Gainsborough is a murderess. Do you think Lily will die ? "

" I hope not ! "

" What will they do to Mrs. Gainsborough ? "

" They will not punish her more than she de-serves."

Essie looked back over her shoulder. Maud Gainsborough still lay on the sofa.

" Uncle," said Essie, " how still Mrs. Gainsborough lies ! She must have fainted. Look ! "

Anthony Gainsborough turned round. Maud Gainsborough certainly lay motionlessly still. But he would not have concerned himself about the fact had not Essie insisted.

" She has fainted, surely, uncle. You ought to see."

Anthony Gainsborough re-entered the room. Essie followed a step or two behind him.

The widow lay half on her side, with her head low on the sofa-cushions, and her right arm hanging down, so that the hand nearly touched the floor. Her eyes were fast closed, but her lips were parted slightly. She was evidently unconscious, and no heaving of her breast was perceptible.

Anthony Gainsborough stood over her, trying to assure himself whether she breathed. Essie had come to his side.

Slipping his arm under the unconscious woman's shoulders, Anthony Gainsborough gently lifted her head to place it higher upon the pillow. As he moved her, something rolled out of the folds of her dress to the ground.

Essie stooped and picked it up.

" What is it, Essie ? " asked her uncle.

" A little empty bottle."

He took it from her hands and examined it. Then, putting his hand on her arm, he said :

" Come with me."

He led her out of the room.

Maud Gainsborough had poisoned herself with the aconite in the little phial in her pocket.

CHAPTER XLVI.

A single flat slab of white marble—nameless and dateless—in a lonely corner of the little churchyard at Lynham, covers a grave over which no prayers for the dead were said.

The spring sun gleamed upon it brightly as Frank Warrington, with his young wife on his arm, made their way towards it, past many other graves.

They had come home from the Continent only yesterday, Lily completely recovered, and without a trace on her beautiful face of the peril through which she had passed.

In her hand she carried a wreath of white flowers, which, when they reached the lonely slab, she put down upon it.

" Poor Maud ! " she said, leaning on her husband's arm, and dashing a tear from her eyes. " Ah, Frank, I would give all my big fortune to have her back again. You have not forgiven her, Frank, for trying to poison me. I suppose you never will. And I know I should find it hard to forgive any one who tried to injure you. But I—I loved Maud. I loved her up to the hour that she died, and afterwards—one could not bear malice against the dead, and I shall love her always." Bending, she put her hand gently on the marble slab, and said, "I hope you have been forgiven, dear, as I have forgiven you."

Stepping back, but still looking at the stone, she asked :

" Frank, do you ever wonder who *he* was ? "

" He ? Who ? "

" That man. The man whom poor Maud met, and fell in love with in a moment; for whose sake she wished to get the fortune that she might marry him. I *do* wonder who he was."

" I don't believe that there was ever any such person. That was all a fabrication—a story invented in the forlorn hope of persuading Mr. Gainsborough to have the poisoning hushed up."

Lily shook her head.

" No, Frank. There was some one. I could give you quite a little history about him. At the time, I thought nothing about it ; but afterwards, after poor Maud had destroyed herself, and Mr. Gainsborough told me all that she had said, when I began to question my memory, I recollected a number of things. There was some one. And he must have come to

Lynham about the time that I was laid up with that bad cold I had after our adventure on the beach. Maud must have met him on some occasion when she was out, whilst I was unable to leave the house. Immediately afterwards, when I was well again, I noticed a change in her. She was anxious and nervous. And then they either met again, or she heard something that was satisfactory, for she became more like herself. Afterwards, things went wrong. At that date, she was never the same for two days together; but sometimes in the highest spirits, and then again unhappy, and then thinking, thinking for hours together, and strange and absent. I think that it must have been about that time that he proposed, and that they found they could not afford to marry. Afterwards, Maud became more like herself again, and was very, very kind to me— that was when you and I had quarrelled—and then I fell ill. And that was, of course, when she began giving me poison. If she had only told me about the fortune, I would gladly have shared it with her, and that would have been quite fair; fairer than that I should have it all, because it was she who was clever enough to find it out, and to get all the papers together. And there would still have been more than enough for you and me, dear. But I do wonder who he was. He must have been a man out of the common. Maud could not have loved a man who had not something in him. And, I believe, he had dark hair, because of a remark she made to me about dark-haired men. And, somehow, I have a suspicion that he loved her much less than she loved him. So few people come to Lynham, that one ought to be able to find him out easily. But I hate to ask people about anything relating to Maud: they speak so bitterly of her; and it makes my heart ache. I wonder what he has thought of it all, and whether he will ever come to see her grave. I should like him to do that—and to be very sorry."

"You will never know who he was," said Warrington. "If there ever really was such a person. She has taken her secret with her."

"Then she has taken with her the dearest thing she had on earth," said Lily, gently; and they turned to go home.

Anthony Gainsborough and the Chesterfield girls were at Lynhurst. They had come back from the Continent with Frank Warrington and his wife. After dinner, in the evening, whilst Violet was playing, Essie and Lily and Warrington and Eustace sat talking in a little group.

"Did you go to Mrs. Gainsborough's grave?" asked Essie.

"Yes."

"Lily," said Warrington, "has been hoping that the unknown man, whoever he was, with whom Mrs. Gainsborough fell in love will pay it a visit. She thinks that he should."

"Are you sure that he has not done so already?" asked Eustace.

Essie bent over, and whispered something to Lily, and she, turning to Eustace, asked:

"Eustace, you see everything that no one else sees: do you know who he was?"

Eustace answered, slowly:

"He did not care for her. But, if she had had money, he would have married her: at least, I used to think so."

"But, who was he? Who was he?" demanded Essie and Lily at the same moment. "You know!"

"Who was he? Why should I tell you?" answered Eustace, pensively "Are you sure that

it would do you any good to know If you had
taken your secrets with you into another world,
would you thank any one for telling them here?
Who was he? That no one will ever know."

Rising, he went across the room to speak to
Violet at the piano. And as he went, he said to
himself:

"These people who see, how blind they are!"

PRINTED BY BALLANTYNE, HANSON AND CO.
LONDON AND EDINBURGH